THE EAGLE'S SHADOW

THE COVERT WAR CHRONICLES BOOK 1

MICHAEL REIT

Copyright © 2025 by Michael Reit

ISBN (eBook): 9789083536309
ISBN (Paperback): 9789083536316
ISBN (Hardcover): 9789083536323
ISBN (Audiobook): 9789083536330

All rights reserved. No part of this publication may be reproduced, distributed, or transmitted in any form or by any means, including photocopying, recording, or other electronic or mechanical methods, without the prior written permission of the publisher, except in the case of brief quotations embodied in critical reviews and certain other noncommercial uses permitted by copyright law.

DISCLAIMER

This is a work of fiction. Names, characters, businesses, places, events, and incidents are either the products of the author's imagination or used in a fictitious manner. Any resemblance to actual persons, living or dead, or actual events is purely coincidental.

Title Production by The BookWhisperer

Cover Design by Patrick Knowles

PART ONE

ONE

Vienna, Austria
10 March 1938

Felix Wolff looked up as the front doorbell announced a visitor. A burly man entered the shop and strode purposefully over to the counter. "I'll be with you in a second, just need to get this down." Felix quickly refitted a front tire before gently lowering the old bike back onto the workshop floor. Felix wiped his hands on his apron as he approached the counter, where the man was reaching into a large briefcase. As soon as Felix saw the contents, he frowned. "I know what you're going to ask, and I don't think it's a good idea."

The man looked up in surprise, holding out a large sheet of paper. "Are you the owner of this establishment?" The tone of his voice betrayed the question was rhetorical, his *Hochdeutsch* accent instantly grating on Felix. "This is a Jewish store, isn't it?" Felix didn't extend his arms to take hold of the document, so the man placed it on the counter.

The poster showed a red-and-white Austrian flag, prominently printed in the middle, surrounded by large typeface prompting readers to vote for independence. *Vote Yes!*

He sighed. "We prefer to keep our political affiliations to ourselves."

"But surely you don't disagree?" The man's eyes focused on the area behind Felix. "Is the proprietor around?"

Felix shook his head and slid the poster back across the counter. "If that's all, I'd like to get back to work." He turned and eyed one of the bikes in line for repair.

The man placed his elbows on the counter, studying Felix as he hoisted the bike up on two chains attached to the ceiling. Felix pursed his lips and rummaged busily through his toolbox. *I couldn't have been any clearer.*

"If we all look away, they're going to win. We need to stand up for our country. People like you and me." The man spoke confidently. "Are you from Leopoldstadt? You strike me as someone who's grown up in the district, in this shop."

Felix continued working on the bicycle, his back to the man, who kept droning on. After a minute, he closed his eyes in frustration, turned, his voice rising. "Look, I already told you—"

"What's going on in here?" A baritone voice cut him off as Anton Wolff appeared from the back of the workshop. He gave Felix a barely perceptible look of disapproval as he strode toward the counter, his voice turning businesslike as he addressed the man. "How can I help you?"

The man's eyes lit up, and he reached for the poster. "I was hoping you would support a free Austria in the upcoming referendum. We need every vote." His superior air, and his Hochdeutsch accent, had faded as he spoke to Felix's father. "A man such as yourself surely understands the importance of the voice of the common people in this election."

Anton picked up the poster, studied it, and turned to his son. "What do you think, Felix? Should we put this up in the shop window?"

Felix shook his head resolutely. "It might bring trouble."

His father looked thoughtful, stroking his beard.

"The trouble will be worse if we don't win the referendum," the large man on the other side of the counter said, his hand signaling to the street outside. "Most of the other shopkeepers have already put up the poster. They understand the importance of showing a united front."

Felix bit his lip. Graffiti supporting Austrian independence from Germany had appeared on walls and sidewalks: Their store was positioned in one of the busiest thoroughfares in the district.

"I agree with you." Anton lifted the gate in the counter, poster in hand. He walked to the door and fitted the poster at eye level. "Can you hand me some tape, Felix?"

"I still think this is a bad idea, Papa." Felix took a small roll from under the counter and tossed it to his father. "We shouldn't expose ourselves like this."

"Nonsense. We can do as we damn well please." Anton secured the poster, to the delight of the other man. "This is still a free country."

"And it shall remain that way, as long as people like your father stand up for it," the man added with a smile. He picked up his briefcase and tipped his hat to Anton. "And now I must take my leave. Thank you for doing the right thing, sir." He opened the door and stepped out into the Vienna sunshine.

THE DAY PASSED QUICKLY, and Felix was bringing in the bikes lined up in front of the store when he saw five men walking abreast on the sidewalk. They were some twenty meters away, and while Felix pushed one of the bikes inside, he noticed the group bullying anyone unfortunate enough to get in their path.

Just as Felix parked the last bike indoors, the doorbell clanged a little more aggressively than usual. The men piled into the small shop, every single one eyeing the poster with disdain. The tallest moved uncomfortably close to Felix, who was determined to keep his composure.

"This your shop?" The man spoke with a thick Viennese accent, the words coming out menacingly. He didn't wait for an answer as he swung around toward the front door, pointing. "Noticed the poster on the door. Me and my friends don't like it."

"Be a good little Jew and take it down, eh!" one of them added, much to the amusement of the others, who burst out laughing.

Felix felt the blood pounding in his ears, but he calmly clasped his hands together, fingernails digging into his skin. He sized the men up: bulky and each at least a head taller than him. He needed to control himself—if it came to a fight, he wouldn't stand a chance. They fanned out through the store. The tallest stood by one of the bikes, his hands running over the handlebars. Felix took a step forward, then caught movement from the corner of his eye. Anton appeared beside him.

"Is there a problem, gentlemen?"

His father's composure calmed him, and he took a deep breath.

The leader of the group turned his attention to Anton, his beady eyes focusing on him like a bird would its prey. "We was just telling him we don't like that poster on the door. We want it gone."

"Hmm." Anton tilted his head, effortlessly holding the much taller man's gaze. He appeared to be measuring his response, and seemed entirely comfortable with the ensuing silence. Some of the brutes shifted on their feet, unsure how to respond. The leader took a step closer, now almost towering over Anton. Felix purposefully shifted his weight to his toes in an effort to hold his ground.

"I'm afraid I'm unable to comply with your request." When Anton broke the silence his words sucked the air from the room. He straightened his back, his face rising a few centimeters closer to his would-be assailant. Felix suppressed a satisfied grunt.

"Is that so?" Despite the fire increasing in the brute's eyes, there was a slight hesitation in his voice.

"This is my shop, and I can put anything I want in the storefront." Anton's voice only increased in strength. "This is still a free Austria, unlike what you'd like to believe."

The jibe struck home and the brute's face twisted in fury, his hand clenching into a fist. He bent down a little, his nose almost touching Anton's. Felix inched forward, making a fist of his own, ready to pounce if the man struck his father. The adrenaline coursing through his veins numbed any fear. If his father was willing to take a stand like this, he would proudly go down with him.

The leader's eyes narrowed. He opened his mouth, then appeared to change his mind. His scowl transformed into an ugly smile before he broke into a high-pitched laugh. His friends joined in, somewhat nervously. The leader took a step back, then jabbed a finger in Anton's face.

"You're a fiery one, old man. I respect that. But you better remember we're not the only ones who feel this way. There are plenty of us, and they might not have the same self-control. Tread carefully." He turned to Felix. "And you. Watch your back."

Felix bit his tongue. His head was pounding, and he tightened his fist. He nodded at the man, then caught his father's look. *Calm down. They're almost gone.*

"Let's get out of here. It's clear these Jews won't listen to reason." The man turned around to his friends, who eagerly shuffled out of the store. "I'm sure we'll find people with reason in Leopoldstadt. People who see sense." He stopped at the door, where he focused on the poster. Felix held his breath. *He's going to rip it off after all.*

Anton moved forward and took the door handle, stepping between the man and the door. Felix found himself moving closer as well. Together, father and son stood.

The brute looked at them for a few seconds, his eyes going between them and the poster, then smirked as he left the store. "That's okay. We'll be back."

Felix stepped outside and watched him join his friends and disappear down the street. The man's last words lingered in his mind. Looking around, there were plenty of people moving about in a seemingly carefree manner. But he knew it was all an act. The Jewish people of Leopoldstadt all harbored the same fear. The upcoming referendum drew closer, and Felix feared there might be more thugs voting in favor of joining Adolf Hitler's regime.

TWO

Vienna
11 March 1938, morning

"There will be no referendum."

The man at the head of the table announced this with a tone of finality. Karl Vogt beamed as he studied the equally pleased faces sitting around him.

"I spoke to the Führer this morning, and he made it clear Chancellor Schuschnigg's attempt at undermining the reunification of Austria is wholly unacceptable." Arthur Seyss-Inquart, the man chairing the meeting and Austria's current minister of the interior, leaned forward in his chair. "He is furious with the proceedings, and will address his grievances with the chancellor later today."

"What will his demands be?" Odilo Globočnik, chief of staff of the Nazi Party in Austria, asked.

"An immediate cancellation of the referendum, along with the chancellor's resignation." A smile crept onto Seyss-Inquart's face, and Karl understood even before the next words came from the minister's mouth. "To be replaced by me."

Applause filled the room as those present hurried to shake the future chancellor's hand. Ever since Karl's arrival in Vienna six months ago, Seyss-Inquart had spared no effort in introducing him to Austria's political elite. Karl was by no means a big political player, and Seyss-Inquart wasn't required to invite him to meetings such as today's, but Karl knew the future chancellor valued his input. More so, he suspected he valued his ability to get things done.

The room settled down as the men returned to their seats, and Seyss-Inquart spoke again. "We don't know how Schuschnigg will respond to these demands, but he has little choice in the matter. The Führer has ordered the *Wehrmacht* to begin staging at the border in case the chancellor fails to comply with our demands." He paused and made eye contact with each of the men at the table. "Now, the reason we're gathered here today is because I want everybody to be aware of what will happen once Schuschnigg resigns. I'd like to go over the status of your individual plans one more time." His eyes fixed on Karl. "Vogt, why don't you start. Are your men in position?"

Karl glanced at Globočnik, who nodded. "Very much so, Herr Minister. As soon as the signal is given, loyal men will spring into action all over the city."

"Including those within the police departments?" Seyss-Inquart's eyes went to the man sitting opposite Karl, Josef Garhofer, criminal investigator within the Vienna police department. Garhofer nodded, and Karl continued.

"We've identified potential troublemakers within the police department, and we'll make sure those are nullified once power is transferred."

"And you're certain those loyal to the Reich will do what's right?" Seyss-Inquart said, raising an eyebrow.

"There is no doubt, Herr Minister." This time Garhofer spoke up. "I vouch for all of these men. They are my colleagues and friends, and every single one of them is eagerly awaiting the *Anschluss*—the reunification."

Karl suppressed a grin. While he had no doubt Garhofer's friends would support the reunification, their motives weren't as pure as Garhofer made them out to be. Most of these men were stuck on the periphery of the police force. Their involvement in the putsch would see their positions instantly elevated. Nevertheless, they were useful pawns in a greater scheme.

Seyss-Inquart nodded in satisfaction at Karl's and Garhofer's explanations, and he moved on to discuss several political allies. This morning's news didn't come as a surprise; Karl had spoken to his boss in Berlin the day prior, who had indicated big changes in the coming days.

"Right, I think that's all for today, gentlemen." Seyss-Inquart stood, and the rest of them followed, stuffing their papers and files into their briefcases. "Please remain close to your phones, as things can and will change quickly. Thank you for your time." As the room emptied, he signaled for Karl to stay.

"Karl, just between you and me, I want to make sure that whatever you have planned, there is minimal violence and damage to the city. I know you've been preparing with Globočnik, and I feel his men can be, how should I put this delicately, overly enthusiastic at times."

"I understand, Herr Minister, but I assure you we have them under control." Karl spoke with more confidence than he felt. In truth, he shared Seyss-Inquart's concerns about the Brownshirts of the *Sturmabteilung*. "I agree they can be somewhat brutish in their ways, but Odilo and I have made it very clear there is to be no looting or destruction of property."

"Just the semblance of civil disorder is enough, Karl." Seyss-Inquart lowered his voice conspiratorially. "And if there is to be any collateral damage to make it look more authentic, perhaps we can limit it to certain districts in the city."

"Absolutely. I will see to it."

The future chancellor's face relaxed as he let out a long sigh. "Very well. Soon, our hard work of the past months will pay off. I'm sure you have some last preparations to make, so I'll let you get to it. *Heil Hitler!*"

"*Heil Hitler!*" Karl raised his arm in salute, then left the room, his pulse racing with excitement.

THE EAGLE'S SHADOW

Karl stepped out onto the cobblestones of Herrengasse and smiled when he spotted Odilo waiting across the street.

"It's fitting to think we'll soon occupy all of these former Habsburg palaces," Karl said, waving a hand at the ornate Palais Modena, where the Ministry of Interior was housed.

Globočnik shrugged in typical Viennese fashion. "I don't really care where my office is, as long as the Führer appreciates what I've been doing these past few years."

"Come, let's get something to eat while we wait for things to be set in motion." Karl slapped his friend on the shoulder. "I'm sure they have a nice spot at parliament lined up for you."

"You're sure, or *really* sure?" Globočnik looked at him in anticipation. "Has Heydrich mentioned anything to you?"

Karl shook his head. "Not specifically, but he's aware of your dedication. He rewards those loyal to the cause. And fewer have been more so than you." In addition, Karl had made sure to prominently include his friend's activities in his reports to his boss in Berlin. "Let's worry about getting us some lunch first. I'm starving."

They navigated the narrow alleys of the city center to reach Franziskanerplatz. The unassuming square was home to Globočnik's favorite restaurant. A queue had formed at the entrance, which they ignored as Globočnik opened the door. The air was heavy with the smell of frying oil, the warmth enveloping Karl like a welcome blanket, his mouth watering as he realized he'd skipped breakfast that morning. All seats were occupied, but for a small table in the back.

"Ah, Herr Globočnik, how lovely to see you!" The immaculately dressed owner appeared out of nowhere and motioned to the vacant table. "We've kept your table free. I had a feeling you might come in today." Karl knew Odilo's table was always free.

"*Danke*, Herr Mayrhofer." Globočnik was curt as he took his seat, declining the menu offered by their host. "I'll have the usual." He turned to Karl. "You'll have the *Schweinebraten* as well, right?"

Karl nodded, eager to get their order in. "And a *Krügel, bitte*."

"For me as well," Globočnik said, and as the owner disappeared, he leaned forward on the table. "What did you think of the meeting? You already knew, didn't you?"

"I knew something was going on." Karl leaned back in his chair, inspecting the diners around them, avoiding Globočnik's piercing, eager gaze. "I spoke to Berlin this morning, and they said we'd have to deal with the referendum, and quickly."

"Did you speak with Heydrich?" Globočnik's eyes sparkled.

Karl shook his head. "He was meeting with the other big chiefs." He paused as a waiter placed two half liters of beer in front of them. "I don't speak to him nearly as much as you think, Odilo." He allowed himself a smile and picked up his mug, holding it out to his friend. They clinked glasses and both took a large sip. Karl relished the slightly biting sensation, as the cold liquid made its way down his throat. He took another sip before setting the mug back on the table. "When it happens, we need to assume control of the city quickly."

"Of course." His friend nodded from across the table. "Our men are in place. They know what to do."

"I know. But one thing is very important." Karl took a small sip and lifted his index finger. "No looting or destruction of Austrian property."

A twisted smile appeared on Globočnik's face. "Oh, don't worry. Most of them are unthinking ruffians, but their leaders have them under control. Most importantly, they know the enemy. Like us, they have been waiting for the right moment to strike. They're not going to bother any good, upstanding Austrian citizens."

Their food arrived, and Karl studied his friend. Odilo Globočnik was ruthless, and he surrounded himself with capable people. Managing an army of eager Brownshirts lurking in the shadows was what he did best. Karl picked up his knife and fork and cut into his honey-roasted pork. He brought a piece to his mouth, then paused. "If any of your men want to have some fun, send them across the canal."

Globočnik took a bite, smiled and nodded. "Don't worry. We'll take care of those *Juden* in Leopoldstadt."

THREE

Vienna
11 March 1938, evening

The cold evening air rushed at Felix as he pedaled his bike a little faster along Vienna's Ringstraße. The heavy traffic moved as it always did on the broad boulevard encircling the inner city, but the air felt different.

Football training had been suspended as soon as Schuschnigg's voice interrupted the regular broadcast, and the boys were called inside the clubhouse. There, they huddled around the single radio set and listened in shock. The chancellor had canceled the referendum, and stepped down from his position. Worse, he accepted that the Nazi factions within the government would take over. The chancellor signed off, and the national anthem of Austria came through the speakers. The boys stared at the radio in disbelief, but there was no time to linger. Training was canceled, and they were urged to go home as quickly as possible.

When Felix passed the university on Schottentor, he saw a group of students had gathered on the steps to the main entrance. A crowd of Brownshirts carrying homemade wooden weapons approached from the main street. Felix kept his head low, careful to avoid eye contact. They did nothing to hide their disdain for the students.

"Leeches!"

"No-good, left-wing Bolsheviks!"

"Jew-lovers!"

The last of the Nazis had passed Felix when a chant grew from the front. "Heil Hitler! Down with the Bolsheviks! Death to the Jews! This is our time!" It quickly picked up, and the sight and sound of some fifty armed men wearing the uniform of the Sturmabteilung feverishly moving toward the unarmed students sent a shudder down Felix's spine. Without another thought, he pedaled his bike along the Ring. Despite the increasing distance between him and the Brownshirts, their chant only appeared to grow louder. He clenched his jaw and focused solely on the street ahead.

His legs ached, but he hardly noticed. Schuschnigg's words reverberated in his mind. *For the good of Austria. To avoid the spilling of blood between German brothers.* His head was spinning, and he almost missed the crowd blocking the road. He squeezed the handles of his brakes, his bike coming to an abrupt standstill. Felix returned to the present as dozens of voices speaking at the same time came at him. People moved about and between the cars blocking the road. Police cars were parked haphazardly along the sidewalk and the street; he was standing in front of the Vienna police headquarters.

The crowd swelled, and as Felix looked for a path through, Brownshirt uniforms encircled, along with even more people in regular clothes. Despite their more casual exterior, they wore the same satisfied, menacing scowls as the members of the Sturmabteilung. The air was thick with anticipation, and even though Felix knew he should move on, he found himself fixed in place.

The doors to the police station opened with a crash, and two Brownshirts escorted a uniformed police officer between them. A cheer erupted from those gathered outside. The Brownshirts paused atop the steps for drama, then stepped down and bundled the man into a waiting car. It slowly moved through the crowd, with plenty of onlookers banging the hood and roof.

"Out with the old!"
"Traitor!"
"This is our time!"
"Heil Hitler!"

The frenzy made Felix's skin crawl. A terrible thought struck: The people hurling abuse at the police weren't just Brownshirts. They were regular people, like him. The chants at the university echoed in his mind. *Jew-lovers.* His blood turned cold, and he looked at the faces around him—his fellow Viennese no longer hid their true, pent-up feelings. They were looking for someone to unleash their fury on. A little farther down the Ring, across the Danube Channel, was his home, Leopoldstadt. *Papa. Mama.*

Felix began pushing his way through the crowd, no longer caring who was in his way. *I need to get home.* A large man wearing a gray overcoat stood in his way, and Felix hesitated before pushing his bike on. The man turned to him, a scowl on his face.

"*Bist Du deppert?* You can't push your bike through here, you idiot." The man kicked the front wheel of Felix's bike, turning the handlebars sideways. Felix only just managed to keep his balance as the bike swerved and fell onto the ground. The man glowered at him. "You touch me one more time, and you'll end up over there with your bike. You got that, boy?"

Anger rose inside Felix as he turned away and picked up his bike. He balled his hands into fists. As he turned around, ready to pounce, he was surprised and slightly disappointed to see him gone. He scanned the faces around him, but the man had melted into the crowd.

The sound of screeching brakes followed by a revving engine drew everyone's attention. A large truck turned the corner from Wipplingerstraße, honking its horn as the people on the street in front of the police station parted to make way. The crowd moved forward as one when the driver got out and opened the rear doors. The disappointment was palpable when the truck turned out to be empty.

However, the mob didn't have to wait long. The double doors of the police station swung open once more. More Brownshirts poured out, this time accompanied by armed police officers. The officers walked with their heads held high and formed a corridor leading down the stairs toward the truck. Felix watched the spectacle in horror, certain this is what the crowd had come to see.

Uniformed, senior police officers in various states were dragged down the stairs. Their uniforms were torn, their insignias and badges ripped off. Some sported bloodied but defiant faces, others trod past the jeering onlookers with their heads bowed, their gazes fixed on the street a few steps before their feet. As they climbed on board the truck, finding a spot on the hard wooden benches on either side, the crowd spilled forward, closing any potential escape route. People spat at the policemen, or failing that, on the side of the truck. The Brownshirts and policemen in charge allowed the violent spectacle to proceed for a few minutes before gently dispersing their brethren. The truck doors were then closed with pompous ceremony.

Felix stared at the grotesque scene from a distance. When the crowd moved forward, he stood where he was, holding his bike. The truck slowly started moving, the driver giving the angry mob ample time to release its fury on the toppled men of power inside. Felix felt sick, but he knew he needed to leave before the situation escalated further. He looked around, searching for more sensible minds to intervene and end this madness. Then he realized those very people were in the back of the truck. Sadness overwhelmed him as he cast his eyes on the police headquarters once more. Bright lights shone from every window, but all he saw was a veil of darkness taking over. A window on the top floor opened, and two men appeared. A large roll of red fabric was attached to the building, secured by the men with nails. The crowd below went silent. The men tugged at the fabric and slowly unfurled the roll. Felix's stomach roiled, and he turned away. The crowd had thinned after the police chiefs were escorted off, and there was now enough space on the opposite side of the street for him to fit through. Felix stepped onto his bike and pushed his pedals down with as much force as he could muster. He didn't look back when the loudest cheer of the night erupted behind him. It was the end of Vienna as he knew it.

FOUR

Vienna
12 March 1938, early morning

The wind howled in the darkness of the deserted Aspern airport, and Karl adjusted the collar of his winter jacket, then quickly stuffed his hands back in its deep pockets. His eyes were fixed on the Junkers Ju 52 airplane slowly taxiing toward them. It had touched down with grace minutes ago, carrying some of the Reich's most prominent figures.

Karl glanced at the people standing on the tarmac with him, all but a few prominent Austrian Nazis. Globočnik stood directly beside him. The leader of Vienna's SS, Ernst Kaltenbrunner, stood a few paces farther. Karl let out a chuckle, which was muffled by the wind, when he looked at the face of Michael Skubl, the head of the police in Vienna. Skubl must've felt Karl's gaze, for he turned toward him, meeting his eyes momentarily. Karl offered a curt nod, which the chief of police did not return.

The roar of the plane's three engines increased as it turned to a stop in front of the welcoming party. The pilot switched the engines off, and the propeller noise faded. Karl's heartbeat increased as he heard someone inside the Junkers working the door. He squeezed his hands inside his pockets, telling himself to stand tall and confident. He had carried out his boss's orders to perfection; the senior party officials on board the plane were arriving in a Vienna under Nazi control. Not just Vienna, but all of Austria.

The door opened, and almost immediately the imposing figure of his boss appeared in the opening. Reinhard Heydrich strode confidently down the short flight of steps and onto the tarmac. The head of the Sicherheitsdienst then waited for the next person to disembark.

Heinrich Himmler, the bespectacled Reichsführer, carried himself gracefully, holding on to the handrailing of the stairs. A wave of pride surged through Karl as he watched Heydrich and Himmler approach the welcoming party. He had never been this close to the second most powerful man in the Reich—Himmler had Hitler's ear. He took his hands from his pockets and drew his shoulders back. As soon as the senior officials were within earshot, Felix and the other men saluted them in unison.

"Heil Hitler!" Their voices were masked by the wind as Heydrich and Himmler raised their right hands in return.

Heydrich ignored the other men as he approached Karl, gesturing toward one of the large Mercedes-Benz limousines lined up on the tarmac. "Vogt, which one is ours? I want to get the Reichsführer out of this blasted weather. And I need some breakfast." His tone crisp and commanding, blue eyes full of purpose.

"This one at the front, sir," Karl responded, rushing toward the car and opening the door for his boss. Heydrich didn't get in, instead waiting for Himmler to finish shaking the hands of the assembled Austrian Nazis. "Was your flight okay, sir?" Karl felt uncomfortable making small talk with his boss, but to his surprise, a thin smile crept onto Heydrich's face.

"It was fine. This is a good trip after the events of last night. I'm looking forward to hearing all about it from you on the way over."

"Of course, sir." Karl hid his surprise as Himmler finished talking to Globočnik and made his way over to the car. *He wants me to ride with them?* His throat went dry as Himmler nodded at him as he got into the car. Heydrich had moved to the other side of the car, and signaled for Karl to take the front seat. He closed Himmler's door and did as he was instructed, taking his seat next to the driver, who looked at him expectantly. "Hotel Regina," Karl said, clearing the nerves from his throat. The car started moving, and he saw the surprise on Globočnik's face as he passed them. Karl was unsure how to proceed next, but thankfully, Heydrich took charge.

"Reichsführer, please allow me to introduce Standartenführer Karl Vogt. He's spent the past six months preparing for our arrival." Heydrich spoke matter-of-factly, and Karl turned around in his seat, facing the men in the back. "He's one of our youngest foreign agents, and he coordinated with local party members to ensure we took control of the Vienna police force last night."

Himmler listened patiently, his eyes studying Karl intently. He turned his gaze to the window, where a dark Danube River flashed by as they crossed the bridge into the city. Then his attention returned to Karl. "High praise from Reinhard, young Herr Vogt. How would you say your operation fared last night?" Himmler's voice was more subdued than Karl remembered from rallies.

"I can't take all the credit, Herr Reichsführer. Many of the local politicians helped." Karl glanced at Heydrich, who looked somewhat impatient, as if urging him to get to the point. Himmler, on the other hand, nodded and looked relaxed. Nevertheless, Karl understood he only had until they reached the hotel to debrief his superiors. "We activated the Sturmabteilung to cause minor confrontations, mostly limited to the Jewish district of Leopoldstadt. This made it easier to sell the concept of anarchy in the city after Schuschnigg's announcement. At the same time, the many police officers loyal to the party sprang into action all across the country."

Himmler interrupted him, raising his index finger. "According to the reports I read, we had thousands of men loyal to us spread across the departments everywhere in Austria. Did we run into any trouble or resistance from those colleagues not known to be pro-party?"

"Little trouble, sir. In Vienna, our numbers were even bigger than anticipated, with many on the force joining unexpectedly."

Karl allowed himself a grin. "They were waiting for the right moment to show their allegiance."

Himmler returned the smile. "I take it we've documented those individuals who professed their loyalty to us prior to last night's events? I want to make sure they are properly rewarded."

"Certainly, sir."

"Very well." Himmler's face turned serious. "What was Skubl doing at the airport? I don't recall reading about his support in the earlier reports. Or did I miss something?"

"He did not support us publicly, sir. Odilo Globočnik spoke to him multiple times, but he was unwilling to give us a clear answer. If I may be so frank, I had the impression he was hedging his bets."

"Hmm. That's what I thought." Himmler turned to Heydrich. "Replace him with someone more suitable."

Heydrich nodded and scribbled something on his notepad. Karl suppressed a smile; his boss had a frightfully good memory, and the matter of replacing the chief of police for Vienna would be at the top of his list of priorities. Skubl wouldn't last the day.

"So, we have control of all layers of the Viennese police, with a new chief ready to lead them soon?" Himmler looked at Heydrich. "Do you have someone in mind?"

"I do, sir. I'd like to suggest we put our plan of incorporating the Vienna police into the Gestapo into action, and have a uniform approach across the board."

"Splendid. Let's discuss this later." Himmler turned back to Karl. "You mentioned the Sturmabteilung causing some altercations. Any substantial damage to non-Jewish property?"

Karl had expected the question. Despite his best efforts, some of the Brownshirts had gone about their tasks a bit too brusquely, indiscriminately smashing windows in the inner city. He'd need to speak to Odilo about that. "Some collateral damage, but nothing we can't fix. I'll make sure the gauleiter hears of it and compensates these people adequately."

"Whatever happens in the Jewish district happens, and I don't care. But see to it that we garner the support of the good Austrian citizens. This is the time to make a good first impression on the many new subjects in the Reich."

The car slowed down, and Karl was both relieved and a little disappointed to arrive at Hotel Regina. Karl jumped from the car and opened the door for the Reichsführer. To his surprise, Himmler placed a hand on his shoulder.

"How old are you exactly, Vogt?"

"Twenty-one, sir."

Himmler shook his head and turned his attention to Heydrich, who joined them from the other side. "You recruited this young man yourself, Reinhard?"

"I did."

"We could use a few more of you." Himmler patted Karl on the shoulder before stepping toward the entrance of the hotel. "You have a very bright future ahead of you, young Vogt." He raised his hand in a salute, which Karl quickly returned, and disappeared into the hotel. Heydrich followed him, but not before turning around and giving Karl an appraising nod. When his boss also stepped through the revolving doors, Karl let out a deep, satisfied sigh. He was on top of the world.

FIVE

Prague, Czechoslovakia
12 March 1938, morning

A dela Beran rushed through the quiet streets. She loved Prague best at this hour—the first rays of sunlight reflecting on the majestic buildings towering over her provided a sense of calm. Today, she anticipated a storm waiting at the office.

"Miss Beran, good morning! You're earlier than usual." The man in the kiosk greeted her with a familiar smile.

"I thought I'd get a head start on the day, Georgi." Adela returned the smile. "I hope I'm not too early for the papers?"

He reached for a stack and handed them to her. "You know I always have these ready for you! I've been up a few hours."

"Of course." She quickly scanned the front pages. The news was the same everywhere.

"Say, if you don't mind me asking, Miss Beran." Georgi's voice turned unusually serious, a little insecure even, and Adela glanced up from her papers. "What do you think this means for us?" His eyes went to the headline plastered atop the *Lidové noviny*: *Hitler takes Austria*.

Adela didn't immediately answer, letting the gravity of the deceptively simple headline sink in. Even though the annexation was expected, the way Hitler bullied the Austrian chancellor from office was frightening. "I don't know, Georgi. We're right in the middle of it now." When Georgi's face creased, she quickly added, "But in a way, it was always in the cards that Hitler would try to claim his home country."

"He said Austria was always going to be part of his empire, but I'm not so sure he'll leave it at that. It all seemed to go so easy, judging from what I've read. Nobody has even condemned his actions."

The newspaper vendor echoed Adela's thoughts, but she feigned optimism, patting her stack of papers. "Let's see what the day brings. We might still see condemnation from Britain and France. They had little time to respond." Georgi looked unsure, and before he could say anything, she added, "I must be on my way. Have a good day!"

She continued through the city until she reached the banks of the Vltava River, splitting Prague's east and west. On a good day, she would cross the Charles Bridge and make her way up to her office climbing the many steps on the other side of the river, but today was not a good day. With a sigh, she sat down at the streetcar stop at Staroměstská. She looked up at the stately Prague Castle across the water, impatient to start her day.

"Most importantly, we need to remain vigilant. Hitler's Germany now surrounds us on three sides. I will appeal to the international community to put a halt to this aggressive policy of expansion."

The room was quiet as President Edvard Beneš spoke. Adela stood to the side, near a window overlooking the city. From her vantage point, the dark bags under the president's exceptionally creased eyes bulged.

"Despite Hitler's words, Austria did not ask for this. And if we are to keep our sovereignty, we must take action now. My promise to everybody in this room is that I will work tirelessly to strengthen our alliances within Europe." Beneš paused, taking a sip of water as he looked around the room. Every single person in the room was an integral part of the Czechoslovak government. Having everybody in one room was rare, and it amplified the gravity of the situation. Beneš put his glass down, the sound of it hitting the wooden table exceptionally loud. "We are in Hitler's crosshairs. Make no mistake about it. Maybe not today, but I have no doubt we'll find the Wehrmacht at our borders soon, if we don't take action. I'm counting on all of you to do your duty." The president nodded and sat down, a clear signal the meeting was over. People rose from their chairs, the doors to the hallway opening, and the quiet chatter of a hundred people filing out, hurrying back to their desks.

Adela lingered at her spot a while longer, waiting for the more senior officials to leave first. She studied Beneš, who was talking to his chief of military intelligence, František Moravec. The latter spoke in a quiet voice, but his wide eyes and arched eyebrows displayed urgency. Beneš' explicit reference to the German army being on their doorstep had shocked Adela and she wondered, what information was Moravec relaying to the president?

"Adela?" She looked up to find Martinek Kucera standing next to her. "Do you have a minute?"

"Sure." Martinek and Adela joined the foreign ministry at the same time two years ago, straight from university. Both had made quick advances in their careers since, with Martinek a liaison to the European embassies. "I assume you need me to translate some of the transcripts coming in?"

He shook his head. "Not yet. We're still waiting for the reports to arrive. I spoke to Vienna earlier, and they're scrambling to get more information on the situation with the new government."

"They appointed the Nazi chancellor, didn't they?"

"Seyss-Inquart, yes. But only after Hitler threatened to send in the army he'd massed on the border."

"And yet, he sent it in anyway."

"My contact at the embassy said the new chancellor requested Germany's help."

Adela frowned. "Help with what?"

"There were reports of riots in the big cities following Schuschnigg's resignation. From what our colleagues witnessed, these so-called riots were on a very small scale, and limited to a few districts." Martinek's voice trailed off, and Adela knew why.

"Is your family okay?" She lowered her voice. "I know you want to be professional, but you're allowed to worry."

Martinek shook his head. "I spoke to my father last night after the chancellor's resignation. He said they were fine, but he didn't mention anything about riots." His eyes turned sad. "But then, they don't live in Leopoldstadt, where I suspect most of the trouble was."

"You should call your family."

"I will." He regained his usual confidence, a steely, determined look returning. "But I'm sure they're okay. I'm more worried about the breakdown of the government. If Hitler placed Seyss-Inquart in charge, you can be certain he'll be looking to install a Nazi government as soon as he can."

"And Austria will turn into a puppet state."

SIX

Vienna
12 March 1938, morning

The Wolff family was up early. While Anton appeared to have his usual appetite, Felix settled for a coffee at breakfast.

"Are you sure you should be heading out to the shop? Perhaps it's better to keep it closed and see how things pan out today?" Rebecca Wolff said, echoing Felix's sentiments, but one look at his father's face told him enough.

Felix and his mother exchanged a few looks while his father finished his plate of latkes. On any normal day, Felix would've devoured a good number of the pancakes himself, but he was too nervous about what the city outside would be like.

"We can't afford to close even for a day, Becca." Anton's voice was calm, but it was impossible to miss the edge. "Besides, all seems to be quiet again." He walked to the window and moved the curtains, revealing a quiet street, as if to underline his point. "I'm sure everything will be fine on Haidgasse."

Felix and his mother both knew there was little sense in arguing with him, and Rebecca gave her son a big hug, then kissed Anton. "Just be careful."

The Wolff men stepped outside onto Lampigasse and made their way to the entrance of the Augarten park. They liked to cut through the park on their way to the shop, a ten-minute walk at their regular pace. Felix was especially relieved to avoid the more crowded streets today, and the serenity of the park calmed him somewhat. After leaving the police headquarters on the Ring last night, he'd raced home, determined not to be stopped again. Despite that, he'd seen plenty more gatherings of Brownshirts mixed with what appeared to be regular citizens in front of numerous buildings on the Ring.

"I know you're worried about what's going on, but we can't hide inside our home." His father's voice interrupted his thoughts, and Felix looked up to meet Anton's determined eyes. "Not today, not after what happened last night. We can't cower in the shadows."

"You didn't see what I did, Papa. They were tearing up the city." It was impossible to erase the scenes he witnessed when crossing Salztorbrucke, the bridge connecting the inner city with Leopoldstadt. "Karmeliterplatz was on fire. The Brownshirts were tearing people from their homes, throwing books and all sorts of furniture from the windows. I only escaped because I was on my bike, and they were too busy piling everything onto the fire in the middle of the square."

"There were bound to be riots. People are upset."

Felix stopped abruptly. "These people weren't upset about what happened, Papa. These were the people that were waiting for the Nazis to topple the government. They were attacking our people; they waited for their chance. And worst of all, their neighbors were only more than happy to stand by and do nothing. Or join in, even." A wave of sadness washed over him.

"They must've had previous issues or problems with each other. Riots always bring out the worst in people. Even the civilized ones."

"No, Papa." Felix raised his voice, his frustration boiling over. "This was a planned attack. This was no accident." He took a deep breath while his father's eyes widened. "And not just an attack on us. Seyss-Inquart's appointment as chancellor was the catalyst, giving them the legal power to do as they please. I'm sure the assault on the police headquarters was just one more way to take control. I don't understand how you can pretend everything is fine, Papa."

They walked through the park in silence for a few minutes, the humming of cars passing by on the other side of the walls mixed with the chirping of birds providing a false sense of normality. They neared the park's southeastern exit, and Anton stopped and turned to his son.

"The only thing we can do is to continue our lives as best we can. We run a bicycle shop tucked away in a little corner of this big city of ours. We're little people; we pose no threat as long as we keep our heads down, and do what we've always done."

"Those people last night were little people too, Papa."

"Riots, Felix. Karmeliterplatz was always going to see trouble." He looked thoughtful, then a small, confident smile spread across his face. "But you know the reason why I think we'll be fine?"

Felix didn't respond, shrugging in semi defeat.

"We're Austrians first, Jews second. We don't openly practice our religion. I'd be surprised if half of the people in our building even knew we're Jewish." Anton had a triumphant air about him as he continued. "We'll be fine, Felix. Now come, we have work to do."

IT TOOK LESS than five minutes for two words to crush Anton's reality. *Juden Raus.* The words were painted across the shop windows in a sloppy manner, the red paint dripping down in uneven streams, smearing the entire storefront.

Anton stood in front of his store without speaking for several minutes, as if in a trance. Felix looked up and down the street and saw only a few other stores had suffered a similar fate. Herr Brauer of the shoe store down the road was already at work, plunging a large sponge into a bucket of soapy water.

"We should start cleaning this up, Papa." Felix spoke softly but firmly, and his father snapped from his daze, nodding and digging out a key chain from his pocket.

They spent the next hour silently scrubbing the windows on their quiet street. Very few people passed through, and not a single one of them stopped for a chat, quickly rushing by, pretending not to see the words plastered across their shop windows. Felix suspected something was off as soon as the footsteps stopped behind him.

"You need to come with us." The words were spoken with authority, but the voice was oddly high pitched. Felix turned to find two boys a few years younger than him smirking at him in dark-brown uniforms and lederhosen. The red-and-white armband with the black swastika girded their left arms. *Hitler Youth*. Before Felix could respond, his father did.

"On whose authority? And where to?" Anton spoke with the tone of a father scolding an impertinent child. Felix felt his stomach turn.

The boys looked momentarily taken aback, then the one that spoke earlier took a step toward Anton. "This is your store, isn't it, Jew? We need you to come help on Karmeliterplatz."

"On the Führer's authority," the other chimed in, with a twisted smile. "Let's go."

"Piss off."

Felix gasped at his father's response. He opened his mouth, desperate to diffuse the situation, when his father held up his hand, instantly silencing him.

"I'm not taking orders from you. How old are you, anyway? If the Führer needs me at Karmeliterplatz, he'd better damn well come down here himself. Now leave me alone, I can't run a business like this." Anton pointed at the remaining letters on the windows and plunged his rag into the soap, ignoring the boys.

The Hitler Youth looked at each other in surprise. One of them mumbled something about teaching the old man a lesson, but the taller one—clearly in charge—shook his head and turned around. Felix watched them march down the street toward Karmeliterplatz until they turned the corner, disappearing from sight.

"Papa, what was—"

"Not another word, Felix. Just clean the shop. I'm not taking orders from anyone, let alone a child." Anton scrubbed furiously at the large *J* on the window.

Felix was certain this wasn't the end of the matter, and his eyes kept darting toward the end of the street where the boys had disappeared.

It took only fifteen minutes for them to return. This time, they brought reinforcements. Four bulky men wearing uniforms in the same shade of brown stormed toward Felix and Anton.

"Papa," Felix said, signaling toward the impending danger, seeing one of the boys point at them. Anton got to his feet and dropped his rag into the soap. He held his arms next to his body, adopting a neutral stance. Felix stood beside him, his heartbeat increasing with every step the Brownshirts took.

When the men reached them, they didn't speak. There was no warning as they punched Anton and Felix in the stomach. All air left Felix's lungs as he gasped for breath. Another punch had him seeing stars, and he struggled to stay on his feet. His arms were taken in an iron grip and he had the odd sensation of floating as he was manhandled through the street, the familiar buildings spinning as they passed him by. The face of the tall Hitler Youth appeared in his vision, his lips moving, the words not registering.

His senses returned to him as he was roughly dropped onto the cold, hard ground. His knees hurt, but he was given no time to consider the pain as one of the Brownshirts handed him a dirty rag.

"Start cleaning, *Judensau*—Jew pig." The man pointed at the slogan in white paint on the cobblestones in front of him. *Vote Yes for a free Austria.* The optimism in the words was from another time. A time when people could speak freely, when brutes didn't control the streets. Felix looked around and saw dozens of people on their knees, men and women scrubbing the streets with dirty rags insufficient for the task. His father sat next to him, holding the rag, but not making a move to do as he was told.

"Papa, you're making things worse. Start cleaning," Felix hissed at his father, barely controlling his anger, while he started scrubbing. He noticed a crowd of onlookers forming, laughing and pointing at some of the people cleaning one of the walls on the far side. Felix cast his eyes down, humiliation adding to his anger. It was bad enough to be told what to do by the Brownshirts in uniform, but to see neighbors, people that probably visited their shop in the past, delight in their misfortune was truly disheartening. He scrubbed the cobblestones harder, but it made no difference. The paint was barely coming off. Felix looked up to see his father sitting cross-legged, the rag next to him. Before he could say anything, the Hitler Youth boys appeared. The tallest made a show of taking out a small notebook and pencil. Felix felt all strength sapped from his body when he spoke.

"Names and address, swine."

SEVEN

Vienna
14 March 1938

Karl walked into the spacious suite his boss had secured for himself at the Hotel Regina. He wasn't surprised to find Reinhard Heydrich wearing his complete formal uniform this morning. No doubt the head of the Sicherheitsdienst had a packed day, meeting with people on various rungs of the political and social ladder. Karl was pleased and a little anxious to have been summoned first thing in the morning. It showed the value his boss placed on this meeting.

"Have a seat, Vogt." Heydrich waved at a comfortable chair in the salon area of the suite. "And pour us some coffee. I need a minute."

Karl took two porcelain cups and saucers and did as he was asked. He looked around the room, studying the ornate decorations, catching himself tapping his foot. Luxurious surroundings like these made him feel like a fish out of water.

Heydrich walked back into the room, a frown on his face.

"These *Idioten* are getting on my nerves. Does everything move so slowly in this city?"

"The people in this country need a bit of encouragement, sir. Anything I can help with?"

"*Ach, nein.*" Heydrich waved his hand dismissively. "I'll deal with it. I expected we'd have moved into our new headquarters by now, but apparently some people are making a fuss about the location."

"Hotel Metropole?"

"Some disagreement about some of our refurnishing plans. They should be happy we're compensating them at all." He shook his head, then took a sip of the coffee, which visibly energized him. "But this is none of your concern. I have a different task for you. Well, two, actually." Karl inched forward in his chair while Heydrich reached for a folder, opening it, then quickly closing it again. "Never mind, you don't need this. You've got plenty of connections in the city by now, don't you?"

"I'd like to think so."

"Very well. With the new referendum coming up in less than a month, I don't need to tell you that anything but an overpowering majority in favor of the unification would be considered a failure in the Führer's eyes."

Karl nodded. Austria joining the Reich would validate the previous week's actions. The enthusiastic reception of the Wehrmacht troops crossing the border, as well as the crowds lining the streets to catch a glimpse of the Führer, had sparked an overwhelming sense of optimism in Germany that the referendum was a done deal. Karl, and Heydrich, had their reservations. This was too important a result to be left up to chance.

"How big a percentage of the Austrian people do you think will vote in favor?" Heydrich looked at him with his eagle eyes while he took another sip of coffee.

Karl shifted in his seat. "The majority. If I had to guess, maybe sixty percent."

"That won't do."

"I agree. The reality is that we need influential leaders of the community to support us."

"The church."

Karl's left eye twitched. "Yes, and the socialists. If we can get them on our side, the result will put our legitimacy beyond doubt."

"Can you pull that off? On both accounts?" He leaned forward in his chair, putting the coffee cup down.

"I know just the person."

Heydrich looked pleased. "Perfect. Then there's one other matter I need your assistance with." He pulled out a different folder and held it out to Karl. "It's concerning the Jewish problem in this country. We've got a very able administrator coming in from Berlin to handle this, but he's going to need a bit of help getting acquainted with the landscape. I suggest you pay him a visit and give him some directions."

Karl opened the folder and scanned its contents. "This sounds like fun, sir."

Karl and Globočnik clinked their mugs with force, then downed more than a quarter on the first draw. Karl smacked his lips, enjoying the setting of the small Viennese *Beisl*. Unpretentious and tucked away on a small street close to the city center, it was packed with men enjoying an after-work drink. It reminded Karl of his own simple roots back home in Bavaria. He spent many of his adolescent years in similar establishments. It was easy to blend in, and he was pleased to see that despite Odilo's elevated position within the Nazi Party, none of the working class patrons in this small bar looked at him twice, never mind recognized him. The copious amount of beer consumed also meant those present spoke with loud voices, and listened with small ears. That suited Karl perfectly as he leaned across the table.

"Congratulations on your promotion, Mr. State Secretary. What time is your ceremony tomorrow?"

"In the morning, so I'll have to make this an early night." Globočnik nodded, although Karl knew it to mean the opposite.

"Seyss-Inquart will announce it in the early afternoon as I settle into my new office."

"I told you things would move quickly for you." Karl took another sip. He was genuinely pleased for his friend. "But I'll admit I didn't expect you to climb the ranks at this pace!" He held out his mug again, which his friend clinked with enthusiasm, then signaled to the bartender for another round.

"I'm grateful for your help, Karl. You having the ear of both the chancellor and Heydrich made a big difference, I have no doubt." He waited for the barkeep to set down their fresh drinks before continuing. "And there was a bit of luck involved. All those police officers unexpectedly turned out to be sympathetic to our cause, well beyond what our planners estimated."

"Sometimes you create your own luck. Speaking of which, now that you're moving into more traditional politics, I may need to ask you for a favor."

Odilo held out the palms of his hands in an inviting gesture. "Anything for you, my friend."

"We need to make sure the referendum goes our way."

"It will. There's no doubt. Have you not seen how the Führer was welcomed across the border? Hundreds of thousands are expected at his speech on Heldenplatz tomorrow."

"Heydrich wants there to be no discussion about its validity. It needs to be an absolute landslide."

"It will be."

Karl placed his mug down and looked his friend in the eye. "Odilo, Hitler wants at least ninety-five percent. You and I both know this will only happen if we drum up additional political support. This needs to be a fix."

Globočnik looked at him with clarity, the haze of alcohol clearing from his eyes. "There's only one way to do that. We need Renner to support the Anschluss."

"Exactly. The people will listen to him, and if he supports us, so will the smaller parties. He's key to political support. Can you get to him?"

"I think so." Globočnik pursed his lips, thinking for a minute.

"He'll need some convincing, and he's certainly not one of ours, but he's a pragmatist. I can get him to see sense. But just Renner alone won't be enough."

"No, it won't." Karl took a deep breath, but before he could speak, Globočnik finished his thoughts.

"I'll take care of the church. They'll need a slightly different approach, but I'm happy to lean on them a bit. And I know just who to turn the screws on."

Karl felt a deep sense of relief. "Thank you, Odilo."

"Don't worry about it." The state-secretary-to-be raised his glass. "It'll be my pleasure."

KARL REPORTED at the Ministry of Interior early the next morning. As expected, Odilo had insisted they celebrate his promotion properly, and his head was pounding as he announced himself to the woman at the reception desk. He was promptly sent up to the third floor, where he was told to take a seat.

He closed his eyes for a moment, reflecting on the previous evening. Odilo seemed very confident about swaying Renner as well as the church. Karl was secretly pleased he didn't have to deal with the clergy himself. He didn't mind playing political games, but he hated the inclusion of faith, most specifically the deference required when dealing with those pompous men of so-called faith.

"Herr . . . Vogt?" A man with a sharp face and especially high cheekbones approached. He looked slightly annoyed, although Karl felt that could also simply be the face of a busy person. "You're here to see me? I have to say it's a little unusual for visitors to show up to my office unannounced." *Annoyed, then.*

"I apologize, Scharführer Eichmann." Karl stuck out his hand. "I'm here to assist you with the transports of the political dissidents. I thought it best we meet as soon as possible, considering the situation."

Adolf Eichmann reluctantly shook his hand. "What situation?" He made no move to invite Karl further.

"From what I understand, you've been put
nizing the first transport from Vienna. Is that cor

"Where's the situation in that?" Eichmann
Karl decided he needed to take a different app
most disarming smile.

"I believe we may have gotten off on the wrong foot, Scharführer Eichmann. I understand you arrived recently in Vienna?"

"A few days ago, yes."

"I've been here for the past six months, familiarizing myself with the country, its people, and its leadership. We're on the same side, sir. My superior mentioned you're working under a very short deadline to get the first enemies of the Reich transported from Vienna. I'd like to offer my help in making that happen. I have the connections to get things done."

"And you think I don't?" Eichmann's words came at Karl in a collected, condescending tone, his eyes narrowing as he took a step closer to Karl. "How old are you, anyway?"

Karl held his ground, meeting Eichmann's gaze, making a concerted effort not to reveal how he felt about this midlevel bureaucrat's amateurish outburst. "I'm twenty-one years old, not that it matters. I don't feel we're making any progress here. Would you like me to return to my superior and report that you have everything under control, and that his offer of assistance is unnecessary?" He produced the folder Heydrich had given him the day prior and held out a list of a hundred-something names. "Shall I tell him that you'll track down the locations of these men, and have them on a train out of Vienna by 1 April?"

Eichmann's arrogant stance melted as he fixed his eyes on the list. "Where did you get that?" Then something appeared to click in his brain. With a much softer voice, he asked, "Who . . . who is your superior?"

Karl smiled and shook his head. "Do you think that's the most relevant question you should be asking at this point? A better response would be to accept my help. I think we both know access to this information is limited to a very small number of individuals within the Sicherheitsdienst."

Eichmann nodded, his cheeks a little pale. "Yes, come to think of it, I think I may have been too hasty in my assessment of your capabilities based on your age."

"That's all right, Herr Eichmann. Your assignment is important to the party leadership, and I understand you're a busy man. I would probably have responded in the same manner if someone showed up at my office out of the blue, badgering me about the project." He wouldn't have, but Karl knew when to keep his ego in check. "Would you mind if I asked how you're faring with the arrests of the people on the list?"

"Not as well as I would like." The bespectacled man sighed. "I prepared that very list myself back in Berlin, making sure to double-check the home and work addresses with our informants in the Vienna police force." For the first time, Karl was impressed. If Eichmann compiled the list from Germany, gathering information and cross-referencing with his Austrian contacts, he was perhaps not as useless a bureaucrat as he at first seemed. "But when I sent the first *Einsatzgruppen* to arrest these dissidents, most of them were gone."

"Gone? How so?" Karl feigned ignorance. He was well aware of what had happened.

"The Austrian Sturmabteilung and police beat me to it. They took swift action on the night of the Anschluss. A bit too swift, to my mind." Eichmann looked exasperated. "It was supposed to be a well-coordinated round of arrests. Now these people are scattered around jails across the city, with poorly administered police stations unable or unwilling to help. Worse, it's given the scoundrels that weren't picked up ample warning. They've gone into hiding."

"Well, Herr Eichmann, it sounds like you find yourself in a bit of a pickle with the locals." Karl couldn't suppress a smile. "The good news is that I've made this particular part of networking something of a specialty. Why don't we head over to your office, and we can get started on tracking these people down. We don't want to delay the first transport to Dachau now, do we?"

EIGHT

Prague
22 March 1938

Adela was pleased to leave the office at seven; she deserved to unwind and not take the weight of the world home for one evening.

It was already dark when she stepped out of the main entrance of Prague Castle. The lights along the walkway in the garden made the surroundings even more beautiful than usual, and she stopped to appreciate her place of work. Terraced gardens lined the hillside, with green lawns, flowers preparing to bloom for spring, and commanding trees that had stood for decades. Adela greeted a groundskeeper trimming one of the bushes across the walkway. She walked on, the sight opposite the castle equally impressive. The river below was illuminated by a sea of lights coming from the windows of the houses, shops, and offices in the city. She hurried toward the tram stop down the road, catching a tram just as it started moving.

The ride into the city gave her a moment to reflect. Ever since the annexation of Austria, Adela's days had bled into one another. While each brought new developments, they all felt the same, the forces at work far beyond President Beneš' control. Try as he might, Beneš was unable to garner assurances that England and France would stand with them in case Hitler decided Czechoslovakia was to be the next country to be assimilated into the Reich.

She almost forgot to alight, jumping off the tram just before the doors slammed shut behind her. The cold air refreshed her, and she crossed the busy Náměstí Republiky, cutting through a series of smaller streets to make it to Grand Cafe Orient. The sudden rush of dozens of voices chatting as she opened the door, warm air hitting her cold cheeks, and the sweet smell of freshly baked strudels welcomed her. The cafe felt like home. Adela scanned the tightly packed tables and found her friends gathered around two booths in the back.

"Adela! You're here, just in time!" Her best friend, Greta Pereles, approached her before she could make it to the group, giving her a big hug.

"Otik isn't here yet?" Adela took off her coat and hung it on the simple coat rack next to their booth. "I lost track of time at work, and I thought I'd miss the surprise."

Greta gave her a cheeky smile. "No, he's late, as usual. Like you, really." Her face turned serious. "Rough day at work?" She held up two fingers to a passing waiter.

"Much like any other day."

"Is it true what the papers say? Is Beneš losing control of the talks?"

Adela waved her hand dismissively. "It's not as bad as they make it out to be. Judging by some of the narratives you'd think it's us, not the Austrians, who have been invaded. But it's not great: The Brits and French are taking Hitler's promise about not grabbing any more land at face value. They don't want to get involved."

The waiter returned with a tray filled with drinks. Greta helped distribute them, handing Adela a foaming glass of beer. She took a large sip and looked around the room. It was good to see normal life continuing, with people laughing, eating, and drinking like they always did. It reminded her she needed to get out more, instead of spending her days and evenings at the office.

"Speaking of Austria, I have some relatives who are trying to get out." Greta took a sip of wine. "My uncle and aunt's bakery was ransacked the other day. The Brownshirts came in and tore their supplies to pieces." She tried to keep a brave face, but Adela could see the hurt in her friend's eyes.

"I'm so sorry, Greta. They should leave the country." Adela had read numerous reports about violence against the Jewish community in Austria. Greta's family's experience was depressingly common. "Where are they looking to go?"

Greta shook her head. "I'm sorry, Adela, I don't want to ruin your night. I'm sure you get enough of this at work."

"No, no, come on. Tell me what's going on. I can see you're upset." Adela felt her chest contract, and she took her friend's hand. "Is there anything we can do for them?"

"Despite what the Nazis say about wanting all Jews out of the Reich, they're making it nearly impossible. They'll only issue an exit visa when they have an entry visa to a country outside the Reich."

Adela frowned, understanding. "And those countries will only issue a visa when they have an exit visa."

"Exactly. It's a never-ending loop. My uncle says only those with good connections are getting out. It's either that or bribing senior officials. But my family doesn't have that kind of money."

"Do you know which countries they've applied to?"

"They went to the Czechoslovak embassy first but were informed the borders are closed, and that Czechoslovakia isn't taking in any Jewish refugees. They then tried Britain and America, but they will only consider applications when they have affidavits from relatives in the country, or confirmed jobs. They don't know anyone there."

A cheer rose from the table, and Adela turned to see the familiar figure of Otik Mares making his way across the room. "There's the birthday boy."

"Good!" Greta's tone was a little too cheerful. "Let's enjoy the evening and not think about what's happening in the world for a few hours. There's nothing we can do about it now." Her smile couldn't mask the sadness in her eyes. The men at the table started a birthday song, and as Adela joined in, she couldn't help but shake the feeling her government was doing Greta's family wrong. There had to be something she could do.

Adela was at the office early the next morning. Otik's birthday celebration had been the break she needed, and although she had been one of the first to leave, she was feeling the effects as she poured herself a cup of coffee. She moved to her desk, sighing at the stack of files waiting for her. After leafing through the papers, she started reading a transcript of a rally held by Germany's propaganda minister Goebbels. It was Adela's job to assess whether the information in the document was valuable enough to be sent to the translators down the line. It meant she'd become quite accustomed to the words of some of the most prominent Nazis. She especially despised Goebbels, whose speeches were silky smooth, but unapologetically inflaming and hateful when one scratched only a little beneath the surface.

After two pages she tossed the folder aside. There was nothing new in the speech apart from Goebbels, as expected with the upcoming referendum, ramping up his efforts to legitimize Nazi Germany's annexation of Austria. His words only worsened Adela's headache, and she needed to move about a bit. She checked the clock. Ten. *He should be in by now.*

She made her way up two floors and stepped into a large hallway. It was quiet but for a few hushed conversations in the offices she passed. When she reached the end of the hallway, she turned and knocked on the open door. A man looked up and smiled.

"Adela, what a lovely surprise. What brings you here?" Martinek got up, waving her to a chair. "Sit, yes?"

"I need a favor." Adela took a few steps into the office but didn't sit. Martinek's face turned serious.

"Okay, no time for pleasantries. What's going on?"

She held up her hands and let out a nervous chuckle. "I'm sorry. Where are my manners. It's just that this has been on my mind all night." She told Martinek about Greta's family's situation in Austria. He listened attentively, only humming in acknowledgment a few times.

"And they live in Vienna?"

"Yes."

He sighed and leaned on his desk. "Your friend isn't wrong. The official line is to decline all visa applications from Jews, no matter what. The truth is that we've been overwhelmed with refugee requests since Austria was annexed. I don't agree with it, but it was the easiest way to create policy."

"I understand. But that doesn't help my friend's family. They're stuck, and it wouldn't surprise me if things turn even worse for them soon. It's only a matter of time before they impose their anti-Jewish laws in Austria as well."

"I know. My contacts in Vienna are echoing those sentiments." Martinek pursed his lips, then looked up in contemplation for a minute. Adela envisioned Greta's family in Vienna, living in fear of the next assault on their business. *There has to be something I can do.*

Martinek cleared his throat. "I think we may need to get a little creative about this. Because of the official policy, there is no way they'll get a visa in Vienna." Adela felt deflated, but he raised a hand. "But if we were to get something arranged from Prague, and hand it down to the people in Vienna, it might work. I get along quite well with the people upstairs, and my contact in Vienna is a friend. Between those connections I might be able to pull some strings."

Adela's heart jumped. "That would be unbelievable, Marti."

"Let's not get carried away yet." He held up his hands. "I can't promise anything but that I'll try my absolute best to see if we can get around the rules. Give me a few days."

NINE

Vienna
23 March 1938

Felix crossed Karmeliterplatz, scanning the people around him. It was more quiet than usual, although some of the stalls had reopened. The majority remained shuttered, and where only weeks ago the selection of delicacies from all corners of Europe was impressive, today's offerings were limited to those of half a dozen brave proprietors. A visit from a group of Brownshirts was never far away. But they had to make a living too.

It had been almost two weeks since Felix and his father were forced to scrub the very cobblestones at his feet. When the Brownshirts deemed the square clean enough, Felix and Anton received a dirty piece of paper indicating they had carried out their duty. It was unclear what they were supposed to do with it, but Felix kept it in a drawer at home, just to be safe. When the Hitler Youth boys took their names, they made it clear his father's insolence would be reported and dealt with. It played on Felix's mind every day, and the fact that nothing had happened since did little to calm his nerves.

Felix turned onto Haidgasse, where the situation was only

marginally better than on the adjoining square. In addition to the Wolff's bike shop, about half of the twenty shops had reopened. Business was slow, as more and more people in Leopoldstadt lost their jobs. It gave Felix a lot of unwanted free time, but he was pleased to see a bike parked inside the workshop as he stepped through the door. His expert eye immediately identified the issue.

"Tire needs to be replaced, doesn't it?" Felix placed the small bag containing their lunch on the counter. "I'll get right on it."

"Eat something first," Anton said as he removed the lid of his container of *Krautfleckerln*, the steam rising from the fried cabbage and noodles.

Felix shook his head. "I'm all right. I had a bagel earlier. Besides, I'm keen to do something."

"Suit yourself." His father sat on one of the stools as Felix hoisted the bike up, grabbing the tools to remove the tire from the wheel. The front doorbell clanged, and both men cast their eyes toward it. The sight of a familiar face accompanied by a uniformed police officer was ominous.

Anton hastily put his lunch down, wiping his mouth with the back of his sleeve. "Herr Steiner, what a surprise to see you." He placed his hands on the counter and bent his head in a subtle display of deference, his eyes then darting to the police officer. "I hope nothing is the matter? We're not late with the rent, are we?"

Short, portly, and with a pockmarked face, Herr Steiner cut an unimpressive figure, especially against the tall, handsome police officer accompanying him. When he opened his mouth, he spoke with a thin, raspy voice. "No, nothing like that, Wolff. But I'm afraid I do need to address an issue concerning the rent."

A knot started to form in Felix's stomach as he placed his tools down and moved toward his father. The police officer subtly inched closer. Within seconds, the air in the shop became heavier.

Herr Steiner appeared oblivious to the change of atmosphere as he pulled out a piece of paper. "Effective next week, 1 April, I'm obliged to increase the rent for this space. You'll find all the details in here." He placed a single sheet of paper on the counter, tapping his finger.

Anton lifted the sheet, his eyes quickly scanning the sentences. He sighed, then gasped. "This is outrageous. There's no way we can afford this." He handed it to Felix, who had trouble processing its contents. *This can't be right.*

"I'm afraid the current economic situation doesn't leave me much choice. Many of my tenants are defaulting on their payments." Herr Steiner spoke without emotion, matching the blank expression on his increasingly unseemly face.

"Look at this store. It's not worth four times what we're paying now!" Felix was surprised by the anger in his father's voice. "You're ruining me." He took the piece of paper from Felix and crumpled it up into a ball, then threw it at Herr Steiner. It landed harmlessly at the man's feet. The police officer took a step forward.

"Sir, you need to calm down, or I'll have to take you to the station. Please control yourself." The man spoke calmly, but his hand was on the baton on his belt.

Felix put his hand on his father's shoulder. "Papa, there's no use arguing. We'll work this out." He gently pulled his father away from the counter, then addressed Herr Steiner in an overly polite tone. "Please allow us some time to process this and tally the numbers. We understand you're also feeling the effects of the economy. We'd like nothing more than to find a solution with you."

"I don't care for your words, boy." Steiner's tone was harsh, and he jabbed a finger at Anton. "And that outburst means there is absolutely no chance of any negotiations. If you're unable to pay rent next month, you'll need to vacate the premises."

Anton took a step toward the counter, but Felix strengthened his grip, holding him back. Before his father could say anything, Felix did, controlling his rising anger. "Very well. But you know just as well as us why your other tenants can't pay their rent anymore. This entire neighborhood has lost its livelihood in three short weeks. Raising our rent isn't going to solve anything."

Steiner let out a derisory snort. "We'll see about that. If you can't pay, I'll find more suitable individuals who can transform this area into something more than the backwater Jewish mess it's become." Before Felix or Anton could respond, he turned on his heel and signaled for the police officer to follow him. "Let's go. There's nothing more I have to say to them." He waited for the police officer to open the door, then turned around one more time. "You have seven days. If you can't pay, I'll take anything still inside the store as payment. Your choice." The bell clanged, and the door shut with a thud.

Felix watched Herr Steiner and the police officer cross the street and enter the sewing workshop of Herr Zimmermann. No doubt they would deliver the same crippling message there. He turned toward his father, who had returned to his lukewarm bowl of Krautfleckerln. He stared into space, his eyes vacant, his face pale. All the earlier fight had left him; Anton Wolff was a man defeated.

"Papa, we should take this to a lawyer. I'm sure he can't just do this."

His father slowly shook his head. "It's no use, my boy. You heard what he said. This has nothing to do with the economy. This is not the Vienna where laws and logic prevail. This is Nazi Vienna, and they make up their own rules. Even if we could afford a lawyer, it would do us no good."

"You're going to give up like that?" Felix was amazed by the turnaround in his father. Only minutes ago, Felix was afraid he would attack Herr Steiner, damn the consequences.

"Unless we find a way to pay that rent, there is nothing we can do." He looked up with the saddest eyes Felix had ever seen. "They took away our rights. Now they take our livelihoods."

TEN

Prague
24 March 1938

There was a knock on the door, and Adela looked up, pleased to see a familiar face.

"Do you have a minute?" Martinek stepped in and closed the door. "I have news from Vienna."

"Already?" She waved at the chair opposite her. "You move quickly."

"I thought it was important to get things in motion. The rules can, and probably will, change every day. My contact at the embassy had some interesting news I wasn't aware of."

Adela sat up. "What's that?"

"Despite the official line, some people are getting visas into the country. He said they're well connected, and are calling in favors." Martinek's expression was neutral, but Adela thought she saw a twinkle in his eye. "Mostly with officials higher up in the government here in Prague."

A jolt of hope shot through Adela. "Do you think we might be able to get through to someone for Greta's family?"

"I think so." A smile spread on his face. "I explained the situation to my contact in Vienna, and he's confident he can work with his connections to get them a visa."

"That's incredible!" Adela stood and took a few steps toward Martinek, who held up his hands, palms up.

"There's no guarantee yet, Adela. While it's great that we have someone who will give them a chance, there are still a few conditions they need to meet in order to get the visas approved."

"Such as?"

"They need to be able to provide for themselves, and they need to have a place to stay. Do you think they'll be able to do this?"

"So, they need money and a roof over their heads." Adela considered Martinek's words for a moment. Greta hadn't mentioned anything about her family's finances, but if they ran a bakery, they should be able to raise some money, surely? It saddened her to think about it, but they might even need to sell their business before leaving the country. From everything Adela had heard, Jewish businesses in Germany were struggling to survive, and she couldn't foresee the situation in newly acquired Austria faring any better. She turned back to Martinek. "I'm confident they won't be a burden on society." Greta would have to take care of the housing situation.

"I was hoping you'd say that. I'll just need their names, and we can get the process started." He moved to the door. "You know where to find me."

"Thank you so much, Marti. I'll see her this evening, and I'm sure she'll be delighted."

Martinek closed the door, and Adela looked up at the clock on her wall. Almost four. She eyed the stack of files on her desk and considered leaving early. That would give her enough time to make it across town to meet Greta as she finished work. *I can wrap these up later.* She had stuffed a couple of files in her bag and got up when a figure appeared in her doorway. Tereza, the friendly secretary she shared with the rest of her department, walked in.

"Sorry to disturb, but you're wanted upstairs." Tereza's tone was urgent.

Adela forced a smile, hiding her frustration at her failed attempt to leave early. "Now? By whom?"

"Top floor. They said to hurry."

Adela made it in record time. Her heart was pounding, and it wasn't from the physical effort required to climb the stairs. A summons from the top floor meant one of two things: You either stumbled onto something very important, or you made a serious mistake. Try as she might, she couldn't recall being involved in either.

It was clear the secretary was expecting her, as he guided her into a large conference room.

"He'll be right with you. Help yourself to some coffee or water." Before Adela could respond, the tall man had already closed the door, leaving her alone in the richly furnished room. A large painting of former president Tomáš Masaryk hung on the far side of the conference table, overlooking the proceedings. She considered pouring herself a glass of water but decided against it. Instead, she moved toward one of the large windows and gasped. The view was unlike anything she had seen before, the vantage point providing a bird's-eye view of the city below.

"It's magnificent, isn't it?"

The deep voice startled her, and Adela turned around. She was surprised to find František Moravec standing only a few meters away, a thin manila folder in his hand.

"Mr. Moravec. I'm sorry, I didn't hear you enter." Her heartbeat increased further.

"Please, no need to apologize." The head of military intelligence smiled graciously as he joined her next to the window, his eyes focused on the river below. "It's easy to lose yourself in the proceedings outside. I especially like following the boats on a summer's day." His voice had a soothing tone, his aura calming. "I'm glad you're here, Ms. Beran. I hope the haste with which you were requested wasn't too inconvenient?" He moved from the window, toward the conference table, and Adela followed him.

"Not at all, sir. I have to say I was surprised, though. Is something the matter with my work?"

"Nothing like that, don't worry. Please, have a seat. Would you like some coffee? I'm having some. It's been quite a day." He gestured toward a seat, placing the manila folder on the table. He sat and poured himself a cup of coffee.

"I'm fine, thank you, sir."

Moravec took a sip. A soft, content sigh left his lips before he focused his eyes on her. "I can see you're nervous, Ms. Beran. Let me try and make you as comfortable as possible. Your work is exemplary, and it has caught the eye of both the president and myself." Adela gulped, then caught herself and nodded politely. "Your command of languages is impressive. You speak five languages fluently?"

"Well, four. Czech, German, English, Russian, and a bit of French."

"A bit of French? I've seen your reports and they suggest otherwise." He grinned. "Your ability to translate and process information is second to none."

"Sir, you're being too generous. There are many talented translators in my department."

"Certainly. But that's exactly what they are. Translators. You're more than that. You're an analyst, able to gauge whether the information warrants the attention of your superiors. It's no coincidence President Beneš and I have seen your name on plenty of documents these past months."

Adela felt her cheeks burning. "Thank you, sir. But I assume you didn't ask me up here just to compliment my work?"

"I want you to work directly for me. You'll still carry out your regular work, but in addition, you'll be involved in more classified work."

Adela felt the blood run from her head all the way to her feet, unsure how to respond. "Should I speak to my boss about this?"

"No need. He's already been informed about your new responsibilities. This request comes straight from the president." Moravec leaned forward in his chair. "We're in agreement about your value to the operation, and hope you'll accept." He tapped the manila folder. "I have your first assignment here. The information it contains is known only by the president, me, and a select number of people in the government."

She eyed the folder, excitement bubbling in her stomach. "What is it, sir?"

"Before I can show you, you need to understand that anything we discuss is highly classified. You'll be privy to some of the most sensitive intelligence in the country." He gave her a stern look. "For your eyes only, and you can't discuss anything with anyone but me. Is that clear?"

"Absolutely, sir." Adela spoke without hesitation. She found herself drawn to the thin folder in Moravec's hands. This was an incredible step up in her career.

Moravec smiled and slid the folder across the table, allowing her to retrieve a single piece of paper. He leaned back in his chair and crossed his arms, inviting her to read its contents. The letter was handwritten and in German, dated three days ago. Adela's eyes raced over the sentences, her mouth opening involuntarily as she took in the information. The letter was short, spanning less than half the piece of paper, and she read it twice before placing it back on the table. Her breathing was heavy, her mouth dry.

"Is this real?"

"Yes, this comes from a source I trust with my life." Moravec looked at her without flinching. "I should probably expand on this a little. This agent first reached out to me about a year ago. The manner in which he approached us was unusual, to say the least, but when we met him, he brought documents that instantly made him our most valuable agent in Germany."

Adela looked at the piece of paper again, then met Moravec's eyes. "If the words on this are true, there isn't a moment to spare."

"There isn't. And I will speak to him soon, but I wanted to give you an idea of what you'll be working on. I want you to monitor every bit of German, French, and British information that passes your desk, and if you think it might be even remotely interesting to us, flag it, and send it up to my department."

She took a moment to process her new assignment. Surely the director of military intelligence had dozens, if not hundreds of agents scattered across Europe. Weren't they placed in a much better position than her? "Why me?"

Moravec smiled. "Isn't it obvious? You're one of the few people with access to information coming in from all countries in Europe. You see everything, whether it's French, English, or German. Do you know how long it can take for information from my sources to filter through?" He shook his head. "Ms. Beran, you'll be the first person to spot patterns in what's happening in multiple countries at the same time. Combined with my intelligence network, I am confident we'll be in the best position to identify any threats to our country."

"I understand." Despite the severity of the message on the table in front of her, a jolt of excitement shot through Adela's chest. It was an incredible opportunity.

He produced a piece of paper. "Now, for your first assignment, would you be so kind as to look over my response to our German agent? My written German is a little rusty."

ELEVEN

VIENNA
25 MARCH 1938

Karl's frustration grew as he listened to the men gathered around the table. They were going in circles. He checked his watch. The meeting had taken almost half an hour, but it felt at least double that. Karl reminded himself he needed to keep these men on his side; they would be seeing a lot of each other in the coming weeks, or months. Still, he needed things to move in the right direction. He took a deep breath and exhaled, calming himself, before raising his hand. The man opposite stopped talking and turned to him.

"I'm sorry for interrupting, but I just want to make sure I understand everything correctly." Karl spoke in his most soothing tone, masking his mounting impatience. "I requested this meeting because I know little of railroads, and you know everything about the Austrian railroads." The men around the table muttered affirmatively, some nodding and smiling at the perceived compliment. "I have to admit some of the technicalities are beyond my understanding, so would you mind terribly if I asked some simple, perhaps obvious, questions?"

"By all means, Herr Vogt. We're here to assist you, after all," the foreman of the group, a friendly Austrian railway man called Franz Hermann, said with a smile. Karl minded him least of those assembled; some of the others were so dimwitted that he had already decided to relieve them of their duties as soon as he was presented with the opportunity.

"Thank you. I suppose the most pressing question is whether we'll have the capacity to transport between a hundred and twenty and, say, a hundred and fifty prisoners to Dachau on 1 April."

"Absolutely." Hermann spoke without hesitation. "I've already reserved a locomotive with five cars to depart Westbahnhof early in the morning. The train will receive priority across the tracks west until Salzburg. From there, we would need to coordinate with our colleagues across the border." He caught himself while he spoke the last words. "Sorry, force of habit."

Karl smiled. "Not a problem. I'll make sure the train is cleared from Salzburg to Dachau. Now, you mentioned five cars? What's the capacity?"

"About thirty to forty passengers per car." Hermann rummaged through some papers. "These are all second-class carriages."

"That seems unnecessary. We should be able to get by with third-class carriages. We'd need fewer, wouldn't we?"

"Sir?" Hermann looked confused at first, then understanding appeared on his face. "We most certainly can do that. We'd only need two cars to transport your one hundred and fifty passengers." He looked up at Karl. "It would be rather uncomfortable. Dachau is a long way."

"I am aware," Karl said with authority. "They are prisoners. Enemies of the Reich."

Hermann nodded, then scribbled something on his papers. "Third-class carriages it is, sir."

Karl stepped off the streetcar at Schottenring next. Despite his earlier frustration at the meeting with the railroad men, he was pleased with the results. They had assured him the train would be waiting and ready for departure in the early hours of April 1. Karl would check in with Hermann a few more times in the coming week, making sure there were no unforeseen, last-minute hiccups.

The early spring weather was warm, a soft breeze picking up as Karl walked alongside the Donaukanal. A few small river barges made their way downstream toward the quay at Schwedenplatz, drifting toward their destination. Karl continued and crossed the street to the Rossauer Lände prison. It blended in well with the stately buildings surrounding it, the iron bars in front of its windows the only indication of the perfectly maintained whitewashed building's purpose.

Karl entered through the front door, offering his badge to the guard manning the reception desk. "I'm here to inspect the prisoners in protective custody."

The man shot up from his chair. "Certainly, sir. Let me get someone to escort you. This will take just a minute." He gestured toward a row of simple wooden chairs lining the wall, then disappeared down the hallway.

Karl ignored the chairs but eyed his surroundings. It was his first visit to the penitentiary, and he was curious as to how the Viennese police handled the mass arrests of the past weeks. The first impression was encouraging; the hallway was quiet and clean, the distinct odor of chlorine penetrating his nostrils. Much to his satisfaction, the guard returned within minutes, followed by a man wearing the same uniform.

"This is Officer Frank. He will take you anywhere you need to be, sir."

Karl nodded at both men. "Very well. Take me to the Jews and socialists."

"This way, please." Frank spoke with deference and offered no more conversation as he led Karl through a maze of corridors and stairways taking them deeper into the prison. They ran into a few guards along the way who eyed Karl with a mix of suspicion and curiosity. It made sense, as he was wearing civilian clothing. Frank's curt instructions to open heavy doors meant nobody questioned Karl's presence.

They had reached what Karl expected to be the third underground floor when Frank turned back to him. "We have about a hundred and fifty men, and a few women, down here. Most were brought in by Brownshirts the days following the appointment of Chancellor Seyss-Inquart."

Karl appreciated the officer's tact in describing the events following the reunification. "And the others?"

"The police, and more recently, Gestapo agents." Frank gave Karl a look when he mentioned the Sicherheitsdienst secret service. "We still have new people brought in every day, but not as many as on the days immediately after the reunification."

"Are you able to house all of them in here?"

"Plenty of space here, sir. Why don't you take a look for yourself?" He opened a large steel door, revealing a long corridor with iron-barred doors on either side. Karl was struck by the silence in the hallway. Passing the doors, he noticed the cells were spacious, with inmates sitting or lying on their bunks. Some were even reading books, while others looked comfortable sleeping. Karl was appalled and turned to Frank. "Is it like this everywhere?"

"I'm sorry, sir?" The guard looked taken aback.

Karl stalked down the hallway, barely able to control his emotions as he passed more prisoners looking surprisingly comfortable. They reached the door at the other end of the hallway, and Karl waited for Frank to open it. As soon as it closed, he turned to the guard, lowering his voice.

"Do you have any larger holding cells? With fewer beds?"

"Upstairs, yes." Frank gave him a questioning look. "Three, able to hold about ten prisoners each."

"Nothing bigger down here?"

The guard shook his head. "The cells in the basement levels are all equipped to hold two to four inmates."

Karl made a quick calculation. "I want you to make some changes to the accommodation of the prisoners."

Frank shifted on his feet, his eyes darting around the hallway. "I don't have the authority to make those changes, sir. You'd need to speak to my boss about that."

"Take me to him."

Franz Josef Huber stood confidently in his SS uniform, bearing the insignia identifying him as an officer in the Gestapo. That was a misnomer: He was the most senior Gestapo officer in the country, responsible for its functioning since the Anschluss.

"Herr Vogt, I must admit I haven't heard much about you, but I'm intrigued by your appearance in my prison earlier."

Karl forced a polite smile, picking up on the condescending tone and superior look in Huber's eyes. He bit back a retort, instead switching to his most diplomatic voice. "I was pleased to hear of your appointment to Vienna, sir. Gruppenführer Heydrich informed me we would be working together closely, but I didn't expect to find you at the prison today."

"The Gruppenführer told you directly?" Huber's eyes narrowed every so slightly, and Karl suppressed a smile. "I like to inspect what's happening on the ground. As do you, it appears. My people tell me you had suggestions for improvements?"

"I'm preparing the transportation of the prisoners in protective custody to Dachau next week—"

"Are you now? I thought Adolf Eichmann was in charge of that?" Huber raised an eyebrow. "Didn't he arrive from Berlin for that very purpose?"

"Obersturmführer Eichmann and I are working on this together. I'm taking care of the logistics, while he's making sure the transport lists are in order. Sir." Karl emphasized the last word.

"Right. So you're assisting the Obersturmführer. Well, let's hear what you'd like to change in my prison."

"I was surprised to see their relatively comfortable surroundings, Herr Huber. I'm not sure it reflects their position in our society. Especially compared to what they can expect in Dachau."

Huber sat up and leaned forward in his chair. "I appreciate your insight. What would you do to amend the situation?" Every word came out overly polite, and the hairs on the back of Karl's neck stood up.

"Perhaps we could save some cell space, and move a few more people in together."

"Cram the cells?"

"If you would agree, sir. It would be good preparation for what they can expect in Dachau. Or on the way there."

"On the way there?"

Karl outlined his method of transportation, and Huber nodded in agreement.

"You know, Vogt, I think I misunderstood your intentions earlier. My guards made it sound like you were causing trouble. Now I see it was quite the opposite. I will consider your suggestions." He stood up and held out his hand. "I'm sure we'll be seeing a lot of each other in the next few months. I'll be sure to let Reichsführer Himmler know of your very adequate suggestions to the improvement of our detainment facilities."

Karl shook Huber's hand but didn't miss his not-so-subtle name-dropping. Despite the man's silver tongue, it was clear he felt slighted by Karl. He would need to be on his guard when dealing with him. It wouldn't do him any good to make an enemy of the Vienna Gestapo chief.

TWELVE

Vienna
28 March 1938

The man wearing the gray overcoat inspected the counter, then ducked underneath and reappeared on the side where Felix and his father stood. It felt awkward as the man silently moved about the empty store, now tapping against one of the front windows facing Haidgasse. It was raining outside, adding to Felix's gloom. He glanced at his father, hoping for something to make him feel optimistic, but Anton's face was rigid. Felix's mind wandered back to his first memory of the store. He couldn't have been older than three or four, but he remembered his father appearing from behind the same counter, asking if Felix came in to help him fix some bikes. Anton had run the shop for almost twenty years, and Felix couldn't imagine his father doing anything else. Or anywhere but behind that counter.

The man in the overcoat—Muller, Mayer, whatever—cleared his throat at the door. "It appears everything is in order. If you would be so kind as to hand me your keys."

Anton and Felix moved to the door. As his father reached into his pockets, he turned around and took one last look at the store, a soft sigh marking Anton's only acknowledgment of the impact of the situation. He turned to the clerk and held out a simple key chain containing two keys. "I suppose this is it, then. Twenty years, just like that."

The clerk took the keys and opened the front door, holding it for the Wolffs. They stepped into the rain, and the man shut the door with a clang. He locked up, then left without a word, hurrying down the street, no doubt to ruin someone else's life.

The Wolff men stood in front of the empty store, letting the rain soak their jackets, silently marking the end of a previous life, like one would bid farewell to a loved one. Felix stood with his head bowed, more thoughts of a simple, yet trouble-free youth growing up passing through his mind. He felt a hand on his shoulder and turned toward it. His father looked at him with a determined gaze.

"Let's go home. No use standing here staring at what has been, is there? Your mother must be wondering what's keeping us."

They turned in the direction of Karmeliterplatz. Neither looked back.

Fifteen minutes later, they opened the door to their apartment. The moment they did, Felix's mother raced to the front door. Her eyes were red and puffy, her voice pitched higher than usual.

"Anton! I'm so happy to see you. They were here just now, asking about you." Rebecca Wolff's words came at them rapidly, while she threw her arms around her husband. "They just left, I was so afraid you'd run into them on their way out. You didn't see them, did you?"

"See who?" Anton managed to speak calmly, but his shoulders stiffened, his pupils grew, wrinkles appeared on his forehead. "Who was here just now?"

Felix had a sinking feeling he knew her answer.

"Two men with badges showed up looking for you." She stepped back and took Anton's face in her hands, her voice softening. "Gestapo men." She lowered her face and started sobbing.

Anton's face dropped, then he pulled Rebecca closer, stroking her hair. "It's all right, my love. What did they want?" Felix was impressed by his father's composure, and he took a step back, taking a seat at the kitchen table.

"They said they needed to speak to you. They barged into our home, even after I told them you weren't here. They didn't care."

"Did they hurt you?" A hint of indignation filtered through in Anton's voice.

Rebecca shook her head. "After they were sure you weren't hiding in the apartment, they told me you need to report to the police station down the street within the next day, or they will come back." She sniffled, and Felix handed her a tissue. After wiping her tears, she continued, "And things would be much worse, they said." She buried her head into her husband's shoulder. "What are we going to do?"

Anton stroked her hair, not immediately responding. Felix got up and poured his mother a glass of water. She accepted it gratefully, and it was quiet in the apartment for a few minutes—each of them contemplating the best response to the horrible news. It was Anton who spoke first.

"I'll make my way to the police station right away." His voice was strong and even, determined. Felix and his mother responded with equal horror.

"You can't, Papa. Who knows what they'll do to you once they have you in custody? You've done nothing wrong."

Rebecca was nodding vigorously. "You should go into hiding."

"And hide where? For how long? They'll come for you instead, and you both know it." Anton's tone became firm, almost harsh. "I will never forgive myself if something happens to you because of my actions." Felix opened his mouth, but his father raised a finger to his lips. "Not another word. I will report to the police station and see what's going on."

Felix knew his father well enough to realize when it was futile to try to change his mind. "Okay, Papa. But I'm coming with you."

They arrived at the police station an hour later. Rebecca had convinced Anton and Felix to eat something first. It could take a while, she'd said, and Felix knew she was right. On the way to the station, he'd pondered why the Gestapo would be looking for his father, and he could come to only one conclusion: Their altercation with the Hitler Youth had finally caught up with them. The only thing that puzzled him was why they hadn't come for him as well. Both their names had been taken down. *I'm sure I'll find out soon enough.*

A brusque officer directed them to one of the hard wooden benches lining the narrow hallway before making his way back to his desk. Felix and his father sat in uncomfortable silence while police officers came and went. After fifteen minutes, Felix spoke softly, almost in a whisper.

"If this is about what happened with those two Hitler Youth boys, just admit you were rude to them, and see if you can make up for it, Papa. It's not worth getting into more trouble by arguing with the police."

"If the Gestapo came to the apartment, I don't think I'm going to be talking to the police about this." Anton's eyes darted up and down the corridor. "I'm not sure the Viennese police care too much about a minor argument between a shopkeeper and two boys, even if they're wearing Hitler Youth uniforms."

Felix sat up and raised an eyebrow. "If you don't think it's about that, why do you think they want to talk to you?"

"I have no idea, but you and me speculating about it isn't going to help us much. I'm sure they'll tell me soon enough. But I need you to promise me one thing."

"What's that?"

"Don't get involved. Just let me do the talking, and make sure your mother has one man coming back to her tonight." Anton's voice was firm, and Felix nodded.

"Just don't get into trouble, Papa."

"Wolff?" A voice thundered through the hallway. "Anton Wolff?"

Felix and his father stood, moving toward the burly police officer holding the door at the end of the hallway.

"I'm Anton Wolff."

"Come with me." The man jerked his head toward the doorway. Anton moved toward the door, but Felix grabbed his elbow.

"What are the charges? Why is my father here?" His heart was almost beating from his chest as he forced himself to hold the much larger police officer's stare.

"I don't know, and if you know what's good for you, you'll turn around and leave this building right now, boy," the man snarled at him, signaling at Anton to keep moving. Felix tightened his grip on his father and swallowed hard.

"If you won't tell me, I'm coming with him."

Anton jerked his arm free, an angry look in his eyes. "Felix, we talked about this. Go!"

The police officer took a step toward Felix, towering over him. "Listen to me, kid. I'm not asking you. I'm telling you. Get out. Now." The man spoke urgently, but there was no malice in his words. Felix forced himself to meet the officer's gaze, and he saw concern in the big man's eyes, and took a step back.

"I'll clear up whatever this is about and be home as soon as I can," Anton said, his eyes still spouting fire, but his voice controlled. "Just go." He didn't wait for Felix's answer and disappeared through the doorway. The police officer nodded at Felix, his eyes narrowed, then followed his father and closed the door.

Felix stepped outside and instantly felt uneasy. Should he have pushed harder to stay with his father? He shook his head—that police officer was trying to shield him from something. The realization did little to make him feel better. Was his father in bigger trouble than they all assumed?

THIRTEEN

Vienna
1 April 1938

Karl was pleased with the orderly row of SS troopers securing a narrow path toward one of Westbahnhof's side entrances. Those at the front stood with steel-tipped batons attached to their belts, while those slightly farther back were armed with rifles. There was little need for firearms, but Karl didn't mind the show of force. He didn't want anything to go wrong this morning.

Despite the early hour, a crowd of onlookers formed on both sides of the SS cordon. Passenger traffic toward the main entrance of the station continued as usual, with commuters rushing to catch their connections like on any Friday morning.

The sound of engines neared and Karl moved from his elevated position on the station's steps toward the street. As he passed the SS troopers, he repeated his earlier orders.

"Stay vigilant, and make sure they keep moving. I don't want any delays." The men nodded at him, and Karl was confident his train to Dachau would leave on time. He reached the street as the first truck pulled up, and two young troopers jumped out of the back. They raised their right hands in salute. They then opened the tarp, revealing thirty unkempt and dirty men, with beards of various lengths. Karl couldn't suppress a smile—his request to deny these men bathroom facilities in the past days had been honored by Huber. He turned to see the crowd swelling; the appearance of the trucks had drawn more curious commuters. *Perfect. Let's see how these so-called prominent members of the community like their walk to the train.*

Karl took a step back as the first prisoners disembarked. Immediately, the SS troopers positioned closest to them started barking commands.

"Keep moving! Get to the station! This way, hurry, hurry! Come on!"

The men froze in the barrage, their eyes wide as they took in their surreal surroundings. At that point, some people in the crowd joined in, hurling insults. It caused the prisoners to withdraw further into themselves, with only a few making their way toward the station, navigating the corridor of troopers. With Karl's instructions still fresh in their minds, the involvement of the onlookers encouraged the troopers.

At first, a solitary trooper unsheathed his baton and stepped toward a fear-stricken prisoner, prodding him along. When that didn't work, the trooper smashed his baton into the man's side, resulting in a bloodcurdling wail. More troopers joined in, and soon the prisoners from the first truck were beaten and harried through the narrow station door. The second truck arrived, its occupants witnessing what happened to their predecessors—and they moved along quicker, much to the disappointment of the crowd, which started to thin. That was fine with Karl—the first truck had served its purpose.

When the last truck pulled up, the prisoners made their way into the station in an orderly fashion. Karl approached an SS man standing next to one of the empty trucks, holding a clipboard.

"Was that the last of them?"

"Yes, sir. They're all accounted for. A hundred and fifty men."

The trooper grinned. "There was no chance any of those prisoners would get lost between the prison and the station, sir."

"Very well." Karl turned and moved toward the station and checked his watch: half an hour before scheduled departure. He allowed himself a smile. *That should be plenty of time.* The door they'd used gave almost direct access to one of the tracks on the side of the station; Karl had deliberately picked it to make sure the prisoners would have as little interaction with the regular passengers as possible. He walked through the entrance onto the platform and was pleased to see it was nearly empty. Only a small number of prisoners were boarding on the far side, and he approached a nearby group of troopers.

"Any trouble getting them on board?"

"Not at all, sir," the most senior of the men responded. "Some asked where they were going, and I heard a few grumble about the conditions, but we shut them up quickly enough."

"You didn't tell them where they're going, did you?"

"No, we had our orders, sir." He smiled. "I think they have an idea, though. They mentioned the destination a few times among themselves."

"Let them speculate. Good work."

Karl headed to the front of the train, where four troopers stood guard at the doors. "I'm going to have a word with the prisoners, prepare them for their journey. I don't expect any trouble, but if something happens, I want you in here on the double. Do you understand?"

"If you're expecting trouble, shall we accompany you, sir?" The young man looked back at him with alert eyes. Karl considered the suggestion for a moment, then nodded.

"That's a good idea. Come with me." He boarded the car, the uncomfortable heat and smell of too many bodies crowded in a tight space enveloping him. He wrinkled his nose, then cleared his throat. Some seventy pairs of eyes turned toward him.

"Gentlemen. I see you've all found a spot, and I trust you're comfortable enough for the journey ahead." He spoke with a practiced fake sincerity, which wasn't lost on his crowd. These men were leaders of their communities. They were Vienna's politicians, union representatives, intellectuals, and prominent businessmen. It gave Karl an immense sense of satisfaction to see these men of status crowded in the constricted confines of this third-class car. "We'll be departing soon, but I wanted to make sure you understand your positions on board. There is to be no talking, and no sleeping, unless you're given permission to do so. Any breach of these rules will result in severe punishment." He turned to the troopers crowding in the narrow doorway behind him, raising his voice loud enough to be heard at the other side of the car. "You have permission to use lethal force, if required." The trooper simply nodded, patting the sidearm attached to his hip. Karl turned back to the prisoners, many of whose faces had turned pale. *Good, let them sweat. Half of them won't survive their first month anyway.*

He disembarked and repeated his ominous message in the other car. He watched as troopers boarded the train, while their colleagues secured the doors from the outside. Then, the locomotive's whistle shrieked, and the train slowly started moving. Within seconds, it cleared the station's roof, and a minute later it disappeared from sight.

KARL's next stop was at the office of State Secretary Globočnik. His friend closed the door and waved him to a chair. "I hear a celebratory drink is in order." Globočnik opened a small liquor cabinet and produced two tumbler glasses. "The transport to Dachau was a success?"

"The train departed on time, with all of the *Prominenten* on board. Plenty of SS muscle as well, so it should arrive at Dachau tomorrow morning. I don't think any of these intellectuals will cause any problems on the way. They were scared out of their minds."

"As well they should be." Globočnik handed a generous pour of vodka, his own drink of choice, to Karl. Karl wasn't a big fan, but he was quite willing to indulge his friend. Besides, he did have something to celebrate. Immediately after returning from the station, he'd instructed his secretary at the Gestapo headquarters to send word of the successful departure to Berlin. It had taken less than an hour for Heydrich's call to come through. Karl's boss had been unusually complimentary, informing him the news had been relayed to Himmler as well. Karl knew that meant the Führer himself would hear about it soon enough. He took a sip and enjoyed the stinging sensation of the vodka making its way down his throat.

"Now that we've removed a number of the political elite, how are you faring with Renner? And the church?"

Odilo gave him a wicked grin. "I'm sure they're well aware of the arrests, but I don't think they've heard of today's transport just yet. It doesn't matter. They'll learn of it soon enough. You said there were plenty of onlookers?"

"There was some press present as well."

"No doubt tipped off by you?" The state secretary took a large gulp. "Either way, I'm not sure Renner needs much more convincing. He's been very forward in his intentions to support our referendum. Today's proceedings will give him just that little bit of extra incentive in convincing the stragglers in his party."

"Sounds like it's a fix."

"More or less. I need a little more time with the clergy, but I'm speaking with Cardinal Innitzer tomorrow. From what I've heard, he's leaning toward supporting us as well."

Karl sat up. "The leader of the Catholic Church in the country will publicly support us? That's great news, Odilo. Isn't he worried about the repercussions from the Vatican? They've been rather critical."

"I think Innitzer knows which way the wind is blowing, even if his overlords don't. I'll leave their internal politics for him to worry about. And if he won't support us willingly, I'll find another way."

"Do you need help from my side? I can talk to people at the Metropole, have them exert some pressure?"

"I appreciate the offer, Karl, but I'll manage. The Gestapo can sit this one out. I'm sure they'll be useful at a later stage." He stood and emptied his glass in one large swig, then eyed Karl's almost-full glass with a hint of disappointment. "We should celebrate. The stars are lining up for us, Karl."

Karl smiled and reluctantly downed his vodka, handing his glass to his friend. The warmth of the drink spread through his body, and a slight buzz started forming. Things were looking very promising indeed. Odilo and he were close to securing an incredible victory in the referendum. There was no doubt the Führer would take notice.

FOURTEEN

Prague
2 April 1938

Adela walked out of her department meeting feeling deflated. Their morning meetings were becoming depressingly predictable, the news from across the continent hardly encouraging. She walked through the hallway caught in her own thoughts, and she didn't notice Martinek until she felt a hand on her shoulder.

"Sorry, I didn't mean to startle you. You look like you could use some fresh air. Want to join me?" Martinek looked troubled, and it was clear whatever he wanted to discuss was urgent. She had a bad feeling about the contents of his message.

"Sure, let me just grab my coat."

Adela met Marti outside the main entrance, and they made for the garden within the castle walls.

"I'm afraid I have some bad news. My Viennese contact has run into trouble."

"What trouble?"

"We secured the paperwork for their entry into Czechoslovakia, but the Germans are unwilling to give them an exit visa."

"What?" Adela gasped. "They want the Jews to leave the Reich. This doesn't make sense. Their papers are in order, aren't they?"

"They're requesting an exorbitant fee to even consider processing the exit visa."

"How much?" When Marti named the sum, Adela's eyes watered. "I'm not sure they would be able to afford that. I'll need to check with Greta." She was quite certain they couldn't, considering what Greta had told her about her family's financial situation.

"There's something else you need to know about this." Marti stopped and sat on a bench overlooking a flower garden that was starting to bloom. Adela remained standing and tilted her head. "My contact says there's a good chance they won't receive the exit visa, even if they pay. He's seen instances where people hand over the money, only for another snag in the process to suddenly appear."

"Are you saying they shouldn't even bother?"

"I'm not sure. But they could end up with nothing."

Adela sat next to him, completely dumbstruck. Greta would be devastated.

"There might be another way." Marti spoke softly, but with conviction. "If you can find a way for them to cross the border, we could perhaps call in some favors, and get their visas sorted. They might need to keep their heads down for a while, but you said your friend would be able to house them?"

"Yes, she could look after them while we work on the permits." Adela's mind was racing. "But how would we smuggle them across the border? I'm sure we're not the only ones to think about that. The border's heavily patrolled on both sides, isn't it?"

"We can look into it." Marti stood up and stretched, then pointed at the castle. "After all, we are perfectly positioned to find out." His eyes went about their surroundings.

Adela looked up at the top floor of the building and saw the sun hitting the windows. Marti wasn't wrong. But as she stood and thought about what was needed, she questioned whether she had the credit required to ask for the favor.

A FEW HOURS LATER, Adela stood before a large map of Czechoslovakia. Two dozen pins dotted the northwestern part of the country known as Sudetenland.

"This is where we've had trouble between the ethnic Germans and Czechs in the past week." Moravec tapped two pins near Karlsbad, one of the larger cities in the area. "Henlein was spotted at rallies here, drumming up further support for a reunification with Germany."

Adela frowned. Konrad Henlein was the leader of the Sudeten German Party, and it was clear Germany's annexation of Austria had given him confidence that the same could be accomplished with the Sudetenland, a region with a high number of ethnic Germans. Adela rummaged through some files.

"His last visit to Berlin was only a few days ago. Surely that's connected to the recent rallies and clashes. It's a deliberate provocation."

Moravec nodded. "It further confirms the report we received from our German contact."

"But Henlein hasn't called for autonomy for the Sudetenland yet." Adela sighed. The letter Moravec had shared with her during their first meeting contained the dire warning that Hitler had instructed Henlein to stir up trouble in anticipation of a call for independence from Czechoslovakia. Combined with his recent visit to Berlin, where he was no doubt meeting with Hitler, this gave her the uncomfortable feeling that Henlein was preparing something big.

"I'm sending additional agents to Karlsbad, and some of the smaller cities, just to keep an eye on the situation. I fear the rallies will only increase in size and intensity."

"Especially if the referendum in Austria goes Hitler's way." Adela had kept a close eye on the proceedings to the south. Everything was pointing toward a comfortable victory for Hitler. "Henlein will use that to launch his own campaign."

"And I'm afraid it will gain traction very quickly." Moravec looked troubled, rubbing his chin. "There are over two million ethnic Germans in the Sudetenland. Hitler will claim their situation is similar to that of the Austrians."

"Has our German contact responded to our recent messages yet?" Adela had drafted a reply to the letter informing them of Hitler's plans, but they hadn't heard back from him since.

"No, he's gone quiet. Unfortunately, this is not uncommon. He might feel it's too risky to communicate, or is waiting for the right moment to supply more information. We'll need to be patient, and hope he responds before Henlein and Hitler put their plans into motion."

"What if he doesn't?"

"Then we'll be playing catch-up." He gave a wry smile as he cast his eyes back to the map. "But for now, we can at least keep an eye on what's happening in the Sudetenland, and try to collect our own intelligence. His warning was useful."

Moravec's words did little to comfort Adela, but she understood the need for patience. In the two weeks she'd worked with Moravec, she had quickly learned that the game of intelligence moved either very quickly or very slowly, and patience was a virtue.

"There's one thing I may need from you, but I'm not sure if it'll be necessary," Moravec said, and Adela sat up. "I'm going to ask our agents to keep an eye on the rallies. If they continue to grow, I think it might be useful for you to attend one or two."

"Head to the Sudetenland?" A mix of excitement and trepidation shot through her body.

"Let's see how things develop first. It might help for you to speak to the ethnic Germans, get a feel for the situation. You might even be able to talk to some of the speakers."

"If you think it might help, I'd be happy to go." Adela spoke with more conviction than she felt.

"I'll let you know if it becomes relevant." He smiled, then made a gesture that made it clear the meeting was over. "Thank you, Adela."

She stood and moved toward the door, then stopped. She hesitated, but before she could say anything, Moravec spoke.

"Something else on your mind?"

Adela began to walk away, but she found herself turning back. Moravec looked at her with a curious expression. It was now or never. "Actually, yes. There's something I've been meaning to ask you." Adela outlined Greta's family's situation in Austria, and Moravec listened without interrupting her. As she talked, she questioned if she was going too far, but she pushed on, realizing she needed to at least try to utilize this powerful connection. When she finished, Moravec stood and walked to the window. He stood there for a minute that felt like an eternity. Adela fidgeted with her nails while she waited in silence. Finally, Moravec turned around.

"The border situation isn't really part of my job, nor is immigration." Adela felt her body shake. "However, I do sympathize with your friend's family. Their situation sounds dire, and in any normal situation, I'm sure they would be welcomed into the country. But our relationship with the Reich is strained at best, and while we might not agree with the foreign ministry's policy, there's not much we can do about it."

Adela felt the strength drain from her body. If she couldn't get Moravec on board, it would be hard to help Greta's family. Moravec took a step back to the map, sliding his index finger across the Austrian border.

"Officially, we can't do much. But if they were to make it across the border, I'm sure I can lean on some friends in the foreign ministry." He smiled, and Adela felt a jolt of hope. "The border is long, and the patrols can't be everywhere at the same time. Let me see if I can get some information about the patrol schedules."

"Thank you so much, sir. That would mean the world to my friend."

Moravec held up his hand. "Let's not celebrate yet. I'll look into it, and if something's possible, I'll let you know. Soon."

GRETA, seated across the table, was shaking. Adela had just shared the developments of the day. Her friend had gone from hope to despair in a matter of minutes. Adela felt for her, but when she finished talking, she saw Greta look at her with a glimmer of hope in her eyes.

"Can we trust your contact? Will he really secure visas?"

Moravec's face flashed in Adela's mind, and she nodded. "He's got the clout to do it. And I believe he will help."

"How long do you think it might take until my uncle and aunt can get across the border?"

Adela had pondered the same thing ever since leaving the conference room that afternoon. She was certain Moravec understood the importance of moving quickly, but she was in no position to make any demands. "We'll have to be patient, Greta. But that doesn't mean we can't start preparing for their crossing. Can you get in touch with them? They'll need to be able to move at a moment's notice. Do you think they have what it takes to do this?"

"They'll be ready. There is nothing left for them to stay for. They'll need to give up the bakery soon, as Nazi thugs are standing outside their shop these days, threatening anyone going in."

"That's horrible. I'm so sorry."

"I spoke to my aunt this morning. They're terrified, and were holding on to the hope that you could get them a visa." She let out an apologetic sigh. "I'm sorry. I don't mean to blame you, you're doing everything and more to help them, and I appreciate it. If the only option is to cross the border illegally, and then build a new life in Prague, I'm sure they would jump at that chance."

"They would need to start at the bottom, most likely."

Greta chuckled. "They're already at the bottom. Trust me, Adela, when you give the signal that they can cross the border, they'll be there."

Adela reached out and took her friend's hand. "And we'll be waiting on the other side, I promise."

FIFTEEN

Vienna
2 April 1938

Felix closed the door to the store, struggling to maintain his composure. He stepped into the street, the warmth of the sun doing little to improve his gloom. It was his third rejection of the day, and he questioned whether it made any sense to continue his job hunt. Nobody was hiring. They'd love to help him, but business was slow.

Despite the blue sky and mild April temperatures, the streets were quiet as he made his way home.

"Felix!" a deep voice boomed from across the street. A tall, wiry man waved at him. "Were you just going to walk by without saying something?" He adjusted his glasses, his stern eyes looking at Felix from behind them.

"Mr. Tannenbaum!" Felix made an apologetic bow as he reached the shopkeeper. Mr. Tannenbaum's textile business had been around for as long as Felix could remember. If he had to guess, its proprietor had to be close to eighty years old. A fixture in the neighborhood, it didn't surprise Felix that he was one of the few shopkeepers able to keep his head above water at this time. "How are you, sir?"

"Things have been better." Mr. Tannenbaum took his glasses off and started cleaning them, then paused and gave Felix a sympathetic look. "But I'm in no position to complain. Nobody's come for my store. Yet, anyway. Have you had any news of your father's situation?"

"I'm afraid not, sir. The last time I saw him was over a week ago. I've asked around, but the police won't tell me anything."

"Damn fools. You used to be able to rely on them, but they all crossed over to the Nazi side in a flash." He inspected his glasses and placed them back on his nose. He looked lost for a moment, then appeared to catch his thoughts. "I'm sorry about what happened to you. Losing the store first, and now your father. How is your mother doing?"

"She's holding it together." Felix felt bad lying to the friendly shopkeeper, but he couldn't bring himself to tell him the truth. Rebecca Wolff was not doing well at all. Felix could hear her crying throughout the night, putting up a brave face in the morning, but the dark rings around her eyes grew every day. Seeing his mother like this made Felix more determined to find a job—any job—and secure something of an income for them.

"They can't keep your father's whereabouts from you forever, Felix. At some point, they'll have to tell you what's going on." Mr. Tannenbaum's words were hopeful, but his tone wasn't. Felix nodded, appreciating the man's compassion, and his attempts to ease Felix's worries.

"Thank you, sir. I should be on my way. You wouldn't know anyone who's hiring at this time, would you? I'm happy to do anything."

Mr. Tannenbaum gave him a sad look. "I'm afraid I can't help you with that. I would hire you myself if I could, but there's just too little business to go around. I doubt the situation's different anywhere else in the neighborhood."

"Yes, and I don't think I stand much of a chance on the other side of the channel. People aren't too keen on hiring folks like us these days."

"Try not to blame them too much. How would you feel about hiring someone who'll potentially expose your business to the same violence we've seen here?" His eyes darted around the street, a sad expression lining his face. "It takes a brave man to stand up to the new regime."

"I suppose." Despite Mr. Tannenbaum's pacifying words, Felix had trouble tempering his growing resentment toward his fellow Viennese. "If you hear of anything at all, I'd be much obliged if you could point them in my direction."

"Sure will, young Mr. Wolff. Take care, and send my best to your mother."

Felix continued down Taborstraße. Mr. Tannenbaum's words echoed in his mind as the steeple of St. Stephen's Cathedral rose up from the city center, across the Danube Channel.

He crossed the bridge to Schwedenplatz, marking his entry into the city's first—or central—district. The square was an important commuter transfer point, with numerous tram lines connecting there. As a result, it was busy with people, creating an atmosphere of normality, in stark contrast to Felix's reality across the channel. People were rushing about, running to catch their trams, while others stood patiently waiting, some quietly enjoying a *Kipferl* from one of the bakeries. The thundering of tram cars on rails, combined with the impatient clanging of bells, took Felix back to normal times, and he forgot about his worries for a moment. Then he heard the loud, piercing voice of one of the news vendors above all other noises. That wasn't unusual: These men were a common feature on any busy square. Felix had always been impressed by their ability to stand out in a crowd of hundreds, if not thousands, demanding attention. But it wasn't the man's ability to attract a crowd that prompted Felix's attention. They had the ability to make the most trivial news sound exciting, selling an extra newspaper or two along the way. But that wasn't the case today. Felix stepped closer, joining the people gathering around the man's stall, making sure he'd understood correctly. As the man opened his mouth, sucking in enough breath to carry his message across the square, Felix felt his spine tingle. The words brought him back from his momentary escape from reality, plunging him headfirst into the new reality.

"Renner on board! Socialist leader pledges support to Hitler's referendum!"

SIXTEEN

VIENNA
10 APRIL 1938, AFTERNOON

Karl had a spring in his step as he crossed Stephansplatz, and he looked up at St. Stephen's Cathedral. Despite his misgivings about religion, he couldn't help but appreciate the beauty of the city's magnificent church. He walked quickly, pleased to see a queue outside the polling station. It was much like the other locations he'd visited today. The people of Vienna had come out to vote in masses.

He bypassed the queue, spotting a few familiar faces among the uniformed men milling about the entrance. Two wore the brown uniform of the Sturmabteilung, while the other wore the more smartly tailored black livery of the SS. They asked every person entering for their identification papers, as instructed. An elderly couple moved to the front, and after a short inspection, one of the Brownshirts shook his head and waved them away. The man tried to push his way past them, but his wife pulled him back. The SS man stepped forward and pulled the couple aside, speaking to them in measured tones. The elderly man's resolve melted away as the words registered, and Karl watched with satisfaction when the couple left the polling station, disappearing into the crowd on the square. He approached the SS man.

"Jews?"

"No, sir. These were registered socialists. Their names were on the list to watch out for. We have no use for their votes."

"Good work. Did you mark their names?"

"We did." The man spoke without emotion, his eyes going between Karl and the queue behind him.

"Did many try to make their way in?"

"Just a few, sir. I'm confident we've picked them out of the queue before they could enter. Either way, we have instructions from the Metropole to send the names of whoever ignored our specific instructions not to come to the polling stations."

Karl nodded, pleased with the trooper's report, and stepped inside the polling station. They were taking the precautions seriously, and the word had been the same everywhere he'd been. Only a small number of Communists, Jews, and other unwanted elements of Viennese society had tried to sneak in and cast their illegal votes. The Gestapo would make short work of those unfortunate enough to find their names sent to its headquarters at the Hotel Metropole.

Inside, he cast his eyes over the polling setup. This was one of the largest locations in the city, and he was pleased to see the people in charge following instructions. He watched as a respectable-looking man wearing a tweed jacket was handed his ballot. The man turned toward four tables on the other side of the room, and the lines forming on his forehead betrayed his unease.

"Something the matter, sir?" The man standing behind the table and handing out ballots bore a swastika emblem pinned to his chest pocket.

"Where am I supposed to cast my ballot?" the man asked, his eyes darting back to the four tables. Stacks of red pencils lay on the tables, but there was no sense of privacy. Karl leaned against the wall, fascinated by the situation. The idea of removing barriers and curtains from the traditional ballot booths was discussed and implemented by the Ministry of Interior earlier that week.

The man behind the table smiled. "Oh, you can just fill it out over here. He signaled toward his table, pointing to the large, encircled *Yes* option on the ballot. "It's just a formality, isn't it?" The option to vote against was barely legible.

The man in the tweed jacket took a step back. "I think I'd prefer to have some privacy."

"By all means, sir. You can use one of those tables. Don't forget to drop your ballot in the box over there." The container with barely folded up ballots was positioned in the middle of the room, revealing filled out ballots supporting the unification of Austria and Germany.

The man in the tweed jacket couldn't look more uncomfortable if he tried, but, much to his credit, he moved toward one of the tables. It took less than thirty seconds for him to drop his neatly folded ballot in the box.

"Thank you, sir," the man behind the table said with a silky voice. "We appreciate your vote." The man in the tweed jacket quickly exited, and as soon as he did, the man running the polling station moved toward the container. Making no effort to conceal his actions, he picked up the ballot, unfolding it in full view of the people waiting to vote. He tutted, and took the ballot back to his table. There he deposited it in a different, smaller bin. All other movement in the room had stopped as the eyes of other votes were focused on the man. He produced a sheet of paper and carefully noted some details. Karl saw the number of names on this particular list were few—a good sign.

The man then moved the list to the side of the table, placing his pencil on top of it with a short sigh of satisfaction. He then returned his attention to the next person in line. After she stated her name, he handed her a fresh ballot and red pencil.

She needed no further instructions. The woman placed the ballot down on the table, placed a thick cross in the *Yes* circle and—without bothering to fold it—handed it back to the man. He held up the palms of his hands, and, the smile still on his face, directed her toward the large container in the middle of the room.

SEVENTEEN

Vienna
10 April 1938, evening

Rebecca Wolff placed a cup of coffee on the kitchen table.

"Thank you." Felix cradled it, warmth spreading through his hands. The smell of the coffee, weak as it was, offered comfort. His mother sat opposite him, blowing on her coffee before taking a small sip. They sat in silence for a moment, while the radio played classical music in the background.

It was early in the evening, and they'd both spent most of the day inside. Felix still hadn't found a job, despite going out every day in search of one. With the polling stations open for the referendum, and plenty of Nazis patrolling the streets looking for trouble, they'd decided it would be safer for Felix to skip today. He looked at his mother, who appeared to age a year with every passing day. Felix wished he could say something to cheer her up, but he knew their silent companionship brought her more comfort.

The music ended abruptly, and Rebecca's eyes went to the radio. The voice of the presenter apologized for the interruption but announced the program would be paused while they switched to a nationwide announcement. Felix met his mother's eyes, and they didn't need to speak. It was clear what the announcement would be about.

"Do you want me to turn it off?" Felix rose from his chair, but his mother held up her hand.

"No, let's hear what they have to say." Her voice was oddly passive.

Felix reluctantly sank back into his chair. His father had been missing for over two weeks now, and just as with the announcement on the radio, there was nothing they could do about it.

The radio went silent, only the crackle of the static coming through for a few seconds. Then a new voice, one with a distinct German accent, sounded into their living room.

"Citizens of *Land Österreich*." It was impossible to miss the gravity of adding *Land* to their country's name, and Felix moved uncomfortably in his seat. "We are pleased to announce the result of today's referendum."

"Already?" Rebecca's voice cracked.

"While a few votes still need to be counted, there can be no doubt about the people's wishes. From today onward, Austria will be part of the great German Reich. While this result was expected, we are delighted with the clear margin of victory."

Felix stood and took three quick paces to the radio, switching it off. "I'm sorry, Mama, but I can't listen to this any longer. This referendum was rigged. We didn't even get to vote."

His mother sighed, but nodded. "Even if we had been allowed to vote, it wouldn't have mattered. I suppose a small part of me hoped our fellow countrymen would've come to their senses at the last moment."

Felix bit back a bitter response. In a measured voice, he said, "Me too. But I'm afraid that was wishful thinking." In reality, Felix hadn't for a second considered the referendum going any other way. He thought of Mr. Tannenbaum's words a week earlier. "The only consolation we can take is that most people probably voted in fear."

His mother gave him a sharp look. "You really believe that? What do they have to be afraid of?"

"To be put in the same category as us. They've seen what's happened to the enemies of the Nazis. It's easier to go along with the rhetoric that we are the source of all problems."

Rebecca looked at him for a minute, then a small, sad smile appeared on her lips. "You sound so much like your father, Felix. I'm proud of you."

Her words struck him hard, and Felix was unsure how to respond. He moved to the window and looked out onto the street. The park was in shadows, and apart from a man walking by on the street below, everything was quiet. He imagined the scenes in the city center to be quite different. If the country voted so comprehensively in favor of joining Hitler's new regime, people would take to the streets to celebrate. There would be none of that in Leopoldstadt. Instead, they would switch off the lights in their homes and keep their doors locked. They hadn't forgotten what happened when the Nazis took power, less than a month ago. Would tonight be even worse? Felix felt a cold shiver run down his spine thinking about it.

A knock on the door.

Felix turned around, hoping he'd imagined it, but knew it wasn't so when his mother's face was turned toward the hallway as well. Neither moved, the silence in the room deafening. His nerves were frayed as he wished for whomever was at the door to go away.

Another knock. Louder, more urgent. Rebecca turned to Felix, her eyes wide with fear.

He considered their options. Had the Gestapo finally come for him as well? It was a cruel time to knock on their door, but it also made perfect sense. With the referendum result safe, the Germans now had complete legal and judiciary power within Austria. Not that they needed it, as his father's arrest proved.

Rebecca dimmed the lights in the living room and looked to Felix. He realized she was waiting for him to make a decision. With a deep sigh to try to release some of the tension racing through his body, Felix slowly moved to the hallway, the old wooden floor creaking underneath his feet. He felt the presence of whoever was outside through their front door. He stopped and listened for any indication as to the number of people on the other side of the door, but only silence greeted him. Felix moved a shaking hand toward the doorknob and took a deep breath. *If they take me today, I will go with my head held high.*

He turned the door handle, and light streamed past him into their dark hallway. The sight that greeted Felix made him gasp, his knees turning to jelly.

"PAPA."

Felix hardly recognized the severely malnourished figure standing in the hallway, but there was no mistaking the bright blue eyes, tired as they were, looking back at him. He was shaking on his legs, and Felix took his father's arm, carefully guiding him into the apartment. His mother appeared in the hallway and let out a shriek.

"Anton!" She rushed toward him, tears running down both cheeks. "I thought I'd lost you." Rebecca took her husband's other arm, and together they guided him into a comfortable chair in the corner of the apartment. She knelt down beside him. "Where have you been, my love? We were so worried."

Anton reached and cradled his wife's hand in his own. He produced a tired smile, his eyes turning misty. "I wasn't sure if I'd ever see you again." His voice was raspy, and Felix was shocked by the exhaustion filtering through his father's normally strong voice. "I'm so relieved to see you're both well." Anton looked up to Felix, who had tears brimming in his eyes.

"Let me get you something warm, Papa. How about some coffee?"

"That would be heavenly. I can't remember the last time I had a hot drink."

Felix ground some of their last good beans to brew his father a strong cup. When he returned to the living room, he found his parents deep in whispered conversation, their faces close together. He stopped in the doorway, but his father looked up and gestured for him to come closer. "I'm sure you'd like to know what happened to me."

He handed the cup to his father and shook his head. "It's all right, Papa. We can talk about it tomorrow. You need your rest."

"No." Anton sat up straighter and took a sip of the coffee. He closed his eyes and sighed in pleasure. "I can't tell you how good this feels: being home with you, and having a fresh coffee. These last weeks have been hell." He took another sip, then cradled the mug between his legs. "After we lost each other at the police station, they made me wait in a small room. After about an hour, or it could be two, I don't really remember, they loaded me into a small van with four other men."

Felix sat opposite his father. His mother by his side, holding on to his hand like she'd never let go.

"They took me to the prison on Rossauer Lände. At first, it was tolerable, as I shared a cell with one other man. He had no idea why he was in there either. At first, at least. Then they took him, and I didn't see him for hours. When he returned, his face was bruised, and his clothes were bloody." Anton grimaced, closing his eyes. "He was in pain, and I helped him onto his bunk. I hoped I might be able to avoid what had happened to him. He told me the interrogators suspected him of having links to the Communists but he assured me he was no communist, not even a socialist, but they had continued beating him until he confessed."

Anton took another sip of his coffee, staring into space for a moment. He was back in his cell, and Felix shot a look at his mother. She inclined her head ever so slightly, and Felix understood. *Give Papa some time.*

"In the next few days, every time I heard footsteps in the hallway, I was certain they were coming for me. I was just waiting for the lock to click. But it never happened. Other men were taken away. Some returned, most very much in the same state as my cellmate, but others never came back. They simply disappeared. After a while, I realized the biggest danger wasn't to be interrogated. It was being taken from your cell never to return."

"Did you speak to any of the other prisoners? Other than your cellmate?"

Anton shook his head. "Not really. You had to assume they were listening in on everything. It was usually very quiet. The only person you could speak to was your cellmate. And mine had gone into a stupor after his treatment by the Gestapo. He hardly ate or drank after he returned, never mind speaking. He was terrified they would return, and he'd decided silence was his best chance to avoid that." Anton sighed, his eyes sad. "It didn't help him much, though. The next time our cell door opened, they took him. I never saw him after that. That must've been a little over a week ago. I thought they'd forgotten about me, and I was certain they'd come and fix their mistake. But they never came."

"Did you ever catch your cellmate's name?"

"No, it was better to know as little about each other as possible."

"I think I know what may have happened to him, Papa. And why you weren't taken that night." Anton sat up, energy flashing through his tired eyes. "I think what you're describing is the transport of Vienna's prominent members of society. It was all over the news. They took those men to Dachau on a special transport. They wanted to make sure we knew all about it."

Anton looked thoughtful for a few moments, then nodded. "That makes sense. Whomever he was, my cellmate was probably more important than he let on."

"What happened after that?" Rebecca spoke for the first time, her voice soft and fragile.

"I was moved to a larger cell, which I had to share with about a dozen other men. It was clear we weren't considered important prisoners, as the guards hardly cared about what we did. They brought us water and stale bread every day, and they left us alone. I thought they would simply let us rot, but then things changed abruptly this evening."

"They let you go."

"The guards came in and took us away in pairs. I was so scared, but in an odd way, I was relieved something was finally happening. The waiting and not knowing was driving me mad. When they said we were free to go, I thought it was a trap. But then they almost threw me out onto the street, and when the door closed, I dragged myself away from the prison as quickly as possible. I got onto a tram and here I am." His voice trailed off, and he closed his eyes. Felix stood and took his father's hand.

"Come, Papa. You need to rest." Anton's face was pale as snow, his eyes sunken deep in their sockets, making Felix feel guilty for not insisting his father go to bed earlier. "We can talk more tomorrow morning."

Anton nodded and allowed himself to be guided toward the bedroom. As Felix helped his father sit on the edge of the bed, Anton looked up, a fierce glint in his eyes. "Felix, we can't stay in Vienna. This is only the beginning. Things will only get worse."

Felix knelt and started untying the laces on his father's shoes. "I know, Papa. Let's talk about it tomorrow, shall we? You just rest now. You're safe." He slipped off his father's shoes and tucked his feet under the warm comforter.

His father mumbled something, but as soon as his head hit the pillow, he closed his eyes and surrendered to his fatigue. Felix pulled the comforter up to his chin and looked at his father. He'd aged ten years in the past two weeks, and Felix felt his throat constrict, a tear running down his cheek. Grateful to have him back, he was shaken by his father's last words. The necessity of leaving the country had been on Felix's mind for weeks as well, but to secure a visa they needed money, or a job abroad. And they had neither. There was nowhere to go.

EIGHTEEN

Prague
24 April 1938

The impressive meeting room was packed, with several bleary-eyed latecomers struggling to find a spot near the walls. Adela looked on from her seat and spotted most of her colleagues scattered around the room. The gathering was as close to a full staff meeting of the entire foreign office as could be. It was rare to have everyone assembled, and even rarer for it to be in the middle of the night. The clock mounted behind the single lectern at the front of the room showed it was almost four. People spoke in hushed voices, the anticipation and gravity of the meeting not lost on anyone. Most people in the room had an idea of what the summons could be about, but they weren't certain. Adela, however, knew exactly what was about to be announced.

The door behind the lectern opened, and the room went quiet. President Beneš was accompanied by four men, one of them Moravec. They took their seats at the front, and Beneš placed a single sheet of paper on the lectern. He adjusted his glasses, glanced at the paper, then looked up. His eyes scanned the room, and Adela felt them linger on her for a moment.

"Good morning, dear colleagues. Thank you all for being here this early. I'm afraid the news I need to share with you couldn't wait." His voice was strong and even, his words measured. "A few hours ago, we received a list of demands from Karl Henlein's Sudeten German Party. I won't go into the details at this point, as you'll receive the list momentarily." A murmur of voices arose, colleagues looking at each other with a mix of shock, surprise, and concern. Beneš held up his hands. "I know most of you have been aware of the increasing tensions in the Sudetenland in the past few weeks, but Henlein's list of demands is essentially a declaration of independence by the Sudeten Germans." The last sentence caused a collective gasp to ring through the room.

Adela studied the responses of her colleagues. Beneš was right: Most of the people in the room knew about the growing unrest among the German and Czech Sudeten, but they didn't know Henlein was in constant contact with Hitler. It had only been a matter of time, and that time had come.

"Needless to say, we'll reject these claims." Beneš raised his voice, and the attention returned to him. "Ceding to these demands would mean opening up Sudetenland to become a province of Nazi Germany in all but name."

The room was quiet as Beneš looked down at his notes, then a scattering of applause started from the back of the room. It quickly spread, and soon every single person in the room was bringing their hands together. Beneš looked up and smiled, then held up his hands, quieting the room once more.

"There's much to be done. Their demands will be public in a matter of hours, as soon as the morning papers hit the stands. We need to have a response ready before the end of the morning. Let's get to work."

As Adela and her colleagues rose from their chairs, she caught Moravec's eye. In an almost imperceptible motion, he nodded at her. That was everything she needed.

ADELA RUSHED OUT of the office a few hours later. She'd spent the morning briefing her team of translators, handing over files she'd prepared in advance. The news hadn't surprised her, merely confirming what Moravec and she already knew. In a way, she was relieved about Henlein's so-called Karlsbad Programme coming out into the open, the eight points outlined as part of their demands for autonomy for ethnic Germans living in the Sudetenland. Their contact inside the German government had been true to his word, even if he hadn't responded since his initial outreach.

Beneš would address the press in an hour, and with her team properly briefed, Adela could finally head out to deliver another important message. Riding into the city, excitement bubbled in her stomach, and she jumped off the streetcar at Staroměstská. She stopped by Georgi's newspaper stall.

"You must've had an early start?" His voice missed its usual cheerful tone as he handed the stack of newspapers to Adela, who nodded. "When I saw the headlines, I figured as much. This is bad, isn't it?"

"It's not great." She lowered her voice. "But we knew something like this was coming."

"What's the government's response? The papers all seem to agree this is a revolt from Henlein. Surely their claims can't be accepted?"

Adela stuffed the papers in her bag. "Beneš will speak to the press in a moment."

"But what do you think?"

"My opinion is irrelevant, Georgi," Adela answered abruptly. "But I think you should prepare for a busy afternoon. I can imagine the newspapers will be releasing late editions today."

She was on her way before Georgi could ask anything else. Adela liked the newspaper vendor: He was a good source for getting a feel for the opinion on the street, but he also asked a lot of questions. Adela needed to filter how much she shared with him. In this instance, she decided there would be plenty of opportunities to exchange information with him at a later point. Small queues and gatherings formed around the newspaper stalls as she navigated her way into the city center.

It took another five minutes to reach the large bakery tucked away on a side street off the main thoroughfare. Greta spotted Adela as soon as she walked in, and she motioned her into the back. The smell and sight of freshly baked bread and sweet pastries made her stomach grumble as she passed the counter. Greta guided her to the bakery behind the shop, the heat of the ovens overpowering Adela's senses. Her friend turned to her with her eyebrows raised, her eyes wide with inquisition.

"I just heard about Henlein. Does that change anything for my aunt and uncle?" She sounded worried, the tone of her voice slightly higher than usual.

Adela nodded. "It does. It means all the attention will be on the situation to the north."

"And that's . . . ?" Greta looked unsure.

"It's good. Call your aunt."

THE TWO WOMEN stepped out of the quaint hotel on the outskirts of Znjomo a few days later. They'd arrived half an hour earlier, and they set out to find something to eat in the city center. Located near Czechoslovakia's southern border, the small city perfectly suited their purpose. Adela relished the sensation of the sun kissing her face, and the smell of pollen in the air. Greta looked a little nervous, and she placed an arm around her friend's shoulder as they walked down the gravel path.

"We've done everything we could to ensure this goes well. I've talked to all the right people in Prague, and there will be no better time to do this than now. Trust me."

Greta kicked a pebble down the road and forced a smile. "I trust you, Adela, and I know you called in every favor you could. I'm very grateful. I'm just nervous. There are still so many things that can go wrong. They might be caught on the other side, or get lost."

"I know. But this is the only way to do it. And with everything happening in the north, even the Austrians will be distracted. Henlein is making a lot of noise, and it's big news in Austria as well."

"You think it means they'll ease up in their border patrols?" Greta sounded doubtful.

"Not necessarily, but I'm not sure the Austrian border patrol is the one we should be most concerned about. From everything I've heard, they're not as vigilant as our own."

They reached the city center, where they found a pleasant bench overlooking the main square. They sat and Adela looked at her friend.

"Everything will go as planned, I promise." She took two sandwiches from her bag, handing one to Greta. "Here, eat something. We should relax while we can. It's going to be a long night."

Greta took a bite, and they watched the people going about their business on the square. A steady stream of mostly women went from store to store, collecting their daily groceries. Greta put her sandwich on her lap and turned to Adela with a serious face. "Have you considered what to do if something goes wrong after they cross the border?"

"You mean if someone sees us?"

"Yes, or if we lose each other in the darkness. If someone gets lost?"

"We won't lose each other, Greta. If all goes as planned, we won't be doing any running. We need to stay calm, and take your uncle and auntie back to the car, and head straight to Prague."

"And you're sure it's safe? No one will stop us on the way?"

"Why would they stop us? We're not doing anything wrong. And our country isn't occupied, is it?" She shook her head. "Once they've crossed the border, I'm certain we can get them to Prague. Once we're there, I have the connections to get them the correct papers to stay. Trust me, Greta, everything will be fine." Adela gave her most reassuring smile. She shared Greta's nerves, but she was also confident Marti and, if required, Moravec would come through. She finished the last bite of her sandwich and got to her feet. "Now, let's go explore the surroundings. We still have plenty of sunlight left, and we need to get our bearings. It'll make our journey tonight so much easier."

ADELA AND GRETA found themselves flat on their stomachs twelve hours later. They had spent the afternoon inspecting the woods southwest of Znjomo. Adela had been pleased to find plenty of tree cover, and very few open spaces. It was as she expected, having spent the past days studying numerous maps at the office with Marti. Although they were both unfamiliar with the terrain around Znjomo, they had identified the small forest on the border with Austria as the perfect crossing point.

It had been a gamble up until Adela and Greta arrived to search for a path or rendezvous point that they could tell Greta's family about. Thankfully, they had succeeded in finding a narrow path running along the eastern edge of the woods. After returning to the hotel, Greta had called her aunt, who was waiting in a town on the other side of the border, with their final instructions. It was now half past one in the morning, and the women had positioned themselves on a small incline. Below them was a gravel road cutting through the path they discovered that afternoon. Adela had decided this would be the perfect place to meet Greta's family. The risk that a border patrol would pass by at that very moment was negligible, Adela felt, and it was imperative that they didn't somehow miss each other.

"It's taking too long." Greta's voice was no more than a whisper, but in the silence of the darkened woods it made Adela jump. She had been so focused on the tree line ahead of them that she'd almost forgotten about her friend.

"They're just being careful, as you told them to. You don't know what they may encounter heading this way. Let's be patient." In reality, Adela was also developing concerns. They had been waiting for well over two hours, and her muscles were starting to ache. It was impossible to see beyond the wall of dark tree silhouettes on the other side of the gravel path, and her nerves were frayed. The quiet of the forest gave her mind plenty of time to think and conjure all sorts of scenarios. What if Greta's family were captured, and the border patrol was now looking for them?

"Psst." Greta gave her a soft nudge, pointing toward the road below. "Do you hear that?"

The sound of an approaching engine was impossible to miss, and seconds later headlights appeared from around the corner. The car drove slowly, as if searching for something. Adela's heart skipped a beat as she pressed her body into the thin blanket, willing herself to disappear. Her breathing became heavier, and even with the sound of the car's engine, every breath felt as loud as a hammer pounding in her mind.

The car slowed down further and was now parallel with their position on the small hill. Adela prayed they would continue, suddenly realizing their hill gave them a perfect vantage point, but it surely would stand out to a trained eye as well. She cursed herself and willed the car to continue. It stopped a few meters later.

The engine was still running when the passenger door opened and a tall man exited. He said something Adela couldn't make out before closing the door. The man then crossed the front of the car, and was momentarily illuminated by the headlights. Adela's heart sank when she saw he was wearing a uniform. He paused and signaled toward the driver, who rolled down his window.

"Hurry up, they're expecting us back in less than an hour. We're running behind schedule!" The driver's voice sound tinny coming from the car, but the urgency was unmistakable.

"Yeah, yeah." The passenger moved to the side of the road and took a few steps up the hill. He was now less than thirty meters from Adela and Greta, and she could hear him mutter, "A few minutes won't make a difference."

A twig snapped as he made his way farther up the hill, and Greta softly gasped. Adela quickly grabbed her friend's hand, cold to the touch, and squeezed it. Below, the man stopped in his tracks. The moonlight illuminated just enough to see him turn and raise his head in their direction. Adela felt Greta's grip tighten, and she forced herself to slow her breathing. The man appeared to consider something, then continued his way up the hill.

Much to Adela's relief, he headed away from where they were hiding and found a large oak tree instead. She heard the swoosh of a zipper, then the trickle of urine hitting leaves. For two minutes, Adela and Greta hardly moved while they listened to the man finishing his business. When he started moving down the hill, Adela allowed herself to exhale. He passed in front of the car, then turned around again, looking up at them. To Adela it felt like he was looking straight at them, and she focused on staying absolutely still.

The sound of the car horn was deafening, and if it wasn't for the man standing in front of the car swearing, Adela was certain he would've heard her soft shriek of surprise. Instead, he opened the passenger door and launched a tirade at his colleague. The car pulled away quickly, disappearing out of sight within seconds.

Adela took a deep breath and looked at her friend. Greta's face was ashen, and she was shivering. They were still holding hands, and Adela moved closer to her friend.

"It's okay. They're gone. You did well."

"I really thought he spotted us. Especially when he looked up." Greta's voice sounded oddly detached, and Adela squeezed her hand once more. "He was looking right at us."

"Me too." She let out a nervous chuckle. "But we're okay." She caught herself speaking at normal volume, and she reduced her voice to a whisper. "Are you all right?"

"Yes. But I'm worried about my aunt and uncle. I thought they'd be here by now."

As if on cue, rustling sounds came from below. Adela's ears pricked up and she searched the tree line for movement. It was impossible to miss the two figures emerging onto the road, only a little way from their position. They moved cautiously but with purpose as they crossed to Adela and Greta's side.

"Greta? Is that you?" The woman's voice came in a whisper, layered between hope and fear.

Greta rose from the cold ground, and Adela did the same, exposing their position in the moonlight.

"Aunt Ida. Up here!" Greta responded in a more urgent whisper, unable to hide her joy and relief. "Come, hurry!"

NINETEEN

Vienna
16 May 1938

The Palais Albert Rothschild was a stately building in the middle of the city. Though surrounded by an iron grille fence, it was possible for passersby to catch a glimpse of the three-story building, its Neo-Renaissance façade decorated with large pillars. Previously owned by the Jewish Rothschild family, it was now the location of Adolf Eichmann's Central Office for Jewish Emigration.

Karl thought it fitting that Eichmann had chosen a palace for his offices. The man considered his job among the most important in Vienna, and Karl got the impression he imagined himself as some sort of Viennese kaiser. Despite his early misgivings about Eichmann, he had to admit the man had built up an impressive agency. The queue of desperate people waiting to submit their visa applications snaked far beyond the tightly guarded entrance to the palace. Karl passed the men and women without acknowledgment, nodding at the guard who allowed him entry on sight. Karl grinned as he crossed the perfectly manicured front gardens of the palace;

he'd become a regular guest at the Central Office, removing the need for identification at the gate.

He made his way up to the second floor, heading straight for Eichmann's office. Pleased to see the door open, he knocked. Eichmann stood near the window, turning as Karl entered the office with a Nazi salute.

"Have a seat. Huber should be with us shortly." Eichmann spoke in clipped tones, moving behind his desk while he offered one of two chairs opposite. "Some have been standing there for two days now. And by the time they get inside, they usually find out they don't have the correct papers, or money. Some even dare to show up with neither, expecting us to help them. It's a damn shame."

"Despite that, you're still doing an admirable job getting Viennese Jews out of the country. Whatever it is you're doing, it seems to be working." Karl knew it was better to flatter the man opposite him rather than go along with his negativity. "You've processed how many by now? A hundred thousand?"

"Hundred and twenty thousand." There was pride in Eichmann's voice; Karl had struck the right chord. "But things are slowing down, which is why I wanted to talk to you and Huber. What's taking him so long, anyway?"

There was a silence as they waited for Franz Huber to arrive. Karl was certain Huber was intentionally late, using his elevated position as head of the Viennese Gestapo to make a power play against Eichmann. Karl made sure to steer clear of such political manipulations.

"Ah, there you are."

Eichmann made no effort to hide his annoyance as Huber entered the room. Karl stood and shook Huber's outstretched hand. Eichmann reluctantly did the same, and the three men sat.

"Any chance we can keep this short and to the point? I'm in a bit of a rush." Huber matched Eichmann's tone, dark clouds gathering around his head. "What's the issue here, Eichmann? Why did you need me here?"

"We need to do something about the process of removing the

Jews from the city. The whole thing is cumbersome, and as I just shared with Vogt, it's taking up too many resources."

"Isn't that what you've been appointed to do?" Huber's eyes darted around the room. "They even gave you a palace to work from. And from what I've heard, you've been quite successful in removing these people, no?"

Eichmann shifted in his seat. "I'm afraid things are slowing down somewhat. The Jews that left since March were quite willing and able to pay for their journey to wherever they needed to go. We're running into trouble removing the rabble. The poor, the leeches. And to make things worse, the remaining wealthy Jews aren't willing to leave."

"What about all those people lining up outside?"

"Most of them don't have any means to get out of the country. As I said, wasting our time." Eichmann clenched his jaw. It was a subtle show of frustration, but neither Karl nor Huber missed it. A modest grin played on the latter's face.

"Sounds like you need a way to get more money to ship out the Jews." Eichmann didn't respond, and the room went silent. Huber leaned forward. "Did you mean to ask my help for this?"

Eichmann shook his head. "Not necessarily. Not yet, anyway."

"Very well. Then what do you need me for?" Huber crossed his arms.

Karl decided enough was enough. "It sounds like a problem that also touches the Gestapo, sir. If you'll indulge me, I think I have an idea that would make both your departments look good to Berlin." Huber and Eichmann turned to him, the hostility on their faces replaced by curiosity. Karl pushed on. "The Führer wants the Reich to be *Judenfrei*, and he doesn't really care how we do it, as long as it gets done. We're making good progress, but we need to make sure all Jews, not just those willing or financially able to move, are removed from the Reich as quickly as possible."

"This all seems rather obvious, Vogt. What's your great plan?" The sharp edge had returned to Eichmann's voice.

"If the Jews aren't leaving willingly, we've not made their lives difficult enough yet."

Huber leaned toward Karl. "What are you thinking? Do you need my men to knock on some doors?"

"In due time, yes." Karl turned to Eichmann. "Do you have a list of all the Jews in the city, including their property?"

"More or less."

"Would you say you could identify most of the rich Jews still living in the city?"

"Yes."

"We should target them first. Make their lives unbearable. Take away their businesses, their livelihoods. They need to have no other option but to leave the country. And that's when they come here, and we hit them with the emigration tax."

Eichmann looked back with interest while Huber looked neutral.

"I like your idea of stripping the rich Jews of their assets, but that won't work with the rabble. They're struggling to survive as it is. How do we get them to leave?"

Karl had anticipated the question and smiled. "By taking everything worth living for from them. We exclude them from the public sphere, restrict their movement and freedom. They'll have no other choice but to leave. And this is where the Central Office will make it as easy as possible for them."

"Using the money we took from the rich Jews."

"Exactly."

"This is all well and good, but how do you expect to execute this?" Huber said, crossing his legs. "Between Eichmann and me we have substantial power to execute a good part of your plan, but not everything. We'd need approval from Berlin for some of these policies, at the very least."

"I'm aware." Karl spoke calmly, but his palms were sweaty. He needed both men on board with his plan before he could take his next step. "If I arrange approval from Berlin, will you work with me on the execution? If we carry this out successfully, it's bound to put us in the Führer's good graces." As he spoke the last sentence, he could see the glimmer of ambition in Eichmann's eyes. Huber looked more composed, but Karl sensed the head of the Gestapo was making the calculation of success in his mind.

"If you're so confident of getting Berlin's approval, I'm happy to see you try," Eichmann said, trying—and failing—to keep the greed from his voice. "I'll make sure the lists of wealthy Jews are updated and ready once you receive the go ahead."

Karl turned to Huber, who slowly nodded as well.

"My men will be available to assist wherever they're needed. But if you're looking to change city policies, I think you need one other person on your side before you take this to Berlin."

Odilo Globočnik leaned back in his comfortable chair and laughed. "You got Huber and Eichmann to work together on this? Well done, Karl. I don't recall anything other than seeing those two bicker and fight about every little detail. How did you manage this?"

Karl smiled and waved his hand nonchalantly. "The deportation and persecution of Jews unites a lot of people in the party."

"True, but that on its own is hardly enough to get them to work together, or stick out their necks for each other in Berlin."

"Technically, I'm the one sticking my neck out, but you're not wrong. I underlined the potential upside to their careers if they pull this off together. I may have mentioned this having the Führer's attention."

"Well, it does."

"Yes, but I'm not sure he's aware of all the efforts on the ground. It's mostly Heydrich's responsibility, and any news of progress goes through him."

"And you, in turn, report directly to Heydrich. Nicely played, Karl." Odilo stood and moved to his liquor cabinet. "I suppose you need my official support on formalizing some of the changes to the city policies?"

"That would be very helpful, Herr Gauleiter." Karl addressed his friend with his formal title. Globočnik had recently been appointed gauleiter of Vienna, which made him the most senior

Nazi official in the region. Odilo now wielded the power to change policies and run the city as he saw fit, provided this was done within the scope of the party line. There was no doubt Karl's plan was very much that.

Odilo poured two generous glasses of vodka and handed one to Karl. "I may be the gauleiter, but you are the one moving all the pieces on the chessboard in the background, my friend. Together, we will rule this city."

They clinked glasses, and while Karl enjoyed the moment, the job was only half done. With three of Vienna's most important Nazis on his side, the most daunting part of the plan remained: convincing Heydrich this was the right approach to solve the Jewish problem in Austria.

TWENTY

Vienna
23 May 1938

The Prater Hauptallee ran straight through Vienna's largest park. Located in the middle of the city, the Prater park hosted an amusement park but also plenty of pathways, playgrounds, and open fields. It was a popular place for Vienna's citizens to spend their weekends, especially on a sunny day like today.

Felix and a dozen friends traversed the four-kilometer avenue as they made their way to their favorite field. People on bikes overtook them on both sides, while runners huffed and puffed, improving their fitness. The majestic Praterstadion rose in the distance, reminding Felix of the days when the Austrian national football team played their games there. That team was dissolved last month, their best players forced to join the German national team.

"So, my father was fired from the hospital yesterday." Wolfgang caught up with Felix, kicking the ball the group was passing between each other to someone else.

"Just like that?" Felix was only mildly surprised; he sympathized with his friend. His father was a well-respected surgeon, and it was still somewhat shocking to hear of him being removed. "I thought the AKH was keeping everybody on?"

"Well, apparently policies can change very quickly. His supervisor came in yesterday morning before his shift and told him not to bother changing. Said his services are no longer required." As Wolfgang continued, his voice remained calm, but his eyes told a different story. They burned with an intensity that almost made Felix want to take a step back. The corners of Wolfgang's mouth twitched downward, fighting to maintain his composed façade.

"How did your father take it?" Felix remembered his own father's initial refusal to accept reality, only accepting his fate when it was too late.

His friend shrugged. "Remarkably well, actually. He told us not to worry about it too much. Said we have enough savings to get us by, but that he's certain to find a job soon enough. He says there are never enough doctors, especially in a big city like Vienna." Wolfgang didn't sound like he shared his father's optimism, but Felix decided not to press the matter. The ball was passed to him, and he controlled it, letting it spin on his foot for a moment before passing it to a friend making a run on the other side of the avenue. It brought a cheer from the rest of the group.

"How is your father doing? And you, for that matter? Any luck finding work?" Wolfgang asked cautiously.

"Nobody will even consider hiring us. I'm seeing more and more companies go out of business as I make my way around the district. It's depressing, Wolfi."

"Hmm. Must be especially hard for your father. How is he coping with the prison and all?"

"He's become very quiet since. He really needs something to keep his hands occupied, to keep his mind from wandering back. Sometimes when I walk into the room I see him staring out into space."

"Doesn't sound like Anton at all."

"All he knows is work. He's run that shop for over twenty years, often spending time there even while it was officially closed. Even on the Sabbath." Felix couldn't help but chuckle. "He'll take any job now. As would I, as a matter of fact."

"You know, I might be able to help you with that." Wolfgang looked thoughtful before continuing. "It's not the most glamorous job, but if you don't mind a bit of dirt and hard work, I can ask."

"What do you think? I've never been picky, and certainly not now. What's the job?"

"Let me check with the owner first. I don't want you to get your hopes up. But the man's friends with my father, so I'm hoping he might be willing to take on a Jew."

"Thanks, Wolfi. I appreciate it. We're struggling to get by."

They reached the field and the boys split into two teams. As they warmed up, Felix momentarily forgot about his worries, enjoying the grass under his feet, even if it was just in the park, and not the football training ground across the city.

They kicked off the game and while Felix followed the action on the other side of the playing field, he couldn't help but feel optimistic about Wolfgang's cautious promise. With all the doors closing, it was nice to think his friend might be able to find him a job. He didn't care how dirty it would be; if it brought in money to support his parents, it was worth it.

"Felix, go left!"

Too caught up in his thoughts, Felix was late to respond, and the ball ran harmlessly out of play. Felix held up his hands. "Sorry! I'll go get it." He turned around and sped up to get the ball, but the sight greeting him stopped him in his tracks.

Six boys a few years younger than him approached, one of them holding the ball. Each sported the brown Hitler Youth uniforms that had so tormented him these past weeks. Felix remained frozen in place as the boys closed in on him. He could feel his friends gathering behind him. Wolfgang showed up by his side, and he felt a little better.

"This yours?" The boy holding the ball tossed it into the air casually, effortlessly catching it.

"Yes," Wolfgang answered before Felix could say anything. "Mind handing it back?"

"Actually, we can't let you continue playing." The boy spoke with an authority that belied his age. Felix felt the veins in his neck popping, his forehead throbbing. The boy didn't wait for a response. "This *Wiese*, field, is now closed to people like you."

The words, as simple as they were, hit Felix like pellets. *People like you.*

"You've got to be kidding me." Aaron, the tallest of the boys standing behind Felix, stepped forward. "Says who?" Felix admired Aaron's calm demeanor, speaking calmly and precisely.

Another uniformed boy stepped forward and produced a sheet of paper. "By order of the gauleiter of Vienna. From this point on, Jews are prohibited from visiting public parks. That includes this Wiese. You'll need to find somewhere else to play football. Maybe you can try one of your squares in the second district." His tone was condescending.

It took every bit of Felix's self-control not to dash forward and plant his fist in one of the smug Hitler Youth faces. Wolfgang's presence was calming, and he decided to let the others do the talking.

"So, what's it going to be, Jew boys? Would you like us to take your names and report you, or are you going to leave? We'll give you a minute to think about it." One of the boys that had been standing in the back came into view. To Felix's horror, he recognized him. They used to play on the same football team. Now, the boy looked at Felix without recognition. Felix felt deflated, and as his friends moved to grab their belongings, he noticed the boy at the front holding the ball.

"Can we have that back, please?" He managed to keep his tone polite.

The boy appeared surprised at the question, studied Felix, then nodded. "Sure, of course." He held out the ball, but when Felix took a step forward, he produced a pocketknife. In one quick motion, he tore a deep gash in the ball, the air escaping with a quick hiss. The boy then tossed the ball to Felix, the rest of the group roaring with laughter as he caught the empty leather shell.

In a haze, Felix stepped forward, his right hand forming a fist, his arm swinging back. The Hitler Youth was distracted, laughing among his friends, and Felix had a clear swing at his face. He then felt a strong hand grabbing his wrist. Wolfgang's worried face brought him back to reality. "Are you mad, Felix? You're really going to start a fight with those boys? Over a ball?"

Felix felt woozy, his anger dissipating. He shook his head. "I'm sorry, Wolfi. I don't know what I was thinking."

"You weren't thinking." His friend pulled him away from the Hitler Youths, who were too focused on themselves to have noticed. "Come, let's get out of here."

They left the field, and as Felix looked back one more time, he noticed a truck pulling up to the side of his favorite Wiese. A man jumped out and grabbed a sign, preparing to mount it on a streetlight. The words confirmed his beloved Vienna was taking another hostile turn: *Für Juden verboten.*

TWENTY-ONE

Prague
25 May 1938

Adela tapped her foot while she watched the traffic go by on the main street. She turned up the collar of her coat. It had been a warm day for this time of the year, but the evenings could still be a bit chilly. A streetcar that was stopped opposite let out a stream of commuters, many running to make their connections.

"Hey! I hope you haven't been waiting for too long." Greta appeared next to her. "I couldn't get away any sooner. It was so busy in the bakery today, we had people coming in well after we closed." Her friend leaned in for a hug.

"No problem. Come, let's go. I want to pick up a bottle of wine on the way." Adela started toward the main shopping street. "Apart from work, how are you? How are your uncle and aunt settling in?"

Greta needed a few extra paces to catch up with her. "Remarkably well. My uncle started working in the bakery this week. My nagging the boss about giving him a chance may have had something to do with it, but he's taken to the job really well. I think he was teaching some of the old-timers a thing or two this afternoon."

"That's so good to hear. They seem like really nice people." Adela thought back to the night they smuggled Greta's family across the border. While nervously navigating the dark woods toward the car, they had hidden down a small road. The sounds of every snapped twig or swishing leaf had seemed like thunder in the silence of the night, and she expected border guards to appear from behind every tree. In the end they'd made it to the car, and Adela had driven very carefully back to Prague. She'd initially preferred to stay on back roads, but when dawn broke, the group decided they could return to the main roads. They'd arrived in Prague during morning rush hour, and Adela had never felt so relieved to be inconspicuous in the slow-moving traffic.

"Will a bottle of red do?" They reached the liquor store, and Adela paused before entering. "What does your aunt like?"

"Anything is fine. It's quite unnecessary to bring anything; they're just happy to get to know you better."

Adela went inside and picked out a nice bottle. They continued on toward Greta's family home, where her parents provided a room to her uncle and aunt.

"How are things for you, at the ministry?" Greta's voice was tense, and she appeared troubled. "I'm reading so many contrasting things in the papers. Did President Beneš really send the army to the Sudetenland?"

"He did, but it's mostly a precaution." Adela had to tread carefully. The recent mobilization of the army was public knowledge, and it had sent shock waves through the country. Suddenly, war was a real possibility many people hadn't considered before. Greta wasn't immune to these feelings either. "He needs to show Hitler and Henlein they can't bully us into giving the Sudetenland independence, just because they asked for it." Demanded, more like, but Adela didn't want to alarm her friend further.

"I read he asked the Brits to intervene. Didn't he just return from England?"

Adela nodded. It had been a disaster. Beneš thought he could convince British prime minister Neville Chamberlain to side with him. Instead, he found the Brits strongly in favor of giving in to Henlein's claims for independence. "He's still hopeful he can find a solution with the Brits." Adela tried to keep her tone airy, but Greta's clenched face suggested her friend was unconvinced.

They reached the large apartment building where Greta's parents lived, rang the doorbell, and waited in silence. Adela was torn. She wished she could tell Greta more, including some of the information from the recent reports she'd received from Moravec. The government purposefully fed as little information as possible to the press, keeping the Czechoslovak population in the dark about the real developments. To most people, it looked like they were standing up against the danger from the west, the mobilization of the army a strong signal. In reality, the diplomatic game played at a much higher level revealed a very different situation. Without the support of Great Britain and France, Beneš would have no choice but to give in to the German Sudeten's claims for independence. Worse, with Britain's policy of appeasement toward Hitler, Beneš would lose all power in negotiating a respectable deal. It looked more and more likely that he would have to give in to all German demands.

The buzzer sounded and Greta pushed the front door open. They mounted the stairs to the second floor, where her mother stood waiting for them in the doorway. She greeted Adela with a generous smile and embraced her warmly.

"I can't remember the last time I saw you, my girl. It's so lovely to see you. Please, come in."

Adela hung her coat on the rack and momentarily forgot about her worries. She'd spent many hours of her childhood in this home, and Greta's parents felt like family. After her own parents passed away in a car accident, now three years ago, the Pereles' home brought even more comfort to her life. As she entered the dining room, Greta's aunt and uncle were sitting comfortably at the table. When she dropped them off three weeks ago, they'd looked every bit the refugees they were: stressed, haggard, and unkempt. Now, they looked respectable as they rose to greet her. Aunt Ida's cheeks were even a little rosy from the warmth of the apartment. It suited her well. As Adela hugged them, she felt proud of what she'd accomplished. But as she sat and accepted a glass of wine from Greta's father, she couldn't shake the feeling of impending doom building up in the back of her mind. The winds, political and military, blowing across Europe looked to be bringing trouble back into the lives of Greta's family. They may have escaped the Nazis once, but for how long? Adela took a sip of wine, and despite its calming effect, she worried trouble was unlikely to be limited to the people surrounding her in the room tonight.

TWENTY-TWO

Vienna
1 June 1938

The door to the large office on the fifth floor was closed. Karl paced up and down the hallway, passing more numbered doors. When the Gestapo took over the Hotel Metropole as its Viennese headquarters, they'd removed the beds and most of the furniture in the rooms. All but a few were now furnished as offices, but they retained their hotel room markings. That, and the traditionally decorated hallways—complete with red velvet carpeting and polished gold wall lamps—meant the offices of Nazi Germany's secret police in Vienna still felt more like a hotel than a government institution.

"Vogt!" The voice of the most senior man in the building sounded from the room, and Karl hurried to the now open door. He stepped inside, where Reinhard Heydrich had returned to his chair. "Close the door and have a seat."

Karl did as he was told, taking no offense at his boss's brusque manners. He was used to it by now.

"You wanted to speak with me?" Heydrich picked up his coffee cup, then looked annoyed when he found it empty. "What is it about?"

"I think I've found a way to move things along with the Jewish question in Austria, and Vienna especially." Karl observed his boss pouring coffee, and paused for a moment. He wanted to make sure he had Heydrich's full attention for the next part.

The tall German put the coffeepot down and looked at Karl impatiently. "Well? Out with it."

"How would you feel about using the Führer's orders of the *Aktion Arbeitsscheu Reich* to remove many of the undesirable elements of the city of Vienna?"

"What do you mean?" Heydrich's eyebrows arched. "We've rounded up a good number of useless mouths using the decree so far."

"Absolutely. But I feel our efforts in rooting out the work-shy elements of society could be combined with a more general purge." Heydrich put down his coffee cup and leaned forward. "What if we expand the criteria for expulsion to the camps to not just the work-shy, but also those we feel are disruptive, undesirable elements in society?"

"The Jews and Bolsheviks." The beginnings of a smile formed on Heydrich's face.

"To begin with, yes. I've spoken to Gestapo chief Huber about this, and he would be happy to allocate resources to seek out and arrest whomever we identify as such. We could present the arrests as part of our efforts to weed out the work-shy elements, while what we're really doing is advancing toward a *Judenfrei* Reich."

Heydrich stood and moved toward the window overlooking the city. When Heydrich turned back around, he said, "We would silently remove them from the city, not causing much of a fuss. And if we classify them as work-shy, there would be no possible legal basis for them to protest their deportation."

"They would be undesirables, in protective custody." Protective custody was the Gestapo's preferred status for its prisoners. This would legally classify them as dangers to the Reich, and made it near impossible for anyone classified as such to reclaim their freedom without the Sicherheitsdienst approving it. Essentially, their fate was in Heydrich's hands.

"I like it, Vogt. How do you want to play it out?"

"Apart from the obvious work-shy, I'd like to target wealthy Jews. We've been struggling to get them to leave voluntarily, and by classifying them as work-shy undesirables in protective custody, we can seize their assets."

Heydrich was nodding. "You've given this a lot of thought, Vogt. I suppose I shouldn't be surprised, but I am certainly impressed."

"Thank you, sir. There's one more thing. Working with Scharführer Eichmann, we'd like to allocate some of these assets to facilitate the departure of the poorer Jews in the city. We can use this money to pay for their relocation elsewhere."

"When would you be able to action this? It sounds like you've got Huber and Eichmann on board already? How far along have you planned this?"

"I've compiled a list of over two thousand Jews in Vienna. We could get started as soon as you give your approval."

"And if anyone asks, they could be classified as work-shy or antisocial?"

"I'm confident we can make either of those claims stand, sir. In many cases, both."

Heydrich nodded. "This takes Jews off the streets, and it provides income to further the deportations. I couldn't have come up with a better plan myself, Vogt."

"That's very kind of you, sir. When can we start?" Adrenaline rushed through Karl's veins, and his throat went dry in anticipation.

"Immediately. I'll inform Huber and Eichmann this afternoon. Make it happen, Vogt."

TWENTY-THREE

Vienna
6 June 1938

The smell of the stables no longer bothered Felix. In fact, he only recalled ever really sensing the smell on his first day. After that, he cared more about getting his work done, while enjoying the company of the horses, their frequent whinnying providing a comfortable sense of camaraderie. He was finishing up when Hannes, the stable master, walked in.

"I assume that's the last of them?" He pointed at the two bales of hay next to Felix.

"Yes, I was just cleaning up, and then I need to move those to the back stalls."

"I'll give you a hand, so we can head home early." Hannes picked up a pitchfork.

Felix nodded his thanks and continued sweeping the floor.

It took them less than fifteen minutes to finish, and Felix waited while Hannes locked the heavy wooden double doors. He reached into his coat and handed Felix a small envelope.

"Here's your wages for the week. You can count it, if you want."

"Thank you." Felix placed the envelope in his pocket without checking its contents. They walked toward the main gate, passing some of the other stables. The Freudenau racecourse, located only a few hundred meters away, would no doubt be crowded this weekend. The thought of many prominent Nazis attending the races at Felix's place of work made him chuckle. Despite their best efforts to put as many Jews as they could out of their jobs, he was providing a living for his parents and himself right under their noses, and most likely paid for by their gambling. He was grateful to Wolfgang for finding him this job. Hannes waited for Felix to roll his bike out of the gate before locking it.

"Have a good weekend, Felix. Be careful out there."

"Don't worry about me." Felix set off, heading north toward the Danube River instead of the more direct route west, which would take him through the Prater park. The Hitler Youth and even Gestapo agents had recently increased their patrols there, stopping anyone who looked even remotely Jewish. Felix didn't want to risk getting caught. He pedaled hard, and soon reached the narrow path following the majestic Danube. Even though it added fifteen minutes to his commute, it was safe. There were hardly any other people here, and he kept his eyes on the river and let the wind clear his head.

After twenty minutes he reached Lasallestraße, the large thoroughfare running north-south from the river to the Praterstern junction leading into town. As he approached the roundabout, it became clear something was going on. Traffic had come to a standstill, and while Felix was able to snake between the cars, he soon came to a halt. The Praterstern junction was blocked by numerous trucks. Men in black and brown uniforms swarmed the junction, supported by police officers. Men and women were escorted and bundled into the backs of the trucks. They were of all walks of life; some were incredibly well dressed, holding on to their hats while they were pushed and shoved toward the trucks, while others wore simple overalls. They all had one thing in common: They came from the direction of the city's second district, Leopoldstadt.

A sense of foreboding struck Felix, and he turned his bike off the road and onto the sidewalk. Before anyone could stop him, he disappeared down a small alley. He needed to get home as soon as he could.

THE TRUCK in front of his apartment building was an ominous sign. Felix quickly parked his bike on the side of the building. A knot formed in his stomach as he approached the front door. It was open, and harsh voices filtered through the stairwell. He raced up, impatient and terrified about what he would find.

He only had to go up two flights.

Two large uniformed police officers blocked the stairs as they escorted someone down between them. It took Felix less than a second to register what was happening. *Papa.*

Anton's wrists were tied and he struggled to keep his balance as the officers moved him down the stairs. Felix opened his mouth, but his father quickly and resolutely shook his head.

"Not now, Felix." His voice was soft but sharp, not leaving any room for argument.

Felix had stepped aside to allow the three men to pass when a fourth appeared from upstairs. He wore civilian clothing, but his manners marked him as a Gestapo agent. Ignoring his father's instructions, Felix addressed the man. "What's going on? Where are you taking my father?"

The piercingly blue-eyed man stopped and looked down from his elevated position a few steps above Felix. It was then that he noticed they were roughly the same age.

"Your father is detained for being an antisocial element of society." The man spoke in crisp Hochdeutsch German, and Felix took an instant dislike to him.

"Antisocial?" Felix was shocked. That term was reserved for criminals. "On what basis?"

The man took a step down the stairs, making a show out of inspecting the sheet of paper he held. "Your father, Anton Wolff, hasn't worked since he closed down his business more than two months ago. That counts as work-shy." He looked up and narrowed his eyes. "That makes him an antisocial drain on our society. We don't need people like that."

The words felt like a slap in the face, and Felix didn't know how to respond for a second. Shock turned to anger, which he barely managed to control. Through gritted teeth, he asked, "Where are you taking him?"

The man shrugged. "That's up to the police for now. We'll decide later. We still have quite a few people like your father we need to pick up." His expression changed from mild disinterest to curiosity while he sized up Felix. "Say, there's only one Wolff on this sheet. Why don't you get out of my way before I decide there was an oversight?" His eyes quickly darted between the piece of paper and Felix. The Gestapo man's blue eyes had turned to ice, and he took another step down the stairs.

Felix stood in a daze, barely registering the words. The Gestapo agent moved even closer, then a voice brought Felix back to his senses.

"Felix! Move out of the way and come up here!" Rebecca Wolff stood atop the stairs. Her eyes were red and puffy, her cheeks pale. Felix's heart filled with sorrow seeing his mother like this for a second time in two months. He stepped back against the wall. As the German agent passed him, he brushed his shoulder against Felix, and slowed down.

"Smart choice, little Jew. Your mother saved you. For now. I've got my eye on you, Mr. Wolff." He then walked on, and muttered, "Have a pleasant evening."

Felix felt the blood drain from his face while he watched the man descend the stairs and disappear from view. He then rushed up to his mother, catching her just before she collapsed onto the cold floor. Her sobs cut through his bones, and for the first time since everything that had happened, Felix felt truly helpless.

TWENTY-FOUR

Prague
12 June 1938

"I need you to meet with him."

Moravec's words couldn't be any clearer, yet Adela had trouble processing them. *Meet him? Where?* She sat opposite František Moravec in his office on the top floor of the castle, and she wasn't sure how to respond. The chief of military intelligence had summoned her out of the blue that morning, as he usually did. Adela had expected an assignment to translate and assess classified documents, but not this. She composed herself and looked up at her superior.

"Sir, this comes as quite a surprise, if you don't mind me saying. I wasn't aware of any new communications with the agent. In fact, I thought we'd lost contact."

"He went dark for a long time, but he reached out yesterday evening." He slid a piece of paper across the table. "This was left in my mailbox last night."

Adela's eyes ran over the paper. There were only two short, neatly typed paragraphs. She read the note twice, although the wording was clear enough. She put the paper down and looked at Moravec.

"Do you think it's genuine?"

He smiled. "Yes. We've known about the Sudetenland threat since early 1937. It was this very agent who confirmed Germany was behind the initial unrest being stirred up. Many of the ethnic Germans in the Sudetenland long to see the Sudetenland return to Germany. Everything in this short message suggests further escalations are due soon. And with that, a possible armed conflict."

"If he knows about Poland's conditions for supporting us in a potential war with Germany, he's got connections right at the top."

"That's something I've assumed from the first time we met. He's never told me where exactly he retrieves his intelligence from, but my best guess is that he works for the *Abwehr*, the German military intelligence agency." Moravec leaned forward and tapped the second paragraph. "But it's his urgent tone here that really caught my attention. He was quite happy to inform us about the developments in the Sudetenland by letter. But now he wants to meet urgently."

"With information vital to the independence of Czechoslovakia." Adela read the words out loud. "It's the first time he's using such strong wording. I don't recall him referring to the Sudetenland situation in quite the same way."

"I'm glad we agree, and I think we should hear what he has to say. In any case, we'll have a chance to develop the relationship. And that's why I want you to meet him. You're well informed, but officially, you're not part of the intelligence agency." His face turned serious. "Adela, do you feel comfortable meeting with him in a public place? You need to be aware of the potential risks."

Adela swallowed hard. "Do you think it's a trap?"

Moravec shook his head without hesitation. "I don't. He's offering to meet us in the middle of Prague, on our own turf. If German intelligence wanted to try something, they would pick somewhere closer to the border, or even in Sudetenland."

"Do you think he's expecting you? I mean, do you think he'll be willing to talk to me?"

"If he's as smart as I think he is, he'll know there's no way I'll attend the meeting myself. Not in the middle of Prague." Moravec chuckled softly. "He might be surprised to meet a woman, though. But that will only work to your advantage. See if you can connect with him, build a rapport."

She eyed her superior—had he planned for this from the start? It wouldn't surprise her, and she couldn't help but smile.

"What's that, Miss Beran?" He returned her smile. "Is that a yes?"

"I'll go and see what he has to say."

ADELA FOUND herself sitting in a large coffeehouse in Prague's central district two days later. She had picked a table in the corner, away from the window, as instructed by the German agent. It was noon, and the place was packed, voices echoing around the high, arched ceiling. Normally, Adela would enjoy the setting, but she had trouble keeping her nerves in check.

"Ma'am?"

The voice of the waiter interrupted her thoughts, and she turned to find him looking at her with an inquisitive, somewhat impatient expression.

"Have you decided on what you'd like?"

"I'll have a *Wiener Melange* and *Linzer Torte*, please." She spoke the words as casually as possible, then raised her voice slightly to make sure the waiter heard her. "And could you add a sparkling water with a slice of lime, please?"

The waiter nodded and left without a word. Adela followed him with her eyes, watching him approach the ornate bar. She saw him relay her order, then disappear into the kitchen. She spent the next minute or two watching the people in the cafe, when a different waiter appeared with her coffee and cake, setting it down on the table.

"Your water will be here momentarily, ma'am." He disappeared, and before Adela had time to take a sip of her coffee, a man appeared from nowhere and took the seat opposite her. The first thing she noticed were his expressive eyes, confidently demanding her attention. His hair was combed back, revealing the beginnings of a retreating hairline.

"Good afternoon, I hope I'm not interrupting you." He spoke in fluent German, and Adela had no trouble following him. "You were expecting company, weren't you?"

Adela smiled. "You don't seem at all surprised to find me here. Weren't you expecting someone else?"

"A man, you mean?" He waved his hand dismissively. "In my job, it's best not to make assumptions." He held out his hand. "I'm Dieter."

She shook his hand and noticed his firm grip. "Hana. It's nice to put a name to the words." *Even if it's not your real name.* "We were surprised to hear from you after such a long time. A little worried, even."

The waiter returned with Adela's water, and the man across from her ordered a coffee. When the waiter left, he spoke again. "I apologize. It wasn't for lack of wanting to speak with you. It was just that things were quite hectic at work, and my supervisors were keeping a keen eye on everything that was happening. I do hope my information about the developments in the Sudetenland were helpful to you." The waiter returned and Dieter paused. He took a sip of his coffee, then placed the cup down. "From what I saw, your government was at least prepared for Henlein's demands. Your response was as I expected."

"Your information was very valuable, and we are grateful. Unfortunately, there's very little we can do but stall his efforts. As you're well aware, we're a small country, and we're at the mercy of the larger countries in Europe."

Wrinkles appeared on the man's forehead. "Yes, I've followed the negotiations with interest. That's why I felt it was important to meet. I'm aware the United Kingdom and France aren't providing the guarantees your president is asking for."

"They appear more interested in appeasing Hitler. It concerns us."

"As it should. I'm afraid I have more bad news." He lowered his voice, leaning toward her. "Our Führer has carried out several directives that your government should know about."

He paused suddenly, and after an awkward moment, Adela realized he was waiting for her to hand over the envelope Moravec had given her. She took it from her bag and slid it across the table. Dieter peered inside and nodded appreciatively before securing the cash-filled envelope in his inside jacket pocket.

"Thank you. Hitler increased our naval budget, upping the production of our U-boats, as well as prioritizing the construction of two battleships. They are to be ready by spring of next year."

He listed the facts without emotion, but they made Adela gasp in horror. "He intends to counter any British dominance at sea."

"Yes. And it gets worse. Your president's reluctance to cede to Henlein's claims for the Sudetenland is considered as a direct slight by the Führer. The mobilization of your army last month incensed him, although this is only known to his inner circle."

The importance of the last words weren't lost on Adela. If he was speaking the truth, the suspicions she and Moravec had about his connections in the top of the German government had proved correct.

"The Führer considers the Sudetenland a German province, currently annexed by your country. He will continue to press for a diplomatic solution to have it returned to its rightful state." He cleared his throat and took a sip of coffee. "However, if things continue to develop the way they are, he will move on to another option."

"He will attack us."

"Only a few days ago, he ordered his generals to prepare for an invasion of your country no later than 1 October. That is why I'm here. You need to find a way to stop this."

TWENTY-FIVE

Vienna
22 June 1938

It had been over two weeks since his father was taken by the Gestapo. Every day following that terrible night, Felix made his way to the main police station near Praterstern, harassing the officers about his father's whereabouts. None were willing to speak with him, and he was sent away on every occasion.

Today was different. Upon arriving, he was greeted by a new face at the station's reception desk. The man didn't appear to be surprised by Felix's request and had instructed him to take a seat. While Felix wasn't getting his hopes up yet, it was somewhat encouraging not to be dismissed immediately.

Life at home had worsened, and even though he was at the police station, it was a relief to be away from the house. His mother had slipped into something resembling the early stages of depression. Felix had the escape of work at the stables five days a week, but for his mother there was nothing to take her mind off her worries. Felix felt powerless to do anything about it, and it was part of the reason why he went to the police station every day. It was the least he could do for his mother, even if his efforts were in vain. Perhaps today would be better.

A door opened down the hallway, and a large police officer made his way toward him, taking long, determined steps. His expression was neutral, and as he reached Felix, he motioned for him to get up. "Follow me." The instruction was crisp, but there was no malice in his voice.

Felix did as he was told and followed the officer into a small room away from the main hallway. It was furnished with a simple iron table with two chairs on either side: an interrogation room. He reluctantly took the seat offered, while the other man remained standing.

"I understand you're seeking information about your father's arrest." His tone was formal, a little distant, but still held no hint of any ill feeling. "It's Wolff, Anton, isn't it?"

For the first time, Felix noticed the man was holding a thin folder. "Yes, sir. He was taken, I mean arrested, at our home two weeks ago, and I haven't heard anything from him since. We're worried."

The police officer nodded and opened the folder. He barely glanced at the piece of paper before speaking. "I understand. There have been many arrests these past weeks, and it's not always clear where prisoners are taken. Sometimes the Gestapo keep them, other times they're placed in our care." The man's candor surprised Felix, but he managed to keep a straight face. "In your father's case, he was taken by the Gestapo. His location isn't known, but I can tell you he was arrested on account of being work-shy."

"Yes, I was told as much when they took him." Felix bit his tongue. The police officer leaned in closer and looked around the room.

"Look, I'll be honest with you. Things aren't looking too good for your father. Prisoners marked as work-shy are considered antisocials. This means your father will most likely be placed on a transport to one of the correctional camps. Dachau or Buchenwald, probably."

"Is he still in Vienna, or has he already been moved?" The

thought of his father being sent to one of the camps struck terror in his heart.

"I'm sorry, I don't have that information." The man sounded genuine, inclining his head ever so slightly.

"Is there any way for me to find out, or anything I can do? My father is sick, and he wouldn't survive a week in one of those camps."

He gave Felix a hard look, then sighed. "There's only one place you could try. But I wouldn't recommend it."

FELIX HESITATED, as he stood in front of the majestic entrance of the Hotel Metropole. Its polished, gleaming doors had opened only for the rich and famous. Doormen would've turned their noses up at him if he even tried.

There were no doormen left now, just a steady stream of men in black and brown uniforms rushing in and out of the building. Felix took a deep breath and passed between two of the four columns, moved through the revolving doors, and stepped into the lobby.

It still felt like a hotel lobby, the plush furnishings kept intact. Instead of hotel guests sipping afternoon drinks at the bar or preparing their visit to the nearby Staatsoper opera house, the space was populated by stern-looking men who were otherwise occupied.

On a whim, Felix approached a man in a smart suit coming down the stairs. "Excuse me. Where could I find someone to speak to about a prisoner in your care?"

The man stopped and looked at Felix with surprise, then disbelief. "Wait. You're looking for a prisoner? Here?" He recovered his composure, and his tone hardened. "Who are you anyway? And how did you get in here?"

"Please, I'm just trying to find out what happened to my father." Felix heard the desperation in his voice, but he realized there was no room for pride in this building. If he was thrown out on the first attempt, he wasn't sure there would be a second. This was nothing like the police station. "Is there any way you could point me in the right direction?"

"I'm not sure what surprises me more. That you stepped into here of your own accord, or that you'd think I'd help you." A harsh undertone developed in the man's already overly formal speech. "Even if I knew anything, I wouldn't be able to tell you. You do realize the building you just stepped into, don't you?"

"Sir, I beg you—"

"No! Get out, now. If you want information about a prisoner, you can go through the correct channels."

"But the police can't help me." Felix locked his eyes on the exit, readying himself to run if necessary.

"Well, that's your answer then." The man shoved him aside. "You're wasting my time." Without another word, the man headed for the exit, leaving Felix standing in the middle of the lobby.

The police officer had been right: Coming here had been a mistake. He was lucky the man didn't arrest him just now, and Felix resigned himself to reality. Nobody in this building was going to help him. He had turned back to the entrance when he spotted a lonely figure making his way down one of the arching stairways in the middle of the lobby. Something about the man was familiar, and as he descended, Felix recognized him. It was the agent who had arrested his father. As if in a trance, Felix moved toward him. The man reached the bottom of the stairs and headed toward the exit, but Felix blocked his path. A look of annoyance, then faint recognition, appeared on the man's face.

"You look familiar, but I can't place you." The man tilted his head. "One thing I know for sure, though. You're not supposed to be in here."

"Wolff. You took my father. We met on the staircase of my home." The words came easy, and Felix felt no fear. "I want to know what's going to happen to my father."

The man raised an eyebrow. "You have guts coming in here, I'll give you that. You realize I can just have you taken to the basement for your insolence? You know what happens in the basement, don't you?"

Stories of torture circulated on the streets of Leopoldstadt. "Sir, I just want to know what's happening to my father. I don't mean to stir up any trouble."

The man studied him for a few agonizing seconds. His eyes darted over Felix's face, then his clothes. Finally, he nodded. "Very well. It takes courage to come in here. Your father was picked up for what, again?"

"Work-shy." Felix barely managed to speak the words.

"In that case, it's quite simple. He'll be sent to Dachau."

Felix felt an agonizing pain as if he'd been hit by a sledgehammer. They were the words he'd expected, but prayed not to hear. All strength left his body, and he struggled to keep his composure. He raised his chin, facing the German who wielded the power of life or death over his father. "He won't survive that, sir. Please, I beg you to reconsider. My father is severely weakened."

The man shrugged and spoke in an infuriatingly condescending tone. "He should have considered that before making the choices he did."

Felix looked at the cold, emotionless face observing him. If he had any strength left, he might have made the poor decision to strike the German.

"Now, if that is all, I'll be on my way." The man made a dismissive gesture, taking a step away from Felix. "And I suggest you do the same."

Felix had no fight left in him and watched the man stalk away. Then a thought struck, and he rushed after the man. He caught up with him near the door leading back to the street. The man turned around in annoyance.

"What is it now?"

Felix took a deep breath. "What if I take my father's place?" Disbelief appeared on the man's face, and Felix continued before he could reject the suggestion. "I'm strong and a hard worker. You'll have more use for me in a work camp." The thought of Dachau terrified him, but not as much as his mother ending up a widower within weeks. He steeled himself. "Take me instead."

The man looked at him, his gaze distant, and Felix could see the wheels turning in his mind. He rubbed his chin, then slowly nodded. The words he spoke next forever changed Felix's life.

"I'll take that trade." He looked around the lobby, then signaled to a man in a SS uniform, who rushed toward them.

"Sir, is there a problem?" He eyed Felix with disdain.

"No, I'll need you to take this prisoner into custody. Have him processed and send his file up to my office."

Felix's skin crawled while he listened to the exchange. "And you'll let my father go, right?"

The man looked down at him. "I'll handle that when I return." He appeared hurried as he moved toward the exit, signaling to the trooper. "Take him downstairs."

"Yes sir, Standartenführer Vogt."

The man disappeared out of the building, and before Felix could say anything, the trooper grabbed him by the shoulder, dragging him toward a door on the side of the lobby. He opened it, revealing a simple staircase. As they slowly descended into the recesses of the building, Felix closed his eyes, resigned to his fate, whatever it might be. *At least I saved Papa.*

PART TWO

TWENTY-SIX

Somewhere in Germany
15 August 1938

T he train slowed down but none of the passengers in the dark train car stirred. The first few times they had slowed down, some had risen to peek through the slits in the walls. Felix had been among them, but it soon became clear there was nothing discernible at their stops. Only once had they stopped at a small station, where their SS guards disembarked to refill their canteens. The men locked inside the cattle cars received no such luxury.

Felix closed his eyes, as much from exhaustion as despair about his situation. They'd boarded the train at Vienna's Westbahnhof two days ago. He'd spent the previous two months dragged from makeshift prison to prison. After he was taken to the basement of the Hotel Metropole, his captors moved him to the prison at Rossauer Lände. When they struggled to house the many incoming prisoners, he had been moved to the Prater stadium. He spent more than a month camped on the pitch, where he managed to claim a spot in one of the tents. Many of the other prisoners weren't quite as fortunate, sleeping outside and exposed to the elements. Felix had learned to look after himself first, defending his spot in the tent with fervor.

Light suddenly spilled through the cracks in the walls. A few seconds later, the sound of heavy boots running along concrete sounded. Felix opened his eyes and pricked his ears. Men around him woke up with groggy, tired eyes. They all came to the same realization. This was no ordinary stop. Seventy closely packed-together men listened and waited silently for news of what was to come.

Voices shouting orders joined the stomping of boots next to their car. A jangling sound echoed out as someone slid the bar locking their door aside. An instant later the door opened with a crash. The light was blinding, and a number of men let out grunts as it burned their eyes. Faceless figures emerged from the light, only their outlines visible.

"Get out, Jewish pigs! Out, out! Don't make us come in there, or you'll regret it!" After more than forty-eight hours of near silence, but for the rhythmic sound of the train wheels drumming along the tracks, the harsh commands were jarring.

When the men near the door didn't respond quickly enough, the abuse started. Two faceless men turned into four, blows raining down on the car's passengers. The passengers bundled over each other to escape the batons indiscriminately hitting their faces and bodies. The coppery scent of blood joined the stale smell of sweat they'd become accustomed to during the train ride.

Felix managed to dodge the blows as he jumped off the train. Hundreds of men were driven across the single platform of a small station. In the distance, he saw the outlines of a forest on rolling hills. Small lights dotted the landscape, suggesting the presence of civilization in the darkness. The mood on the platform was anything but civilized, where the swell of the terrified crowd pushed him toward the exit. Troopers wearing the distinct skull-and-bones-decorated uniforms of *SS-Totenkopf* stood spaced evenly down the platform. They harried the prisoners along with cudgels and steel-tipped batons.

"Keep moving! Come on! Don't stop!"

Anguished cries mixed with incessant shouts from the troopers left the prisoners in no doubt of what was expected of them.

Within minutes Felix found himself running through a picturesque town. The curtains of the houses they passed were drawn, as if the inhabitants wanted to shield themselves from what was happening outside their homes. Felix wondered if the locals were aware of what was going on. *Where am I?* He had no time to contemplate, as someone barged into him, almost making him lose his balance.

"Keep moving, you idiot!" the man hissed at him. He slipped to the side, trying to get past Felix, then lost his footing and crashed to the ground. Felix continued, now hearing those behind him swearing at the man obstructing the way. A gunshot rang through the air. Felix instinctively ducked, then turned his head to the source of the sound. One of the SS troopers stood in the middle of the group, the barrel of his pistol still pointing down to the man who had tripped. A pool of blood was quickly forming around the man's head. The crowd had stopped, their faces lined with shock.

The SS trooper turned to the man standing closest to him and pointed the gun at his head.

"Why have you stopped moving? Did I tell you to stop?" he roared at the man, who froze, unable to respond. "No! I didn't, did I?" Another gunshot, and the man's head exploded, his limp body collapsing on the ground. That was enough motivation for those gathered around to start moving at breakneck speed again.

The houses made way for a dirt road. Dawn broke and the sun illuminated the open countryside surrounding them. All the while, the SS troopers continued their abuse, shouting and beating them forward. Those who couldn't keep up were immediately finished with a bullet to the head. The others jumped over their corpses, their lungs burning, their tired bodies screaming for a break. But there was to be none. Felix's tongue stuck to the roof of his mouth: He would kill for a drop of water.

A densely forested hill rose up, and the men started their ascent. The gunshots became more frequent, and Felix forced himself onward. The sun was rapidly making its way up in the sky, but the trees obscured their view. It was impossible to tell how much farther they had to go. He battled against the cramps that surged through his legs.

Finally, the road turned sharply and into a clearing. Barracks stood scattered around, many under construction. The men were driven forward through a towering gatehouse and into another large open space. They were now encircled by a three-meter-high, barbed wire fence. Felix could hear the crackle of electricity flowing through even from a distance.

"Line up, pigs. Rows of ten. Quickly! Go, go!" The guards whipped the prisoners into formations, again unleashing their violence with alarming zeal. Felix was fortunate enough to find a spot in the middle and escaped most of their blows. It took less than five minutes for the thousand or so men from the train—minus those who'd fallen on the run—to line up in the silence of the beech forest.

It took all of Felix's strength to stay on his feet, gritting his teeth as his muscles burned. A handful of men collapsed onto the sandy ground, their bodies failing them. They were finished with a bullet to the head, their bodies left where they were. Giving up was no option.

A door in the gatehouse opened, and three men in SS officers' uniforms emerged. They moved to a small platform in front of the assembled prisoners. One of them produced a microphone, taking his time scanning the crowd. From a distance, Felix couldn't make out anything notable about the man, but his confident demeanor made it clear he was a man of power.

"Well, well. There you are, then." His voice shrieked through the loudspeakers mounted on the gatehouse. "*Judensau*, Jew pigs. I take it you had an invigorating run here." As he spoke, a truck pulled into the camp. Its open flatbed was littered with the corpses of the fallen, clearly tossed onto the truck without any ceremony. Despite his exhaustion, fury built up inside Felix. The truck stopped a little distance from the platform, and the man continued.

"Take a good look. This is your future. No matter what you do, you will end up like this." A sinister smile played on the man's face. "Welcome to Buchenwald. This is where you will die."

TWENTY-SEVEN

Prague
17 August 1938

Adela's desk was buried in papers. She reached for her coffee mug—her fourth this morning—and found it empty. Ready to slam the mug back on the desk, she instead reached for another thick folder. It was heavy, and after scanning the first pages, she placed it on the discarded pile. There was no need to send everything to her translators, and from what she saw, this news report from a small German publication near the border offered few new insights. She checked the clock above her door: It was almost ten thirty. Half an hour before the briefing. Her hands trembled and she took a deep breath. The pile containing discarded newspapers and clippings was growing, and significantly larger than what she considered important, on the other side of the desk. That might have frustrated her a few months ago, but her position was very different now. In addition to her regular work sifting through the morning papers, she was also receiving daily intelligence reports from Moravec and, when she was fortunate, updates from her German spy. The latter were sparse, but when he did come through, his information was worth a hundred times more than anything scattered on her desk. If only he had given her something new to bring to Beneš later.

"Adela, do you have a minute?"

"What is it?" She caught her harsh tone the minute the words left her mouth, and instantly felt horrible. She felt even worse when the bemused face of Natalia, one of the translators on her team, poked her face around her door.

"I'm sorry, I can come back later. This is a bad time." Natalia looked mortified, already taking a step back into the hallway. Adela held up her hands and shook her head.

"I'm sorry. I shouldn't have snapped at you like that. Please come in." She stood and waved her colleague to a chair. Natalia reluctantly entered and sat. Adela put on a friendlier, more patient tone. "What can I help you with?"

Natalia held up a piece of paper. "I'm sorry, I know you have your meeting with the big shots later. I didn't want to disturb you, but I ran into something I think you would want to read before talking to them." She handed the paper to Adela. "Normally, I wouldn't flag another report on the activities in the Sudetenland like this, but there's an alarming amount of detail in this one."

Adela caught the source of the article at the top and frowned. "This is from the *Völkischer Beobachter*." She read on, recognizing the familiar tone of one of the largest pro-Nazi newspapers in Germany. Then she caught the author's name. "Ah."

"Yes, this one's published by Goebbels himself. Again, this wouldn't be enough to disturb you, especially not this morning, but I thought the wording was—" She paused for a moment, searching for the right words.

"More extreme and graphic." Adela finished reading the article and placed it on the useful pile, then returned her attention to Natalia. "Thank you for bringing this to me. You're right, this needs to be addressed later."

Natalia inclined her head slightly, then rose to leave. "Good luck with your meeting." She turned for the door, but it was clear from the way she moved that something was on her mind.

"Thank you. Was there anything else you needed from me?"

"Well." Natalia hesitated as she turned to Adela, who encouraged her on with her eyes. "He's becoming more extreme in his phrasing, don't you think? Goebbels is a gifted writer, if not the most interesting public speaker."

Adela wasn't surprised by Natalia's observation. The Nazi minister of propaganda's addresses mirrored the increasingly aggressive stance she knew Hitler was requiring the higher political and military echelons to adopt. But Natalia wasn't privy to that information. "Yes, he's ramping up the accusations. Most likely to put pressure on the negotiations with Henlein."

"Are you worried?" Natalia's voice was surprisingly small.

Adela didn't immediately answer. "Not as long as we can show their accusations are false."

PRESIDENT BENEŠ SAT at the head of the large table. Dark rings lined his eyes, deep grooves had formed across his face. Despite this, his eyes were focused on Adela with a clarity that showed little sign of fatigue.

"Can you repeat that please, Ms. Beran? I want to make sure I understand correctly."

Adela glanced around the table, making sure she had the attention of the other men assembled. "The number of media sources reporting attacks on ethnic Germans in the Sudetenland has increased over the past few days." She held up the clipping from the Völkischer Beobachter that Natalia handed her less than an hour earlier. "While we always suspected the involvement of the Nazi government in spreading these rumors, I believe this publication by Goebbels indicates they're now comfortable presenting this as the official Nazi government line."

A few of the men at the table moved uncomfortably in their chairs. Adela's eyes briefly met František Moravec's. The military intelligence chief looked unfazed. Beneš looked equally unshaken. Even though Adela wasn't included in the conversations between them, she was in a sufficiently well-informed role that she knew these developments were no surprise to either man. Judging by the response from the majority of the other men at the table, that wasn't the case for everyone.

"Trouble between the Czech and German inhabitants of the Sudetenland isn't a new development," Beneš said. "The German and pro-Nazi newspapers in Sudetenland have been keen to blow them out of proportion ever since the region was allocated to us after the Great War. The frequency increased over the past months, but I believe this is the first official Nazi government publication on the matter."

"It is, Mr. President."

"Has anything happened to warrant Goebbels' direct comments on this? Any escalations?"

Adela glanced at Moravec, who gave her a quick nod. "The German media have been reporting alleged attacks on towns populated primarily by ethnic Germans. They claim these attacks are organized by Czech nationalists with support from our army. Some papers even go as far as to claim that this is the main reason for the presence of our troops along the border."

"Alleged attacks?" Beneš raised his eyebrows and turned to Moravec. "Can we deny these allegations, or do the Germans have proof?"

Moravec leaned forward in his chair, placing his hands on the table. "We can categorically rule out our involvement in any of the reported incidents. I've sent a large number of agents to border towns, and while we can't deny there is friction between the Czechs and Germans in the Sudetenland, it's nothing out of the ordinary. Isolated incidents. Certainly nothing to warrant Goebbels speaking out in a national newspaper."

"So his claims are false. Our army isn't involved?"

"Our soldiers have orders to guard the border. Their focus is to the west. The German claims are wildly exaggerated, as is to be expected." Moravec cleared his throat before continuing. "But we should still take this escalation seriously. Goebbels is serving as

Hitler's mouthpiece in what we believe is a bid to increase international support for their claims on the Sudetenland."

When Moravec stopped talking, Beneš sat back in his chair. The room was silent, and Adela could feel the air thin as the gravity of the situation sank in. All eyes were on the president, who rubbed his chin while gazing out the window. Adela chanced a glance at Moravec, who gave her a thin, appreciative, but humorless smile. The tidings she brought were grim even before she received Natalia's news.

"What can we expect next?" Beneš snapped back to the present, addressing Moravec. "Do we have any indication of what Hitler's, or Henlein's, response to these news reports will be?"

"I can only foresee further escalation, sir."

Beneš nodded his agreement. "We've acceded to nearly all of Henlein's demands, but it appears it's not enough. I'll return to the negotiating table, and I'm sure they'll cry outrage at these supposed attacks. What escalations can we expect?" He spoke slowly, as his shoulders drooped for the first time in the meeting.

"We have strong indications most of the reported altercations are staged by the Germans themselves. I can only imagine they'll continue to increase the intensity of the incidents in the next few days or weeks. That would be the first escalation that I foresee, Mr. President." Moravec's voice was businesslike and analytic. Based on what Adela had read, she agreed. But then he surprised her, a trace of emotion filtering through when he continued. "We shouldn't, however, rule out the more serious escalation of a German invasion into the Sudetenland."

ADELA SPENT the rest of the day with Moravec's ominous words ringing in her head. After the meeting was adjourned, she returned to her office, but she had found it hard to focus. She'd expected a summons from above, but it never came. Poring over Goebbels' article multiple times, she searched for hidden messages that may give her more insight into what they should expect next. There were none, and she desperately wanted to speak to Moravec to discuss their approach.

Despite her unease, Adela controlled herself. If Moravec wanted her to look into something, or take action, he wouldn't hesitate to call on her. For Adela, the next course of action was clear: She needed to speak to their German spy.

She managed to get through the next hours, and she felt a small sense of calm when she packed up for the day. Walking down the hallway she was surprised to find most of her colleagues had already left. The clock in the hallway showed it was a little past eight. She rushed down the stairs and, as she crossed the large hallway on the ground floor, was surprised to hear someone call her name. A young man she recognized as an aide of Moravec rushed to catch up with her. A tingle of excitement shot through her body—she was being summoned after all. She walked toward the aide, preparing to head back up.

"I'm glad I caught you before you left." The aide handed her a sealed envelope. "Mr. Moravec is quite busy, but he wanted to make sure you received this."

Adela took the envelope. "He doesn't need to see me?"

"No ma'am, he'll be wrapped up in plenty of meetings through the evening." Adela felt a pang of disappointment at the words. "I'm sure he'll want to see you tomorrow morning. Enjoy your evening." The aide hurried back toward the elevator, leaving Adela standing in the middle of the large space.

She headed toward the exit, the envelope feeling oddly heavy. Outside, the temperature was balmy, the heavy August evening air soothing and comfortable. The sun was setting over the city, and Adela sat on one of the small benches lining the front square. She tore open the envelope to reveal a neatly folded sheet of paper. She opened it to reveal a single sentence scribbled in Moravec's handwriting. As her eyes shot over the words, she gasped, almost dropping the paper. Six words that would change everything.

Wehrmacht soldiers massed on western border.

TWENTY-EIGHT

Vienna
19 August 1938

It was rather convenient that the Gestapo and Sicherheitsdienst shared the same headquarters in Hotel Metropole. Karl's small office was housed on the second floor of the building, although he preferred to spend as little time as possible there. Offices were for bureaucrats. Karl liked to roam the streets of Vienna, getting a feel for what was going on, and expanding his ever-growing network, keeping his ear close to the ground. It was this very skill that got him where he was. Every now and again, however, he was required to make his appearances at the headquarters. He tried to make sure that those visits always served a purpose, preferably to his advantage.

Today was such a day, as Karl strode through the heavy rotating doors of the Hotel Metropole. Ignoring the chatter in the lobby, he made his way to the third floor. He reported to Franz Huber's office at precisely a minute to ten in the morning and was shown right in. Naturally, Huber wasn't there yet, but his aide provided coffee, and Karl stood at one of the windows overlooking Morzinplatz. Located close to the Ringstraße and the Schwedenplatz interchange, foot traffic was always abundant on the square. Karl watched from his elevated position as people rushed from their streetcars into the city or across the Danube Channel.

The door opened and Karl turned to see Franz Huber walk in.

"Ah, Vogt. Enjoying the view? I like to stand in the same spot when I have a minute. It's not a bad office, is it? Where is yours again? On the other side, no?" The head of the Gestapo spoke cordially, with a trace of familiarity.

"Mine overlooks the channel." The men shook hands and sat in two comfortable chairs in the corner of the office. "It's not too bad. Although I'm hardly ever there."

"Yes, I think that's what Heydrich likes so much about you. Always on the move, never time to sit, right?" Huber spoke casually, but Karl recognized the quip. Huber was a career administrator posing as a man of action. Especially since becoming one of the most powerful men in Vienna. But he was useful, and Karl needed him on his side.

"I go where I'm needed, sir."

Huber leaned back in his chair. "I haven't forgotten your usefulness in the deportations. It's all moving along rather smoothly."

"Thank you, sir. I much appreciated your men taking over the operation. Which is why I'm here. I've been tasked by Obergruppenführer Heydrich to assist in setting up a new Einsatzgruppe."

"Yes, I've been informed. I assume you need Viennese recruits from the Gestapo for your task force?"

"I'd like to have them on board. We could use their experience. I expect we'll be recruiting from a variety of organizations."

"Brownshirts as well?" Huber practically spat out.

"They make useful brutes, sir."

Huber smiled and slapped his thigh. "I suppose they do. What can I do to help?"

"I need men with military experience. I can't recruit from the Wehrmacht, even though they'll most likely assist. Limited military experience is fine."

"Talk to Eichmann. He's set up an entire system of index cards."

Now it was Karl's time to smile. "I thought he reserved those for enemies of the Reich." Eichmann's index card system had been invaluable in the early days, when the Gestapo could easily pull up information on Jews, Bolsheviks, and other troublemakers based in Vienna and other cities. Karl had to admit Eichmann had done his due diligence preparing for the annexation.

"Let's just say his approach caught on." Huber got up. "He should be in the building today. Best you talk to him. I expect the Obergruppenführer wants this new group set up quickly?"

"They should be operational by the end of the month."

"Not a lot of time to train. Who's overseeing them?"

"A man named Stahlecker. I'm meeting him later today."

"Sounds like you've got a busy day ahead." Huber's eyes narrowed and he moved a step closer to Karl. "Do you think the Einsatzgruppe will be operational up north?"

"I haven't been informed of where it will be deployed, sir." He raised his hand in salute, then opened the door. "Many thanks for your cooperation. I'll keep you posted."

Once in the hallway, he smiled. The lie came easy.

A FEW HOURS LATER, Karl left Adolf Eichmann's office. The head of the Central Office had been remarkably cooperative. He had been happy, proud even, to run Karl through his index of Gestapo men in Vienna. It gave Karl confidence that, in addition to the volunteers he would recruit, he would be able to get the new unit together in the next two weeks.

He moved toward the elevator and checked his watch. It was almost two, which meant Stahlecker would arrive in half an hour. Karl was pleased with his progress so far, but from everything he'd heard about Stahlecker, he knew he would have to play his cards very close to his chest. Heydrich had informed him Stahlecker was an extremely ambitious member of the SS, one who would be reluctant to cede any control over the new Einsatzgruppe to Karl. That was fine with him: Karl had no interest in leading the new unit. He did care about the composition, though.

Karl spent his free time in his office, and he had just finished his quick lunch when a knock at the door announced Stahlecker's arrival. The tall, blond man in full SS uniform took large, confident strides toward Karl, his right arm shooting up in salute.

"Heil Hitler! Standartenführer Vogt, I assume?" Stahlecker extended his hand, which Karl shook. The man's grip was like iron, his cold, calculating eyes giving nothing away about his opinion of Karl, who matched the stare.

"Yes, thank you for coming in at such short notice, Standartenführer Stahlecker." Karl was keen to highlight they were of equal rank. "And congratulations on receiving command of the Einsatzgruppe." Stahlecker sat without being invited, and Karl moved across the desk. "Can I get you something to drink?"

"No, I'm fine. Let's get to business." Stahlecker spoke brusquely, matching his appearance. "From what I gather, you're to assist me in the preparations?"

Karl ignored the condescending undertone of the statement. "I believe this initiative is important to Obergruppenführer Heydrich, and he'd like us to work together in getting the unit battle-ready as soon as possible."

Stahlecker nodded, but his eyes drifted across the room. Karl thought he detected a hint of disdain in the man's eyes. "Yes, I do believe I'll have them ready well before we move into Czechoslovakia. Do you have any military background?" This time Stahlecker did little to hide his smugness.

"I've worked with Obersturmführer Eichmann to compile a list of potential recruits with military experience. We believe they'll be useful for providing training and leadership along the ranks of the Einsatzgruppe." He slid a folder across the table and allowed Stahlecker a moment to scan the pages before continuing. "How do you feel about completing the unit with men of the Sturmabteilung and recruiting from NSDAP members in and around the city?" Karl made sure his proposal sounded conciliatory, giving the man across the desk plenty of freedom to provide his own ideas. To his surprise, Stahlecker closed the folder and nodded.

"Sounds like a good approach. If we're to be ready by the end of the month, we should be able to count on experienced Gestapo men. And judging by what I've seen in this city so far, there should be no problem recruiting from the general public."

Karl raised a hand. "Not the general public. They need to be party members."

"Of course." Stahlecker agreed just a little too quickly for Karl's liking. Then he dropped the bomb. "But I want to be in complete control of basic training and formation of the unit. I don't want any interference from you." He leaned forward, his eyes dark slits. "Do you understand? I'm happy to look into personnel composition with you, but after that, this is my unit."

Karl suppressed a grin, then held out his hand.

"Deal."

As Stahlecker shook his hand, Karl had found in this man a perfect useful idiot.

TWENTY-NINE

Buchenwald
29 August 1938

The sun was beating down on the prisoners without mercy. Between the man-made cliffs of the quarry, the heat of its rays bounced around ferociously. It radiated from the pale limestone as Felix returned to the ever-growing pile of rocks. On the other side of the pile, two dozen men hacked away at the walls of the quarry. The sound of their pickaxes echoed between the walls, a rhythmic clanging that tormented Felix even in his dreams.

He glanced around and, when he was certain none of the guards were looking in his direction, paused for a moment and used the back of his shirt sleeve to wipe the sweat from his face. The air touching his face brought momentary relief before he bent down to pick a rock from the pile. After two weeks in the quarry he could judge if the weight of the rocks would be sufficient to please the *Kapos*, the prisoners serving as guards. He'd seen men beaten to death for picking up rocks considered too light.

His knees and back protested as he lifted the limestone rock. The sharp edges bit into his fingers, and he gritted his teeth in reflex. He no longer noticed that his hands were constantly bloody. The blisters from previous days had only nighttime hours in his bunk to mend. This brief respite proved inadequate; come morning, the first rock he lifted would rip them open anew. By the end of the day, countless new cuts ravaged his hands and fingers. If he was lucky, there would be running water in the barracks tonight.

"Keep moving, you piece of shit!" A sudden, sharp pain radiated from the side of his stomach and shot through his ribs. Stars clouded his vision, the pain dizzying. He almost dropped his rock, but instinct took over, and he gripped it tighter. His knees buckled, but he somehow managed to stay on his feet. "You think you're some kind of important person? Keep moving, Jew pig, or the next blow will finish you!" The voice faded into the background as Felix continued putting one foot in front of another, moving away from the pile of rocks and toward the cart some two hundred meters across the quarry face. He didn't dare close his eyes; doing so could easily draw the attention of one of the guards.

And so Felix kept going, his head spinning, knees shaking, repeating the same words in his mind over and over. *Don't drop the rock. One step at a time. Don't let go.* He hardly noticed his fellow prisoners moving in the opposite direction, relieved of their burdens for a few blissful minutes. They were apparitions in his peripheral vision, cursed as he was, trying to hide from the attention of the ever watchful eyes of the Kapos.

Armed with sticks, cudgels, and other crudely constructed weapons, the Kapos patrolled the quarry floor, tasked with keeping the regular prisoners in line and productive. They took to their tasks with a zealousness matching that of the SS guards watching from the tops of the quarry cliffs. Just looking at a Kapo in the wrong way could set some of them off, and they would descend on a prisoner with unmatched fury. More often than not, it would mean the death of their victim. Felix kept his head down, and he had been fortunate enough to receive only the regular blows these hounds of the pit dished out indiscriminately across the day. For the fate of a Kapo deemed too soft was to be relegated back to the general population. It never ended well for them.

Felix reached the cart and lifted the rock, then toppled it inside. It crashed onto the hard steel with a clang, marking the end of his journey. One of the men handling the cart gave him a sympathetic look.

"Not long until the break. Hang in there, Felix." He spoke under his breath, his eyes scanning the area.

Felix forced a tired smile. "If only we could have some clouds to get rid of this damned sun, Werner." He turned around and started moving back to collect another rock, keeping his pace steady but not expending more energy than needed. Some of the more experienced prisoners had taught him a trick—if he took small steps, it looked like he was moving faster than he really was. He'd perfected the gait within a morning.

About halfway along the journey he heard a piercing shriek ahead of him. Wary of drawing attention to himself, he glanced up enough to see two Kapos bending over a downed prisoner, one of the limestone rocks on the ground in front of him. The men were yelling at him. Felix sighed. The man hadn't been able to keep hold of his rock. He knew what was next, and averted his gaze, continuing at his purposeful pace. Expecting the sickening sound of cudgels smashing bones and accompanied by the prisoners' death cries, he tried to block it out by focusing on the pickaxes and hammers attacking the limestone instead. To his surprise, the beating never materialized.

Felix approached the pile and saw the man was back on his feet, holding a rock that Felix immediately recognized to be light enough to warrant a beating.

"You'll still carry this to the other side, but before you do, I think you should entertain us. We're a bit bored, aren't we, Richard?" Felix recognized the Kapo talking. Known as Fritz, he was among the worst, taking exceptional pleasure in the demise of his fellow prisoners. There was little chance he would ever be considered wanting in his duties. The SS-issued baton he carried was testament to his dedication. The Kapos and the prisoner now blocked his passage to the rock pile, and Felix and the other prisoners could do nothing but watch the spectacle in front of them unfold.

Richard needed little motivation as he nodded enthusiastically. "Dance, Jew pig! Show us what you can do with that rock!"

The prisoner was frozen in place. After a few excruciating seconds, the man attempted to run toward the cart. His limp made it seem almost comical, but one look at the Kapos made it clear that wasn't even close to what they expected. Fritz easily caught up with the man and smashed his baton into the side of the man's head mid-stride. The prisoner crashed to the ground, the stone rolling a meter or two ahead of him.

"That's not what I asked for!" Fritz roared at him. "Get up and dance for me!"

Felix held his breath as the man somehow managed to get back on his feet. A drizzle of blood came from his nose, and his eyes were glassy, but he slowly moved toward the rock. When he bent to pick it up, he almost lost his balance. Fritz drew back his baton, but the man recovered just in time and rose, cradling the rock in both his arms. For a moment, nothing happened, as the man appeared unsure what to do. Then Fritz repeated his command. "Dance!"

Something in the man's mind clicked, for he started to move in a small circle, lifting his right leg first, then his left leg. It appeared as if all sound had left the quarry, and the Kapo's fool was dancing to a tune only he could hear in the silence. Felix risked a glance at Fritz, who looked on with a disapproving smile.

The macabre performance went on for what felt like an eternity, but in reality took less than a few minutes. Fritz encouraged the prisoner, but the man soon started to tire, the rock slipping a few times. When he could no longer hold it, the sound of the ten kilo rock hitting the sandy ground felt like an explosion. The exhausted man slumped onto his knees to lift the rock, but it was obvious he would be unable to do so. His fingers clawed in the sand underneath the rock, but there wasn't enough strength left in them to clasp them around its sharp edges.

The Kapos moved to either side of him. Without another word, they rained blows onto the man, who no longer had any energy left to shield himself, and it took less than a minute for his soul to leave his broken body. Felix and the other prisoners stood by in silence, unable and unwilling to do anything about it. It could just as easily have been them.

When the Kapos finished their execution, they focused their attention on the group. "What are you waiting for? Get back to work!" Fritz shouted while he waved his baton at them menacingly.

Felix and the other men rushed by the Kapos, some receiving a perfunctory blow. Felix was first to the pile and picked up an especially heavy rock. As he turned around and moved toward the cart, he saw two prisoners approach with a stretcher, then lift the body of the dead man onto it with an air of indifference. Just another body in the endless stream from the quarry. Felix gripped his rock tighter. *Don't drop the rock. One step at a time. Don't let go.*

THAT EVENING, Felix lay in his bunk. He was exhausted as always, but he mustered up enough energy to take out a postcard and pencil. The picture on the front of the card showed an image of the Buchenwald area Felix didn't recognize. The pristine beech forest with a river running in the foreground was so far removed from his reality that he marveled at the thought of sending this to his parents. In the semidarkness of the bunk, he transported himself back to his home in Leopoldstadt. He thought of his parents, and prayed they were doing well.

Putting pencil to paper, he pondered what he could share in the small space he had available. Fellow prisoners had warned him not to write anything about the camp's conditions. If he did, his postcard would never make it to Vienna.

Dearest Papa, Mama,

I'm letting you know I'm alive and well. They're treating me fairly.

His fingers trembled as he focused on putting the words to paper. He hoped they would pick up on his subdued use of the word *fairly.*

I hope life in Vienna is as good as when I left, or perhaps even better. Has Papa found a new job yet?

His stomach grumbled, and he lifted his pencil. Could he ask his parents for a small contribution to spend in the camp canteen? He ran his hand along the side of his stomach, noticing for the first time how his ribs jutted sharply beneath his skin. Obtaining the postcard had cost him half a week's rations, trading with one of the prisoners with money and access to the camp canteen. The thought of a can of beans made his mouth water. The foul, watery broth with a few scattered vegetables once a day wouldn't be enough to get him through the back-breaking work in the quarry for much longer.

He shook his head and concentrated hard to fit the final words in the tiny space left.

Hoping with all my heart to receive news of your good health.

Your loving son, Felix

Felix carefully placed the postcard at the side of his bunk, then put his head down. He would post it first thing tomorrow, before roll call. As he drifted to sleep, his heart ached, but he was glad he had taken his father's place. His mind was filled with thoughts of his parents. At least they were together.

THIRTY

Prague
12 September 1938

Adela awoke with a start. She blinked in the darkness of her room and reached for the small bedside clock. Her groggy mind barely comprehended why she was awake at two in the morning. She turned to get back to sleep, but a banging on her front door had her sit straight up in her bed. The urgency of the pounding fist demanded her attention. Terror shot through her body: Who would be at her door in the middle of the night? Then her mind sprang into action, and she swung her legs out of bed. Whomever it was, they weren't going anywhere. She would need to do something, one way or the other.

She carefully treaded toward the hallway of her apartment, then stopped. The banging of fists had stopped, but she could feel the presence on the other side of the door. She pricked her ears and thought she heard breathing in the hallway beyond. *What do they want?*

"Miss Beran?" The voice startled her, and she jumped with a small gasp. Adela immediately placed her hand before her mouth, but it didn't matter. "If you're there, Miss Beran, would you please open the door? Your presence is very much required at the castle."

Adela didn't recognize the voice, and she remained quiet. Was this a trap? Had the Germans somehow found out about her connection with their informant? She shook her head. That was silly. She was in Prague, in her home, and there was no reason for anyone to come to her apartment. *I'm a small fish.* Still, she stayed in her place, not making a move toward the door.

"The chief of military intelligence sent me, Miss Beran." Adela noted the man on the other side of the door spoke with no discernible accent. If he truly were a German agent, his Czech was flawless. A note was slipped underneath her door. "Please have a look at this if you're there, ma'am."

Curiosity got the better of her and she tiptoed to the door, grabbing the note. When she read it, she let out a sigh of relief. It was impossible to miss Moravec's characteristic handwriting. She unlocked and carefully opened the door. Her relief was further enhanced when she saw the man in the hallway. She'd seen his face at the chancellery many times, although he hardly ever spoke. He smiled wryly.

"I apologize for waking you up like this, but it's imperative you come with me at once. Riots have erupted in the Sudetenland."

THE BRIGHT LIGHTS of the conference room on the top floor of the castle contrasted sharply with the dark Prague night outside. In under thirty minutes, Adela transformed from wearing her nightgown to leaping into the waiting car and arriving at the castle door. Moravec had been waiting for her in the conference room.

"Hitler made a speech in Berlin late last night, accusing us of genocide in the Sudetenland. It sparked several riots." He pointed at a cluster of pins dotting the map on the wall. "Henlein's supporters went into the streets and clashed with the police. We've got things under control, for now."

"You think it will get worse?" Adela counted ten pins on the map.

"This is just the start. While a lot of people will have heard Hitler's speech on the radio, they will read all about it in their papers this morning, no doubt with more details." Moravec shook his head. "It's a declaration of war."

Adela's throat constricted. Moravec was a careful man, keen to analyze the situation based on solid intelligence, and certainly never one to openly speculate. It was the first time he explicitly described the Nazi government's aggression with these words. Nevertheless, it was a situation they had planned for. "I suppose this means they reject President Beneš' latest offer? We've given in to nearly all of their demands."

"Every time we move closer to an agreement, Henlein comes up with new demands. It's been clear for a while we were never going to find a solution."

"He keeps holding out for more." Adela remembered Dieter's ominous words at their last meeting. "He's stalling until the German army is ready to invade."

"We have two and a half weeks until 1 October. Beneš will fly to London in a few hours, in a last attempt to garner support." Moravec looked troubled. "But he won't get it. They are pushing for us to give in to Hitler's demands."

"And hand him the Sudetenland." Adela was appalled. "If we do, who says he won't come back for more later?"

"That's the president's concern, and mine, as well." Moravec gave a wry chuckle. "But we have to try and convince them."

"What can we do?" Adela sat up straighter, a fighting spirit awakened inside her. "What can *I* do?"

"I need you to meet with our contact and find out if there is any way to avoid a war."

"I have no way to contact him." Adela felt flushed.

"He's the reason I summoned you this early. He'll be at your regular rendezvous at eight in the morning." Moravec stood and moved to the map of Czechoslovakia. He pointed at the pins marking the areas where trouble had erupted overnight. "But before you go, I need to catch you up on the latest developments."

"Of course, sir." Adela leaned forward in her chair.

He moved to a cabinet to the side of the map and produced a thick folder. "This has the president's talking points for his meeting with Chamberlain later." He returned to the table, this time taking a seat next to Adela while he opened the folder. "I'll walk you through it. It's important you know exactly what he's taking to the British prime minister."

Adela felt lightheaded as she stared at the classified documents in front of her. "Sir, are you sure?"

"Adela," he said, for the first time addressing her by her given name. "If there is any chance you can obtain intelligence that can influence the decision-making in the higher echelons of the German government, you need to have all information available. I'll leave it to your judgment to decide whether you need to share any of this with Dieter."

"Sir." Adela felt the weight of her country's future on her shoulders.

"Let's begin, shall we?"

THE COFFEEHOUSE FELT normal in every way. The people at the other tables were having their morning coffees and pastries, and some tables even ordered cake at this early hour. It was almost as if those gathered here had decided to ignore the news from the north and go on about their lives like normal. For Adela, it couldn't be any more surreal.

Dieter resolutely shook his head. "There is no way Hitler will allow Henlein to accept these terms, generous as they are."

Adela's heart sank. "Are you sure?" In reality, his response had been anything but a surprise. *But I have to try.* "Is there anything we can add to make it acceptable?"

He took a sip of his coffee before responding, scanning the faces of the people in the cafe. When he fixed his eyes back on Adela's, he dropped his head. "I'm sorry, but Hitler will only accept a full, unconditional surrender of the Sudetenland. You heard his speech last night, didn't you? Claiming torture and oppression of the German minority means he's laid his marker down. If he accepts anything less than full annexation and return of what he considers German lands he will look weak."

"Beneš will never go for that."

"And Hitler knows this. You're right; Henlein is stalling the negotiations. He's under clear orders to do so. They are waiting to see if the British will change their stance, while working on Chamberlain themselves as well. The fact that the Sudeten Germans are openly revolting means they're confident the Brits won't come to your aid."

"And what do you think?" Adela held her breath.

"I think they're right." His response was instant, without hesitation. "Chamberlain wants to avoid conflict at any price. He won't allow his country to get involved in what he considers a Czech-German conflict. Same for the French. They will follow Britain's lead."

Adela felt the blood drain from her head all the way to her feet. Her expectations for the meeting had been severely tempered after Moravec's briefing. When she left the castle, she was convinced President Beneš' visit would yield few results, and she had entered the coffeehouse with a heavy heart. Despite this, the confirmation of her suspicions by the one man who could provide a sliver of hope had been brutal. She looked down at her untouched, cold coffee and let out a deep sigh before looking back up. "Is there anything we can do?"

"If your president can't secure British support, expect Hitler to issue an ultimatum soon. You know your options, but be aware that he won't hesitate to move the entire might of his army into the Sudetenland. Do you think your country will fight?"

THIRTY-ONE

Vienna
13 September 1938

Three hundred men wearing their new SS uniforms lined up on Ballhausplatz. It had been less than a month since Karl and Walter Stahlecker discussed the composition of the new Einsatzgruppe. Now the men stood at attention at their formal presentation. The significance of Ballhausplatz as a location wasn't lost on Karl either. It was close to Heldenplatz, where Hitler had addressed over a hundred thousand new citizens of the Reich in March. More importantly, the square had always been the home of Austria's ministry of foreign affairs. When Stahlecker suggested parading the new Einsatzgruppe here, Karl had been impressed by the man's sense of symbolism.

"What do you think, Vogt?" Stahlecker appeared by his side, observing the men on the square with a satisfied look on his face. "I think I've whipped them into shape quite well, considering the time we had available."

"Yes, they look quite disciplined." Karl kept his voice neutral when he turned to Stahlecker. "Are you confident you've addressed the earlier issues?"

The grin disappeared, and a shadow crossed over his face, but he caught himself and answered in a agreeable tone. "Quite so. I believe they all responded to my training rather well. May I remind you it was our joint decision to recruit a larger number of men from the Sturmabteilung than we initially intended to?"

Karl didn't miss Stahlecker's use of overtly formal language. *He's covering himself.* The number of applications from the Austrian Brownshirts had been overwhelming, in sharp contrast to the interest from the Sicherheitsdienst and Gestapo. Karl had been disappointed, but Stahlecker was encouraged by the influx of Brownshirts making up the new Einsatzgruppe.

"Have you encountered any recent breaches in discipline?" It was a seemingly offhand question, but Karl knew he'd struck a nerve when Stahlecker's jaw clenched and his eyebrow twitched.

"It was dealt with internally, as per my report."

"So they're still part of the group?"

"They've shown a willingness to improve their behavior moving forward. I will keep an eye on it." Stahlecker refocused his gaze on the group, purposefully ignoring Karl's look.

Karl decided he'd made his point, and he watched as the men finished their initiation ceremony and were dismissed. They walked away in groups, excitedly chattering about their day off, and would report as fully fledged members of the SS in the morning. Reports from Berlin indicated they could be sent to the border with the Sudetenland within a few days. As the men passed by, Karl observed them. Most of them were still in their late teens; Karl had his doubts about Stahlecker's claims of keeping them disciplined.

"Standartenführer Vogt, did the ceremony please you?" Karl turned to find a man in his mid-forties standing next to him, a smile on his face.

"A proper show of force and discipline, Oberführer Winkelmann. You must be looking forward to taking command."

"Thank you, and certainly, sir. I don't mean to overstep, but from what I gather, it sounds like it will be sooner rather than later." The tone of his voice implied he hoped Karl would confirm.

"Quite likely indeed." Karl was happy to encourage the man who would lead the troops on the ground. He turned to Stahlecker, who stood next to Winkelmann. "Standartenführer Stahlecker has made the right decision in handing the unit's reins to you. The timing is perfect, with his recent promotion to lead the Central Office surely taking up most of his time now."

Karl watched Stahlecker's face closely, and he was pleased to see the man's eyes narrow ever so slightly, his jaw tightening once more. He could almost hear his teeth grinding. Stahlecker's appointment was on paper only, as everybody was well aware it was Adolf Eichmann leading the agency. Karl wondered what Stahlecker would do now that the formation of his Einsatzgruppe was complete and Winkelmann was taking over.

"Yes, I look forward to working under Standartenführer Stahlecker's command." Winkelmann must've sensed the change in atmosphere, and he looked keen to leave. "If there is nothing else, I will join my men."

Stahlecker was quick to speak. "Yes, enjoy your success, Winkelmann. We will convene tomorrow morning, and we will discuss the next steps for the unit. We must make preparations to head out as soon as possible."

Winkelmann saluted both men, then hurried off. Stahlecker turned to Karl, barely containing his rage.

"If you have a problem with the way I run my affairs, you can tell me to my face." The tall man took a step closer and waved a finger in Karl's face. "But don't ever pull that shit again."

Karl suppressed a grin. "What shit?"

"Questioning my authority in front of my subordinates."

"I'm not aware I was," Karl replied smoothly. "I just congratulated you both on your new roles. From what I can tell, the Oberführer was thrilled. Aren't you?"

"It's still my unit," Stahlecker snarled at him, then shook his head and stormed off.

KARL ENTERED his office at the Hotel Metropole the next morning to find a note summoning him to Franz Huber's office at his earliest convenience. He frowned, surprised to receive an out of the blue summons from the Gestapo chief. It spelled little good, and his suspicions were confirmed when he was led into the man's office thirty minutes later.

"Have you lost your mind, Vogt?" Huber didn't waste any time with pleasantries, not even inviting Karl to sit down. "Why are you picking a fight with Walter Stahlecker? I thought the two of you were getting along fine with the Einsatzgruppe. Didn't the unit finish its training just yesterday?"

"It did, sir, and I'm not aware of picking any fights." Karl remained standing, his voice calm, and he made deliberate eye contact with Huber. The man on the other side of the desk looked furious.

"He wasn't very pleased with your remarks about perceived ill discipline in his new unit, claiming you were questioning the inclusion of some of the men. To be frank, I was more than a little surprised to hear this. Weren't you involved in the recruitment phase?"

"And I raised those concerns at the time. I think there are too many Brownshirts in the unit. Most of them are louts, sir, if you don't mind me calling a spade a spade."

"You didn't block their inclusion, so why bring it up now? This reeks of covering yourself, Vogt."

"I merely asked Standartenführer Stahlecker if he felt comfortable sending these men to the front lines in the Sudetenland, in light of the reports of ill discipline during training. He assured me he had it under control. That's enough for me, sir."

Huber sat down and indicated for Karl to do the same. "Vogt, you need to be aware of a few things. I know you have Heydrich's ear, as do I."

"I am aware, sir."

"Why do you think Stahlecker was appointed to lead the

Einsatzgruppe, and then to head up the Central Office?" Huber paused for a moment. "Because he is well connected. Between you and I, we both know his new role at the Central Office is ceremonial. There's only one man running that show, and the men in Berlin who appointed Stahlecker also know it."

"Eichmann."

Huber nodded. "The point is, don't overestimate yourself. I like you. But you won us over by doing what you do best: fixing things in the background, making us look good in the process. You know it, I know it, and Heydrich knows it. But the other people involved mostly see the façade." He pointed at himself. "That's how you rise to the top, Vogt. Not by making enemies with men like Stahlecker."

Karl listened to Huber's words with growing concern.

"You're right, sir. I appreciate your warning."

"We're not friends, Vogt. I don't even consider us allies, but you're useful. I like to keep useful people around, and not see them sent off to the front lines because they make the wrong enemies." Huber waved to the door, and Karl inclined his head before leaving.

In the hallway, Karl walked to the stairs. As he made his way down, it became clear to Karl what he needed to do with the information concerning Stahlecker's flawed sense of discipline in his unit. It would serve as Karl's insurance policy.

THIRTY-TWO

Buchenwald
14 September 1938

Another day in the quarry ended, and Felix found his spot among the lines of prisoners. The guards did a quick head count, which was nothing like the roll calls in the central square they experienced in the mornings and evenings.

The count was mercifully quick, and the mass of prisoners started their short ascent along the tracks used to ferry the heavy carts filled with rocks up to the camp. Carts were parked at the bottom, patiently waiting for their handlers to return the next day. Felix was pleased to have avoided cart duty so far. It took a dozen prisoners to push and pull each heavy cart up the hill, and as the day progressed and men tired, limbs were crushed underneath haywire carts racing down the tracks. There was no mercy after such accidents, and these now useless men were promptly finished off beside the tracks.

The group of prisoners emerged from the quarry, the bleak surroundings serving as a stark reminder of the futility of contemplating escape; the narrow incline out of the quarry led straight back into the camp, and it was heavily guarded. The only way men escaped the endless grind was by forfeiting their lives. To their right were the living quarters of the SS: barracks properly built and no doubt comfortably furnished. The group followed the Caracho Path; it was here that many new arrivals often found themselves beaten to the ground, unable to keep up with the murderous pace set by the SS. Apart from a few shouts to keep moving, this afternoon's guards appeared content with the quarrymen's pace.

The procession passed through the gatehouse, the sound of the humming three-meter-high barbed wire on either side leaving no doubt as to the deadly current running through it. They were back in the prisoner camp, and rows of neatly lined-up barracks were spread out in front of them. The wooden structures were barracks in name only. Felix had experienced the unbearable heat of summer, and the older prisoners warned him it would be freezing cold in winter. The walls were pierced with cracks, giving the wind free rein, tormenting the prisoners at all hours.

They reached the roll call yard in the middle of the camp. Prisoner work details poured in from all directions, taking their places for the final torture of the day. Felix's muscles ached, his legs burned, but he forced himself to stand upright and not give the guards any excuse to single him out. He stared at the back of the head of the man in front of him, keeping his eyes rigidly straight as the guards passed by.

The count only had to be repeated twice, and for some reason the SS guards decided no further torture was required today, dismissing the men to their barracks. As they fanned out, Felix was looking forward to an unexpected hour of rest in his bunk. It was rare for roll call to be finished this quickly, and a jolt of energy shot through his exhausted bones.

A strong hand gripped his shoulder, a voice barking at him a second later. "Volunteers needed in the kitchen. Come with me." Felix was moved to a side of the square, where more prisoners soon joined him. Two guards then moved them north, to the part of the camp where the kitchen, among other facilities, was located. Felix cursed his luck, but signs of discontent would only result in a beating.

The kitchen was mayhem. Massive pots with the dodgy stew they were fed every day boiled on large stovetops. Despite knowing its questionable contents, the smell made Felix's mouth water. He didn't have time to enjoy the aroma, as a kitchen hand pulled him along, ordering him to cut potatoes. After an hour he was dismissed and practically thrown from the kitchen. Standing outside, he knew it was for his own good. He'd almost given in to the temptation of stuffing a few pieces of raw potato into his mouth. If he were caught, it meant a flogging at the very least, depending on the mood of the guard catching him.

He walked back along the fence shielding them from the SS quarters. Directly opposite the kitchen was the zoo. It was an odd thing to have in a labor camp, but Commander Koch had it built for the entertainment of his staff. In what Felix was certain was meant as further torture of the prisoners, it was built in full view of them. Access was, of course, strictly forbidden to prisoners. As was stopping to watch from their side of the fence, but the scene at the deer enclosure made Felix do exactly that.

Two young guards stood on the far side, sticking a piece of bread through the fence, attracting a young buck. As the animal reached for the bread, the guard dropped it, getting the buck to reach down. To Felix's horror, the guards grabbed the animal's antlers and produced pieces of rope. The buck struggled, but the men were too strong, and they expertly wrapped the rope around its antlers before securing it to the fence. Felix stood frozen, watching as the helpless animal struggled to break free. The guards stood laughing and pointing at the buck's futile attempts.

Then they spotted Felix on the other side of the fence. They looked at each other, suddenly realizing they had a witness. Felix stood frozen, considering his options. Should he run? It would make no difference, they would find him somehow.

One of the men pulled out his pistol and moved toward the gate. "Don't move." He signaled to the other guard, who rushed off. Felix and the guard stood in silent deadlock for what felt like an eternity before he heard footsteps running toward him. The guard was now on his side of the fence and roughly grabbed him.

"Not a word." Felix was manhandled through the main gate, to the side of the SS encampment. He was weak with fear, his hands trembling, heart beating in his ears. The lives of prisoners were worth nothing in Buchenwald, but Commander Koch was extremely protective of the zoo's animals. This was the end of the road.

From there, the guard pulled him through the zoo entrance, where the other guard stood by the now-exhausted buck. "Untie him," he ordered Felix.

Felix moved toward the animal and reached for the rope. As soon as he did, the animal came back to life, struggling with all its might. The rope snapped taut, and Felix pulled his hands back only just in time to not have them tangled between the rope and fence. The guard was unimpressed and slammed a fist into the side of his ribs, knocking the wind from his lungs. Felix gasped for air while the guard yelled at him to try again.

Felix struggled toward the buck again. This time, he whispered soft words, hoping it would soothe the animal. As he reached for the rope again, a firm voice sounded behind him.

"What the devil is going on here? Get your hands away from that buck!"

Felix did as he was told, taking a step back and looking to the source of the voice. The first thing he noticed was the lack of a uniform. The man wore a comfortable jacket and loose-fitting pants. He did have the standard issue SS boots, and from his posture it was clear he held rank. The two troopers deferred to him as they saluted him. The tallest spoke up.

"We caught this prisoner abusing the animal."

Felix's surprise was only temporary. Now that they were caught, it only made sense for them to blame him. He remained silent, as speaking would only make things worse.

"Is that a fact?" The man eyed the guards suspiciously before focusing his attention on Felix. "How did you get on this side of the fence?"

"I had nothing to do with this, sir." Felix gambled the man was sufficiently senior to overrule the guards. Anything to get from their clutches. *I'm dead if I stay with them.* "I was only trying to untangle the rope."

The senior SS man looked thoughtful for a moment, then took out a knife and moved toward Felix, who took an involuntary step back. Ignoring Felix, he cut the rope, freeing the buck. The animal stormed off to the other side of the enclosure. After securing the knife, the man addressed Felix.

"I don't know how you got here, or why you wanted to hurt my animals, but we'll let the commander decide. For now, I'm taking you to the Bunker. Perhaps they'll get a straight answer from you there." He then looked to the guards. "I'd like your names as well."

Felix saw the flash of fear in the guards' eyes as the man took out a small notebook. After he jotted down their names, he grabbed Felix by the arm, his grip like iron. "Come with me. We don't tolerate animal abuse in this camp."

AFTER LESS THAN an hour in his cold cell, the door opened. A burly guard grunted at Felix to follow him. The man practically shoved him through the hallway and into a dark room in the back. As soon as the door closed, all outside sound vanished. The room was soundproof. The only sound came from a single buzzing light bulb emitting a faint glow in the middle of the room.

His eyes quickly adjusted to the darkness. The room was completely bare, but for a single chair chained to the wall. Felix stood awkwardly in the middle, unsure what to do next. Then the lock clicked, and the door opened, revealing a young man only a few years older than himself. He wore a crisp SS uniform, his hair was neatly combed, and he carried a small bag resembling a doctor's bag. He closed the door and placed his bag on a small table in the corner that Felix had missed in his initial observation.

"Sit down." The man pointed at the only chair, and Felix reluctantly followed the order.

The door opened again and two guards walked in. Without a word, they secured leather straps around Felix's wrists and ankles, tying him to the steel chair. Meanwhile, the other man opened his bag and started sorting through it with his back to Felix. It was impossible to see its contents, which only heightened Felix's terror. The guards left and locked the door.

The man turned around, his youthful face devoid of emotion while he took a few steps toward Felix. He had an unremarkable face, but for the eyes. They bore into Felix's as he spoke his first words.

"Do you know who I am?"

Felix shook his head. An instant later, a force so powerful hit him that Felix thought his head would be knocked off his body. A searing pain shot through his head, and he tasted copper as blood filled his nose and mouth. The room was spinning, and nausea almost overtook him. Taking a gulp of air, he managed to stave off the impulse to vomit.

"You will answer me properly when I ask you a question!" the man yelled a few centimeters from his ear. "Do you hear me? Do you know who I am?"

Felix swallowed the blood in his mouth, then managed a weak, "I don't, sir. I'm sorry."

Another blow to his head, now from the other side. This time, he was unable to stop the wave coming from his stomach, and his body convulsed to bring up the bile from his stomach. He vomited on the floor, gagging for air as he did.

Felix's assailant stepped away in time and looked on from a distance. "Pathetic." He waited while Felix took deep, ragged breaths. Sweat gushed down his forehead, and he felt raddled as the room spun quicker and quicker.

To his surprise, the man produced a jug of water. *Where did that come from?*

"It looks like you could use some of this." Before Felix could answer, the man pushed his head back and forced open his mouth with one hand, then started pouring water down his throat. Felix was unable to keep up, and he soon felt like he was drowning. He spluttered and coughed, his eyes tearing up while the stream of water continued. For a moment, the world went black, but then the man released him, and his senses rushed back to him.

"Why did you hurt that poor animal?" the man screamed at him, his face so close that their noses were almost touching. "What sick sort of pleasure do you take from that? And how did you get out of the prisoner camp?"

Felix looked into the furious eyes and lost all willingness to fight. He couldn't produce more than a croak. "It wasn't me." He braced himself for another blow, but it never came. Instead, the man walked to his bag in the corner and closed it. Then he walked back to Felix, and leaned down. In a soft voice, he said, "I think this was enough for our introduction. We'll meet again soon, and get to the bottom of this." His voice was like ice, and he walked to the door, casually rapping a couple of times.

It opened moments later, with two guards appearing.

"Take him back to his cell. Make sure he stays alive. I'm not done with him yet."

"At once, Obersturmbannführer Sommer."

As Felix was dragged back to his cell, the name echoed in his mind. He wouldn't make the mistake of forgetting it.

THIRTY-THREE

Vienna
21 September 1938

There was a knock on the door, and Karl looked up to see a secretary walk in.

"This came for you just now. I was told to deliver it with haste." The young man placed a folded piece of paper on his desk and left, softly closing the door behind him.

Karl reached and unfolded the piece of paper. He quickly read the words, written in the staccato hand he recognized instantly. His mouth opened a little, and he read the message one more time, making sure he understood correctly.

Placing the paper on his desk, he leaned back in his chair, clasping his hands behind his head, and closed his eyes. The contents of the message were clear, but they were unexpected.

Karl sat motionless for a few minutes, going over the reasoning for the message. Was it his handling of the Einsatzgruppe? He sat up. Had Stahlecker exerted his influence and called in a favor at Karl's expense? He wouldn't put it past the man, even though they hadn't spoken since the unit's inauguration, more than a week ago.

He picked up the phone and dialed a number he knew by heart. A knot of anxiety grew as he waited for the other end to pick up. Then the line clicked, and he heard the familiar voice of his best friend in the city.

"Odilo, we need to talk."

ODILO GLOBOČNIK HANDED the telegram back to Karl. "And you haven't spoken to Heydrich about it at all before? He didn't mention this the last time you spoke with him?"

"No, this is completely out of the blue. We spoke earlier this week, and everything seemed fine." Karl took a sip of his beer. "We even discussed the readiness of the Einsatzgruppe."

"That makes sense, with things escalating up there. Did you receive any new information about the Führer's intentions to reinstate the *Sudetendeutsch Freikorps*? That would be a bold move, but I applaud it." He drained his beer and looked around for a waiter.

"I think he'll follow through with that. With the continued assaults by the Czechs, he has little choice. And the Brits don't look like they're going to do anything about it."

Globočnik grinned. "I think we both know those attacks aren't quite as severe as they're made out to be. In truth, I'd say the revolts by our own people are doing more to escalate the tensions, don't you think?" He managed to get the waiter's attention and held up two fingers.

"Fair enough." Karl kept a close eye on the reports coming from the Sudetenland, and Hitler's intentions to reinstate the banned and disbanded paramilitary Freikorps in the region was a reasonable response to the perceived violence against the ethnic Germans. According to the Führer, the people in the region needed a way to defend themselves. In reality, the Germans were at least as complicit in stoking the fire as the Czechs were in responding. "It's all going exactly to plan. Which is why it's so frustrating to be recalled to Berlin."

"Didn't you say you pulled your hands from the Einsatzgruppe?"

"Only until it becomes interesting again. I don't want Stahlecker to think I'm getting in his way."

"So you'd like to join the unit when they're sent to the Sudetenland?"

Karl took a second before responding, then shrugged. "I don't know exactly. But as long as I am based near the unit, it is a possibility. It won't be the same from Berlin."

"I wonder what Heydrich has in mind for you." Odilo paused while the waiter placed two large mugs on the table.

Karl quickly drained the remainder of his beer. They clinked their fresh beers and each took a sip. Karl felt a little woozy, having skipped lunch.

"I'm thinking this might not be such a bad move for you, Karl. You'll be close to leadership. And Heydrich hasn't shown any displeasure with your performance, has he?"

"No, I really think this was a political play from Stahlecker. He wants to get rid of me before he sets off. It's a smart move."

"I'm not so sure. I mean, I can see why he would want you away from Vienna, but it makes no sense for you to then be recalled to Berlin. You'll have even more of Heydrich's ear. Heck, you might even run into Himmler frequently." Globočnik shook his head. "Politically, it makes no sense. I think you need to consider other reasons."

His friend's words did little to lift Karl's spirits. "It still feels like a demotion. I need to be in the field, Odilo. Not stuck in an office in Berlin."

"Look, Karl. I've been in this game a lot longer than you. I'm not saying you're not good at it, you most certainly are. Better than most with your experience. But I think you're missing something here, and you're getting yourself down for no reason. Things can change quickly." He snapped his fingers, and Karl met his strong gaze. "Wait until you've spoken to Heydrich. If you're right, and you're on desk duty, suck it up for a bit. Outperform everybody else, and make sure Heydrich and the other big shots notice. You'll be back in the field sooner than you think. But when you step into that office, exude confidence. You've done big things in Vienna, and make sure nobody forgets that." He raised his mug. "Now, let's drink and celebrate your last evening in Vienna."

Karl lifted his mug and reluctantly smashed it against his friend's.

THE PLANE LANDED in Berlin early in the afternoon. A car was waiting, whisking Karl into the city in record time. Upon arrival at the headquarters of the Sicherheitsdienst on Prinz-Albrecht-Straße, Karl was escorted up to a spacious office on the third floor.

"The Obergruppenführer will be with you shortly." The clerk left without another word, leaving Karl on his own. He walked to the window and overlooked the broad street below. Apart from a few cars passing by, the sidewalk was deserted. People avoided the building if they could, and given what went on in the basement, Karl understood why.

He paced the room, his nerves threatening to get the better of him. The car waiting at the airport had been a surprise. It wasn't common for people of his rank to be given a private escort like that. Whatever Heydrich wanted to share with him was important. Karl remembered Odilo's words of the previous night. *Perhaps there is something going on.* Or Heydrich was busy and wanted to make sure Karl was in the office when he wanted to demote him. He rubbed his hands, surprised to find them clammy. *Get ahold of yourself.*

The door opened and Reinhard Heydrich walked in, alone. Karl wiped his hands on his pants, then saluted his boss. The second-most-powerful man in the building returned the salute, then signaled for Karl to sit in one of the comfortable chairs in the corner.

"Did you have a good trip? I trust the journey was smooth?" The words came at Karl rapidly, and Heydrich didn't wait for an answer. "You must be wondering why you were recalled here at such short notice."

"It crossed my mind, Herr Obergruppenführer."

"The developments in the Sudetenland are moving along at a faster pace than anticipated." Heydrich's face was stern. "We'll be sending in the Einsatzgruppe you assembled with Stahlecker soon." Karl failed to suppress a groan, but Heydrich didn't notice, or ignored it. "They'll be attached to some of the advance Wehrmacht forces, and among the first to cross the border. I take it you're confident they'll be able to carry out the tasks we discussed?"

Karl considered his response for a second, then nodded. "They know what's expected of them."

"Good. And how do you feel about Stahlecker and Winkelmann taking control?"

"I have no real opinion, sir. I'm sure they will be capable leaders."

A slight grin appeared on Heydrich's face. "Would you have preferred to join them?"

"I go where I'm required." Karl realized he needed to play this very carefully. Heydrich hadn't given him any indication as to his intentions with him.

"So you don't feel overly attached to the unit?"

Something in the way Heydrich phrased the question made Karl think his boss wanted him to distance himself from the Einsatzgruppe. Considering he was in Berlin, that felt like the right conclusion. "No sir, I assisted in setting it up, and I'm sure it is now in very capable hands."

"Very well, Vogt. Because I think your talents would be wasted tagging along with them." Heydrich's words lifted a great weight from Karl's shoulders, and he sat up. "The Sudetenland will return to Germany sooner rather than later. I don't know if it will be through force or diplomacy, but we need to prepare either way."

"Sir." Excitement surged through Karl's body.

"We've spent the past months mapping out the situation in the Sudetenland. We know where our allies are, and we've identified most of our enemies. But I need a trusted agent on the ground. Someone who can prepare and initiate the essential tasks once our forces cross the border. Do you understand?"

Karl knew exactly what his boss was asking.

"I need you in the Sudetenland tomorrow. You'll establish and judge the validity of our information. You'll talk to community leaders and prepare them for when we retake the region."

"Just like in Austria, sir."

Heydrich gave him a satisfied look. "Just like in Austria, Vogt." He handed him a thick folder. "This is the essential information, with locations and names of known allies. It also contains multiple invasion plans for the Wehrmacht. Study them, and tailor your approach. You leave for Karlsbad in three hours. You have my full authority to make preparations as you see fit, and we will be in constant contact."

Karl was buzzing as he leafed through the first few pages. This wasn't a demotion at all. He would be at the tip of the spear. *No. I am the arrowhead, surging ahead.*

THIRTY-FOUR

Buchenwald
22 September 1938

The door of the cell opened, the beam of light blinding Felix in the darkness. He shirked away to a corner, desperate to avoid another trip to the room at the end of the hallway. He'd lost count of the number of times he'd been dragged to the torture chamber, exposed to Martin Sommer's sadistic ways. Despite this, he'd remained true to himself, repeating his innocence. It didn't help. Each time he'd been certain the Nazi butcher would murder him in the impending session. He passed out in the room, but not before thinking it was all over. To his surprise, he awoke in his cell. Days and nights bled into each other, the dark, windowless room taking away all sense of time. The only indication of time were the sparse sounds seeping in through the walls. Felix didn't know how far down he was, but he sometimes heard voices of people moving about outside. It was the only semblance of normality in this hell he'd resigned himself to dying in soon.

"Get up and come with me, you piece of filth." The guard's words were as harsh as always, but he didn't drag Felix out like he normally did. The change was almost enough to provide him with a speck of hope, and he opened his eyes. "Come on, I don't have all day." The guard gave him a sharp kick in the ribs. The pain jolted Felix to his knees, and with an effort, he rose to his feet. After two steps, he lost his balance and crashed onto the cold, hard floor.

It was enough to break the guard's patience, his strong hands lifting him off the ground. In the hallway, Felix braced himself, knowing this could very well be the day Sommer finished him off. To his surprise and relief, the guard turned in the opposite direction. He had trouble keeping his balance while the guard dragged him through the hallway. The sound of a heavy bolt sliding, then the loud creaking sound of a door opening.

Bright sunlight streamed in, and Felix breathed fresh air for the first time since he was taken into the Bunker. Adjusting to the sunlight, he found himself near the main gate, at the front of the *Appelplatz*, the roll call square. He thought he was hallucinating when ahead he saw thousands of prisoners lined up, facing him. Felix squinted and saw some of the men's eyes trained on him. They looked at him with a mix of emotions. Most looked disembodied, their broken bodies and souls revealing nothing. A few looked on in horror, while some averted their faces, avoiding eye contact.

Felix turned around and saw commander Otto Koch on the platform above the main gate, just beside him. The man wielding the power of life and death looked down at him condescendingly. In the flash their eyes met, Felix saw death, and he quickly averted his gaze. That was the moment he realized. *They're making an example of me.* A deep sadness overcame Felix as he scanned the Appelplatz for the gallows. He'd witnessed hangings during roll call before, and he'd sported the same detached gaze the men opposite him had. Now it was his turn to dangle on the rope until all light was squeezed from him.

"What are you waiting for? Get to your position in roll call," the guard hissed at him, pushing him toward the mass of prisoners some twenty meters away. "Off with you, before the commander changes his mind."

Felix looked at the guard in disbelief. Was this some sort of cruel trick? He chanced a look at Koch on the platform, but the commander had fixed his eye on something happening on the other side of the square. Mustering all the strength his broken body could produce, Felix dragged himself through the sea of prisoners. The guards walking by for the count ignored him until he made it to his spot.

There, the guard stopped and looked him up and down. Felix was certain the man would order him back to the front to collect his punishment, but after a few tense seconds, he moved on. Felix struggled to stay on his feet for the next half hour, waiting for the words that would haul him back to the front. It wasn't until they were dismissed for the night that he breathed a sigh of relief. His knees buckled, and if it wasn't for the men around him, he would have remained in the middle of the roll call square.

As soon as his face hit the hard, wooden frame of his bunk, Felix was out.

THE NEXT MORNING he learned the reason for his miraculous release. Felix hadn't been the only person witnessing the guards' abuse of the buck. Two guards had reported the incident, and when Koch heard of it, he promptly demoted the two culprits. This was a mere two days after Felix was locked up in Martin Sommer's hellish Bunker. Nobody had given Felix another thought, until the man who had put Felix in the Bunker asked what had happened to the wrongfully accused prisoner. That had gotten the ball rolling, and Koch ordered the release. It was a miracle, but it showed that even the ruthless commander of the camp had some sense of what was wrong and right.

Felix was dismayed to learn he'd been locked up for more than a week. In his mind, it could easily have been twice as long. Most importantly, though, he was alive. As he struggled to climb down from his bunk the next morning, he was delighted to see his only friend in the camp approach.

"Back from the dead, my friend." Werner gently helped him down from the bunk. "How are you feeling?"

"Probably about the way I look." Felix had trouble speaking, his throat raw from the lack of water. He'd managed to drink something the night before, but he had become dehydrated again since then. "Just grateful to be alive at this point."

"Here, have this." Werner handed him an open can of beans. "I'm sorry it's only half a can. I was saving it for later, but I think you need this more than me at this point."

Felix took the can, holding on to it like it was pure gold. Tears welled in his eyes. "Thank you, I can't tell you how much this means to me."

"Regain your strength. You'll need it to survive."

It was Sunday, their day off. The timing couldn't have been better for Felix as he stepped out of the block, still holding on to the can of beans. He sat on the ground and carefully removed the lid. He brought the can to his lips, careful not to cut himself, and took a mouthful of beans. Somewhat stale, they still tasted like heavenly nectar. Making himself not eat too quickly, he paused and took a breath of the fresh morning air. It was mid-September, and the fall chill was in the air. The weather would soon turn, and Werner was right. He needed to regain his strength.

He finished the beans, then joined the stream of men for roll call. The energy of his first proper meal flowed through his body, and he got through the ordeal without issue. After eating his morning bread and a thin slice of sausage, he made for the camp post office. The prisoner working there took a long time searching for his mail, and Felix was about to leave when the man held up an envelope with his name.

He found a quiet spot between two blocks overlooking the birch forest and sat down on a patch of grass, his back resting against the outer wall of the block. The envelope was light, and he removed the seal placed by the camp censors with trembling hands. He recognized his mother's handwriting, and he thought he caught a whiff of home on the paper. He closed his eyes and his hazy mind conjured fragmented elements of his mother's loving face. Ignoring his frustration at not seeing a clear picture of her, he began reading.

Rebecca Wolff's letter started well, letting him know she was relieved to hear from him. Life in Vienna was tolerable, and she was doing all right. A stab of pain cut through Felix's heart. His mother would never describe herself as doing "all right." She was clearly not. Then she dropped the bombshell. Felix's breath caught in his throat, his heart skipped a beat. The world stopped turning.

Your father has passed away abroad.

The letter suddenly felt heavy. He read the words again. Warm tears rolled down his cheeks, clouding his vision as he wished for the words to change shape. Grief overtook him as he dropped the letter and buried his face in his hands.

It took him five minutes to collect himself, and he finally wiped away the tears from his face. He picked up the letter, and read the remainder. His mother had transferred some money into his account, so that he could buy food and soap in the canteen. Felix was overcome with emotion. His mother had lost the love of her life, and surely was struggling to make ends meet in Vienna. Guilt replaced his grief as he realized she was starving herself for him.

He read the letter again. His mother had very deliberately added that his father had died *abroad*. The gravity of that one word hit him hard. This could only mean one thing—Anton hadn't been released when he offered himself in his place. The Gestapo man had lied. He balled his hands into fists and stared at the birch trees behind the electrified fence. There, in a rare moment of silence in Buchenwald, Felix made a solemn vow. *I will survive this camp, and avenge my father's death.*

THIRTY-FIVE

Prague
23 September 1938

The squares of Prague were filled with people, bringing the city to a standstill. Adela was among them, proud to stand alongside her compatriots. It was late morning, but she had ventured outside from the castle to witness the crowds. She looked at the faces of her fellow Czechoslovaks, seeing all sorts of emotions. Anger, disappointment, resilience, and fear. The developments of the past few days had been tough on everyone, Adela very much included.

It had been less than a week since Hitler escalated the conflict by claiming ethnic Germans were being systematically butchered in the Sudetenland and openly threatened war if the Sudetenland wasn't surrendered to Nazi Germany. It was a blatant lie, but the British and French government had accepted it at face value, ordering the Czechoslovak government to concede the region. Despite protestations from Beneš, the Czech parliament ceded Sudetenland on 21 September. When Hitler added further demands the next day, people took to the streets. They wouldn't stand by idly while the Sudetenland was stolen from them.

It was now 23 September, and a new parliament had been installed. They promised swift action, but it was unclear what that meant. As it stood, the country would still need to hand over the Sudetenland to Germany. Anything less than a reversal of that capitulation would result in anarchy. The crowd simmered with indignation at the previous parliament's willingness to cede such a large part of their country without a fight.

Adela took a deep breath and turned back toward the castle. She had positioned herself on the edge of the crowd, and she made it back to the streetcar interchange across the bridge with relative ease. When she got there, it became clear she had underestimated the impact of the crowds. No trams would arrive anytime soon. A strange feeling of calm overcame her as she crossed the bridge over the Vltava River. Something monumental was happening. The Czechoslovak people wouldn't be bullied into giving in to Hitler's demands. Hope was in the air.

ADELA'S HOPE was converted into action by the new parliament a few hours later. President Beneš ordered the general mobilization of the army, with more than a million men ordered to take up arms to defend the country.

A sense of excitement was palpable in the hallways of the castle, and Adela had a spring in her step as she returned to her office. She had little doubt Hitler would follow through with his threat, which terrified her, but she also felt pride in her country for taking a stand against the Führer's endless expansion of his empire. She was secretly hopeful the Brits and French would come to their senses, reverse their standpoints, and come to Czechoslovakia's aid. It would avoid war.

A secretary poked her head around the door. "Adela, you're needed upstairs. Urgently."

Adela took the elevator to the third floor and joined a stream of people entering one of the larger conference rooms. It was so crowded she had to remain on her feet, and she was grateful to find a spot against the wall. Senior members of the government sat at the large table, speaking among themselves in hushed voices. It was impossible to make out their words, and Adela resigned herself to waiting to hear what the summons was about.

She didn't have to wait long as President Beneš entered a few minutes later. He looked tired, which was no surprise. He'd been flying back and forth between Prague and London so much that she was sure he never spent more than a few hours in one place. She didn't envy him. He took a seat at the head of the table and the murmurs died down, making way for a sense of anticipation from those gathered.

"As most of you are aware, immediately after the previous parliament's decision to cede the Sudetenland and the imminent declaration of war from Nazi Germany, we received word from Moscow." The president spoke clearly, but there was an edge to his voice. Adela held her breath; she knew of the talks with Russia, but very few details had been shared. "They offered to assist us in the defense of our sovereignty. Unfortunately, we won't be able to take them up on their offer, as Poland and Romania are unwilling to let their troops pass through their territories." Beneš' voice sounded strained.

There was no need for Beneš to expand further. Everybody in the room knew Poland and Romania were in an impossible situation. If they allowed the Russian army to march through, they risked agitating Hitler.

"This means we remain on our own. While we still have the support of France in case Hitler decides to move beyond the Sudetenland, we now know this is as good as worthless. The British and French have shown they will do anything to avoid getting involved in any form of conflict with Germany." It was the first time Beneš sounded bitter, and Adela was surprised. He had previously refrained from making any public judgment of their supposed allies. Was the situation really that dire?

"We're receiving reports of increased violence against our

people in the Sudetenland. Czech citizens are being targeted, some even abducted from their homes. That, and the additional demands placed on us by Hitler, means we will continue our mobilization, with the first troops moving into the Sudetenland as we speak."

This resulted in cheers and a round of applause from the people in the room. Adela was pleased to see this show of support for the president from all layers of government. Beneš looked uncomfortable but nodded as he held up his hand, and the noise died away.

"We will not back down without a fight. Our army is well equipped, and our government is united in the belief that if we give in to the German demands now, they will return to take the rest of our country soon enough." Murmurs of assent spread through the room. "Meanwhile, I will continue to exhaust all political means available to avoid bloodshed. We must avoid war at all costs."

Adela looked around the room. The emotions on the faces mirrored those she saw on the square earlier. She balled her hands into fists, goose bumps forming on the skin of her arms. The country was united, and they would fight for their independence, whatever happened.

THE NEXT DAYS passed in a blur. Hitler responded to the Czechoslovak mobilization by issuing an ultimatum of unconditional surrender of the Sudetenland by 28 October. Beneš continued to reject these claims while still lobbying for support from Great Britain and France.

Less than a week later, it became clear they would receive no such thing.

"Have you heard?" Martinek stepped into Adela's office on the evening of 28 September.

She nodded. "They're meeting in Munich tomorrow." *They* were Britain, France, Italy, and Germany. "Deciding our future without us."

"After everything the president has done, I can't believe this is how it's turning out. Do you think it will actually happen?" Marti wasn't really asking, he was talking to himself before turning to Adela. "They can't bypass our sovereignty like that, and force us to surrender a part of our country."

"Considering what's been going on these past weeks, it feels like we've already lost our grip on the region." Trouble in the Sudetenland had only increased, with the German-backed Freikorps expanding its reach, terrorizing the Czech citizens of the region. Many had fled in anticipation of the German invasion. Adela had no doubt more would follow soon.

"Do you believe Hitler when he says the Sudetenland is the final territorial claim he'll make?" Marti sat and looked at Adela with interest.

"Does it matter what we think? President Beneš has many times repeated that he places no value on Hitler's promises. I tend to agree with him. But it appears the ruling powers of the continent feel differently."

"Cowards, all of them. Especially that Chamberlain." Marti's words were uncharacteristically harsh, and Adela sat up. "He's been stringing Beneš along."

Adela nodded in agreement. "From what I've heard, the president is furious at not being invited to Munich."

"He is. Can't blame him."

They were silent for a moment, then Marti stood. "Good luck these next few days. You must be on permanent duty."

"Pretty much. We're trying to keep track of every press report, insignificant as they may seem. What about yourself? Are the embassies providing good insights?"

Marti shook his head. "They give an indication of the feeling on the ground, but I think you're getting a more complete overview from the different media you're tracking." He smiled wryly. "Let me know if you hear anything interesting. I might be able to verify with my sources." He moved toward the door.

"Will do, Marti. Take care." Adela watched him step into the hallway, then returned to the pile of reports on her desk. Despite Marti's words about her being well informed, it wasn't because of the foreign papers coming in. She'd seen the storm brewing long before most people in the building, along with Moravec.

To their great frustration, their German source hadn't reached out to them after their last meeting, and she'd felt left in the dark, unable to do anything about the current developments. As she picked up a German newspaper, she dragged herself back to reality. The forces in motion currently were many times above her scope of influence. It was up to Moravec to use the limited information they had gathered from their source accordingly. She questioned whether it was enough to change anything.

Twenty-four hours later, it became clear the meeting in Munich was beyond the Czechoslovak's sphere of influence. In a joint declaration, the governments of Great Britain, France, Italy, and Germany ordered Czechoslovakia to unconditionally surrender the Sudetenland to Germany.

A day later, despite protestations from the armed forces, President Beneš had no other option but to give in to the demands. Nazi Germany would formally take control of the region within ten days.

Great Britain and France offered a guarantee that they would protect the newly formed borders against unprovoked aggression.

Adela sat in her office, unable to focus on her work. The hallways in the castle were quiet, her colleagues no doubt experiencing the same feeling of defeat. The Czechoslovak army would start its withdrawal from the Sudetenland soon, and she had few illusions as to the British and French promises of protection. This annexation was only the start of the dismantling of her country, and for the first time, she felt absolutely powerless to do anything about it.

THIRTY-SIX

Eger, Sudetenland
1 October 1938

Karl watched as cars, trucks, and soldiers streamed past. People lined the streets stretching from the border all the way into the heart of the city of Eger. He allowed himself a smile as he witnessed the Sudeten Germans saluting the Wehrmacht soldiers with outstretched arms. Women blew kisses while children held out their hands, looking to catch a glimpse of the soldiers in their finely tailored uniforms.

It was Karl's third week in the Sudetenland, and preparations for the German army's arrival had been smooth. Heydrich had kept him well informed on the developments, and while he initially had to take a potential war with the Czechoslovak army into consideration, it soon became clear this was very unlikely. It wouldn't have mattered to Karl, for he had had plenty of time to observe the Czech soldiers occupying the border. They were well trained and equipped, and if this were any other region in Europe, Karl had no doubt the Wehrmacht would've had a tough fight on their hands. But in the Sudetenland, the German influence was felt everywhere.

With over two million ethnic Germans, Karl had felt right at home, especially after Hitler intensified his efforts to rally the pro-German militias.

He moved along with the stream of people heading into the center of town. Many of the soldiers paused to enjoy the festivities set up by the citizens of the town, populated mostly by ethnic Germans. Tents had been erected, and citizens stood chatting with the soldiers or among themselves. Many held large mugs of beer, and the atmosphere was convivial. There was little evidence of the Czechoslovak part of the population. Many had fled the border city in the past week after it became more and more apparent that their city would be one of the first to be annexed. Not all had left, with a number of prominent members of the city council refusing to give up their positions. It was for this very reason that Karl needed to speak with some of the Freikorps leaders. The reestablishment of the Freikorps had made Karl's work a lot easier. Where the more partisan Germans in the region had operated largely in the shadows, they were now confident enough to step into the limelight. Assaults were no longer restricted to the evenings, with any repression of the ethnic German population now handled firmly for everyone to see. For Karl it meant he could easily identify his allies, and he'd rapidly built up a rapport with many of the Freikorps leaders. It helped that these men were often also elevated members of their communities, and thus well connected and informed.

He headed for his office overlooking the city square and was pleased to see a familiar face waiting.

"Thomas, good to see you're already here." Karl shook the large Freikorps commander's hand and motioned to the stairs. It was a single flight to the second floor where Karl's office was located. "Would you like something to drink? I've got a good selection."

Thomas shook his head. "I'm fine, thank you. Perhaps some water?"

"Of course." Karl was relieved, preferring to function with a clear mind. There was much work to be done in the next hours. Karl placed two tall glasses of water on his desk and invited

Thomas to sit opposite him. "You must be pleased to finally see the end of the Czech occupation."

Thomas took a large gulp of water, then smiled. "I'm glad to see Hitler and Henlein keeping their end of the bargain. We've been preparing for quite some time, and while I have faith in the Führer, we were never informed about the inner workings of what was happening in the grander politics."

"I understand. Just know that your efforts haven't gone unnoticed in Berlin. There's a reason why the Führer and Reichsführer will be arriving in Eger in a few days." Karl was pleased to see his flattery had its intended effect, as Thomas' chest puffed up. "Before they do, I'd like to make sure we have the city completely within our sphere of influence."

"Naturally, sir. I take it you've seen my report?" His eyes went to a thick folder on Karl's desk.

Karl nodded. "Very impressive. You've practically done most of my work for me. I just wanted to verify the list of Prominenten." He pretended to leaf through the pages. In truth, the names of the most influential enemies of the Reich were engraved in his mind. "How did you obtain these?"

"Why, I used my network, sir." Thomas looked surprised by the question. "Are you questioning the validity?"

"Not at all." Karl was quick to put on a placating tone. "Impressed, more so. These people come from all walks of life. Politicians, doctors, leaders of the labor unions." He paused while his eyes went down to the piece of paper. "But also plenty of regular people. The baker, teachers at the local schools. I was curious how you managed to obtain such a complete and varied list of potential enemies."

"I can assure you there is nothing potential about our enemies. This information comes from trusted sources. We've been part of this community since the annexation after the Great War. It means we're well integrated into the community. We know these men and women from our sports clubs, political gatherings, and cultural events. It's not hard to know people's loyalties when your children go to the same ballet classes."

"Perfect." Karl closed the folder, making no effort to hide his delight. The twenty-plus years of living alongside each other had resulted in some form of shared culture between the German and Czechoslovak inhabitants of the region. Whether they liked it or not, they needed to work together, and friendships had blossomed. That came in especially handy now, as it provided Karl with an unexpectedly accurate list of targets. He smiled and tapped the folder. "Are your men ready to start the arrests tomorrow morning?"

Thomas looked pleased. "They can't wait, sir."

It was early morning when Karl approached the large house just outside the city center. He accompanied a squad of five Freikorps men, specifically selected for this mission, as their target was of high importance. It was also why Karl had decided to come along with them—he wanted to see firsthand how one of the most prominent members of the city would respond.

They reached the front door in silence. Communicating with hand signals, the most forward-placed man indicated for the rest to stand back. He then pounded the front door with surprising force, the sound appearing even louder in the silent morning.

Nothing happened for the first ten seconds, and the man rocked the front door again, now adding a vocal command for the people in the house to come outside.

After thirty seconds the lock rattled, and a tall man opened the door. Fully dressed, he glared at the men, but he did not appear surprised. Karl frowned—the man knew they were coming.

"Herr Prokisch, you are to come with us. I suggest you do so willingly, or we're authorized to use force." The leader of the group spoke politely, but there was no doubting the validity of his threat. "You are relieved of your function."

Karl watched Andreas Prokisch, the mayor of the city, calmly observe the faces of the men on his doorstep. It was clear he recognized them, and he paused for a moment when he met Karl's eyes. He looked taken aback, his eyes showing surprise at the stranger, then he appeared to realize who Karl must be, or what he was part of. Prokisch then nodded and stepped forward with his head held high.

"Where will you take me?"

"You'll be detained in one of the hotels in the city." The man guided the mayor away from the house. "Until it's decided what's to be done with you."

Karl was impressed by the mayor's calm acceptance of his fate. They escorted the man toward a waiting car. One of the Freikorps men was opening the door when a rock crashed against the windscreen of the car. Another sailed by and narrowly missed one of the men's heads. Karl and the other men turned toward the source and saw six men in their early twenties approaching.

"Where are you taking the mayor? Come here, you Nazi scum!" The men were only twenty meters down the road. Nothing happened for a moment while the Freikorps sized them up. Then, to Karl's utter surprise, the young men charged and ran down the road screaming obscenities.

They crossed the distance at alarming speed, nearly surprising the experienced Freikorps men. Then their training kicked in as they bundled the mayor into the car before they took up defensive positions next to it. The Germans were outnumbered, but Karl was confident their training would see them through.

The groups clashed seconds later, and Karl found himself in the back. Balling his fists, he suddenly realized he was carrying his sidearm. A young man appeared in front of him, a scowl on his face. Karl had little time to think. The man was twice his size, and clearly a trained fighter. He reached for his pistol and took a step back while he pointed it at the man.

All confidence left the man's posture. His face went white as a sheet, and he raised his hands, stumbling on his feet.

"Back off!" Karl shouted, steadying his aim on the man's chest. "Or you'll be a dead man."

Fear was etched on the man's face. Behind him, however, the Czech thugs were winning. Some of the Freikorps men had gone down to the ground. Karl considered his options, and just as he was about to fire a warning shot, he saw something that turned his stomach.

One of the Czechs pulled a gun from a fallen Freikorps trooper. Time appeared to slow down as he inspected the gun. Even from a distance, Karl could see the man's trembling fingers. *Excitement or fear?* Karl's heart pounded in his ears, and his throat was uncomfortably dry. The young Czech rose to his full height while he observed the fights around him, holding the gun loosely by his side. Karl took a step toward him, tightening his grip on his own gun, slowly raising it. The movement must've alerted the Czech, for he turned around, locking eyes with Karl. There was indecision in his eyes, then he started raising the gun. Karl quickly aimed his gun at the man's chest. Without hesitation, squeezed the trigger. The force of the gun surprised him, and he ignored the hammering sound. Another loud bang echoed, then the man fell to the ground, his gun clattering harmlessly on the street.

It ended the fight instantly, the remaining men freezing.

"Hands up now!" Karl shouted, aiming his gun at the first Czech in his sights. "On your knees!"

One of the Freikorps men snatched the gun from the ground and pointed it at the man near Karl.

"Load them up," Karl said when the Czech men were on the ground. "And get the mayor to the hotel." His heartbeat slowly returned to normal as he holstered his pistol. He walked to the man who'd picked up the pistol. A pool of blood had formed around him, and he no longer moved. Karl felt for a pulse, and found none. Oddly enough, he felt nothing. No remorse, but no satisfaction either. As he walked toward the car with the mayor, he understood why his emotions were muted. He was now at war.

THE NEXT DAY Karl watched from his office window as the city went into a frenzy. The streets were reduced to the narrowest of thoroughfares as citizens from all across the Sudetenland came to welcome their Führer.

Adolf Hitler drove in his open top Mercedes-Benz for only the second time, mirroring his victorious entry into Austria over half a year ago. The symbolism wasn't lost on Karl, as the Führer addressed an adoring crowd before disappearing into the very building Karl occupied.

The newly appointed mayor of Eger had organized a reception for the Führer and his party, and Karl was naturally invited as well. He kept his distance as Hitler shook the hands of prominent members of the Sudeten German Party. Karl felt a tap on his shoulder and was surprised to see a young aide.

"Please come with me. The Reichsführer would like a word."

Karl's heart was beating hard as he followed the young man toward Heinrich Himmler, who stood somewhat to the side while Hitler made conversation in the middle of the room.

"Ah, Vogt. Good to see you again. I see you've been carrying out useful work here. It all looks in order."

Karl didn't know exactly how to respond, but quickly found his words. "I've been hard at work making sure everything was properly prepared for your visit, Herr Reichsführer."

"Very good. The Führer would like a quick update on the situation on the ground." He looked at Karl inquiringly.

"Of course. We've taken most of the names on our lists into custody. I was part of the mayor's arrest myself."

"I heard there was some trouble there." Himmler sported a thin smile. "But I also gather you took care of it."

"I did what needed to be done. Apart from that incident, we've had very little resistance."

Himmler looked out the window, where the crowd on the square had barely thinned. "Yes, it appears the people of Eger are pleased to be part of the Reich."

"I can confirm they are, sir. The Freikorps have been exceptionally helpful and useful. We'll continue with the arrests tonight. I expect we'll have almost everyone in custody by tomorrow morning. But for the ones that have fled."

Himmler made a throwaway gesture. "Let them run. As long as they're not around to stir up trouble here. I'll inform the Führer of your progress." He nodded at Karl, then sauntered off. He went straight to Hitler, interrupting one of the men talking to the Führer. Two aides made hand gestures suggesting the men needed some space, and the Sudeten Germans quickly obliged.

Hitler listened attentively while Himmler spoke close to his ear. Then, to Karl's surprise, Himmler turned and nodded at Karl. From across the room, Karl met Hitler's stare. At first, the Führer looked at him with his customary cold, detached stare. As Himmler continued speaking, a glimpse of warmth appeared in his eyes, and he gave an almost imperceptible nod. The moment passed quickly, as the Führer was escorted away from the room.

Karl stood fixed in place. Pride swelled in his chest. His Führer had graced him with his attention. No, not just his attention. His approval.

THIRTY-SEVEN

Buchenwald
20 October 1938

Roll call took much longer than usual. The October wind had free rein on the open Appelplatz, and Felix shivered. He now understood what the other prisoners meant when they said he should cherish the heat of the summer. He still wore the same prisoner garments issued upon arrival in August. While slightly better than the shirt and shorts some prisoners were forced to wear, his sweater was littered with holes. He'd patched a few up, but new ones appeared every day. Felix wondered how bad it would have to be before he could ask for a replacement.

He looked around the roll call square. The guards had long since finished the count, and most had retreated into the warmth of the guardhouse building. Only a few remained in the yard, their rifles drawn. The ever-watchful guards in the guard towers were also sheltered from the wind. *Why are we being kept out in the cold?* There had been no mention of any outstanding punishments. Felix shifted his weight from one leg to the other, stretching to avoid cramps.

It felt like he'd been standing there for another hour when the main gate creaked open. Felix, along with the other prisoners, glanced at the movement. A minute or so later, the sound of many trampling feet approaching from the other side grew louder. A gunshot sounded, followed by harsh commands. Felix knew what that meant.

It didn't take long for the first men to stumble through the gate. They were stunned by the mass of prisoners awaiting them, their tired eyes bulging from surprise. The guards gave them little time to catch their breath, beating them toward an empty corner of the Appelplatz. The men continued pouring into the Appelplatz until some three hundred of them stood near the fence to the side of the main gatehouse. They all handled their new surroundings differently. Some looked around with curiosity, while others kept their gazes firmly focused on the sandy ground beneath their feet.

More guards emerged from the gatehouse, immediately shouting at the men. When the prisoners didn't respond quickly enough, they took out their batons and beat them, harrying the men along the fence toward the registration blocks.

Buchenwald's existing prisoners followed the introduction of the new arrivals with trained detachment. Felix knew how the men felt but three months of survival in the camp had hardened him. Expending energy feeling sorry for other people was a luxury he didn't have.

When the last of the new arrivals disappeared, the men on the Appelplatz were finally dismissed. Felix collected his watery soup and paced himself to eat slowly, savoring every bite. He then retreated to his block, where he used the final bit of strength from his weary bones to lift himself up into his bunk.

It was quiet in the block; most men were exhausted and longed for rest. Unfortunately, the guards had different plans.

The door to the block opened, and the raspy voice of their Blockführer drew everyone's attention. "Get up, inspection!"

Three hundred men jumped from their bunks, then lined up next to them. The SS man remained at the door, and Felix waited for the Kapos to arrive for the inspection. They would rummage through the bunks, looking for anything that could incriminate their occupants. Felix detested the men: prisoners like him, but doing the SS's dirty work in exchange for a more comfortable life.

When the door opened again, a Kapo appeared, immediately followed by a stream of prisoners. Their heads were freshly shaven—new arrivals. The men looked frightened and overwhelmed, their eyes shooting across the block.

"Make room for the new prisoners." The Blockführer spoke with a detached air. "Whoever isn't in a bunk within five minutes will find accommodation in the Bunker instead."

The words took a moment to sink in as prisoners—old and new—looked at each other in disbelief. There was barely enough space to accommodate the current occupants of the block. It was impossible to fit another thirty men into the bunks. Some of the men near the door hastily exchanged words in a different language. Their compatriots translated the Blockführer's message.

The situation in the block changed in an instant. Prisoners hastily made their way back to their bunks. New prisoners scrambled for free spots, which were impossible to find. New prisoners were pushed from bunks, some crashing three meters down onto the hard wooden floor. Most continued their search for a free spot, while some stayed down, too exhausted to continue the cruel exercise.

Felix had climbed back into his bunk when the face of a man of similar age appeared.

"Can I please stay here?" His pleading eyes showed exhaustion even beyond Felix's own. "Please." The man spoke German with a thick accent.

Felix nodded and moved over. His previous bunkmate hadn't returned to roll call that evening. He remembered the Bunker, and he couldn't condemn someone to such a fate.

"Stay quiet, and don't draw any attention to yourself," Felix whispered. He watched as only a few men continued to scramble along bunks. They were pushed away everywhere, and it was no surprise. Most bunks now had three, sometimes four, occupants. They simply couldn't fit any more.

A shrill whistle pierced the air. "One minute!" The Blockführer's voice thundered through the room.

The man in Felix's bunk looked at two men frantically searching for a spot, now making their way down the aisle. His eyes went to Felix, the same pleading look still there. Felix gave him a quick understanding nod. The young man made a soft whistling noise, and Felix didn't think the men, some ten meters away, would hear it. But they looked up, relief evident from their eyes when they spotted the young man next to Felix. They ran to the bunk and climbed in, just as the whistle of the Blockführer sounded again.

Felix looked back and let out a sigh of relief. No men were making their way across the rows of bunk beds anymore. The Blockführer looked disappointed, but then someone shouted from the far side of the block.

"I've got two hiding on the floor, Herr Blockführer." Felix recognized the voice of one of the Kapos.

"Bring them forward."

Two Kapos ran to assist their colleague, and they soon dragged the two prisoners to the SS man at the door. He gave them a quick look, then cocked his head dismissively in the direction of the door.

"Take them to the Bunker. Tell Sommer to have his fun with them. There's no room for them in here." The SS guard spoke like he was ordering the men to dispose of trash. He watched the Kapos leave, then addressed the prisoners. "This is the new way we will run this block. Anyone who doesn't have a place in a bunk in the evening will be moved to the Bunker instead."

Felix kept his face composed while he listened to the horrible announcement, waiting for the man to leave. But the Blockführer wasn't done yet, and as he continued, a smile spread across his face. "We'll have many new prisoners arriving in the next few days. Better make sure you claim your place in time."

THE NEXT MORNING, Felix gave his new bunkmates a quick introduction to life in Buchenwald.

"Make sure the bunk is cleared, and leave nothing behind. Store your tin and utensils in the small space underneath the bunk. If there is an inspection, the Kapos will look for anything they can find to report. Stay away from them, and never trust the Kapos. Only speak when spoken to."

They exited the block to find the camp illuminated by bright lights. It was only four in the morning, and still dark outside, but the camp was well and truly awake. Felix motioned for the men to follow him.

"If you need to use the latrines, make sure you do it first thing in the morning. You might not get another chance. Nothing is certain in the camp. The guards can change the schedule whenever they want."

Petr, the man who'd climbed up first the evening prior spoke up. "When will we receive something to eat?"

"Not before morning roll call is finished. And that's just a slice of hard bread. You'll need to earn your hot meal in the evening." The disappointment was clear on the young man's face, and Felix added, "Don't expect too much from that either."

He showed the men to the latrines, then told them he would see them at roll call later. Felix was keen to get some time to himself, but an announcement from the loudspeaker at the main gatehouse made short work of that.

"*Häftling* Wolff, 245011, report to camp security. Prisoner Wolff, 245011, report to the gatehouse."

The word echoed through his mind while he stood on the main thoroughfare. Other prisoners passed by, moving like apparitions in his peripheral vision. Despite the cold, he felt flushed, a trickle of sweat running down his spine. It really had been his name; it was him they wanted. A summons to the security office almost always meant a trip to the Bunker. He racked his brain but couldn't think of anything he'd done to deserve that. He'd kept his head down, broken no rules, and reported to his work detail on time. There had been no complaints, as far as he knew.

Despite his mounting terror, he had no option but to report as quickly as possible. Things would only get worse if they had to call for him a second time. He made his way to the front of the camp as fast as his tired legs would carry him.

The door to the Gestapo office looked unassuming; a simple wooden door next to the main gate, but Felix knew better than to enter with hope. The men behind the door were rumored as evil as the guards dishing out the beatings in the yard. The difference was that these Gestapo agents had the means to a whole new level of terror available to them in the soundproof rooms of the Bunker. With his heart in his throat, Felix knocked on the door.

THE GESTAPO MAN across the table wore regular clothes. It made him look normal, but Felix knew this man was anything but.

"Your family is still in Vienna, is that correct?" The man's tone was cordial, almost friendly. It got Felix's defenses up; no Nazi in Buchenwald spoke to a prisoner like this.

"My mother is still there, as far as I know."

The man marked something on the form in front of him. A photo taken upon Felix's arrival in the camp was attached to the top right corner. "What was your job back in Vienna? It says here you were unemployed."

"I worked odd jobs to try and make ends meet." Felix thought of his father's bicycle shop, but decided not to mention it.

"Yes, I'm sure that was challenging." The man sounded indifferent now, as if he'd heard the story many times before. *He's testing me.* "I see here you volunteered to come to Buchenwald."

Felix opened his mouth to explain what had happened, then thought better of it. There was no sense in sharing the real reason he'd ended up in Buchenwald. A stab of pain shot through his chest. It wouldn't bring back his father anyway. He swallowed hard, then nodded. "I did."

"Odd decision to make." The man scanned the sheet with Felix's details again, then looked up. "How would you feel about going back to Vienna?"

Felix looked up in disbelief, not sure he'd understood the man correctly. *My mind must be playing tricks on me.* "Back to Vienna?"

"Yes. We feel you've spent enough time here. You've learned your lesson, haven't you?"

"I would very much like to return to Vienna." Felix barely managed to speak the words. *This isn't real. It's a cruel joke.*

"There's one catch, though." The man paused, and Felix met his gaze. "We'll put you on the train to Vienna, but only for you to retrieve your belongings, and leave the country immediately. You and your mother."

"Where would we go?" As soon as Felix spoke the words, he regretted them. It didn't matter. He was being given a chance to leave Buchenwald.

"I don't care. As long as you leave the Reich." He looked down at Felix's file again. "The Central Office in Vienna can help you with this."

Felix's head was swimming. He still couldn't tell if the man on the other side of the table was playing him, or if he was really giving him a chance to leave this hell. Then the man slid a piece of paper across the table.

"Sign this, and we'll prepare for your departure."

The words on the paper danced in front of his eyes. He tried to focus, but the words wouldn't remain in one place long enough for him to read the sentences.

"I can also just take the offer away, if you'd prefer to stay here." The voice of the Gestapo man sounded distant, but his hand moved from the other side of the table, ready to snatch Felix's potential freedom away.

Without another thought, Felix grabbed the pen and signed his name at the bottom of the form. *It can't get worse than this.*

THIRTY-EIGHT

Prague
22 October 1938

It had been a little over two weeks since President Beneš resigned. It hadn't been a surprise to Adela, who could see the political vultures circling the moment the Munich Agreement was announced. Beneš' position became untenable when public opinion turned against him. He was personally held responsible for not fighting to keep the Sudetenland. Evil whispers even claimed he'd been pleased to cede the Sudetenland.

Adela knew the president had no choice but to accept the decision handed down from Munich. Great Britain and France had clearly chosen Hitler's side, even if they tried to spin it differently. Chamberlain had even dared to claim victory upon his return to England, to have secured peace in Europe. Adela's mouth twitched with fury thinking back to the moment she heard those words on the radio. Peace in Europe at the cost of her country.

She adjusted her scarf and pulled up her collar before exiting the streetcar. Crossing through several small streets, she arrived at an unassuming coffeehouse. The smell of freshly roasted coffee entered her nostrils as soon as she stepped inside, and she greeted the woman behind the counter.

"Your guest is already here, Adela. I placed him at the table in the back."

Adela smiled and pointed at a poppy seed *koláč* in the display. "Can you bring me one of those and a strong cup of coffee, Irena?"

The tables in the coffeehouse were placed close to each other, but Irena had reserved a more private table in the back. Adela even thought Irena had moved some of the tables away. It didn't matter, for it wasn't noisy and crowded enough, and she smiled when she greeted František Moravec, who was waiting for her. He stood as she approached, then waited for her to sit before doing so himself.

"It's good to see you." He pointed at the piece of half-eaten apple pie in front of him. "The waitress tells me it's all baked in house?"

"You should try the koláč. Best in the city."

As if on cue, Irena appeared with Adela's order. "Enjoy. Let me know if you need anything else." She quickly disappeared back behind the counter, and Adela looked at the head of military intelligence.

"How have you been, Adela? I'm sorry we've been unable to meet in the castle recently. There have been so many changes in staff, I wanted to make sure we keep our contact minimal. I need to find out who I can trust first."

"I understand. How are you finding President Hacha?" Adela took a sip of her coffee.

Moravec shrugged. "I'm not sure. He's harmless, which is also the biggest problem with him. He's happy to agree with pretty much anything the Nazis demand in the Sudetenland."

"I've been hearing much the same in the hallways. I haven't had the pleasure of working with him yet."

"And I don't think you will anytime soon. He's quite hands off, happy to let parliament and other officials make the tough calls."

"Including you?" Adela's tone was hopeful.

"Yes, but that's not necessarily a good thing. He's not involving me in as many of the meetings as he should. Hacha shows too little interest in my department, which means he's making too many uninformed decisions."

"Have you told him as much?"

Moravec nodded. "I've talked to him twice now, stressing the value of our intelligence network. He keeps saying he appreciates it, but then I find out I'm kept out of the loop again."

"It sounds nothing like the relationship you had with President Beneš."

"For everything he was accused of, you can't fault Beneš for trying. You and I know how hard he fought for the Sudetenland. It's a shame most of it was done behind closed doors. People will never know how hard he fought for our country." Moravec looked downcast and sliced a bite from his apple pie. He lifted his fork, then changed his mind. "How are you doing? I can imagine your department is quite busy with the Germans moving into the Sudetenland?"

"It was very hectic right after the annexation, with articles exclaiming the brilliance of the Third Reich's influence on the region. I'm quite certain Goebbels personally ramped up his output. But right now, things appear to be heading to a business-as-usual state."

Moravec chewed on his apple pie while listening, then let out a small grunt when she finished. "Adela, it's now more important than ever that we cultivate the relationship with Dieter."

A spark in excitement shot through her body. Moravec had initiated the meeting after nearly two weeks of radio silence. She had almost resigned herself to merely carrying out her regular job, but then an aide delivered a message. Adela had hoped he'd rekindle their partnership.

"You're aware of the strategic importance of the Sudetenland, right?" Moravec's eyes bored into hers, and he didn't wait for her response. "The region accounted for about 70 percent of our strategic resources and military production capabilities. After the Munich Betrayal, the Nazis overwhelmed us, forcing us to leave much of our equipment behind."

Like most Czechs, Adela had read the alarming reports in the newspapers. "So it's really as bad as the press says?"

"Worse. This was never mentioned, but they knew where our border fortifications were set up. We really were ready for war, but the cost would've been too great. An armed conflict without France's support would've crushed us. We'd have lost hundreds of thousands of men."

"So you agreed with Beneš in ceding the region?"

"I did. We could've beaten the Wehrmacht back for a long time, but we would never have stopped them in the long run. But it does leave us virtually defenseless against future German aggression."

"Which is why Hacha is placating the Nazis like this."

"It's one of the reasons. But the biggest issue is that he's acting on assumptions. He doesn't know what to prepare for. Hitler says he won't go beyond Sudetenland, but it has to be tempting to move for the rest of Czechoslovakia at one point. Hacha is flying blind."

"And you want to do something about it."

He leaned forward in his chair. "I don't know who to trust in the new parliament yet, but I do know I can trust you. We need to obtain reliable information from Germany. We need to know their intentions, their moves. Heck, I'm sure they're already looking for ways to spread their poison farther than the Sudetenland."

"And that's why you want me to meet with Dieter again."

The man across the table nodded his head. "Yes. We have to assume I'm being tracked by the increased number of agents pouring into the country, and I don't know who I can trust in the government. It's best if you continue to meet with him for now."

Adela didn't hesitate. "How do I reach him?"

THIRTY-NINE

Karlsbad, German Sudetenland
31 October 1938

The train waiting at the Karlsbad station wasn't especially long. The steam locomotive with just four third-class cars attached differed little from the other trains passing through. What made it different was the large number of armed SS and Freikorps troopers surrounding it.

Karl looked on as a now-familiar spectacle unfolded in front of him. The entrance to the small station was closed off to the public, who were kept at bay some fifty meters down the street. While Karl enjoyed the public attention in Vienna when he organized a similar transport, he preferred to wrap this one up with minimal fuss.

Trucks turned off the main road and stopped in front of the station. Men belonging to the Freikorps enthusiastically stepped forward and assisted the prisoners down from the trucks. Once their feet touched the street, they were pushed toward the station entrance, where they needed to cross only a single platform to board the train.

Karl observed the faces of the men disembarking from the trucks. If they didn't realize their destination offered no hope, they would soon enough. In contrast to the transports in Vienna, none of the men resisted, and boarding went on in a surprisingly orderly fashion. Karl couldn't help but be disappointed and, judging from their faces, so were many of the troopers.

After double-checking all the prisoners on the transport list were on board, Karl gave the signal for departure. Slowly, the train started moving, taking the last of the political dissidents and prominent Jews from the Sudetenland. It marked the end of the time Karl would, very successfully, labor there, and he was keen to celebrate.

The train disappeared out of sight, and Karl approached a group of senior Freikorps men. "How about we mark this rather successful transport downtown?" There was a bar Karl knew the men liked to frequent, and it took little to convince them to join him. "I just need to pass by the office, and I'll join you momentarily."

He left the station and reached the Karlsbad Freikorps headquarters just before five in the afternoon, and he raced up to his second-floor office to collect some of his things. His train to Vienna would leave early in the morning, and he didn't know when or if he would return to Karlsbad. His work here was done. All that was left was to keep the region under control, and that could be managed by men less capable.

He stepped into the hallway ten minutes later and ran into an old acquaintance on his way down the stairs. It was impossible for Walter Stahlecker to ignore him, and Karl plastered on his best smile.

"Fancy running into you here, Stahlecker." Karl's surprise was completely feigned, for the men had worked in the same region for most of the past month. Stahlecker had traveled from Vienna to oversee Winkelmann's command of his Einsatzgruppe in the region. He had been exactly the overbearing superior Karl had expected.

"Yes, although from what I hear, this won't happen that much more often. You're on your way back to Vienna soon, aren't you?" Stahlecker looked keen to continue on his way.

"Tomorrow morning. We just sent the last transport to Dachau. Well, last transport for now, anyway." An idea popped into Karl's head. "Say, I'm celebrating the successful completion with some of the senior Freikorps men. Why don't you join us? Your Einsatzgruppe has been crucial to our success in the region."

Stahlecker wrinkled his nose, but he knew it was poor form to reject Karl's invitation. "All right, one drink."

"Excellent. My car is right outside."

THE TAVERN WAS FILLED with Freikorps men, and Karl and Stahlecker struggled through the packed room to find the officer's table in the back. Two of the men got up to make room. As Standartenführers, Karl and Stahlecker outranked everybody in the bar.

Large mugs of beer soon arrived, and Karl made sure to sit next to Stahlecker. After their second round of beers were placed on the table, Karl turned to Stahlecker, raising his mug.

"I think you and I got off to a bad start in Vienna. But look at what we've accomplished in just a month in the Sudetenland." He smiled, and Stahlecker hesitantly clinked his mug. Karl decided he needed to up his charm once more. "And I'm big enough to admit I was wrong in my doubts about your unit's discipline. They behaved impeccably." That wasn't entirely true, as there had been plenty of incidents with the Einsatzgruppe.

"Yes, I appreciate you seeing the error of your assumptions," Stahlecker responded tersely, keeping his eyes averted from Karl while he scanned the room. "I believe the unit has performed rather well, and it appears the men who matter agree."

Karl put down his beer. "How so?"

"You haven't heard?" Stahlecker appeared a little too smug for Karl's liking. "Heydrich has asked me to meet with Henlein later this week, and to see how we can assist him in expanding our influ-

THE EAGLE'S SHADOW

ence across the Sudetenland." He took a large gulp, then leaned conspiratorially to Karl. "Although I highly doubt we'll restrict that sphere of influence to just the region, don't you think?"

Karl felt lightheaded, and it wasn't from the beer. He hadn't expected Stahlecker's revelations. He had invited his peer along to make him aware of his own success in the area, to gloat somewhat, and certainly not to be upstaged. Heydrich had made no mention of continued Sicherheitsdienst efforts in the Sudetenland. At least not in the way Stahlecker framed them. Karl felt stung and passed over for an important assignment. Suddenly, the prospect of his return to Vienna no longer seemed so enticing.

"Will you leave the command of the Einsatzgruppe more to Winkelmann, then?" It was all Karl could manage as he searched for the right words to mask his shock.

"For now. But I'll stay involved. I expect it will be rather useful in the future." Stahlecker was visibly growing in confidence. "I'm sure we'll encounter more resistance in the region soon enough, and it will be good to have a trained unit nearby. In addition to the Freikorps, of course."

"Sounds like a good idea." Karl's response was almost robotic, and he took another sip of his beer. All his desire to be in the tavern had evaporated. He needed space to think, to consider what Stahlecker's assignment meant. Had Heydrich passed him over this time? Or was this Stahlecker's belated revenge? The same doubts he'd felt when he traveled to Berlin some six weeks ago resurfaced.

"Are you all right?" Thomas appeared next to him. The Freikorps leader looked concerned, and Karl caught himself. He couldn't appear weak, not in front of these men, and certainly not in front of Stahlecker. He smiled and nodded. "Just considering when I'll return to the area. I've enjoyed my time here, and I think there's a lot of good work to be done still." He turned to Stahlecker. "And I've just learned you'll be working more closely with this good man in the future." He lifted his mug and held it out to the middle of the table, attracting the attention of the other men. They did the same, and when the chatter died down, Karl forced himself to announce in his most cheerful voice, "Cheers to Standartenführer Stahlecker!"

As Karl took a large swig of beer, he eyed the man to his right. There was no doubt in his mind the man was plotting against him. Karl would keep him close. He would never be caught out like this again.

FORTY

Buchenwald
2 November 1938

Felix approached the main gate, where he was surprised to see another fifty men waiting. They clasped the bags containing their few belongings, their faces indicating their confusion. Two guards stood to the side, chatting with each other but otherwise looking unconcerned. Felix didn't see anyone familiar, and he joined the mostly silent group of men.

The anticipation was tangible. Their names had been called out in the morning's roll call, and they were ordered to collect their things and report to the gate after the regular work details had left. It had come as a surprise, as it had been nearly two weeks since Felix signed the piece of paper offered by the Gestapo man. His initial suspicions at the whole thing being a cruel game had only grown when nothing happened. Until this morning at the Appelplatz.

Felix still wasn't convinced he was being sent home. They could still be transferred to a different camp. He wouldn't believe it until he was really back home in the small apartment in Leopoldstadt. The thought warmed his heart; he couldn't wait to see his mother.

A few more prisoners arrived, and then the guards sprang into action. They called out the numbers and names of the prisoners, confirming all were present. The fact they were was hardly a surprise: Despite the possibility that they might not be going home, Felix was certain every single one of the men surrounding him was willing to take a risk if it meant leaving the hell of Buchenwald. It couldn't really become any worse.

The gate was opened, and the group of prisoners methodically streamed through. Felix was at the rear and glanced back at the rows of barracks behind him. *Good riddance.* He passed through the gatehouse, thinking back to the first time he went in the opposite direction. To the moment his freedom was taken from him.

They walked down the Caracho Path, and Felix prepared to make the brutal five-kilometer trek back down Blood Road, to the town of Buchenwald, and hopefully onto the train to Vienna. He was shocked when he saw two flatbed trucks waiting, the first prisoners already climbing aboard. *We won't have to walk?* It was encouraging.

The drive took less than ten minutes, and when Felix jumped from the flatbed, he found himself in front of the small Buchenwald train station. Nothing had changed since his arrival three months ago. More SS guards awaited them, and they halfheartedly drove them into the station. There was none of the violence they had become accustomed to as they were told to wait at the end of the platform.

The rest of the station was deserted, and while the SS guards puffed on cigarettes, the prisoners sat on the ground. As the group waited, they became more emboldened, whispering among themselves. A man who looked at least twenty years Felix's senior sat next to him.

"Do you mind if I sit? Where are you headed to?" His voice was raspy, his eyes kind.

Felix was slightly thrown by the question. "Vienna. Aren't you?"

"They told me I was going home to Salzburg. Well, my town

close to Salzburg, but you've probably never heard of it. I suppose they're making a few stops along the way."

"I guess so. How long were you in Buchenwald for?"

The man scratched his head. "I can't remember exactly, but I must've been among some of the first arrests after the Nazis came." The man apparently caught Felix's surprise, for he smiled. "You're wondering how I survived for so long, aren't you? I worked in the kitchen, and I may have done some things I wasn't supposed to." He brought his hand to his mouth in an eating gesture. "Just need to make sure you never get caught."

"Do you have someone waiting for you at home?"

"My wife. She wrote to me every week. Not that I received every letter, but I got most of them. They kept me alive." A tender look crossed his face as he looked away into the distance. Then he turned back to Felix. "What about you? Someone waiting for you?"

"Just my mother." He couldn't bring himself to mention his father's passing. Keen to change the subject, Felix turned his attention to the tracks. "I wonder how long we'll have to wait."

The man shrugged. "We have time. What's meant to happen will happen." He closed his eyes and was snoring softly less than a minute later. Felix decided to follow the man's lead and closed his eyes as well.

HE WOKE up to the sound of screeching brakes. The prisoners were on their feet, and Felix quickly did the same. The train was similar to the one that had taken him to Buchenwald, bar one difference; it was much longer. Felix counted fifteen third-class carriages attached to the large steam locomotive.

The guards directed them to the back carriage. Passing the other cars, they saw similar looking men—shaved heads, gaunt faces—observing them without emotion. Felix wondered where they came from.

Felix was one of the last to board, and the door was quickly shut behind him. He found an uncomfortable spot in the crowded car, but he didn't care. As soon as the train started moving, the sense of freedom he'd missed when leaving the camp slowly started to build. They picked up speed, and soon the birch trees of the Buchenwald area made way for towering mountains in the distance as they headed south and into Austria.

THE JOURNEY TOOK over two days as the train made many stops along the way. Provided only with water and scraps of bread, Felix was torn by hunger when the train rolled into their destination: Vienna's Westbahnhof. He could hardly believe it, and he was on his feet even before the train came to a stop.

He felt queasy as the doors opened and he breathed in the familiar smell of the city he'd grown up in. There was something about coming home, even more so in these circumstances. He looked down the platform and saw a squad of SS men barring the passage toward the main station hall. Despite his exhaustion and hunger, he found himself making his way toward them with renewed energy. The adrenaline of being home would carry him these last few steps.

Two dozen men were ahead of him, milling about and trying to hide their impatience, as the SS men waited for all prisoners to assemble. When the last prisoner had disembarked from the train, one of the guards spoke in a loud voice.

"You're back in Vienna, and you may think you're free now. Let me assure you you're not." He left the words hanging in the air before continuing. "The conditions for leaving the camps were very clear: You are to leave the Reich at your earliest opportunity, but no later than the end of the year. I suggest you make your way to the Central Office as soon as possible, and secure your exit visas." He looked around menacingly, while the hissing of the engines of arriving and departing trains continued in the background. The chatter and clattering of heels of commuters rushing to and from their trains sounded a lot like freedom to Felix. "If you're still in the country at the end of the year, you will return to your camps: no amnesty. Make haste and leave the Reich." He then turned to his colleagues, who stood with clipboards. "Report to these men, and don't leave until they clear you."

The line moved quickly, and after Felix confirmed his identity, he was allowed to pass. As he walked into the crowded hall of Westbahnhof, he took a deep breath. People moved in a familiar hurry, too busy to notice the emancipated men staring at them. It was overwhelming, and Felix found tears welling in his eyes. He was home, and for now, he was free.

FORTY-ONE

Prague
3 November 1938

Dieter was clean-shaven and looked rested. His clear eyes met hers without wavering.

"Thank you for responding to my message so quickly," Adela said after the waiter had placed two coffees on the table. "We were a bit worried about you."

Dieter waved his hand casually, the hint of a smile on his face. "It's not me you should worry about. Not with everything that's happening in your country."

He was right, but Adela was pleased to have him sitting opposite her regardless. After she left the meeting with Moravec a few days ago, she had been nervous about establishing contact with Dieter. It was the first time she would initiate a meeting, and she was worried their German contact would not take her seriously. It was quite a different prospect to have the head of the Czech military intelligence agency instead of one of his underlings reach out. Much to Adela's relief, he had responded a day later, suggesting a small cafe on the outskirts of Prague. Apart from Adela and Dieter, only one other table was occupied; an elderly gentleman was buried in his paper, paying them no attention.

"Moravec wants you to know he still values your commitment to our cause. He's unable to communicate with you directly—"

"Because of the new government," Dieter interrupted, holding up the palms of his hands. "Trust me, I understand the intricacies of the situation. These are challenging times. But in a practical sense, it doesn't really change anything." He gave her an intense look. "We're the ones meeting in the real world anyway. I'm glad you're still involved."

It was clear from his face that he was genuine, and Adela appreciated his words. She had woken up shaking with nerves, and more than once considered turning back on the tram ride over. Now she was glad she hadn't.

"I'm glad you reached out, though. And your timing couldn't have been better." Adela didn't like the ominous notes in Dieter's voice. "As Moravec is probably aware, the Sudetenland isn't the final piece of land in Hitler's sights. Judging from what I see from my position, plans to invade the rest of your country are well underway."

Adela made an effort to keep her face passive. Inside, her heart was beating against her chest. Dieter's words weren't a surprise, but the matter-of-fact way he announced the Führer's plans made her bones ache. "Can you share some of those plans? A timeline or dates, perhaps?"

"There's no date for any invasion or such. Our focus is on the Sudetenland for now." He whistled softly. "But the bounty from that annexation is rather plentiful, and it will only strengthen the Wehrmacht when they do march for Prague."

"We're aware of this. We didn't have enough time for an orderly retreat after what happened in Munich." The thought of German soldiers attacking her country with its own weapons sickened Adela. "Apart from the weapons in Sudetenland, what plans are you aware of? Is there anything we can do?"

"Dozens, if not hundreds, of Abwehr and SD agents are pouring across the border. Many assisted in the cleansing of the

Sudetenland, but now that most of that job has finished, they continue farther west. They're infiltrating all parts of Czech life. Their job is underway: unsettle the population, weaken the government's position, and prepare for imminent German invasion. It's the tried and trusted method we used for Austria and the Sudetenland. I'm sorry to say that it is highly effective."

Adela was aghast. "How long has this been going on?"

"Since well before we took the Sudetenland. Ask your boss, he'll know. But now that that region has been taken, the focus shifts to the rest of your country. The number of agents moving into Czechoslovakia has increased significantly in the past two weeks. Moravec is right to be cautious."

"What can we do about it?" Adela was hesitant to ask, for she suspected she knew the answer. Her mind raced while Dieter took a large gulp of coffee. She thought about the people working in the castle. With the new parliament, lots of new faces roamed the hallways. She had no doubt that at least some of them were part of the German infiltration network Dieter was talking about.

"Not an awful lot, I'm afraid. These men and women are some of the best agents of the Abwehr and Sicherheitsdienst. They know how to blend in. In fact, it's quite likely they recruited Czech nationals and people who grew up here. It won't be as easy as looking for someone who speaks with a German accent." He gave her a sympathetic look. "But you can do one thing. Keep your circle small. You have a chance of exposing these spies, because they don't know you have someone on the other side."

"Can you help us in any way?"

"I thought about that, and there might be a way for me to find out where focal points of the spy infiltration and attacks are aimed. It may take some time, for this is very sensitive information, and I need to be careful. Even with my clearance level, too many questions will raise suspicions."

"Anything that could point us in the right direction would be most welcome." *And hopefully catch some of them in the act, and make an example of them.* She didn't share her thoughts. "But from what you're saying, the spies are only the prelude to our problems. It sounds like it's a matter of when, rather than if, the invasion takes place."

"I fear it is. Unless your government can strengthen your allies' pledges."

"Their words are meaningless. They handed Hitler something that wasn't theirs to give away to avoid confrontation. I have no faith in the promises of our so-called allies." Nor did she trust president Hacha to make any sort of fist.

"I agree. Nevertheless, I will pass any information about the invasion along to you and Moravec." Dieter made a move to get up, reaching for his coat. "I do have one demand to continue our future partnership. And it's not financial."

Adela raised an eyebrow. It was the first time Dieter asked for anything other than money.

"I will only meet with you, and I trust that this information goes to Moravec, and only him."

"Naturally." Adela felt relieved. Moravec had already agreed on this approach.

Dieter stood and wrapped his coat around his body. "Keep the circle small, Hana. I will do whatever I can to assist you." He held out his hand, and Adela handed him a thick envelope. He stuffed it into his coat without looking inside.

As she watched him leave, she hoped he would come through with information that could break the crushing wave coming from the north. From what she'd heard in the past half hour, she wasn't too optimistic.

A FEW HOURS LATER, Adela found herself in the warm, familiar company of friends. They sat at their favorite spot in the corner of the Grand Cafe Orient. It was as crowded as ever, and they sat closely packed together in the booth. She looked at the faces at the table and tried to forget her troubles at work. These were the people she loved most, and she was happy Greta was sitting next to her, their knees touching.

Two of the men at the table were in a heated discussion about an assignment they were given at the university that afternoon. The rest of the table feigned interest for a minute or two, and everybody was relieved when the waiter checked in. They ordered a new round, and they were silent for a moment, until one of the men, Karel, spoke.

"At least we can still discuss this. We've lost about a quarter of our class since the annexation of the Sudetenland." His voice was heavy as he looked to Jiří. They both studied at Prague's prestigious Univerzita Karlova and took most classes together.

"What do you mean? Did they leave, or were they sent away?" An uncomfortable feeling rose in Adela's stomach. Greta gave her a sad look.

"Many have family in the Sudetenland, and when the Germans took over, they went home." Now Jiří spoke up, his deep voice ringing clearly around the table. "Many tried to convince their families to move away in the weeks building up to the annexation, but they wouldn't listen. I haven't heard from a few since they left. I would've expected them to be back in Prague by now."

"But others were picked up from class." Karel lowered his voice. "The police showed up, called their names, and they were taken away, just like that."

"The Austrian Jews," Jiří added. "When we asked what happened to them the other day, we were told they needed to return home. I'm not sure they had any choice in the matter."

"I'm sure they don't consider Austria much of a home anymore."

Adela felt bile rise in her throat. She knew nothing about this.

"People in my parents' circle have also been picked up and sent back to Austria," Greta added, then quickly shook her head when she saw Adela's distraught look. "Not my uncle and aunt, thankfully. But it was very similar to what they're saying." She nodded at Karel and Jiří. "People are saying the Hacha government is working with the Nazis to deport people back to the Reich. Political opponents, they call them."

All the faces at the table turned to Adela, whose neck was

burning up. "I knew nothing about this." Her frail voice surprised her, and she was relieved by her friends' sympathetic looks. "But I do know the Germans are trying to disrupt life in our country." She wasn't supposed to share information, but judging from what her friends witnessed, it was hardly a secret anymore.

"Many of my parents' friends are considering leaving the country before someone knocks on their door," Greta continued, her voice quivering. "We thought we were safe from the Nazis, but their influence is growing from beyond the borders."

"Is there any reason why these people are taken away?" Adela asked without much hope, and Greta shook her head.

"Other than being successful members of the community, none."

"And being Jewish," Jiří added. The words hung heavy in the air. There was no denying it.

Tears welled up in Greta's eyes, and Adela placed an arm around her shoulders. Her heart ached for her friend.

"Are your parents considering leaving? Are you?" She was horrified that she was asking the question, but felt compelled to. She held her breath while Greta dried her eyes and cleared her throat.

"We've discussed it. Maybe, if things get worse. But my father really doesn't want to abandon his business. For now, we'll remain where we are."

The tremor in Greta's voice suggested her family were doing more than merely considering it. A sudden feeling of deep loss overcame Adela at the thought of her best friend leaving—no, fleeing—the country. She tightened her grip on Greta's shoulders and pulled her closer.

FORTY-TWO

Vienna
7 November 1938

The man leading Felix into the small room said nothing, merely pointing at the examination table in the middle of the space. He then closed the door and disappeared, leaving Felix by himself. He sat on the table, legs dangling, his eyes drifting to the small, empty desk in the corner. It was the only other discernible feature in a room that smelled like disinfectant.

Felix had reported to the municipal office in Leopoldstadt in the morning and was promptly directed to the top floor. There he spent a good two hours in a long, slow-moving queue before he arrived at a single desk. The woman taking his details snarled and growled at him along the way, his mere presence clearly offending her. He was then told to take a seat, where he spent another hour and a half feeling ignored. Finally, the man who had just left had escorted him to this windowless room. It brought back memories of his time in Buchenwald's Bunker. Tiny beads of sweat collected on his spine, and his head spun while the walls closed in on him. He took a deep breath and calmed himself; this was nothing like the

Bunker. *I just need to get through this to get my passport. It can't take much longer, surely.*

After returning to Vienna, he was keen to find a way out of the country. He had no doubt the threat about being returned to a camp would be followed through on. But to leave, he needed a new passport. The Nazis had recently passed mandates that required the front of his passport to be marked with a *J*, indicating his Jewishness. A physical examination to determine the extent of his Jewishness was part of the application.

The door opened, and a man wearing a shoddy doctor's coat walked in, followed by an SS trooper in uniform, a pistol prominently dangling on his hip. The trooper's presence startled Felix, but he wasn't given any time to reflect, for the doctor looked at him with annoyance.

"Why haven't you undressed?" He held up his hands, impatience clear in his voice. "Take off your clothes, hurry. Do you think I have time to waste?"

Felix jumped from the table and started undressing. The doctor moved to the table in the corner and placed a folder down. The trooper stood by the door, his eyes never leaving Felix. Humiliating as it was, he obliged and stripped to his underwear. The doctor turned back around and shook his head.

"Everything. I can't very well tell if you're Jewish without looking at what's in your underwear. Come on, off."

Felix did as he was told, and he unconsciously placed his hands over his privates and cast his eyes to the floor. He sensed the trooper's stare burning into him, but he tried to ignore it.

"On the table." The doctor's command was businesslike. The steel felt cold on his bare skin, and goose bumps formed. "Move your hands." The doctor stood between Felix and the trooper, and he reluctantly moved his hands, feeling extremely exposed and vulnerable. The doctor took a quick look, then hummed his approval while he ticked something off on his sheet. "Clearly circumcised. You identify as Jewish?" His gaze went to Felix's face, his eyes narrowing as he appeared to search for something.

"Yes, sir." Felix didn't know what else to say. The fact that he was here for his new passport should've been sufficient indication of his heritage. The whole medical ordeal appeared designed simply to humiliate him.

The doctor grabbed Felix's chin, lifting his face. The bright fluorescent light on the ceiling caused Felix to close his eyes. The doctor pinched his nose, appearing surprised. "You don't have very clear Jewish features. The size of your nose is rather . . ." The man paused, as if searching for words. "Normal." He scribbled a longer note on the paper, illegible to Felix. "Stand up."

Felix got up from the table, and the doctor moved about him without explanation. The trooper smirked at him, his eyes on Felix's genitals. He heard the doctor scribbling some more, then he exclaimed, "Well, you're a rather unremarkable specimen. Nothing that makes you stand out, and no clear Jewish racial features." He handed a small piece of paper to Felix. "You can get dressed and hand this to the front desk. They'll take care of the rest of the paperwork." Without another word, he turned to the door, which the trooper hastily opened for him, and disappeared from the room. As Felix reached for his underwear, he had never felt more humiliated.

Wolfgang was waiting outside. As soon as he saw Felix come down the steps of the municipal building, his face turned serious.

"Are you all right? Did you get the new passport?"

Felix tapped the breast pocket on his coat while he kept walking at a steady pace. "I did. But I can't believe what happened in there."

His friend gave him a compassionate squeeze of the shoulder. "I know. I was there a few weeks ago. We all have to go through it. It's just another way for the Nazis to dehumanize us."

"At least I can now apply for the visa. I should head to the Central Office." Then he realized it was already dark. "What time is it?"

"A little past five. You won't be getting into the Central Office today. Besides, there's no point in going unless you have a job offer, or someone willing to vouch for you."

Felix turned to him. "When did that change? I thought they were keen to get rid of us."

"I mean, sure, they want us to leave. But even if you'd somehow procure an exit visa, you wouldn't be able to go anywhere without proving you add something to the country you're going to. The other countries in Europe, or the United States for that matter, aren't exactly welcoming us with open arms."

"But you're leaving soon. How did you manage that?" Felix felt disheartened. Everything from the Gestapo agent in Buchenwald to the guards on the train back to Vienna suggested obtaining the exit visa was a formality. Why had he gone through the humiliation and journey to receive his new passport if it was an almost impossible task?

"It wasn't easy. My father reached out to distant family in New York. They didn't respond at first, but then he received mail from a lawyer in America. The family have signed an affidavit that they will take care of us. My father says we won't need their generosity. He's quite confident he'll find a job in New York soon enough."

"I have no doubt he will." Wolfgang's father was a skilled surgeon, something the people running the American hospitals would realize as soon as they talked to him. He was happy for Wolfgang, but he also envied his friend. Even more so, he was going to miss him. Wolfgang had been a permanent fixture in his life for as long as he could remember. *I wish I could go with them.* "What will you do in America?"

Wolfgang shrugged as they made their way onto Karmelitermarkt. "I don't know. I would love to go back to school. Perhaps one of the universities will take me? But I think it's more likely that I'll need to get a job first, to support the family as much as possible. That's okay, though. I know I'm lucky to be going to America."

They crossed the square, and Felix pondered his situation. He had no connections in foreign countries, and he hadn't broached the subject of leaving with his mother yet. He smiled when he remembered coming home a few nights ago. She had almost collapsed when she opened the door, almost as undernourished as him, instantly making him feel guilty about using the money she sent him in Buchenwald. Rebecca Wolff knew her son well, for she immediately assured him he needed it more than she did. She was right, of course, for Felix wasn't sure how he would have survived the final weeks without the extra tins of food from the prison canteen. He hadn't mustered the courage to tell her they would need to leave the country soon. It would be even harder to convince her if he didn't have their visas arranged. Felix decided he would only tell his mother once everything had been set up for their departure.

"What's going on over there?" Wolfgang interrupted his thoughts, pointing at the newsstand on the corner of the square. People crowded around it, and they could hear the vendor yelling in excitement, although they were unable to make out the words from a distance.

Felix frowned. "There's only one explanation for an evening crowd at a newsstand."

They moved closer, the murmurs of the crowd increasing, the words of the vendor becoming clearer. A woman was reading a newspaper, and Felix could see her mouth opening in shock as her eyes flashed across the page. An uncomfortable feeling was building in the pit of his stomach.

"Special evening edition! Get your special edition!" The vendor's words came through clearly as he turned in Felix and Wolfgang's direction. "German diplomat attacked in Paris embassy!"

Wolfgang grabbed a paper, handing a few coins to the vendor in the process. The headline covered almost the entire top third of the page, with a photo of a man he'd never seen before taking up half of the remaining space. Felix's stomach dropped. Wolfgang turned to him, his face pale. The words danced in front of his eyes, and he willed for them to change. But they were there, screaming at him in a black, bold typeface.

GERMAN DIPLOMAT SHOT BY JEW IN PARIS EMBASSY!

Wolfgang's words sounded muffled, as if he was underwater. But there was no denying their truth.

"This changes everything."

FORTY-THREE

Vienna
9 November 1938, early evening

Karl was back in the familiar surroundings of the Hotel Metropole. He'd initially planned to stay in Vienna for a week, but as he was preparing to return to Berlin, news of the attack on Ernst vom Rath in Paris broke. It meant Karl was instructed to stay in Vienna until further notice. That was fine with him. His old office was still available, and he'd spent the past two days awaiting news from Paris and Berlin.

The attack on the German diplomat had been big news across Europe, with Goebbels making sure it received as much attention as possible. Karl knew the propaganda minister had struck gold with the assailant. Herschel Grynszpan was a Polish Jew who'd been raised in Germany and emigrated to Paris a few years ago, leaving his parents and two siblings behind. When his family lost their Polish citizenship last month, and Germany announced all residence permits for foreigners were revoked, they were deported back to Poland. No longer citizens of Poland either, they were stuck in appalling conditions on the German-Polish border. It drove Grynszpan mad enough to enter the German embassy and shoot vom Rath.

There was a knock on the door and a secretary walked in.

"Sir, you requested to be kept updated regarding the vom Rath situation." The man spoke without emotion. "Berlin reports he's succumbed to his injuries about half an hour ago."

"Thank you." Karl waved the man off, and as the door closed, he couldn't help but smile. Everything was coming together perfectly. He had no doubt Goebbels would broadcast the news shortly. He leaned back in his chair and focused on the telephone on his desk.

It rang an hour later, and Karl picked it up on the second ring. When the connection from Munich came through, so did the familiar voice of Reinhard Heydrich.

"News of vom Rath's death spread quickly here." Heydrich was at the annual commemoration of the 1923 Beer Hall Putsch. It was a wonderful coincidence to have many of the party's most influential members gathered together at a time like this. "Goebbels just finished his speech. He stated the party will not intervene against spontaneous retribution."

Goebbels' words were deliberately vague. It was one of his greatest strengths, for he hardly ever explicitly called for action, but did enough to imply something needed to be done. His underlings were generally happy to oblige.

"Many of the local SS leaders are on the phone to their constituents, encouraging them to participate in this retribution." Heydrich sounded neutral, and Karl was slightly confused. His boss had been critical of the riots that erupted in Vienna earlier this year.

"What are your instructions for Vienna, sir?" Karl wanted to make sure there was no misinterpreting what Heydrich wanted.

"Our official line is that the police won't intervene if the citizens of the Reich take matters into their own hands. If these spontaneous actions are what the people see as the correct retribution, so be it. Just make sure any damage is restricted to Jewish property."

"I understand, sir. Would you like me to reach out to anyone in the city?" Karl managed to suppress any excitement in his tone.

"That won't be necessary. I'll reach out to Huber and Müller myself. Coordinate with them. I'm sure you can make yourself useful." There was a pause. "On second thought, this might be a good opportunity to inspect the functioning of the Gestapo and police force firsthand. Why don't you make sure you're close to the fire, and observe and assist where necessary? This will be an eventful night, Vogt. This attack can not go unanswered."

"Understood, sir. I will report to Huber immediately."

Karl put down the phone and exhaled deeply. Heydrich had been as calm and calculating as always, but the meaning behind his words was beyond anything Karl had ever heard before. The years of carefully building up the case against the Jews in the Reich had cultivated a powder keg within German society. The spark needed to set things into motion had just been provided by one of their own. All Karl and his colleagues needed to do was fan it in the right direction.

KARL PICKED up the phone a few minutes later, dialing a number he knew by heart. It was promptly answered, and he waited patiently while the operator connected him.

"Karl, I was wondering when you'd call." Odilo Globočnik sounded upbeat, the Vienna gauleiter no doubt informed of the developments. "It looks like things are about to get interesting."

"Heydrich just briefed me, and I'm sure you'll receive a call from the Gestapo soon enough. Just wanted to give you a heads-up." He relayed his boss's instructions about not intervening with the expected unrest.

"I appreciate your call. I spoke to a friend at the festivities in Munich. He already received reports of unrest in smaller cities in

Bavaria. I'm sure it will spread to the larger cities soon, especially when Goebbels' speech is broadcast."

"Naturally." The newspapers had given the Jewish attack front page attention for the past two days. Besides constant updates on vom Rath's condition, they included plenty of opinions and analysis about the motives of the attack. None had served to temper the growing anger against the Jews of the Reich. "It could be the final push in taking away any doubts about the Jewish problem."

"It's already happening. Brownshirts are gathering all over town, and they're joined by many regular people." Globočnik spoke calmly, but there was purpose in his words. "From what I gather, they're preparing to march to Leopoldstadt."

"It's similar to the evening of the annexation."

"Yes, but with one big difference. We had planned most of what happened that night. This is the people responding to a murder of one of their own."

Karl smiled.

A knock on the door drew Karl's attention, and he placed his hand on the receiver while the same secretary that had come in earlier poked his head around the door.

"Sir, I'm sorry to bother you, but your presence is required upstairs."

"Huber?"

"Yes, sir. And Gruppenführer Müller. You're wanted urgently."

"I'm on my way." He dismissed the secretary, then took his hand off the receiver. "Odilo, things are moving along quickly here. I need to report to the chiefs upstairs." He couldn't contain the excitement in his voice.

"I'm sure I'll be hearing from them soon enough. This will be a historic night, Karl, mark my words."

Karl put down the receiver and stood, taking a brief moment to compose himself. As soon as he stepped into the meeting with the two most senior officials of the Sicherheitsdienst in Austria, there wouldn't be another moment to spare. Odilo was right: It would be a memorable night.

FORTY-FOUR

Vienna
9 November 1938, evening

The air on Stephansplatz was thick with tension. He was normally happy to cross the city's most central square, but today Felix kept close to shops lining the square. Men of all ages had gathered in groups beneath the towering spires of the majestic St. Stephen's Cathedral. Many wore the brown uniforms Felix had come to fear and despise, and he was keen to give them a wide birth.

He had gone into the city, despite his mother's protestations, to mail another pile of job applications. The man at the post office had been curt as he processed the envelopes marked for England. Felix had felt the energy change as soon as he crossed the Danube Channel, leaving the relative familiarity of Leopoldstadt behind for the Inner City district. News vendors on Schwedenplatz were hawking more special editions confirming the death of the German diplomat. Felix had considered turning back, but he had decided against it. Every day his applications remained unsent was a day lost. A feeling of impending doom had gnawed at him upon learning of the vom Rath's passing. The crowd at Stephansplatz confirmed his fears, and it proved to be just the tip of the iceberg.

The street connecting the city center to the Danube Channel, Rotenturmstraße, was backed up with cars and trucks honking their horns. More Brownshirts filled the sidewalks, their bloodshot eyes and vicious chants striking fear into Felix's heart. Blood and terror were in the air, so he dashed into one of the side streets and navigated his way to the Schwedenbrucke.

What he found there made him stop in his tracks. Streetcars were backed up as hundreds of people marched across the bridge, into Leopoldstadt. What shocked Felix most weren't the many Brownshirts, but the number of people without uniforms alongside them. Their faces were lined with the same bloodlust.

"Justice for vom Rath! *Juden Raus!* Out with the Jews!" Their chants bounced off the walls of the buildings on either side of the Danube Channel. They raised their fists, and Felix was dismayed to see many swinging crude weapons. More crowds emerged from the streets around Felix, and he was swept along by the masses. He kept his head down, fearing someone might recognize him.

The mob crossed the bridge, where they split, as one section continued farther north up Taborstraße. The other group moved along the channel heading west. Felix had no choice but to continue with the first group. It meant the crowd thinned somewhat, giving Felix more space to move. As he looked up, he witnessed the first stones sailing through the air. A moment later, the sound of shattering windows and broken glass hitting the cold pavement was everywhere. People whooped their encouragement, and more windows were smashed.

"Death to the Jews! Out with the traitors!"

The first looters made their way into a pharmacy, their victorious cries clear as they pillaged the store. Others took their cue and soon people—Brownshirts and regular Viennese—came running from stores, carrying whatever they could. A fight broke out between two groups of men as they entered a jewelry store at the same time.

Felix looked at the mayhem, frantically searching for some form of authority to restore order. It was in vain; the streets were taken over by the people. And they were on a mission. He realized he needed to get inside, and quickly.

Careful not to draw attention to himself, he walked down Taborstraße as quickly as he could, his head low, glass crunching underneath his feet. Every step brought him closer to home, and it was obvious the rioters were too focused on securing their bounty from the stores to care about Felix moving among them.

That changed when he cut through the district and had to cross Karmeliterplatz. The rioters had converged in the packed square. Felix wanted to bypass the square, but it was too busy, and he was sucked back into the mayhem. The scene was similar to what he'd witnessed along Taborstraße, glass littering the cobblestones. Not even the small market stalls had been safe from the violence, their windows smashed, canopies torn to shreds. But things were about to get worse.

Panicked screams sounded from across the square, and Felix couldn't help but look. What he saw filled his heart with terror. The rioters had broken into one of the apartment buildings, and they were dragging people onto the street. An elderly couple was struggling to keep up with the four young thugs pulling at their arms. The woman lost her footing, slipped, and crashed onto the ground. She let out a cry of pain, and her husband broke free from the two young men to help her up. Her skirt was ripped, and blood started to soak her stockings. She shook her head, indicating she was unable to get up. The thugs tried to pull her husband away from her, but he lashed out, hitting one of the young men square in the face. Felix's heart skipped a beat. The look on the older man's face showed he, too, realized his terrible mistake, for all the fight appeared to abandon him.

The thug needed no further encouragement as he rubbed his cheek, a glowering look on his face. He draw his arm back in a flash, then the sickening crunch confirmed his fist had connected—and broken—the elderly man's nose. He never stood a chance as he slumped to the ground. The other thugs descended on him, savagely kicking his head with their heavy boots. More gathered around;

some with the same bloodthirsty look in their eyes, as if they would like to join in, but most looked on with something perhaps even more terrifying: indifference.

The man on the ground was no longer moving. His wife's initial wails had stopped and turned into sobs as she retreated within herself. With the killing, the thugs thirst for blood appeared to have been sated, for now, and they moved away from the distraught woman. Felix wanted to comfort her, to help her, but the dead body less than ten meters away warned him to steer clear.

There was no time to recover, as shouts sounded from above.

"Move out of the way!"

The faces of two men appeared from an open window three stories up, waving their hands at the people below. They moved out of the way, clearing the area in front of the building. The men's faces disappeared, only to be replaced by the outline of what appeared to be a wooden cabinet in the window opening. It balanced on the windowsill, then it was pushed farther out for gravity to take control.

An instant later it landed on the square, wood splintering in a mighty crash. A cheer went up from the crowd, and soon more objects rained down from above. When there was a pause, men on the ground started piling up the shattered possessions. A few minutes later, the first fire roared on the square, its flames reflecting off the shattered glass on the ground. Soon, the spectacle was repeated in buildings all around the square. With the thugs entering more buildings and fires starting up, Felix decided he could no longer witness the destruction and hurried away.

He moved quickly through the side streets. Having spent his entire life in this district, he knew every nook and cranny, every shortcut through Leopoldstadt. *If I can get to the Augarten park, I might be able to get lost in the darkness.*

The smell of smoke and fire was everywhere. The night sky lit up bright orange, and Felix tried to block out the sounds of violence from every corner. But his mind didn't afford him that luxury, as the memory of the elderly man getting beaten to death kept returning to him. Felix felt cowardly for not stepping in to help him, but he also knew it would only have meant the same fate for him. The beating had subconsciously triggered memories of the atrocities he'd witnessed in Buchenwald, and his hands wouldn't stop shaking. His knees felt weak, but Felix clenched his teeth, not allowing himself to give in to the overwhelming feeling of despair. It would be easy to stop and sit for a moment, to give in to the crippling fear. But that would only attract attention. The will to survive, an instinct he'd honed to perfection in Buchenwald, was stronger than anything, and he forced himself forward.

He reached a crowded intersection. On the other side was the Augarten park, but one look made it clear passing through there wouldn't be an option. Brownshirts carrying torches, screaming and chanting the same vitriolic slurs that had become a constant background noise moved in and out of the park. There would be no hiding from the violence anywhere. Felix looked down the street running alongside the park's edge. His home was so close he could see the outlines of the building in the distance. He took a deep breath and gathered his courage. *One step at a time. Don't draw attention to yourself. Don't drop the rock.*

Felix was back in Buchenwald, the four-story apartment buildings transforming into the towering walls of the quarry. People passing him on the streets turned into the apparitions that surrounded him while he carried his heavy load to the cart. *One step at a time.* He was careful not to make eye contact with the kapos. He could see the cart ahead of him. *Almost there.*

"There's one! I know him!" The words cut through the cold evening air and instantly transported Felix back to the streets of Vienna. "It's Wolff!" Felix looked up to find four men blocking the sidewalk in front of him—each wore an SS uniform, and one was pointing a finger at Felix. "He's a Jew!"

Felix vaguely recognized the man's face, but he couldn't place him exactly. An odd deadlock ensued, where Felix's brain worked furiously to identify the man. It only lasted a few seconds.

"Get him!"

The SS men, spurred into action, dashed toward Felix, who turned and ran in the other direction. His hands were no longer shaking, his legs stronger than ever as adrenaline took over. The sounds of the street faded as he focused on his breathing. The steady rhythm gave him confidence, and he pushed himself harder. He didn't know where he was going, but he knew he had no choice but to keep running.

The voices of the men chasing him sounded distant, the pounding of their boots on the pavement mere distractions as he forced himself to keep looking ahead, not back. He was vaguely aware of more voices joining the existing ones then abruptly turned into a narrow alley. If he could get over the fence, he could escape.

The fence was only twenty meters down the alley, and his vision narrowed, the walls of the buildings enclosing the alley blurring. *Keep going.* The voices of his pursuers echoed along the walls, appearing closer than they were. Ten meters to go, and he spurred himself on, the muscles in his legs now protesting.

Five meters, and Felix could almost touch the fence. He prepared to jump and mount the fence, his hands tingling, his stomach clenched.

He crashed into the fence, but not how he'd expected. A moment later, his body slammed onto the cold pavement, and a heavy force crushed all air from his lungs.

FORTY-FIVE

Berlin, Germany
11 November 1938

Two days after the night that shook the Reich, Karl was back in Berlin. The night of the pogrom that spread across the cities of Germany like a wildfire had been hectic and, quite frankly, unbelievable. Unrest and rioting up to a certain extent was expected, but the widespread wave of violence that washed over the Reich was beyond anyone's expectations.

During his meeting with Huber and Müller in the Hotel Metropole, they had received additional instructions from Heydrich in Munich. Businesses and apartments belonging to Jews were to be destroyed but not looted. Foreigners were not to be harmed, be they Jewish or not. But the most important order was saved for last. As many healthy male Jews as could be accommodated in the prisons were to be arrested, with a special focus on affluent ones. These men would then be transported to various concentration camps.

It was this particular order that Karl had found most interesting. The rioting had gone off the rails during the night, with thousands of Jewish businesses destroyed and looted. The fires enveloping the homes and synagogues painted the skies of Germany's cities a fiery orange and red. Heydrich had sent a late-night telegram ordering all looters to be arrested immediately, but by then it was already too late. Karl had witnessed the devastation firsthand as he assisted the Gestapo in the execution of what he considered Heydrich's most important order.

Despite the destruction's economic damage to the Reich, the riots had provided the perfect cover to pick the Jewish men up from their homes. An early estimate from Vienna's overcrowded prisons suggested more than four thousand Jewish men had been arrested during the night now referred to as *Kristallnacht*, a reference to the broken glass littering the sidewalks of every street in the country. Karl was keen to learn how his colleagues across the Reich had fared, and he knew just who to check in with now that he was in the Sicherheitsdienst's headquarters.

"Well, well, well, if it isn't the legendary Karl Vogt!" The tall man stood and moved from his desk to embrace Karl in a brotherly manner. "What brings you to Berlin?"

"Max, it's good to see you." Karl didn't see much of one of his few true friends in Berlin. More often than not, Max Vogel operated in the field, much like Karl. It was a rarity for both men to be in the Berlin offices. "What have you been up to?"

Max pointed to a chair while he sank back in his own comfortable seat. "I've spent more time in the office than I'd like, if I'm being honest. With people like you running around Austria and the Sudetenland, some of us need to look after the shop." He grinned cheekily.

"I'm sure you'll manage to talk your way out of the office just fine."

"No, I'm serious. Heydrich has me working on a lot of policy documents these days. Says I know what it's like out there, so he pairs me with some of the administrators." Max pulled a face.

Karl couldn't suppress a grin. "Doesn't sound like something you'd enjoy."

"I didn't, at first. I thought it was just pencil pushing. But then I saw the policies implemented in the real world. You work with Eichmann in Vienna, don't you?"

"Sure, not as much as before, but I helped him with some of the first deportations." Karl made a mental note to check in with Eichmann when he returned to Vienna.

"He's a bright guy. Asked me to look into ways to expand his Central Office policies across the Reich a while ago. You can imagine my delight at recent developments. This has put my work front and center with the leadership. I had Heydrich in my office twice since Kristallnacht."

"Sounds like you're making a nice transition into becoming an administrator."

"Hey, I work where I'm needed! But you didn't answer my question. What are you here for?"

"Summons from the boss. I'm not sure he's too happy about how Goebbels' pogrom turned out." Karl summarized the phone call, meeting with the Gestapo chiefs, and Heydrich's late-night telegram. "He's at Göring's conference about the future of Jewish policy today, but I imagine I'll be speaking with him tomorrow."

"On the positive side, Huber and Müller are responsible for the security forces in Austria. You were merely assisting. You'll focus on the number of arrests, won't you?"

"Of course, but I'm sure he'll vent about the damages to the economy because of the looting."

"Well, he's right, no arguing with that. And again, it's not your fault."

"True. About those arrests. Did you hear anything about the number in Germany?"

Max shrugged. "There's all sorts of figures going around. One day it's twenty thousand, the next it's double that. I'm sure the truth is somewhere in the middle. Safe to say, though, it's a lot." He checked his watch. "Say, what are your plans for the evening?"

"No plans. I just need to read some reports before my meeting with Heydrich tomorrow."

Max got up and grabbed his coat. "Perfect. Let's head into town and catch up. My treat."

Karl was led into Heydrich's office early the next morning. He was pleased with his decision to go back to his hotel early and not follow Max into the capital's nightlife. To his surprise, the director of the Sicherheitsdienst was already at his desk, going through a file. He seemed remarkably rested as he looked up to greet Karl with a curt nod.

"Vogt, have a seat. Good to see you. Coffee?" He snapped his fingers and the secretary that accompanied Karl almost jumped, and he dashed to a side table to pour Karl a cup. Karl sat down and waited while his boss scratched some markings on the sheet of paper in front of him. The secretary set down his cup and he nodded his thanks. Heydrich closed the folder and placed it to the side.

"Well, there's much to discuss. I think we can agree the people's retribution turned into quite a disaster." He didn't wait for Karl's response. "Reichsmarschall Göring and I are in agreement that the economic damage is unacceptable. We're looking at several hundred million Reichsmarks. At the end of the day, someone needs to pay for this."

"Naturally, sir." Karl had an idea where this was going.

"It's only fair that the instigators of this injustice are held accountable. After careful consideration and numerous discussions at the conference yesterday, I convinced the Reichsmarschall of the value of expanding Eichmann's Central Office setup to the rest of the Reich. It will expedite the expulsion of Jews everywhere, and we can claim the damage of Kristallnacht from them. It's only proper."

"Sounds about right to me, sir." Karl marveled at his boss's quick thinking. No, he corrected himself, this hadn't been a spur-of-the-moment thing Heydrich had come up with at the conference. He'd been very involved in the early days of the Central Office in Vienna and had constantly requested feedback on its functioning. It was no coincidence that Max—whom Karl knew was one of Heydrich's brightest agents—had been assigned to the project. Heydrich had been preparing for this moment, and Kristallnacht had given him the perfect opportunity to push the policy. "Would you like me to return to Vienna to assist Eichmann?"

"Not exactly, Vogt. You've done enough in Vienna." Heydrich raised his coffee cup and slowly took a sip. Karl felt his brow dampen, and Heydrich must've sensed his anxiety, for he shook his head. "I mean that in the best way possible. I don't blame you for what happened during Kristallnacht. Between you and me, that's mostly on Goebbels. He incited the crowd in Munich, and called for retribution, but even he couldn't have expected this response." Heydrich shrugged. "Or maybe he did. Either way, it didn't turn out the way he wanted, I understand."

"How so, sir?" Karl asked carefully. He didn't want to get involved in top-level politics, but Heydrich's forthright mood intrigued him. It wasn't often his boss confided in him like this.

"After the speech in Munich, he was going around the room, making sure as many of those present relayed his message. At the meeting yesterday, he was trying to claim Kristallnacht as a victory for the party, saying it showed the people's true feelings about the Jews. Göring didn't like that tone, stressing the economic damage of the night. It was as much of a dressing down as you'd ever witness at that level."

"And that's when you suggested expanding the Central Office approach." The pieces were falling into place, and despite Heydrich's casual recollection of the meeting, it confirmed Karl's earlier suspicions: He had planned this.

"Yes, and that's where you come in. You're better informed about the workings of the Central Office than anyone in this building. And your preparations prior to the annexation of the Sudetenland didn't go unnoticed."

Heydrich paused briefly, and Karl's mind went back to that afternoon when the Führer had acknowledged him personally. A burst of excitement shot through his body, and he held his breath as Heydrich continued.

"I'm sure you've seen the way the people of the Sudetenland have responded to joining the Reich. It makes little sense to leave the rest of Czechoslovakia withering away under weak leadership.

Although nothing has been decided officially yet, I'm making preparations for the day that happens. I want you to travel ahead."

"Like in Vienna and the Sudetenland."

"Yes, but with one big difference. You'll be the agent on the ground, but you'll have a large team at your disposal. You won't be operating on your own as much as you're used to."

Karl was surprised. He had always excelled at working alone. "Where will this team be based?"

"Initially, here in Berlin. But you'll need to prepare for a large part of them moving to Prague when the country becomes part of the Reich." Heydrich must've seen some of the confusion on Karl's face. "Don't worry, you'll still be running your own operation, but you'll need help. In Austria, you had the advantage of tapping into an established network of party members. That you were so successful was still very much to your credit, but Prague hands us a completely new challenge. We have a good number of existing connections and a small number of prominent members of the community who support further annexation, but you'll find more opponents. Especially in government positions."

"You need me to smoke them out."

Heydrich smiled. "Let's start with identifying them first. Get the lay of the land, see who will stand with us in a possible conflict, and who poses a threat. Do what you always do, build your network."

"Sir, with all due respect, I appreciate having support in Berlin, but what you're describing sounds like something I'm perfectly able to carry out on my own, reporting back to you."

"Yes. But there's one more thing you need to do." Heydrich scratched his chin. "Apart from the obvious threats in power, I need you to document all smaller threats as well."

"Smaller threats?"

"I don't want a repeat of Kristallnacht, ever. And the best way to ensure that is to take away the cause."

"The Jews."

"The country, and Prague especially, is rife with them. I want a list of all Jews, with as many details as you can obtain. The people back in Berlin will make all preparations, guided by your knowledge and experience on the ground. Eichmann will be consulted as well. We'll have all preparations for a Central Office prepared before we set a foot in Czechoslovakia."

Karl had trouble containing his joy at the assignment. Of course he'd heard the rumors of an impending invasion of Czechoslovakia. But he never expected his boss to place him at the forefront. "I'm honored to take the assignment, sir."

"I didn't expect anything else." Heydrich got up, signaling the end of the meeting. As Karl saluted him and turned for the door, the Gruppenführer cleared his throat and said, "One more thing, Vogt. You report to me, and me alone. Consider the entire apparatus of the Sicherheitsdienst and Gestapo at your disposal."

"Understood, sir."

As he stepped into the hallway, the door closing behind him, he exhaled deeply. The magnitude of the mission was slowly dawning on him. He wasn't just an agent in the Sicherheitsdienst anymore. He was Reinhard Heydrich's right-hand man in Czechoslovakia.

FORTY-SIX

Vienna
13 November 1938

More than forty men had been packed together for four days, and with no way to wash themselves, the smell of sweat and other human odors made it difficult to breathe inside the prison cell. When the door opened, a cool breeze brought immediate relief from the thick air inside. Felix, like those around him, took a deep breath that tasted as sweet as he could ever remember.

"All of you, out! One by one, and form an orderly line in the hallway," a bulky guard's deep voice thundered through the cell, and the prisoners got to their feet. Anything would be better than staying in the overcrowded cell a minute longer. "When you pass by, clearly state your name. Don't make me ask you twice."

The cell was cleared within two minutes, and Felix soon found himself escorted up the stairs and through the labyrinth of the prison. As he slowly moved closer to the surface, the air warmer with every step, he recalled his arrival four nights earlier.

He'd returned to consciousness as he was bundled into a truck filled with other men. He recognized a few from the district, but nobody was foolish enough to start a conversation. They acknowledged each other with solemn nods, then rested their gazes on the wooden boards that served as the truck's floor. Felix didn't remember how long they'd sat there, with more men getting loaded onto the flatbed, but when they finally moved, they raced through a city that appeared on fire. The smell of smoke was everywhere, and even from their limited perspective from the open back of the truck, raging fires lit up the dark Vienna sky.

Soon after they arrived at the prison, the group was herded down into large holding cells. Felix spent the rest of the night uncomfortably standing on his feet, jostling for space with the men pushing against him. It wasn't until the next day that they were processed and placed in only slightly more spacious cells. At least they could sit back to back. And in this cell he remained, the monotony interrupted only when the guards brought water and stale bread once a day. The worst was not knowing what would happen next.

Felix reached the top of the stairs, and an icy breeze shocked him back to his senses. He followed the man in front of him toward the open door that led into the prison's yard. Expecting a roll call, Felix was surprised to find a row of trucks lined up instead. Felix and the group were bundled inside, with only a few guards providing additional motivation in the form of their batons. Soon enough, the trucks rolled through the prison gates and into the quiet Vienna streets.

The drive was short, and this time, the destination provided little surprise. He was at Westbahnhof train station, and the situation as Felix disembarked the truck was eerily similar, although everything seemed bigger than the last time he made this journey. More people watched from behind a larger cordon of SS troopers. Most looked on with morbid interest, but others shouted obscenities at the prisoners as they were harried toward a side entrance. There was only a hundred meters between the road and the entrance, but Felix felt the force of the crowd as they pelted them with all sorts of vitriol.

"Off with you, leeches!"

"You'll finally do some actual work!"

"Jew pigs!"

"Enjoy Dachau! Die!"

Felix made the mistake of looking up and saw a boy at the front of the crowd. He couldn't be older than twelve, if even that. His eyes were fixed on Felix, and while his words were drowned out in the wave of noise, the hatred shone brightly in his eyes, as if the devil himself had taken control. Felix quickly looked away, his heart beating faster as he moved forward, mindful to avoid the attention of the men in uniform wielding sticks and cudgels.

A whistling sound close to his ears made Felix pause. The man walking next to him let out a sharp, surprised shriek, and this was followed by a dull thud as he collapsed onto the ground. Blood poured from a large gash on the side of his head. A large rock lay a meter away. The man didn't move, his eyes staring lifelessly into the afternoon sky.

Felix looked up and was dismayed to see more rocks sailing in their direction. All but one missed their mark, as another man went down a little farther along the cordon. The guards appeared unconcerned, and Felix had to keep moving and get inside the train station as quickly as possible.

He upped his pace, and at that moment something changed in the crowd beyond the cordon. People turned their faces, their interest piqued by something more interesting than the prisoners heading into the station. The shouting intensified, and the barrage of rocks stopped. Felix slowed down, craning his neck to see what was happening on the square.

Suddenly, the cordon of guards stumbled back, as if pushed by an invisible force, constricting the perimeter near Felix. The crowd moved as one to get out of the way of something. A few seconds later, the guards turned their attention to the threat coming from outside their cordon. A fight between two groups had broken out, and it was moving toward the cordon. Not wanting to be caught up in the struggle, the bystanders rushed to get out of the way. In Felix's direction. With the guards distracted, the flow of prisoners toward the station stopped, as everyone watched to see how this would end.

Seemingly in a flash, the fighting mob reached the row of guards. The inexperienced SS troopers did not react in time and were overwhelmed by the force of bodies crashing into them. Their ranks broke, and the fight spilled into the now-sundered cordon. Felix was in the middle of it, and he ducked and backed away as best he could. He moved and wriggled, catching a stray punch here and there.

Suddenly, he found himself on the outside of the fight, among the people fleeing from the station. He didn't look back, moving along with the men, women, and children hurrying in the direction of Mariahilfer Straße, the city's largest shopping street. His temples pounded, blocking the sound of his surroundings, and his throat felt bone dry. He continued at a steady but measured pace, expecting a blow from a guard watching him escape.

None of that happened as he left the unrest of Westbahnhof behind and joined the crowd of shoppers. Despite the many boarded-up windows, there were still plenty of shops open, while others were under repair by their new Aryan owners. When Felix reached the intersection with Zieglergasse, some two hundred meters into the main shopping street, he deemed it safe enough to stop and turn.

The crowd eventually began thinning as the SS regained control of the situation. There wasn't a trace of any troopers in pursuit. No time to waste. Felix kept a brisk pace as he made his way down the street, toward the Ringstraße.

Fifteen minutes later, he boarded a tram headed toward Leopoldstadt. It wasn't until the doors closed and he was whisked past the Volkstheater that his heartbeat returned to something resembling normal.

HE REACHED his apartment building half an hour later, after walking the last part through the Augarten park. Half expecting Gestapo or SS thugs to be lying in wait for him, he carefully slipped inside, pricking his ears for any unusual sounds in the hallway as he stalked upstairs. He almost tiptoed to his front door and listened for any voices. When he was confident no one was waiting for him inside, he opened the door.

"Felix!" His mother's cry startled him as she appeared at the other end of the hallway and rushed toward him. "I thought you were gone!" She threw her arms around him, gripping him so tightly he had trouble breathing. "What happened to you?"

Rebecca's glistening eyes triggered his own tears to surface, and he took a moment to compose himself while they entered the living room. His mother rushed to the stove and put a kettle on, then turned back to him, looking at him expectingly. He took a seat and recounted the events of the past days.

"But I can't stay here any longer. They'll find out I'm missing soon enough, if they haven't by now. This will be the first place they'll come."

"Where will you go?" She placed a mug of tea in front of him, and he warmed his hands. A feeling of restlessness overcame him as his own words sank in. He jumped to his feet and headed for his bedroom.

"I'm putting you in danger with every minute that I'm in this house." He bent down, opened a drawer, and stuffed underwear and socks in a small bag. Where would he go? There was only one place he could think of. He looked up at his mother standing in the doorway on the verge of breaking down, her lip quivering. His heart broke seeing her like that. She had gone through enough, and now he had to leave her yet again.

He got to his feet and put his arms around her. "I'm sorry, Mama. But I think it's better if I don't tell you where I'm going. The Nazis will be on your doorstep soon, and the less you know, the better."

"I know, Felix." Rebecca Wolff's voice was weak, the words coming through without conviction. "Just promise me one thing. Do whatever you must to survive. And don't worry about me. I'll be fine."

Felix put his hands to her face, wiping away tears as he did. "I will. And when it's safe, I will let you know where I am. You will hear from me, Mama, no matter what." He hoped he could keep his promise, but he could offer her nothing more.

He put some more clothes in the bag, then moved to the front door. Felix placed his hand on the doorknob and listened for any sounds outside. He looked back to his mother, who stood in the doorway to the living room. She looked frail, but her eyes showed determination.

"Stay safe, Felix. I will always be here, waiting."

Battling the tears burning in his eyes, he swallowed hard. It did nothing to move the lump caught in his throat. He inclined his head as he turned the doorknob. "I'll see you soon, Mama."

He stepped outside, his heart heavy from making a promise he doubted he could keep.

"I DON'T WANT to put you in danger."

Felix had gone straight to his best friend's home. He realized his presence was a risk to them, but he had no other place to go. He couldn't think of a better man to turn to than Wolfgang's father.

"We'll look after you for as long as we can, but you're right. You can't stay in the city, and certainly not here. If the Nazis are intent on tracking you down, they'll find out about your friendship eventually." Leo Klein brushed his beard and looked at his son. "You'll need to take Felix to the house at Neusiedlersee. It won't be comfortable, but that's also an advantage. There will be very few people around: no tourists, and certainly no Nazis."

Lake Neusiedl was about an hour's drive from Vienna, on the border with Hungary. Felix had been at the Klein's lake house before. It was unassuming and, more importantly, detached, with a large yard. He liked the idea of hiding there, even if it would be especially quiet.

Wolfgang looked out the window. "It's too late to go now. We'll be stopped the instant we step off the train in Neusiedl. Better to travel tomorrow morning."

"Felix, do you mind spending a night in the basement? We'll

bring you some extra blankets to stay warm." Though Wolfgang's father phrased his words as a question, only one answer was acceptable.

"Of course. I'm grateful for your help."

Leo Klein nodded, then looked thoughtful. "Your stay at the lake house is a temporary solution. We're leaving for America in four weeks, so we can look after you until then. But you can't be seen coming and going from the house. I don't trust the neighbors."

Wolfgang raised an eyebrow. "You look like you've got something on your mind, Papa."

"We need a more permanent solution. Leaving the city is a good start, but the reality is that you're not safe anywhere in Austria. You need to leave the country."

"I've still got my passport." Felix patted his pocket. "But that's little use now. Even if I managed to get a positive response from England, I'll still need to go through the Central Office. That's impossible now." He had no doubt his disappearance from Westbahnhof made him a marked man.

"There might be another way, but it's extremely dangerous, and by no means certain to get you out."

Felix sat up in his chair. "What is it?" Staying put in Austria felt like a terrible risk as it was, bringing danger to anyone harboring him. With the Nazis actively hunting him, he couldn't imagine Mr. Klein's idea being more dangerous. "I'll do anything."

Leo Klein sat back in his chair and folded his arms. He looked hard at Felix, as if weighing up his options. Felix felt self-conscious, but forced himself to hold Leo's stare. After a minute, the older man nodded.

"Very well. I'll reach out to some people. You'll go to the lake house first, and wait. Once I'm confident this is the right path for you, we'll come and get you."

PART THREE

FORTY-SEVEN

Prague
3 March 1939

Adela reached the street on the outskirts of the city a few minutes before ten in the morning. She focused on walking at a normal pace, and she kept her trembling hands in the pockets of her spring jacket. It was a street like any other, and she casually walked on, scanning the house numbers until she arrived at a nondescript house at number 25. Her eyes scanned the street behind her one last time. Certain that she wasn't followed, she entered the perfectly kept front yard and reached the front door. Adela knocked twice, waited, then quickly rapped her knuckles another three times. *Some password.*

The door opened a second later, and Adela quickly entered the dark hallway. She didn't recognize the man who nodded at her, but it was clear he knew who she was.

"They're in the upstairs master bedroom." He signaled up the staircase, and Adela took it two steps at a time. The upstairs hallway was dark, but light filtered from one of the open doors, and Adela entered. Inside, four men hovered around a table, two of them familiar.

"Hana, glad you're here." František Moravec, using her cover name, moved to take her jacket. "Please have a seat."

From across the room, Dieter stood and inclined his head. "It's good to see you again."

"It's been quite a while," Adela answered while she moved to join them at the table. Her eyes went to the two unfamiliar young men, waiting for Moravec to introduce them. He didn't, instead signaling to their German agent.

"Dieter sent word last night, indicating an urgent meeting was required. That's why we're all here." He looked at Adela with his piercing eyes. "He insisted on your presence."

Adela looked to Dieter, and she thought she detected a barely visible smile. It vanished as quickly as it appeared, but she couldn't help but return the gesture, her eyes sparkling. She wouldn't admit it to anyone, but she had been pleasantly surprised when the messenger bearing Moravec's last-minute summons arrived on her doorstep the evening prior. The night had been restless, her mind churning with possibilities. In the end, she'd fallen asleep convinced Dieter had returned from the dead.

For months, it seemed like Dieter had fallen off the face of the earth. Moravec and Adela had assumed he'd lost interest in working with them, the fate of the doomed Czechoslovakia sealed. The touch of the German agents was felt everywhere in Czech life, but nowhere quite as keenly as at Adela's place of work. German-speaking aides appeared in the hallways, and Adela understood Dieter's reluctance to collaborate. It placed him in direct danger; especially since Moravec had openly admitted he didn't know who to trust in the government. He'd confided to Adela that even his own organization wasn't safe from outside infiltration. But looking across the table, it heartened Adela to see Dieter hadn't abandoned them. Despite that, she had no doubt the urgency of his request to meet signaled the importance of his message.

Dieter stood, the solemn look on his face confirming Adela's suspicions. The tension in the room heightened as he opened his mouth. "I'm afraid I have some grave news to report, but in light of our cooperation these past years, I deemed it essential to meet." He looked directly at Moravec, then at Adela. "The plans for the invasion of Czechoslovakia have been finalized. Our armies will invade in eleven days, on 15 March."

News that Czechoslovakia would cease to exist as an independent country was met without surprise by all present. Adela felt no shock at Dieter's words, but an odd form of acceptance of the inevitable. The threat of Hitler's invasion had hung above their heads for so long, it was almost a relief to learn the sword would soon fall on them.

"Four army corps will enter the western stump of Czechoslovakia at dawn on 15 March. They will push through Bohemia and Moravia to arrive in Prague by midmorning. Then they will split, and half of the army will continue toward Brno." Dieter spoke with finality and full conviction. "At the same time, Slovakia will declare independence, accepting protection from the Reich."

Adela gasped. The invasion from the west was expected, but Slovakia turning its back on the country was not. Her eyes shot to Moravec, who looked oddly calm, as if nothing Dieter was reporting was news to him. Then she realized it made perfect sense. Rumblings about Slovak independence had been growing in recent months, but Adela never considered them credible.

"Hitler will demand Slovak independence to fracture our country," Moravec said, looking at Dieter. "It will be nothing more than a Nazi puppet state, won't it?"

The German agent nodded. "If the Slovak parliament doesn't give in to Hitler's demands, he will divide the country between Hungary, Poland, and the rest of Czechoslovakia. It's an ultimatum, there's no choice." He paused, then continued. "There's one more thing. We're expecting this to be a bloodless invasion, much like in Austria. Your president will be informed at the very last moment, and given no choice in the matter." Dieter chuckled dryly, humorlessly. "If he does choose to resist, it will come at a terrible price to the Czech population."

Dieter didn't have to expand on those words. Everybody in the room knew the Czechoslovak army was in no shape to mount a significant defense. That opportunity had passed when the German army was allowed to march into the Sudetenland unopposed five months ago. The new government had demobilized most of the army, focusing its efforts on appeasing Hitler.

"There's one more thing you need to see." Dieter handed a document to Moravec. "This is the original order from the Gestapo directing their agents to arrest all Czechoslovak intelligence officers following the invasion. You'll agree from the wording that there is little doubt as to how they will be treated."

Moravec's eyes scanned the document. "They'll be tortured to reveal the identities and whereabouts of our agents operating within the Reich." He handed the document to Adela.

"How will you evade the Gestapo?" Dieter focused keenly on Moravec.

"We have some things planned."

"If those things involve leaving the country, may I suggest avoiding France?" Adela looked up from the sheet of paper. Had Dieter just revealed France as Hitler's next target? "But it doesn't matter. Wherever you go, I will find you."

For the first time, Dieter's words caught Moravec off guard. The head of military intelligence raised an eyebrow. "You want to continue working together, even when my country has fallen?"

"You're well connected within Europe's intelligence networks. I believe my information will continue to be valuable to your allies. The fall of Czechoslovakia is just the start." Dieter spoke without hesitation, his confidence unnerving but completely in character.

"But why do you care?"

"As I've stated before, I still believe a large-scale war across the continent can be avoided. It's too late for Czechoslovakia, but with your influence and my intelligence, we have a chance to stop this madness."

Adela wasn't quite as optimistic. France and Great Britain hadn't acted on their intelligence before, and she doubted they would see the danger before it was too late. She hoped she was wrong.

"Very well." Moravec scribbled down two addresses and handed them to Dieter. "These are safe houses in the Netherlands and Switzerland that can facilitate communication."

Dieter carefully folded the piece of paper and stuffed it in his jacket. "I have one more request before I leave, Colonel, if you don't mind."

"Of course."

"Would you do me the courtesy of making sure that anything that could expose me isn't left behind?"

Moravec nodded gravely. "We've taken precautions for the scenario you described. Rest assured your invading countrymen won't find a trace of our cooperation."

"I thank you, and I wish you good luck. This is not goodbye, but *Auf Wiedersehen*." Dieter moved to the door and, as he turned the handle, looked back to Adela. She caught only a glimpse of his eyes, but it told her everything she needed to know. His promise was true. They would meet again.

FORTY-EIGHT

Prague
7 March 1939, morning

A weak spring sun provided some warmth as Karl waited for the traffic light to change. He closed his eyes for a moment, savoring the rays hitting his face, listening to a streetcar clattering by. He'd quickly become used to the sounds of the city, and he couldn't help but admit the Czech capital had grown on him.

It had been almost four months since Heydrich had assigned him to Czechoslovakia, and his boss hadn't exaggerated about the mission being something new. From the moment he touched down in Prague he realized the Czech people would pose a challenge. They were wary and suspicious of foreigners, especially German-speaking ones like himself. It meant Karl spent much of his first month intensively learning the language. As his Czech proficiency improved, so did the city's sometimes downright hostile atmosphere. He practiced at every opportunity in shops, bars, and cafes, always keen to strike up a conversation.

At the same time, he made contact with the German-speaking

community in the capital. The Sicherheitsdienst had given him a list of local contacts, warning him he might have limited success tracking these people down. Karl had taken it in stride but found their warning depressingly accurate. It only made him more determined to build up his own network, and he took it as further motivation to prove Heydrich he'd sent the right man into Prague.

The traffic lights changed and Karl crossed, turning onto Wenceslas Square. He merged into the crowd of shoppers, listening in on conversations. It pleased him that he could follow along, understanding nearly everything that was said. The square was one of his favorite places to practice his Czech; lined with shops and theaters, it was always lively and provided him with plenty of people in the right mindset to have a casual conversation.

He moved away from the square and navigated the narrow, winding streets in Nové Město, the city's inner district. Karl no longer needed to look at the street names; he knew this area like the back of his hand, and he soon reached a small bar tucked away in a corner. It was one of those places that you could pass by every day for years and never notice. Perfect for Karl's purpose.

The door jammed a little, and Karl pushed harder. The place was empty but for the barkeeper barely acknowledging him from behind a row of tap handles, and a solitary man sitting at a table in the back. Karl ignored the barkeep and went straight to the other man, who looked up from a newspaper and smiled when he saw Karl approach.

"Right on time as always." The man greeted him in German with a thick Czech accent. "I think you're going to be pleased with what I have."

"Can't wait to hear it. I could use some good news." Despite his Germanic name, Leopold was born and raised in Prague's Holešovice district. His simple working class background was evident in everything he did, and Karl liked him the moment they met.

Leopold reached for a bag on the seat next to him and produced a thin envelope, sliding it across the table. "I received this from my source in the castle last evening." His eyes were glimmering. "I'm sure you'll find it very useful."

Karl opened the envelope, revealing four pages of neatly typed out names. "Where did you get this exactly?" His eyes grew wide when he noted some of the departments and positions of the people listed.

"I can't reveal my source, but let's just say they're placed pretty high up." Leopold sounded a little smug.

"And you're certain this is accurate?" Karl tore his eyes away from the list to focus on Leopold. If this was genuine, it was an incredible piece of intelligence.

The man across from him lifted an eyebrow. "Are you questioning my work?" There was a trace of hostility in his voice. "I didn't get to where I am by providing shit intelligence, you know? I'm good for it, and so are my sources. This is real."

Karl realized his mistake and held up his hands. "I'm sorry, I just didn't expect this." He tapped the small pile of paper. "I haven't had my hands on this many names since arriving."

"Some will be happy to work with you, others not so much." Leopold leaned forward and placed his finger on the last column. "This shows their dedication to the cause, as judged by my source. As you can see, quite a few of them would join the cause as a matter of principle, while others would need some motivation." He smiled, revealing crooked teeth. "Then there's also the group I marked as troublesome. I'm sure you'll find a way to deal with them."

Karl nodded, still overwhelmed by the wealth of information at his fingertips. When Leopold reached out to him the evening prior, he had expected some names, but nothing like this list. He couldn't wait to send it to his team in Berlin and have them investigate these individuals in more detail. For now, Leopold's insistence the list was real gave him confidence.

"This is great work." Karl slid the sheets back into the envelope, placing it safely inside his jacket pocket. "I don't think I need to tell you this will greatly strengthen your career prospects in the near future."

"Happy to assist." Despite the man's cool response, the greed in his eyes was impossible to miss. Karl had no problem with that; people were driven by different motives, and it was up to him to find the best way to motivate them. If the information proved correct, Karl was happy to put in a good word for Leopold.

"How are you progressing with the other list?" Karl asked almost casually, but following Leopold's response closely.

"I've got a few of my subordinates working on it. They're making sure the information is accurate, but there's quite a few more names to look into, so it might take a bit longer."

"When can you have it ready?"

Leopold hesitated, his eyes shifting before he responded. "In two weeks."

"I need it sooner." Karl's tone was harsh for the first time. "Put more people on it. This is as important as the document you provided today."

"We don't want to attract the wrong attention. I need to keep this under wraps. Involving more people might expose us," Leopold responded firmly, and Karl decided not to push any harder.

"The sooner I have it, the better. Provide it in parts, and send the information when it's ready."

Leopold nodded in understanding. "That's reasonable. I can do that." He stood, revealing a holstered pistol strapped to one hip, and handcuffs dangling on the other. "I should return to the station and speed things up. I know of a few officers who could use some extra money."

The hint couldn't be any clearer, and Karl produced a thick envelope of his own. "This should help."

Leopold glanced inside and nodded appreciatively. "It will, indeed. I'll be in touch." He put the envelope in his bag and moved from the table, the squeaking of the door confirming his departure from the bar a few seconds later. Karl hardly noticed, a wide grin appearing on his face as he scanned the pages once more. Heydrich would be pleased.

FORTY-NINE

Prague
7 March 1939, afternoon

F elix wiped the large counter top and checked the clock. Almost three in the afternoon—they'd finished cleaning early. He removed his apron and shook the flour off, judging it clean enough for another day's work before hanging it on the rack in the corner. The other bakers had already changed into their regular clothes as he took off his overalls.

"Are you still coming over for dinner tonight, Felix?" Gerhard Löwy spoke in his thick Viennese accent, reminding Felix of home. "Ida is cooking her famous *cholent*."

"I wouldn't miss it for the world." Felix enjoyed speaking in his native tongue with Gerhard who, along with his wife Ida, was Felix's only Austrian connection in Prague. Whenever the other bakers were around, they spoke Czech, which Felix picked up remarkably quickly. "I just need to run a few errands, but I'll be there around five, if that works for you?"

"Absolutely. We'll have everything ready by then. Perhaps we'll even have time for a drink before dinner." He put on his coat and waved as he walked to the door. "The girls are also coming."

Felix put on his regular clothes and was the last to leave the bakery. He turned off the lights, then went through the shop in the front, greeting colleagues still selling bread to the last patrons of the day.

Stepping out into the street, the crisp air on his face made him relax. Felix enjoyed working in the bakery, stepping into the warm, oven-filled room from the early morning cold, but it was equally satisfying to step into the fresh air after his workday. It was quiet for the time of the day as he ventured farther into the inner city, stopping to get a bottle of red wine for his hosts tonight. He was looking forward to the evening; he'd mostly kept to himself after arriving in Prague some three months ago, but he liked Gerhard's family. Ida was a lovely woman who always spoiled him with her cooking. Together with their niece and her best friend, the Löwy family had really made him feel at home.

With plenty of time before dinner he decided to take a detour along the Vltava River en route to his small apartment. The area was quiet, with only a few other people strolling along the waterfront. The smell of the river reminded him of the Danube River in Vienna, and his mind wandered to his home in Leopoldstadt. His mother's face appeared, and he felt a pang of guilt, as he always did. Rebecca Wolff was on his mind every day, and he missed her terribly. Worse, he cursed himself for not trying harder to convince her to come to Czechoslovakia with him when the opportunity arose in December.

Felix had spent almost three weeks in the lake house in Neusiedl before Wolfgang's father came in one morning. After apologizing that it had taken a while, he explained he'd spoken to friends who'd fled to Czechoslovakia after the Anschluss. They were willing to take Felix in and help him find his feet. The only condition was that he would need to make his own way to Prague. Fortunately, the couple had crossed the border illegally themselves, and they had shared their route with Leo Klein.

There had been no hesitation in Felix's mind. The walls of the lake house were rapidly closing in on him, and he cherished the chance to build a new life up north. Most of all, he was tired of looking over his shoulder all the time.

He had once again packed his small bag and, before leaving, called his mother. The Gestapo were no longer knocking on her door every other night, hoping to catch Felix, but she worried they might one day find out where he was hiding. When he asked if she would come with him, her response had been unsurprisingly resolute. Vienna was her home.

Wolfgang's father had taken him to the train station, and together they rode north, changing trains in Vienna before stepping off the train at Laa an der Thaya, near the Czechoslovak border. This is where Leo Klein handed him a few hundred koruna and said his farewells, and Felix was on his own. When night fell, he stepped into the darkness of the nearby woods, and he crossed into Czechoslovakia a few hours later. The next morning, he boarded a train for Prague, where he found Gerhard and Ida's flat in the afternoon.

He smiled at the memory as he picked up a pebble and skimmed it at the river. It skipped once before disappearing into one of the gentle waves. He looked at the castle and the St. Vitus Cathedral, a view that he never tired of. The spires of the cathedral reminded him of St. Stephen's Cathedral in Vienna. It gave him an odd form of comfort, as did many of the buildings in Prague.

The sun was rapidly disappearing behind the horizon, reminding him of his evening plans. He headed back into the city, to his very small apartment, to change into more suitable clothes for dinner.

The small but cozy Löwy living room was filled with guests when Felix arrived a little before five. He handed the bottle to Ida, then smiled when their niece Greta rose from her chair to give him a hug.

"Felix, so good to see you. My uncle tells me you're doing well in the bakery."

"I'm allowed to do more than just rolling out dough these days. They're letting me cut some of the cookies as well." He smiled and took a step toward Greta's best friend, her sparkling brown eyes making his breath catch in his throat.

"I'm sure you'll be running the place soon enough," she said in Czech while she, too, gave him a hug, her hand lingering on his back. "I tried some of those cookies the other day. I could tell something was different."

Felix smiled and pretended to be embarrassed, but there was something in Adela's voice that was off. She was hiding something behind her easy smile.

"Now, how about a glass of wine?" Gerhard uncorked Felix's bottle with much fanfare and poured everyone a glass. When he took a quick sip, he nodded his approval. "A true Austrian, Felix knows his wines."

They all clinked glasses, and as Felix took a sip, he looked around the room. These people had welcomed him into their lives without reservation, opening their homes to him, and making him feel at home. His eyes lingered on Adela, who had been especially determined in making sure he landed on his feet. He'd spent the first month staying with Gerhard and Ida, but Adela had found him his own place at a very reasonable rent. He suspected she'd pulled some strings, using the influential job she didn't like to speak much about, and he was very grateful.

Gerhard had taken him under his wing at the bakery, and he had quickly picked up the skills to become useful. Despite Felix moving out, Ida and Gerhard insisted on a monthly dinner, although Felix found himself at their place more often than that. Gerhard frequently invited him for a drink that rolled into dinner after work.

They enjoyed the wine, and then Ida announced dinner was ready. They found their places, and Gerhard recited the hamotzi blessing before dinner. After a brief silence, they started eating, and

Felix was amazed by the richness of the flavors. He was about to compliment Ida when Adela spoke.

"There's something I need to share with you." Her tone was serious as she put down her cutlery. All eyes focused on her. "I learned of something rather distressing at work today. It's confidential information that I'm not supposed to share with you."

The table was silent but for the soft, constant ticking of the wall clock. Adela fiddled with her hands and cast her eyes to the table. She appeared to weigh her next words.

"You shouldn't tell us if it gets you into trouble," Greta said unconvincingly, her slightly higher-than-usual voice betraying her curiosity.

Adela looked up and resolutely shook her head. "I'm not worried about getting into trouble at work. I'm worried about our future." She took a deep breath, then her eyes focused on Felix's. "A week from now, the German army will invade Czechoslovakia. The plans have been approved by Hitler."

Her words sucked the oxygen from the room. Felix felt as if he was underwater, his senses numbed but for a rhythmic pounding in his head. Adela's words bounced around his mind, their weight increasing as the consequences unfolded in his brain. He scanned the faces at the table, where the rest of the guests appeared stuck in a similar daze. They looked at each other with glassy eyes as they tried to comprehend Adela's terrible announcement.

"But what about the French assurances?"

Felix's senses snapped back at the sound of his host's voice.

"Aren't they supposed to guarantee our borders? That was part of the Munich Agreement, wasn't it?" Gerhard spoke in a trembling voice and swayed in his chair, his face pale. Ida gently grasped her husband's hand, attempting to maintain a brave face, but her glistening eyes betrayed her true emotions. The table went silent for a moment, until Adela spoke up in a surprisingly strong voice.

"We have little faith in the French honoring that promise. They backed out last time, and we shouldn't expect anything this time. They're dismissing the evidence, as is our own government. I'm so sorry." Adela looked at Felix again, her eyes like dark wells.

The freedom he had tasted for the past three months would soon come to an end. This time, he didn't know where to run.

FIFTY

Prague
14 March 1939

Adela was in her office when it happened. At first, there was a bit of commotion, with more people walking and whispering up and down the hallway. The whispers quickly turned into regular voices, and before long her door opened and Zdenka, one of her team members, burst in.

"They've done it!" Her cheeks were flushed, eyes wide. Adela knew the words that would come next. "Slovakia has declared independence!"

Adela nodded solemnly but didn't speak, prompting Zdenka to retreat from her office in surprise. As her door closed, Adela buried her head in her hands and closed her eyes.

The Slovakian declaration confirmed Dieter's words. Reports of a meeting between the Slovak People's Party's leader Jozef Tiso and Adolf Hitler emerged yesterday.

Adela opened her eyes and stood, taking a deep breath. It calmed her somewhat as she moved to the window overlooking the inner garden of the castle. It was a sunny day, and many of her colleagues streamed out of the building. The excited chatter confirmed that the news was spreading through the castle, and it would be a matter of hours—if not minutes—before the public would hear about it.

Adela moved from the window and sat back in her chair. Methodically she collected pieces of paper from different folders and placed them in one file. All the time, she kept one eye on the door, her ears pricked.

The knock she expected came a minute later. She was on her feet before the secretary could open the door.

The head of military intelligence sat at his desk with dark bags under his eyes, ghostly pale. "Adela, thank you for coming up so quickly." Moravec's voice sounded raspy and strained, as though he'd been in negotiations all night. "I don't think I need to tell you what the news from Bratislava means."

She shook her head. "Dieter was right. We only have hours left."

"Hacha just departed for Berlin. Summoned by Hitler."

Moravec's words were no surprise. It was an odd sensation to consider an event of this magnitude with quiet acceptance.

"You know, it feels like we've been rolling a boulder up a very steep hill for the past months, and it's finally become too heavy," Adela said candidly.

"Our eastern borders are in turmoil, which is exactly what Hitler planned after convincing Tiso. The troops stationed on the Slovak-Hungarian border will take time to return. It won't matter, though, because Hitler will convince Hacha to stand down."

Adela was afraid to ask the next question. "What about the French?"

"Our government needs to formally ask for help. I've briefed the men upstairs on the impending invasion numerous times since we spoke with Dieter, all to no avail. They're not accepting the intelligence. They're confident they're doing enough to appease Hitler and don't believe in an invasion."

"Sticking their heads in the sand."

Moravec looked defeated as he nodded. "I've instructed my staff to destroy all documents. They'll be working through it throughout the night."

"What will you do? When will you leave?"

Moravec seemed troubled as he moved in his seat, avoiding eye contact before looking up. Adela spotted an emotion she hadn't before seen on the face of one of the most powerful men in the country: guilt. "Tonight. I leave for London in a few hours. The Brits are sending a plane."

Adela nodded solemnly. Even though she knew this would happen, the thought of Moravec leaving made her feel uneasy and worry about her own future. Moravec had been a fixture in her life ever since he asked her to work for him. He'd given her purpose, and she felt useful.

"Senior officers are currently packing the most vital national intelligence."

"Are you going on your own?" Adela caught her tone being hopeful, and quickly added, "Are any other government officials leaving the country?"

"Just some of the most important men from my office. We'll make ourselves useful from London. We'll continue the fight there."

"I see." Adela felt oddly hurt at not being considered part of Moravec's inner circle, and she had trouble hiding her feelings. She silently cursed her unprofessional behavior. Moravec, ever the intelligence officer, picked up on her mood.

"Adela, there's a reason you're not joining me on the plane." He spoke softer than ever before, and she couldn't help but meet his gaze. "Officially, you're not part of my team. There's no trail of your involvement in any of the missions. Nobody even knows we're speaking right now. The only times you had access to any classified or covert information, it was handed directly to you by me."

His words did little to make her feel better.

"I'm doing my best to take as much vital information with me before the Nazis arrive. But there are things I can't take with me. There are people in power who know about the operations I've run over the past years. Some highly placed government officials will be eager to align themselves with the Nazis. People will be betrayed. But you, Adela, you're the ghost nobody knows about."

It was the first and only time she considered being called a ghost a compliment, and Adela managed a cautious smile. She was starting to see what Moravec was getting at. "But what if the Nazis decide I'm no longer of value within the administration? Won't they install their own government and clerks?"

"It's possible, but judging from their approach in Austria and Sudetenland, I doubt it. They're too practical to sever the head off a functioning public administration. Sure, they'll replace plenty of highly placed politicians and administrators, but only if they're convinced they might present a problem." He paused for a moment, observing her. "I expect the services of your department will be in great demand. You'll have plenty of Germans requiring translations of anything you can think about. Not to mention a need to monitor potential Czech resistance communications."

Adela raised an eyebrow. "I can't work for the Nazis like that. It's treason."

"I'm sure you can find creative ways for some of that information not to make it up the chain." Moravec's mouth curled into a smile for a moment, then his serious look returned. "But the most important reason why I need you in Prague, Adela. I think you know."

"Dieter." This time she spoke softly. He had lingered in her mind ever since the news of the Slovakian independence filtered through, but it had taken Moravec to bring him to the forefront of her attention. "He's still useful." She spoke hesitantly, unsure of the statement.

"Very much so. We've been able to at least prepare for the German aggression of the past six months. If it wasn't for his warning about the impending invasion, I wouldn't have been able to prepare my intelligence agency the way I have. Some agents would've been horribly exposed without that knowledge, and others have been reassigned to collect valuable intelligence in Slovakia." He leaned forward and placed his hands on the table, a flash of energy returning in his eyes. "I know the future of our country looks bleak, but we will continue fighting, even when we're occupied. I will continue my work from London and find ways to communicate with you and Dieter. It might be easier for him to blend into the masses when many of his colleagues are also stationed in Prague. Dark times lie ahead, but we will come out stronger on the other side, Adela. And you will play a vital part in our country's future."

The words roused Adela, her heart beating faster as she listened to Moravec's impassioned plea. She had looked at her position in the wrong way, and Moravec revealed her true worth. There was nothing she could do about the inevitable capitulation to Nazi Germany. Her country would be occupied, and the best she could hope for was a bloodless transition of power. When Moravec announced he was leaving the country, she had taken it as a sign that her usefulness was at an end. But now she saw her true calling, her new role in her occupied country. She would operate in the shadows, a true spy for Czechoslovakia.

FIFTY-ONE

Prague
15 March 1939

The next morning the streets of Prague were covered in snow, and it didn't look like it would stop anytime soon. It did little to deter Karl, who donned the same standard-issue boots as the soldiers marching onto Wenceslas Square.

Curious citizens peered from their windows in the apartments above, a few daring enough to brave the snow to greet the victorious Wehrmacht entering the capital of Czechoslovakia. Or the Protectorate of Bohemia and Moravia, as the country would soon be known. The snowflakes landing on his exposed cheeks did little to extinguish the pride radiating from deep within him. Endless rows of soldiers goose-stepped past Karl, the snow dampening the stomping of their boots, their disciplined gazes straight ahead, unbothered by the snow.

After some fifteen minutes Karl found shelter in one of the large coffeehouses on the square. It was nearly deserted, with only two of the forty-something tables occupied. Karl had never seen it this quiet, and he found a table by the window. He ordered a coffee and an *Apfelstrudel*, deciding to indulge in the Führer's favorite pastry. This momentous day called for it.

He looked outside while he waited for his coffee to arrive. Apart from the soldiers, the streets were empty, which he knew was only partly due to the snow. Despite his triumphant feeling, he knew they would've received an equally frosty reception if it had been sunny outside. This wasn't the Sudetenland, where the large German population had welcomed the conquering army with open arms. If his time in Prague had taught him anything, it was that the Czech people were proud and fiercely nationalistic.

The waiter placed his coffee and strudel down and left without another word. Karl was unbothered and raised his cup to his lips, savoring the bitter taste of the perfectly brewed coffee.

Karl set his cup down and pondered the future. He'd done everything possible to prepare for the arrival of his Führer. According to the schedule, he would arrive early in the evening, accompanied by Heydrich. Karl was in awe of how quickly things had developed. In the space of three days, Hitler had brought Slovakia into his sphere of influence voluntarily—Karl chuckled at the thought—and forced that weak president Hacha into unconditionally surrendering the rest of the country. From what he'd heard from Berlin this morning, Hacha had collapsed during the talks when Hitler threatened to bomb Prague to the ground if he didn't agree. Karl hoped someone would've given him a call if that was actually going to happen, but was pleased the threat alone had been enough. It would've been quite a waste.

The strudel was a bit dry, and Karl pushed it aside. That was disappointing, but he wouldn't let it ruin his day. He signaled for the bill, and the waiter was especially prompt. As he stepped back into the snow, the endless stream of soldiers continued.

THAT EVENING KARL found himself overlooking Prague from the most elevated position in the city. The snow had stopped, and the lights of the city were reflected by the snow-covered streets and roofs. It was a majestic sight, especially from the top floor of the Prague Castle. Karl turned away from the window and back to the room, clutching his glass of champagne. Some fifty prominent members of the party had gathered to celebrate the addition of the new protectorate to the Reich. The Führer was slated to speak momentarily, and Karl felt anticipation bubble in his stomach.

He scanned the faces in the room: Many occupied high positions in the Sicherheitsdienst, SS, and Gestapo, and keen to play up their efforts in the annexation, despite most of them arriving this very day. None of the men assembled would know their way around town, let alone know who to approach in the current government. Karl took a small sip of his champagne. It was fine; he would show them the way.

"Vogt." The familiar voice of Reinhard Heydrich appearing by his side startled him, and he saluted his superior.

"Sir, good evening. I trust you had a good trip? And the hotel meets your approval?"

"It's quite adequate." His boss responded in his characteristic measured way. Karl stifled a grin. He'd arranged suites for Heydrich and Hitler in the Hotel Steiner, the most luxurious hotel in the city. "Can you give me an update on what's happening outside?" He turned down a waiter offering him champagne, and Karl placed his half-empty glass on the tray.

"Our agents started their arrests early in the morning, assisted by the local Prague police. The Einsatzgruppen will assist as soon as they arrive, which is expected to be in the next few hours."

"They're using the lists you sent back a few weeks ago? The ones that were sent for my approval?" When Karl nodded, Heydrich added, "Did you add any new names in the meantime?"

"A few came through at the last moment. I did add them. Easier to interrogate them and decide they're harmless than the other way around, I figured."

"Good man. These are mostly government officials?"

"Not just the government, sir. Plenty of community leaders and local party leaders not directly linked to the government. Many Bolsheviks, Communists, and plenty of Jews. They've got their sticky fingers in quite a few pies in town. I thought it was best to round them up before they can cause any trouble."

"Smart thinking. Wouldn't want a repeat of the November pogrom. What about the public's response so far? Any trouble?"

Karl shook his head. "Apart from a few small student protests at the university, nothing. I was in town this morning, and I think the sight of our soldiers occupying the streets made people think twice about rising up."

"That and the horrid weather." Heydrich frowned as he looked outside. "Let's not kid ourselves, Vogt, there's a reason we declared martial law and the curfew. These Slavs don't like us. We need to be careful."

"I agree, sir, but I've cultivated a strong network of allies in the police force. Many of them are very much in support of our strong rule of law." Karl proudly puffed out his chest. "I can introduce you to some of the most important players, if you'd like."

Heydrich waved his hand dismissively. "Maybe later. Let's focus on striking down any opposition before it has a chance to rise. Good work on preparing all those lists. I look forward to seeing the numbers tomorrow morning." Heydrich then moved on to a group of high-level Sicherheitsdienst men standing near the window, greeting them curtly.

A loud cheer went up, which could only mean one thing—the Führer himself had entered. He was all smiles as he worked the room, shaking hands and even making time for a quick word or two. Then he mounted the podium and took his place behind the lectern. As he started speaking, his eyes darted across the room, making everyone feel like he was talking directly to them. When his gaze landed on Karl, he appeared to pause for a moment, a spark of recognition before his eyes moved on to the next person. It was enough for Karl.

When Hitler finished his speech half an hour later, they moved to the balcony overlooking the river and city below. In the biting cold, with the wind howling across the castle's ramparts, Hitler pulled a cord, unfurling a massive red-white-and-black Nazi swastika flag. Pride filled Karl: The first part of his mission had been accomplished.

IT WAS STILL DARK when Karl returned to the castle the next morning. He was pleased to see a group of his subordinates from Berlin preparing empty offices on the second floor.

"Sir, we're ready to start the interviews." The youthful face of Heinz Neumann belied his experience and value to Karl's operation. Barely twenty years old, he'd been with the Sicherheitsdienst from the moment he was eligible at seventeen. This was his first field assignment, but from everything Karl had observed he had the makings of a great asset. His reports were concise but complete, and he handled himself especially well in meetings with more senior operatives. It was why Karl had placed him in charge of preparing the interrogations of the general staff at the castle.

"Very good. Did you get my room set up as well?"

"Certainly, it's right here." Heinz led him to a small room at the front of the hallway. It was exactly as Karl had instructed: uncomfortable chairs, a rickety table, and the temperature turned up a few degrees too high to be comfortable. He rubbed his hands in anticipation. "Let's get started. Did you distribute the lists yet?"

Heinz shook his head while handing him a thick brown folder. "I thought you'd like to do that yourself."

"Good thinking. Assemble the rest of the crew. It's going to be a busy day."

FIFTY-TWO

Prague
16 March 1939

The castle's groundskeepers had cleared the main walkway and now focused on some of the smaller paths. The deep layers of snow covering the castle gardens would normally be enough for a childlike excitement to lift Adela's spirits for the rest of the day, but today it did little to distract her from the nerves raging through her body. She nodded at one of the men shoveling snow to the side of the path, but her mind was elsewhere.

It was her second day as a spy, but her first walking into the wolf's den. Moravec had left shortly after their meeting, entrusting her with the exclusive handling of Dieter. The head of military intelligence had made it out of the country with ten of his most trusted agents and a host of files, just hours after the first Nazi soldiers crossed the border.

Adela and her colleagues had been ordered to stay at home the previous day, as the Nazis took over. Moravec hadn't made it very clear how they would communicate, but he said he would find a way. For now, it was her job to keep her eyes and ears open.

Adela cautiously approached the castle's main entrance. A short queue of employees had formed as two uniformed soldiers stopped everybody, demanding to see their papers. Joining the queue, she observed the men. From the many photos that had crossed her desk in the past months, she recognized the uniforms to be those of low-rank Waffen-SS. In their late teens, the soldiers appeared confident and capable, the line moving along quickly.

When she reached the front of the queue and handed over her government ID, she was surprised to be addressed in Czech.

"Your papers are in order, Ms. Beran. Please report to one of the tables set up in the main hall. We're interviewing all mid-level employees and higher today." Couched in courtesy, the trooper's request was clearly a nonnegotiable order.

Adela did as she was told, and another uniformed trooper looked up her name. "Please proceed to your office, and carry out your tasks as usual. We'll come and get you."

She resisted the temptation to ask when that might be, but he was already focused on the person behind her.

As she closed the door to her office, she collapsed into her chair and exhaled deeply. She had run into more SS troopers on the stairs, and each eyed her suspiciously. Or had she imagined their looks? Perhaps they were just alert and doing their job. She took a deep breath. *Calm down, Adela.* It was the first time she felt uncomfortable in her own office, as if she were somewhere she didn't belong, pretending to be someone else.

She sat up: In a way, she was. After she accepted Moravec's assignment, she went from one of the many employees that made the government function to someone who was actively looking for ways to undermine the new powers that be. And on her first proper day, she would be hauled into an interview. No, an interrogation. This was her first test as a spy. She needed to prove to whoever was waiting for her that she was a valuable member of the new regime, worthy of keeping her job.

Her mind started to churn at full speed. Could she get away with pretending to be the woman she was just a few days ago? How much should she share about her duties? Her job heading up a team of translators meant she had intimate knowledge of the situation in the countries surrounding them. Would her interviewer consider that a plus, or a reason to fire her? Adela felt flushed, and she wished she could talk to someone about these questions.

A short rap sounded, then the door swung open. A tall trooper entered her office, his face passive, eyes devoid of emotion.

"Fraülein Beran?" Adela got to her feet and nodded. "Please come with me. You're wanted on the second floor."

Stepping into the hallway and struggling to keep up with the trooper's brisk pace, there was little time to consider her approach. She would need to improvise and pray for the best.

THE TEMPERATURE in the room was uncomfortably hot, the radiator on the side crackling. The man waiting for her had evidently prepared, as he was wearing linen pants, and a thin shirt. Adela was dressed for the Prague winter, and instantly regretted her choice of skirt—with thick stockings—and a wool sweater. She hoped the interview wouldn't take too long, pearls of sweat already forming on her back as she adjusted herself in her seat.

"Miss Beran, thank you for joining me." The man spoke in accented Czech, and he even smiled as he sat across from her. The lack of uniform made him less threatening than the other Germans she'd encountered this morning. It only served to put her guard up more. "While I speak a bit of your language, I'd prefer if we could continue in German. From your file I gather this shouldn't be a problem for you. You're a translator, correct?"

"German is fine," she responded in his native tongue, drawing another smile.

"Thank you. You're probably wondering what this is all about. Let me first introduce myself. I am Standartenführer Vogt, and my colleagues and I are getting to know the people working here. Unlike what you may have heard, we'd prefer to keep things as much as they are, where possible." He then appeared to catch himself, although Adela doubted the authenticity of his gesture as he tapped his finger on a closed file on the table. "Ach, what am I saying? Your job is to monitor foreign newspapers and reports, isn't it?"

"It is." She was conscious of keeping her responses as short as this Vogt would allow.

He held up his hands. "Well, then you must know that we've kept most government employees in their jobs in Austria and the Sudetenland."

Adela nodded. "I would very much like to keep my job, sir."

"Tell me a little bit more about what it is you do exactly. You work in a team, correct?"

"We're a small team assisting the foreign ministry. My job is to check any news reports for relevance."

"Define 'relevance.'"

"If we think it helps the foreign ministry in their decision-making and policies, we act on it."

"And these reports come from? Germany mainly, I suppose?"

"We do get a lot of German news reports, but we also like to know what's happening in Britain, France, and Russia." She tried to keep her tone as casual as possible, clipping off the countries without emotion.

"Of course. A foreign ministry needs to be well informed." He casually flicked open the file, his eyes scanning the information Adela was certain he already possessed. "And you lead this team of translators, is that correct?"

"I do."

"Tell me what that means. Are you the most senior of your team? Do they report to you?"

His questions came thick and fast, confirming to Adela that he had prepared for this interview. Even so, he looked completely at ease, exuding a confidence and calmness she hadn't anticipated.

"I make the first judgment, and when the news item is relevant enough to be passed up the chain, I assign it to one of my fellow translators."

"That would make you quite senior."

"I suppose. I've never really thought about it too much. I also translate texts myself."

"It seems to me like you're being overly modest." His eyes went back to her file, and she took note of his words. She shouldn't undersell her importance to the operation. "Which languages do you speak?"

"Czech, German, English, Russian, and a bit of French."

Vogt raised an eyebrow. "Very impressive. Considering the state of the world, I would've expected you'd have received a promotion by now."

"A promotion, sir?"

"I don't know, you must have some kind of espionage division as well, no?" The comment sounded offhand, but Adela's senses pricked up. "I could see you making a strong contribution there."

"I have no training in that department." She hesitated for a moment, then forced a smile. "I don't like the cloaks much. I prefer to keep my work simple."

"How old are you, Miss Beran?"

The question caught her off guard. Adela expected Vogt to continue with the intelligence angle. Relief flooded through her system, and she answered in a light tone, "I'm twenty-two years old."

"Hmm." He abruptly turned toward the door and opened it. "I'll be right back." He disappeared into the hallway, leaving the door open.

Adela felt flushed and dabbed at her face, relieved to find that she wasn't sweating. She ran through the conversation in her head, and she couldn't imagine anything she said revealing new insights to the German. There was nothing linking her to Moravec's division. Unless Vogt already knew about their link, in which case she knew there was little she could do but deny the connection. Even so, that wouldn't be enough to save her. She shook her head and forced herself to focus on what she could control: She was seeing ghosts. *Stick to the story.*

There was movement in the hallway, as two troopers quickly moved by with a man Adela recognized from the hallways. She'd never spoken to him, but she knew he worked in the foreign ministry. The troopers harried him along and spoke in harsh tones. It was clear he was not returning to his desk. A shiver ran down her spine—she was sure he wouldn't be the only one today.

"Okay then, Miss Beran." Vogt appeared in front of her, as if out of thin air. "I checked your story with some of my colleagues that happened to speak to your colleagues earlier. Everything appears to be in order."

"I'm glad to hear that," Adela said, annoyed at the obvious relief in her voice.

"Unfortunately, we won't retain all of your team. With our own intelligence people moving in, it doesn't make sense."

"I see." A feeling of unease settled over her. *Am I being fired after all?*

"Would you be open to working alongside our new people coming in? I think you would be of value, especially considering your experience within the foreign ministry. You know your way around this place. And secondly, but equally important, your command of languages is impressive."

Adela considered the proposal. He effectively told her her team was being dismantled, and she wouldn't just continue her work for the new government, but she would work alongside Nazi colleagues. It was not what she'd expected, but that was not the first thought that popped into her head. *This is better than getting fired today.* In fact, it brought her closer to the heart of the Nazi administration. Her new position was better than the one she had when she walked into the room half an hour ago.

"I would be honored." Her tone was businesslike and formal, and she held out her hand. When the Nazi shook it, a surge of repulsion shot through her body. She would destroy them from within.

FIFTY-THREE

Prague
16 March 1939, afternoon

The mood in the bakery was more subdued than usual. From the moment Felix entered in the middle of the night he felt the anxiety among his fellow bakers. There was none of the joking or laughing, the small pranks they pulled on each other throughout their shifts. The men were quietly going about their work, only speaking when they needed to. Even then, their expressions were tense, their words short and curt.

Felix was relieved when Gerhard tapped him on the shoulder halfway through the morning.

"Come, let's have a coffee together. I'm sure you can use a break."

Felix washed his hands and followed the older man to the anteroom between the bakery and shop. Gerhard went to the front and came back with two steaming cups of coffee, handing one to Felix with a sad smile on his face before sitting down on a large sack of flour.

"How are you holding up? I feel like we're back in Vienna. I've seen it all before."

Felix shook his head. "I overheard some of the people living in my building last night. They couldn't believe Hacha just surrendered the country."

"I've heard the same murmurs. If they really believe that's what happened, they're naive. Hacha never had a choice, just like Schuschnigg didn't. You might argue Beneš could've taken the country to war when they still had their defenses set up in the Sudetenland, but with the Sudeten Germans rioting and causing problems, that would've been challenging."

"The Czechoslovak army would've been facing the Wehrmacht while the Sudeten Germans attacked them from the rear."

Gerhard nodded. "It would only have caused more bloodshed with the same result."

"But where does that leave us?" Felix's eyes went to the door, not for the first time that day. "I'm sure they'll be making life for us as difficult here as in the rest of the Reich. Not to mention we left Austria illegally."

"It might take a while for them to get everything started up here." Gerhard's tone was only mildly hopeful.

Felix frowned. "This doesn't feel like a spontaneous invasion. They planned this. You can be sure they made their preparations even before they crossed the border."

"What do you suggest we do?" Gerhard now sounded worried. "Ida and I have built a new life here, and I'm not sure she could handle another move."

"We should check with Adela. If anyone knows more about what's going on, it's her. She's got connections everywhere." Felix hadn't spoken to Adela since their dinner two weeks ago, and he wondered what the Nazi invasion meant for her job. He couldn't discount the possibility that she had already been fired. But she was their only source of information. "I'll try to talk to her tonight."

"I think that's the best we can do for now." Gerhard rose from the sack and took both cups. "Let's get back to work. We can't afford getting fired from this place."

Felix smiled wryly. Getting fired was the least of his worries.

He finished work early and was first to get changed into his regular clothes. Most of the other men were still cleaning the ovens, a task they rotated weekly. It took significantly more time to finish, and Felix was pleased to step out of the warm bakery and onto the snow-covered street a little past three in the afternoon.

The crisp air gave him somewhat of a reset from the gloomy mood inside. After his chat with Gerhard, his mind kept churning away, weighing the possibilities of what might happen next. His biggest worry concerned his registration with the city of Prague. When he arrived in Czechoslovakia he'd registered with the authorities, who granted him refugee status. It was a prerequisite for being able to work, or renting an apartment. He was so used to the bureaucratic ways of his home country that he'd gone through the process with resigned acceptance. It had given him only a few months of freedom: He would soon have the Nazis hunting him once more. Technically, he was now back in the Reich, violating the terms of his release from Buchenwald.

He headed down the street and toward the city center, still lost in his thoughts, not paying much attention to the surroundings. The only constant was the soft crunching of the snow under his shoes, giving him comfort.

Loud engine noises snapped him out of his thoughts. He turned to the source of the sound, just like the other people on the street. A moment later a large truck turned the corner, its engine roaring as the driver shifted but hardly slowed down. Its large tires slipped for an instant, then gripped the cobblestoned street again, propelling the truck forward. Two German Kübelwagens followed closely behind. The truck slowed, and Felix knew where it was headed well before it skidded to a halt in front of the bakery.

Felix stood frozen in the snow, unable to move. Fear gripped his throat, constricting his breathing. The people in the street watched in morbid fascination as SS troopers emerged from the vehicles.

Two jumped from the bed of the truck and drew back the tarp, revealing the uncomfortable wooden benches Felix had sat on many times before. He shivered involuntarily, feeling helpless as the first Nazis stormed the bakery.

He was less than a hundred meters away, but the snow carried the voices as if he were standing next to the truck.

"Get all of them outside right now. I don't care what they say. If they're on the list, they're coming with us. If they can't prove who they are, the same." A man with a clipboard stood erect, his shoulders back as he waited patiently next to the truck. He didn't have to wait long for the first people to emerge from the shop.

Felix wasn't surprised to see the bakery's owner, Mr. Coufalik, coming out. Even from a distance he looked defiant, scowling as he stomped toward the man with the clipboard.

"What is the meaning of this? Why are you interrupting a legitimate business? I've had no warning of this." Considering his exterior, his tone was surprisingly cordial. Felix suspected he'd decided to temper his anger at the last moment. *Smart.*

"Are you the owner of this establishment?" The SS man glanced down at his clipboard, butchering the Czech surname. "Coufelik?"

"Hynek Coufalik, yes." He pointed at the shop sign bearing his name. At that moment, the first employees were escorted out by the troopers. "Where are you taking my people? They've done nothing wrong."

"We'll be the judge of that," the man responded icily, while turning to a young salesgirl named Hannelore. Felix liked her a lot, and he felt frozen watching her shake as she stated her name. "Can you prove that? Do you have any papers on you?"

Hannelore reached into her coat and handed over her papers. Felix let out a sigh of relief when the German dismissed her. She hurried away from the bakery, not once looking back. The SS man had then signaled for the next bakery employee to approach when Mr. Coufalik moved between them. With the lightest hand signal, the SS man in charge summoned one of his men. Without another word, they picked up the baker, and bundled him into one of the cars. They raced off, leaving the rest of the staff that were exiting the bakery in shock.

Felix stood open-mouthed as the Kübelwagen raced by him. He turned back to the scene in front of the bakery and saw the first men that worked the ovens with him climb aboard the truck.

Then he spotted Gerhard. His friend looked defeated, shivering as he stood in only his overalls and apron while a young SS trooper held onto his arm. He reached the man holding the clipboard and Felix heard him protest he didn't have any papers on him. It was the only thing Gerhard could do. Felix would've done the same. If they couldn't prove he was indeed a Jew, there was a slim chance they might let him go.

Not today. With a brief, sharp nod, the man gestured for him to get into the truck. As Felix watched his friend disappear behind the tarp, he became aware of the movement around him. The people in the street had become bored with the spectacle, and they were moving on with their lives. With a deep feeling of guilt, Felix forced himself to turn away from his colleagues and friends. There was nothing he could do for them, and he needed to save himself. With every step away from the bakery, his heart grew heavier. His lucky escape was short-lived. He was on the run again.

FIFTY-FOUR

Prague
16 March 1939, evening

Adela came home to a dark apartment. She put her bag down, feeling exhausted. The morning's interview weighed heavily on her for the rest of the day. The man who'd introduced himself just as Vogt had made an impression on her. He hadn't stated anything other than his SS rank, but the more Adela thought about it, the more she was convinced he was affiliated with the Gestapo or Sicherheitsdienst. His quick thinking and his air of superiority marked him as someone in a circle outside the regular SS. Whomever *Standartenführer Vogt* was, Adela hoped she wouldn't have much to do with him in the future. Something in the back of her mind told her that could be wishful thinking.

She flicked on the light in the hallway and took off her coat. Just then, the curtains in the living room ruffled. She almost missed it, but in the silence of her apartment, and her current state, her heightened senses would've picked up a mouse scampering away in the upstairs apartment. Adela froze. She pricked her ears while she slipped off her shoes, carefully tiptoeing toward her living room.

Wait. What am I doing? She had nothing to defend herself with. If there really was an intruder, she would be an easy target. Standing halfway between her front door and the doorway into the living room, she had to make a decision. *Fight or flee?*

The sound of someone moving behind the curtain was now unmistakable. Adela made a decision: She turned and dashed for the front door. No longer caring if the person in the living room heard her, she snatched her shoes and coat. Her hand was on the door handle—

"Adela! Wait!"

Her heart dropped when she recognized the voice. Relief flooded her senses when her best friend's figure appeared from the darkness of the living room.

"Greta. What are you doing here? I nearly had a heart attack." She put her shoes down and rushed to her friend. They were both shaking, and—as they embraced—Adela sensed from Greta's tense shoulders that something was very wrong.

"It's the bakery. It was raided." Greta's voice was shaky.

They stepped into the living room, and Adela flicked on the lights. She was shocked by her friend's appearance. Her eyes were red and puffy, the usual glow on her cheeks reduced to pale outlines.

"They came just before closing time. They took everybody." She spoke in quick bursts, barely contained panic in her voice. "Well, nearly everyone. I was lucky to be on an errand when they came. If I had come back five minutes earlier, I wouldn't be standing here."

"Wait, stop. Slow down." Adela heard the words, but they were too terrible to accept. "Who came?" She already knew.

"The Gestapo, the SS, I don't know! As soon as I saw the truck, I got out of there." She put her hands before her face. "Adela, they took all my friends. These people have done nothing wrong."

Adela guided her friend to her dining table and quickly filled two glasses with water. She sat next to Greta, putting her arm around her friend, and handed her the water. "Did you recognize any of the uniforms?"

"I didn't stick around long enough to get a good look, but they were definitely German. Grayish uniforms."

Definitely SS. Adela had seen enough of those in the castle to know for sure. It was then that she noticed Greta was still wearing her baker's apron. "Did you come here straight from work?"

"Yes, I didn't know where else to go. If they know where I work, they might also come for me at home."

"Did you warn your parents?" A growing sense of dread was building in the pit of Adela's stomach.

Greta nodded. "I called them from a pay phone before coming here. They're leaving the city with my aunt."

Aunt Ida. Adela's heart skipped a beat. "Did you see them take your uncle?"

"No, but he was working in the back. I have no doubt he was loaded up." She was silent for a moment. "As was Felix."

"Oh no." Adela gasped silently, a sharp pain shooting through her heart. The thought of him in an SS prison filled her with terror. She turned back to Greta, reminding her of their immediate problems. "You'll stay with me while we figure out what to do next. What are your parents planning to do?"

Before Greta could answer there was a faint knock on the front door. They looked at each other, the shock and terror in Greta's eyes mirroring Adela's feelings. She raised a finger to her lips and slowly turned toward the door. The bright lights from the apartment filtering underneath it betrayed their presence, and she cursed silently. Had the Gestapo interrogated Greta's colleagues and someone deduced she would be at Adela's? Surely they didn't work that fast. Then another—no less terrible—thought entered her mind. The Germans had been keeping tabs on Adela, and they knew about their friendship well before the raid. She suddenly felt very cold. If the Germans were at the door, there was nothing she could do for her friend. Or herself, for that matter.

Another knock, this time more forceful. They weren't going anywhere. Adela stood and composed herself, then met Greta's terrified look. "Hide in the broom closet in the kitchen," Adela whispered. "I'll try to keep them outside."

She waited for Greta to disappear, steeled herself, and went to the front door. A third knock, and she put on an annoyed face. She was determined to show she had nothing to hide, and they weren't going to barge into her home just like that. She slid the door bolt to the side, then twisted the door handle, slowly opening the door. The faint light in the hallway revealed a single figure standing there. Adela let out a shriek, and her heart skipped a few beats.

Carrying nothing but a small bag, there stood Felix, a ghost returned from the dead.

Adela and Greta sat next to each other at the kitchen table, listening open-mouthed to Felix's recollection of the afternoon's events. When he finished, they remained silent for a good minute, Adela cradling her mug of tea, which had long gone cold.

"And you're certain you saw them take my uncle?" Greta asked with a desperate note.

He nodded. "Gerhard was one of the last to board the truck. I feel terrible. We spoke about something like this happening just hours earlier. It's sheer luck I wasn't assigned to cleaning the ovens. That never happens." He looked shattered, and Adela wanted to put an arm around him, tell him everything would be fine. But there was nothing she could do to make it better. "I was supposed to be in that truck as well."

"You can't blame yourself, Felix." Adela's words came out harsher than she intended, and she held up her hand, softening her tone. "You didn't know this would happen. We should be grateful you both made it out. I know I am. I can't imagine losing both of you."

Felix looked back at her in surprise, and then he locked his eyes on her. Looking more vulnerable than ever before, her friends now appeared to her in a new light. Both had faced their share of adversity, but they had always come out stronger. Felix most of all. He'd survived a German concentration camp and crossed into her country in search of freedom, forced to build a new life among strangers. And now his freedom was once again torn away. And Greta, poor Greta, had her life turned upside down in a matter of hours. An urge to protect them overcame her. If she didn't help them, no one would.

On cue, Greta asked, "What can we do?"

"You will stay here for now, while we figure things out." Adela's confident tone belied her underlying nervousness. She had no idea how to fix the situation, but of one thing she was certain. "You can't go outside anymore, it's too dangerous."

"Are you sure? You're putting yourself in terrible peril by hiding us." Felix's objection was surprisingly firm, but Adela shook her head resolutely.

"You will stay with me, and that's the end of the discussion." Relief flooded Felix's face, and she smiled back in response. Hours after retaining her job within the new government, its value proved of lifesaving importance. Now she needed to find a covert way to unlock the possibilities of her new position in the Nazi government. She would do anything to get her friends to safety.

FIFTY-FIVE

Prague
25 March 1939

It was clear from the moment Leopold entered Karl's office in the castle that something was wrong. The Czech police captain looked annoyed, and his greeting was more blunt than usual. Karl was undeterred, waving him to a chair with a smile.

"Is this your first visit to the castle?" He didn't wait for a response before moving to the liquor cabinet to the side of his desk. "Can I offer you something?"

Leopold looked slightly less agitated when he pointed at the bottle of premium Becherovka at the front of the rack. Karl poured two glasses, the strong herbal scent of the liquor overpowering his senses. He wasn't a big fan of the Czech spirit, but he decided he needed some common ground with the man opposite him. Sharing a drink usually worked. He handed a glass to Leopold and held out his own in a toast.

"*Na zdraví!*" It had been one of the first phrases he'd learned in Czech, and he found it often broke the ice. Leopold let out a soft grunt before downing the glass in one go. He sighed and smacked his lips, placing the glass on the table next to him.

"Now that you've had a drink, why don't you share what's on your mind. You look like someone insulted your mother." To Karl's relief, the beginnings of a smile appeared on the policeman's face.

"It's been almost two weeks since you took over the country, and as far as I know, my men have been helping you with your assorted efforts in the city, no?" Leopold spoke calmly, and the smile had vanished. "I'm curious to know if our services have not been to your satisfaction?" The words were cautious and diplomatic, but Karl had enough experience to know what Leopold was getting at.

"There is no cause for concern." He picked up the man's glass and sauntered back to the liquor cabinet. He took his time unscrewing the cap from the bottle. "The first weeks of the Protectorate have been eventful. It was of the utmost importance to nip any potential resistance in the bud. At times like those, operational matters precede administrative ones." He poured another generous portion, handing it to the policeman, who looked unimpressed. "You can be certain your efforts have not escaped my attention, nor that of my superiors."

Leopold perked up a little. "I'm glad to hear that." He took a sip, clearly anticipating Karl would continue. Karl returned to his seat and crossed his legs.

"Now that there's a semblance of order in the Protectorate, I had time to bring out a number of reports to my superiors—"

"When you speak of superiors, may I ask who they are?" The alcohol was clearly having some impact as Leopold interrupted him. Karl ignored the transgression, taking this as a good sign. The Czech man was keen. Karl grinned, which Leopold incorrectly took as friendliness.

"I report directly to the top." There was no need to inform him of his direct connection to Heydrich. *Keep him in the dark.* "And they have been impressed by the dedication of the Czech police." He casually waved a dismissive hand. "This was no surprise to me, of course, for all our dealings were rather productive, and you assured me they would fall in line."

This drew a content smile from Leopold. "We're glad to be of service."

"And we appreciate it. So very much that Reichsführer Himmler will this week announce the official incorporation of the Czech police force into the Sicherheitsdienst. He was especially impressed with the physical capacity of your force. Proper, strong men."

Leopold was now beaming. "This is fantastic news, sir. We'll be proud to serve."

It's not like you have much of a choice. "I'm glad to hear it. Your police force will work closely with the Sicherheitsdienst, and be heavily involved in our activities within the country." He didn't mention the incorporation meant the Czech police force would cease to exist as an independently functioning entity. They would take orders from the Sicherheitsdienst. "This also means a promotion for you. You'll be promoted to major immediately, with another promotion in six months. With the appropriate increase in pay, of course."

Leopold did nothing to hide his delight at the news, but he also appeared to realize the error of his earlier moodiness. "I apologize for doubting you, sir. I wasn't aware of the intricacies that came with the Protectorate. I will be more patient next time."

"Don't worry about it. You deserve the promotion. You've been essential in these first months." It was no exaggeration, for the man helped Karl tremendously while he was operating on his own. With Leopold in an agreeable mood, he decided to broach the next important subject. "With that, I need you to assist me with something that goes beyond the scope of your new job."

"Happy to help." Leopold eagerly leaned forward, his gaze a little glassy from the alcohol, but not enough to hide the greed shining through. He hadn't forgotten the generous supplements to his income that Karl provided. Along with his new rank, he could lead a very comfortable life in the new Protectorate.

"The lists you supplied me with were very accurate, and we managed to pick up most of the people on them. But with the new situation, we're receiving plenty of reports of additional resistance rising up across the country."

"We'll be happy to help you work on that."

"Naturally. And with the Sicherheitsdienst expanding its network of agents, it will be easier to identify these troublemakers. We're making good progress setting up and increasing the number of informants in Prague, but I'd like to see if you can help us beyond the capital's borders."

Comprehension dawned on Leopold's face, and he nodded enthusiastically. "I have plenty of connections in the departments surrounding the city. I assume you're looking for similar lists? Communists, Jews?"

"Yes, but in addition, I need your sources to keep their eyes open and their ears close to the ground. It's one thing identifying the obvious threats you mentioned. Let's call that phase one, and we can probably wrap that up rather quickly." Karl paused, gauging the Czech man's response. He looked a little lost, and Karl pushed on. "I want you to help me set up a network of trusted sources that will report any treacherous talk. I don't care how small the transgression, I want it on my desk the next day."

"Would you like us to act on these?"

Karl shook his head. "Only when they're clearly breaking the law, or seem likely to flee. Otherwise, I want you to pass it on, and have us handle it. We'll still involve your men for the arrests and other interesting activities, don't worry. You'll still receive your chance to shine."

"Understood, sir."

"I'll leave it up to you how you recruit these men outside Prague, but I expect to see the first report within a week. At the very least, I want to know the locations of our contacts, so we have a good overview of the reach of our network."

"I'll take care of it, and thank you."

Karl was pleased with how the meeting had gone, and it was time to wrap things up. Leopold had his instructions, and Karl was keen to see how he would fare in less familiar surroundings. He was taking a risk delegating part of the creation of his network to Leopold, but he had faith in the man. Whatever the outcome, it would be more productive than him heading out into the corners of the Protectorate himself. Just to be certain, he added a final incentive before letting Leopold leave.

"Remember, if you make me look good, I'll make you richer than you ever imagined." He intentionally omitted the effect of an adverse outcome, but Leopold appeared oblivious to it. His eyes now glittered with undisguised greed, a big smile fixed on his face as he saluted Karl and left the office.

FIFTY-SIX

Prague
27 March 1939

Felix put down his book and checked the clock. It was only a little past noon. He sighed; it felt like an entire day had passed. He walked to the kitchen and made himself another cup of tea. The sound of the water slowly coming to a boil interrupted the silence. Along with the silence of the units surrounding Adela's apartment, for that matter.

He'd become quite aware of the schedules of the other tenants of the building, hearing them move about in the mornings as they no doubt rushed to get to work. It would mostly be quiet until around three o'clock, when the first neighbors returned. Oddly enough, it gave Felix comfort to know he wasn't completely alone in the building.

He picked up the kettle and made himself a large cup of tea. This was his second week in Adela's apartment, and he was already going a little stir-crazy. Greta had stayed for the first two days but then left to join her parents in their small holiday home in the countryside. He missed having someone to speak to during the day, for Adela left very early, and usually wasn't back until the early evening.

He returned to the living room and sat in the comfortable chair he'd made his own. Sipping on his steaming tea, he studied the large bookcase prominently placed in the middle of one wall. Adela's book collection was vast, and it had reignited his joy in reading. Adela collected a lot of foreign language books, many in German and English. She'd suggested reading the English books to prepare for his journey there. He appreciated her optimism, even though his chances of securing a visa to England were as slim as ever. But he agreed it was a good idea, and he started with some of the slimmer books first. Adela provided a dictionary, and while he was still looking up a fair number of words, he found himself reaching for the little booklet less. It was encouraging, and reading was probably the only thing keeping him sane.

That and the promise of Adela returning every evening. He'd been nervous about staying with her at first, even more so when Greta left. Felix and Adela had always gotten along really well, but living together was quite something else. So far, everything was going smoothly, and they spent the evenings talking about everything and nothing.

They discussed his chances of going to England nearly every evening. Adela had cautiously inquired with a few colleagues, and they said they would see what they could do, but it hadn't yielded any results so far. She thought it was because many were waiting to see what changes the Nazi government would make. Afraid to lose their jobs, they didn't have exit visas for Jewish refugees high on the list of priorities at the moment. Felix understood, and he was content to wait within the relative safety of Adela's apartment.

For there was always the fear of being found. He was careful to keep the blinds closed during the day. Adela's apartment was on the third floor, with no building facing them. It was unlikely that anyone would spot him from street level, but he was extra careful. He didn't want to think about what would happen to Adela if she were caught harboring him.

Felix picked up his book and sat back in the chair. It took ten minutes before he had to reach for the dictionary. A new record.

THE DOOR OPENED, and Adela appeared carrying two large bags filled with groceries. Felix jumped up and carried them to the kitchen while she took off her coat and shoes. She inquired about his day from the hallway, and he grinned at the domesticity of the situation.

"I finished the Steinbeck book."

"*Of Mice and Men?*" Adela walked into the kitchen and poured herself a glass of water. "Did you like it? It's one of my newest books."

"Yes, and I didn't have to use the dictionary on every page anymore."

"Perfect." Something appeared to pop into her head, and she looked a little downcast.

"What's wrong?"

"I wonder how easy it will be to expand my collection of English books now that the Nazis have taken over. Their policies on popular culture aren't very liberal."

He started unpacking the groceries. "I'm sure you'll find a way."

"Speaking of ways." Adela's voice rose a little while she propped herself on the kitchen counter. "I may have some good news about your chances of getting out of the country."

Felix's hand froze midair—holding an apple—while his head jerked to Adela. "How?"

"One of my more daring colleagues says he might have a way. It's not a certainty, and you'll still need to go through the visa process later, but it's the best shot we've got."

"I'll do anything, you know that. Tell me more." He placed the apple down and leaned against the counter. Struggling to contain his excitement, he tried to control his shaking hands.

"He's not just a colleague, he's also a friend. He's been with the foreign ministry for years, and he was placed within the department that maintained contact with our embassies across the continent. Now that the Nazis closed these, he feared they would fire him. But they've made it clear he'll stay on, for now."

"How does that help me?"

"Well, it's a bit of an odd situation. You can imagine he's not very busy at the moment, as the people he used to speak to every day have all been recalled. So it's given him time to look into what's going on in the foreign ministry under new leadership. Turns out, many of his colleagues have kept their jobs. Again, this is odd, considering the Nazis will run their own foreign policy."

"Yes." Felix was getting a little impatient. "So, what's he found out?"

"The Nazis are happy to have these people working on meaningless tasks for now. My friend thinks they're trying to create the illusion of a shadow government. The clerks are still busy with real work, but that's pretty much it. They're bored." Adela smiled as if that explanation should make everything clear. She must've noticed Felix's blank look. "Felix, it means these people still have access to all the diplomatic tools, including the means to issue identification documents."

Felix gasped, then considered something. "But not Nazi-approved documents, surely?"

"Technically, no." Adela didn't seem deterred. "But it's a small matter of backdating the document."

Adela's news was overwhelming, and Felix's mind raced, considering all possibilities and outcomes. He wanted to share her optimism, but he didn't want to get carried away. "Do you really think it'll work?"

She shrugged, eyes sparkling. "I think it's worth a shot. We'll only know when we try. And I've known Marti for years. If it's possible, he'll make it work."

Felix looked around the kitchen. An odd sensation overcame him: He'd started to like living with Adela. He felt safe in her home. The thought of leaving tore him up, which was ludicrous. Her news should delight him, providing a chance to leave the country, and escape the Nazis. The perceived safety in Adela's apartment was an illusion. Looking at her, he felt a wave of affection, and he knew the apartment had nothing to do with his conflicted feelings. He took a deep breath, forcing himself to put his feelings aside.

"What does he need from me?"

FIFTY-SEVEN

Prague
2 April 1939, morning

It had been almost a week since Adela handed Felix's passport photo to Marti. He'd been confident of obtaining the papers, and Adela's hopes had grown. If this worked, they might be able to do the same for Greta and her family. She missed her friend: They hadn't spoken since she'd left to be with her parents, and the home didn't have a phone line. Oddly enough, she didn't worry about Greta, for she was in such a remote location that she couldn't imagine the Nazis showing any interest in the people living in the town.

Walking to her office, she'd become accustomed to the other offices on the hallway being empty. Quite a few of her colleagues had been let go after the first round of interviews, now almost a month ago. In the following weeks, other familiar faces had gradually vacated their offices. Adela wasn't sure if they were fired or if they decided to leave on their own terms. If they did, she couldn't blame them. Marti's position wasn't the only shadow job in the castle. Adela knew she was fortunate to have a job that still mattered

THE EAGLE'S SHADOW

somewhat, even if it meant she had to train the young Germans coming in. She had been surprised by their language skills, for many understood a decent amount of Czech. It was clear the Nazis had been preparing for their annexation of her country for quite some time. They were easy enough to get along with, with a few exceptions. Not a day went by without her longing for the days when she was working for Beneš and Moravec.

The thought of the head of military intelligence reminded her why she was soldiering on, despite her misgivings about the new leadership. How she felt about her job was irrelevant in the grander scheme of things. Moravec hadn't reached out yet, and she had no way to contact him, so she made sure she appeared busy and useful to the Nazis. She also made an effort to build relationships with the new arrivals. She wondered how Dieter was doing. He was resourceful enough to find a way to contact Moravec, even in England. But had he? Or was his promise to continue working together just a nice way of saying goodbye, after all?

Adela entered her office and was pleased to see most of the morning's papers had already been delivered to her desk. She still stopped by her favorite newsstand every morning, but Georgi couldn't compete with the ability of the Nazi apparatus in obtaining newspapers from across the continent and beyond. It was impressive.

She sat at her desk and checked the clock. It was a little past seven, and most colleagues wouldn't be in for an hour, at the earliest. She reached for one of the newspapers and opened a drawer to get her notebook. Sitting atop the notebook was a small, scrunched-up piece of paper. Someone had stuffed it into her drawer. Adela's breath caught when she read the short message. *Docs in. M.*

Excitement bubbled inside her stomach, and she had to control herself not to immediately race up to the second floor. Marti most likely wouldn't be in yet, and it made no difference: She could pick up Felix's papers on her way home. That would be the safest way to go about it. She wouldn't want to be caught carrying them around.

With her mind racing, she reluctantly settled in to go through the morning's newspapers. It was normally her favorite part of the day, but this morning she found the letters dancing in front of her eyes. She checked the clock again, and told herself she wouldn't go up before midday.

She managed to control herself until half past twelve. Her excitement gradually increased over the course of the morning, and she bounced up the stairs to see Martinek. The papers had been a constant source of discussion between Felix and her. Adela was positive they would be able to secure a visa once he received his new identity. They agreed he would receive Czech identification papers dating back a year. His Czech had improved enough to be able to fool any German patrol asking for his papers. That was the first step in their plan, although Felix was hesitant about going outside again. Adela didn't blame him, and she hadn't even told him about the increased number of German patrols on the streets. Still, Felix could venture outside soon was an encouraging thought. The month he'd spent indoors was taking its toll. He needed some fresh air.

Once the papers were sorted out, they could work on the second phase of the plan, which was even more important. Marti was confident he could pull some strings with friendly contacts in the British government. The only problem was reaching them, as diplomatic relations between Germany and Great Britain were frosty at best. That it had taken Hitler's occupation of her country for them to see his true colors embittered Adela.

She put those feelings aside as she reached the second floor and made her way toward Marti's office. Nodding at acquaintances along the way, she felt upbeat about the future. Felix would be headed for safety soon.

The door to Marti's office was open, and Adela was about to walk in when the sound of unfamiliar voices stopped her in her tracks. They spoke in German, and Adela immediately heard something was amiss. She slowed her walk, preparing to pass Marti's office, and suppressed her shock when she casually glanced inside.

Two men were clearing out Marti's desk, making no effort to be subtle. Sheets of paper and files lay scattered on the desk, some spilling onto the floor. The men were oblivious to her.

"Where do you think he hid the important stuff? This is trash. It must be somewhere else."

"Let's check those filing cabinets." The other man walked to the cabinet on the opposite side of the office. Adela stood frozen in the hallway, unable to look away. The man tugged at one of the drawers. "Locked. We'll have to force it." At that moment he turned and saw Adela. His face registered surprise, then annoyance. "Who are you? What are you doing here?"

She recovered quickly. "I was just passing by. I need to see one of my colleagues farther down the hall."

"Then why are you stopping here?" The man took a few steps toward her, now standing in the doorway. "We're carrying out an official search here. Move along."

"Of course, I apologize. I didn't mean to intrude."

The man opened his mouth, but a cry from the other agent cut him off.

"Rudy! I think I found something." He lifted a thick folder, and held out one of the papers. Adela's heart froze as she saw Felix's face staring back at her. It was the passport application paper she'd filled out. "There's at least ten of these."

"Ha!" Rudy moved to the desk, seemingly forgetting about Adela. She needed no further encouragement to get out of there, and she quickly but quietly snuck away. Careful not to run, she moved down the hallway as fast as possible, fully expecting to be called back by Rudy or his colleague. When the stairs were in sight, she almost launched herself down the steps, not looking back until she reached the safety of her office.

She shut the door and leaned on her desk, allowing her heart to slow down. What had happened? How had they found out about Marti? He was so careful, and she was certain he hadn't shared what they were doing with anyone he wasn't absolutely certain he could trust. Then the words of the Gestapo man played back in her mind. *There's at least ten.* Had Marti bitten off more than he could chew? She shook her head; that was nothing like him.

The evidence suggested otherwise, but Adela still struggled to believe her friend had taken such a big risk. She sat down, and as the adrenaline wore off, the consequences of Marti's arrest became chillingly clear.

He would be on his way to a Gestapo prison, if he hadn't yet arrived. Faced with the irrefutable evidence of his crimes, they would sooner or later demand to know who else was involved. The temperature of the room appeared to drop ten degrees at the thought. The stories of the Gestapo's torture techniques were notorious: Everybody talked. Some held out longer than others, but the end result was the same. Whether he wanted to or not, Marti would break. And when he did, would he mention her name?

FIFTY-EIGHT

Prague
2 April 1939, evening

The group of men amassed on the inner plaza of the police station wasn't particularly large or impressive. Ten wore the uniform of the Czech police, another dozen the field gray of the SS. They looked relaxed, chatting among themselves in two groups: Germans and Czechs separate. Looking down from a window two stories above was Karl Vogt.

"You're certain the meeting is tonight?" He turned to Leopold, who looked rather comfortable behind his desk. The big Czech gave a quick, confident nod.

"No doubt. My informants have been tracking this group for weeks. They've had several smaller meetings, but tonight sees their brethren come in from surrounding towns."

"Hmm." Karl turned back to the window, his eyes running over the men below. He had insisted on full operational gear, including sidearms, but no rifles. The raid would be carried out in a confined space, which made the handling of rifles cumbersome. If all went well, they wouldn't even have to unholster their pistols. "How many people are you expecting at this meeting again?"

"Around fifty. These are mostly leaders of the Bolshevik parties from the surrounding counties, meeting with the Prague leadership. Even if only half of them show up, it will be quite a coup. One of my informants has been at four of the last meetings, and the plans these men are sprouting are quite radical. Getting rid of them would save us a lot of trouble further down the road."

Karl made the calculations. Even if all fifty showed up, their group of twenty-four—including Leopold and him—should provide plenty of strength to take them down. This was their first test of loyalty, and he wanted to see them in action before entrusting them with guns.

"Okay, let's get ready. We don't want to be late."

They arrived at a warehouse on the outskirts of the city an hour later. Darkness had descended, and nothing from the outside of the building indicated anything was going on inside. Most of the surrounding buildings were in a state of decay, and Karl questioned whether they were at the right address. Leopold assured him they were as the men piled out of the two small trucks.

"There are just two entrances to the building. Front and back. My man on the inside scouted the building a few days ago. We should enter from both sides at the same time." Leopold spoke quickly and with authority. He was clearly in his element, and Karl was pleased to see the operational side of his informant come through. "Would you like to use anything to disorient the people inside as we enter? I brought some smoke grenades."

Karl considered it, then shook his head. "I don't think that'll be necessary. But I'll instruct my men to draw their weapons as they enter. That should give those small-time politicians a good scare."

"Fair enough." Leopold looked disappointed, but he was professional enough to move on. "Would you like your men to enter from the front or back entrance?"

"The SS will take the front." Karl checked his watch. It was twenty past eight. They were perfectly on schedule. "Any latecomers will have arrived by now. If someone does show up, keep them quiet, but no violence. We'll enter at exactly a quarter to nine."

"Sounds good. I'll take my men to the back entrance."

Karl walked to the corporal who was in charge of leading the SS troopers. He relayed the final instructions, which the man calmly delivered to his troops. Karl watched their faces as he did. They looked eager but calm, and when the corporal finished speaking, they silently assembled in formation. Their leader looked to Karl, who followed in the back and nodded.

They stalked toward the front door; their mission was simple, but they understood the power of surprise. Karl's breath sounded in the cold night air as they reached the door in silence. He checked his watch: ten minutes to go. As they waited, nobody moved or talked. The men at the back kept their eyes focused on the narrow street approaching the warehouse, mindful of potential latecomers.

At exactly eight forty-five a single command from the corporal sprang the seemingly dormant group into life. They unholstered their pistols as one, then streamed through the door into a well-lit warehouse hall. On the opposite side, the door also opened and the Czech policemen poured in. They were closer to the gathering sitting on simple chairs. The policemen shouted for the assembled men to get down and put their hands on their heads. The group of SS troopers stormed toward the Bolsheviks, who were complying with the orders.

They were some fifty meters from the assembled crowd when Karl heard a controlled cry from one of the men in his group. "Up top, concealed enemies on the second floor!"

Karl looked up and was blinded by bright lights. He shielded his eyes and then spotted the men on the elevated walkways spanning the warehouse's walls. They stood on opposite sides, and as the SS men lifted their pistols, chaos erupted.

Rocks rained down from above, and Karl instinctively tried to shield his head by putting his hands up. A loud whoosh followed by an explosion of light and heat radiating in his direction confirmed their assailants were equipped with Molotov cocktails.

More rocks came down, but the SS troopers held their ground. The corporal shouted the command to open fire, and the explosion of twelve pistols in close proximity dulled Karl's senses. Time slowed down as the final rocks hit the warehouse floor, followed by shouts of pain from above. A dull thud behind him confirmed the first of their attackers had been struck down.

It was then that the first Czech policemen appeared. Leopold was with them, and his commands sounded distant in the haze of gunshots. Slowly, the gunfire died down, and Karl's senses came flooding back.

"Are you all right, sir?" Leopold's concerned face was in front of him. "Did you get hurt?"

Karl didn't feel any pain, and his clothes showed no sign that he was hit. "I'm fine." He regained his composure, and looked around. The warehouse floor was littered with stones, glass, and bullet casings. Next to him lay two SS men writhing in pain. Along the sides of the warehouse lay five bloodied bodies of their attackers. They weren't moving. "What the hell happened? This was supposed to be a gathering of Bolsheviks. This was a bloody ambush. They knew we were coming."

"I'm as surprised as you." Leopold's voice was flat, but his eyes were burning with rage.

More shouts in Czech as the policemen pointed their guns up, forcing the assailants to climb down. They were immediately beaten to the ground. Karl had to control the urge to confront them. Instead, he focused on his men, bending to check on the troopers struck by stones, who turned out to be fine despite the beating. He turned back to Leopold. "Seize everyone and lock them up. We'll decide what to do with them." He had trouble controlling his fury, certain his superiors would feel the same way about an ambush on German citizens.

THE EAGLE'S SHADOW

A FEW HOURS LATER, Karl hung up the phone and called for an aide. When the man walked in, he looked at him expectantly.

"I need you to relay an order for a public execution tomorrow afternoon." The aide didn't flinch as his pen raced over the page to keep up with Karl's instructions. "Tell the chief of police I want it to be carried out at a prominent location in the city center. We'll need a gallows for twenty men."

"You want all the prisoners strung up at the same time, sir?" The aide looked up and spoke with the casual tone of someone who was taking a lunch order. "That might be difficult to accomplish at such short notice. They'll need to build the gallows from scratch. We've not done anything like this in the Protectorate before. Certainly not in Prague."

Karl considered the man's words for a moment, then nodded. "Fair enough. It'll be more dramatic if we have them watch each other. A smaller gallows will do."

"May I suggest five spots? That should be manageable for the carpenters."

"Make it so. Thank you."

"I'll keep you informed of the progress, sir." The man left as silently as he'd come.

Karl leaned back in his chair and felt a conflicted sense of satisfaction. The raid had been a disaster, and he blamed Leopold. His information had been incorrect, but that wasn't what most concerned Karl. The Czech police major had shown little sign of surprise at the ambush. It was almost as if he'd expected it. Karl could hardly believe Leopold would willingly lead him into an ambush, but something felt off. Karl hadn't said anything, but he would keep a close eye on his supposed ally in the next few weeks. If there was any indication he was crooked, he'd end up on the end of a rope as well.

There was a silver lining to the raid, for it did yield the arrests he'd expected. The leaders of the communist organizations had shown up, and they were currently enjoying the Gestapo's finest hospitality. Karl had told his colleagues to prioritize learning what the men knew about the ambush.

The warehouse assailants were locked up, and they would also be questioned throughout the night. For them, the noose would be waiting tomorrow afternoon. Karl was pleased Heydrich had agreed to his plan. News of the ambush would no doubt spread quickly, and small victories like these bred further resistance. Karl was keen to cut off opposition at the root. A public hanging was the perfect instrument. It would strike terror into Prague's population.

A knock came, and the aide poked his head around the door. "Sir, a call from Berlin."

"Who is it?"

"Him."

Karl carefully picked up the receiver. "Sir?"

"Vogt, I discussed your plans with Reichsführer Himmler, and he is urging restraint." Reinhard Heydrich's voice came through crystal clear on the connection. "He feels we'll be antagonizing the Czech people with such a public display, and I agree."

Karl gritted his teeth. Scaring the Czech population was the point of the execution. "I understand, sir. But we can't let this go unpunished."

"Yes. Have the Gestapo extract every bit of information from them, by whatever means necessary, then send them to Dachau. They'll take care of them. Let's not do it so publicly." His tone left no doubt as to the finality of his words, and Karl reluctantly accepted defeat.

"I'll take care of it, sir. Thank you, and good night."

The line clicked, and Karl felt despondent. As he called for the aide, he consoled himself with the thought that there'd be plenty of opportunities for retribution in the future.

FIFTY-NINE

Prague
3 April 1939

The calm Felix had felt for the past week left the moment Adela came home the night prior. He'd never seen her like that before. Gone was the confident and composed woman who hadn't hesitated in hiding him in her home. After she settled down somewhat, she told him what had happened at work. At first, Felix had been ashamed to feel disappointment at the thought of another chance to leave the country slipping through his fingers. He'd quickly recovered to see the true problem here: Adela could be in big trouble, and if her friend did talk—and Felix had no doubt he would—the Gestapo could be on her doorstep any day. Felix couldn't stay with Adela for much longer, but that didn't change the danger if her colleague implicated her during interrogation by the Gestapo.

"What if he admits to preparing false papers for people but doesn't mention my name? Marti is smart, he'll come up with a way to keep me out of this."

Felix frowned and crossed his arms. "It's not up to him. I've experienced interrogations in Buchenwald. At one point, you'll tell them whatever they want to hear to make the pain stop. He might hold out at first, maybe the second time as well, but he'll crack. And whether he wants to or not, he'll mention you." She looked at him in horror. "I'm sorry, Adela, but we have to accept that he'll compromise you. And he most likely won't even be aware of it. The things they do, and the drugs they use to get people to talk. I don't remember half of the tortures I went through when they held me in the Bunker."

Adela sat hunched at the table, her eyes focusing on nothing. Felix stood and poured two glasses of water. He took a large gulp, refilled it at the faucet, then sat back down next to Adela.

"Here, drink something. It will make you feel somewhat better." He held out the glass, and Adela took it without acknowledging him. She swirled the water in her mouth, then swallowed and abruptly turned to Felix. Her eyes were clear, as if something had come to her.

"If Marti does speak, they will come looking for both of us. I can't go anywhere, I have my job, and my responsibilities in Prague. I need to stay here. But we must get you out."

"You'll be in the same danger. You could come with me."

She resolutely shook her head. "I can't. I wish I could, but I really can't. I need to stay, and if they do show up, I will convince them I had nothing to do with Marti's actions." Pain appeared in her eyes, and she took a deep breath. "Or with you."

"I know. I'll leave tonight." His heart felt heavy at the thought, but every minute he stayed, he put Adela in more danger.

"That won't be necessary." Adela's voice returned to normal, an authoritative note returning, and with it, some confidence. "There's something we could try tomorrow."

Felix's eyebrows shot up. "What's that?"

"I didn't want to think of this option unless we had no other choice. And when Marti was securing your papers, I forgot about it." She corrected herself. "Not forget about it as much as take it out of consideration. But I think this is our only option now."

"What are you talking about?" Felix moved forward in his seat.

"A week ago, some of my friends talked about a communist group operating up north, along the border. For the right price, they're helping people escape to Poland, through an old network of coal mines."

Felix was stunned. "Why didn't you mention this before?"

"I don't know these people, Felix." Her tone was sharp, defensive. "Between trusting Marti to get you the right papers and sending you off to coal miners in the north, I thought the former was the best option." Her eyes spewed fire, then quickly softened. "I'm sorry, Felix. I'm just trying to get you out of the country safely. I should've told you."

"No. I'm sorry. You're right." He slid his hand across the table, reaching for hers. It was just out of his reach, but Adela moved to slip her fingers into his. Her hand was warm, and a tingle of excitement shot through his body. "What did your friends say? Are these people real?"

"Apparently, they've been smuggling their own people into Poland from the day the Nazis invaded. They've expanded their operations to anyone willing to pay their fee. My friends said they knew of numerous Jews who got out of the country this way."

"Can you get in touch with them? I think we've run out of options."

She squeezed his hand and nodded, her eyes sad. "I already did. After I left Marti's office, I didn't know what to do, so I sat in my office for an hour. I didn't have a good feeling about the Communists when I first heard about them, and I still don't. I've never met them, and I don't know if we can trust them."

"I understand. But this is my decision. I can't see another way to stay out of the Nazis' clutches. The only other people I knew in Prague worked in the bakery. Greta and her family have gone to their holiday home. There's nowhere left for me to hide." He stood and moved to the chair next to her. "You've done more for me than anyone, and I can't begin to express how grateful I am. But Adela, if there is a chance for me to get to Poland, I must seize it. The Gestapo will eventually knock on your door, and I can't be here when they do." He wished Adela would come with him, but twice she'd mentioned she couldn't leave. Asking a third time would be useless. "What's next?"

"You're on the train to Ostrava tomorrow morning. I'll take you to the station."

Conflicting feelings raced through him as he looked at her. She gave him a smile, but a sadness filtered through her eyes. Felix's chest felt heavy. He'd suppressed his feelings in the past weeks, but they had only grown as he spent more time with her. Now that this was coming to an end, every fiber of his being wanted to let her know his true feelings. He opened his mouth, then decided he shouldn't burden Adela with them. She had done so much for him already, and apart from taking his hand earlier, there was nothing that suggested she felt the same way.

"I'll sleep in the basement tonight." He got up, and she gave him a surprised look. "If the Gestapo do show up at your door tonight, I don't want them to find me."

Adela stood and put her arms around him. "We'll get you to Poland safely, Felix. And once this is all over, we'll see each other again." Her voice was close to his ear, her breath caressing his neck. A lump rose in his throat as he struggled to keep his true emotions hidden. When he reluctantly pulled away, the cool air rushed in, a stark contrast to the warmth of her body against his.

"I'll never forget what you've done for me, Adela. No matter what happens next, you're the reason I'm still alive today."

SIXTY

Prague
4 April 1939, morning

Adela waited until the train cleared the platform, making sure there was no final German inspection. When the train disappeared from sight, only the smell of the engine's coal smoke remained in the air before she turned and made for the exit.

The crisp spring air brushed her cheek when she stepped out of the station and overlooked the square. Her fellow Praguers went about their business as usual, oblivious to her concerns. Adela took a deep breath, hoping it would ease the pressure on her chest. It didn't. Watching Felix leave for Poland, she should feel relieved danger was now gone from her apartment. However, she couldn't muster up any sense of relief at all. A feeling of loss grew as she crossed the square.

Felix had tried his best to take away her doubts about the journey, even as they said their goodbyes on the platform. He assured her everything would turn out fine, and that he would let her know as soon as he made it to Poland. Adela had gone along with his optimistic outlook, but doubts continued to gnaw. There was so much that could go wrong before he made it across the border.

She caught her reflection in a shop window and gave herself a reproachful look. Her objections about Felix going to Ostrava weren't entirely out of selflessness and concern about the logistics. She had become quite fond of having him around. Or maybe there was more to it than she was willing to admit. Felix had brought a feeling of companionship into her home that she'd never experienced before. The thought of coming home to an empty apartment saddened her. Even last night, when they discussed his leaving, she had steeled herself, not allowing herself to let him know how much the thought of the Gestapo showing up at her front door terrified her. Somehow, the threat of getting caught when Felix was there was something she could've faced, as long as he was beside her.

No, Adela! You can't think like that! Felix wouldn't have stood a chance with the Gestapo, but Adela was confident she could talk herself out of any accusations. Now that Felix was gone, there was no proof. And she still harbored hope Marti wouldn't mention her name.

She walked through the city center, hoping to clear her head before she entered the castle. As she walked her familiar route and turned to stop at a crossing, she caught the gaze of a man who looked oddly familiar. His eyes bored into hers with purpose, not looking away. Adela felt a pang of fear, racking her brain. Why did he look so familiar? The light changed and she hurried along, thankful for the cover of the morning crowd. Not daring to look back, she knew the man was still there—she could feel his eyes burning into the back of her head. *I have to lose him.*

Adela quickened her pace, hoping that would deter him. The tram stop was only two hundred meters away. Once on the tram, there would be too many people in the small space for him to try anything. It stopped in front of the castle, so there would be no way he would follow her inside.

She never made it to the tram. Quick footsteps caught up with her, and the man appeared next to her. He seemed confident and unhurried, despite their quick pace.

"Miss Beran, would you please come with me?" He flashed a disarming smile while speaking calmly in a Prague accent. "I have a message from a mutual friend that I think you'd very much like to hear." He spoke in the manner of an invitation, yet the underlying demand was evident.

Adela didn't slow her pace, but his charm and her curiosity won out. "What friend?"

"One you haven't seen in a while, but that still values your friendship from afar."

That made Adela stop in her tracks. There was only one such person. "How far?"

"I think you know. Please come with me, so we can have a proper conversation, away from all these people." He gestured at a coffeehouse on the opposite side of the street, and Adela found herself compelled to follow him.

They entered and he escorted her to a table in the back, away from the noisy front of the house. The proprietor showed up with two coffees, and the man dismissed him in a familiar way. It was clear he had planned this, and Adela was both impressed and on her guard.

"I'm sorry to surprise you like this, but I had no other way to approach you. I can't very well show up at your workplace."

"Who are you?" Adela was taken aback by the firmness of her own voice. She leaned forward. "Who sent you?"

The man smiled. "Isn't it obvious? Colonel Moravec, of course. He's asked me to deliver a warning."

Adela observed him coolly. "You haven't told me who you are yet."

"Let's just say I'm a friend of the colonel. He warned me you would be suspicious."

"If you really are a friend, you would understand why that would be the case." She crossed her arms.

The man waved his hand apologetically. "You're right. I know your name, it's only right you know mine. I'm Václav, and the colonel wanted me to pass along that he's received alarming reports about your position in the government."

"How so?" Adela's interest was piqued, but she wasn't going to volunteer any information to this stranger.

"The Germans are planning a purge, and your department will be a part of it. He feels it's time for you to move on."

"Move on how? I've heard nothing of these developments."

"That's because you're not supposed to." He took a sip of his coffee, holding the cup while he continued. "Are you enjoying working for the Nazis? I'm guessing not so much. You're only there because Colonel Moravec asked you to stay on." Adela remained quiet. It was true, but the man hadn't given her any indication she could trust him yet. He appeared to sense her distrust, and he put his cup down. "You're right to be suspicious of me. I'd like to take your doubts away." He looked around to make sure no one was watching them, then pulled a small envelope from his inside pocket and slid it across the table. "Read this."

Adela tore open the sealed, blank envelope, revealing a single sheet of paper. She unfolded it and recognized the neat handwriting of Moravec. He had wasted no ink, and the weight of the two short paragraphs hit Adela like a brick wall. She read the message twice, just to be sure she understood everything correctly.

Still reeling, holding the piece of paper, she looked at the man opposite her. "He really wants me to do this?"

Václav looked at her with sympathy. "You see now why there was no time to lose? They could very well start picking up people at your place of work today. They're convinced many people within the government are actively working to undermine the regime." He smiled humorlessly. "I suppose they're right about that, aren't they?"

Adela's head was spinning. When Moravec left and promised he would reach out to her when the time was right, she thought he would need her to supply information from within. Over the past weeks, she'd slowly become convinced he'd forgotten about her. The appearance of this man shattered that thought in an instant. Within the space of a few days her world had collapsed. Marti's arrest had put things into motion, and Adela was left behind, exposed to the coming Nazi storm. There was no longer any doubt about the Gestapo showing up at her doorstep. The question was whether it would be at her home or the office. She glanced down at Moravec's message, then at the confident man across from her. It was no coincidence he showed up when he did. He was here to save her.

SIXTY-ONE

Prague
4 April 1939, afternoon

The train slowed down and the first houses on the outskirts of the city came into view. There was no doubt they were passing into Ostrava, the towering headstocks of the coal mines dotting the landscape. Felix felt a surge of energy as he watched the density of houses grow. At last, the platform of the city's station appeared next to his train, small signs indicating they had indeed arrived in Ostrava.

He stood and moved to the door, his heart rate increasing as the train screeched to a full stop. Felix opened the door and stepped onto the platform, breathing in the air, which carried a whiff of coal. After nearly six hours on the train, he savored the cold afternoon air on his skin.

Felix looked up and down the platform and was relieved to see no uniforms. When leaving Prague, police were visible everywhere. He'd almost turned back, fearing they would ask for his papers, but Adela had pushed him on. There was no way back, she said, and he was glad for her perseverance. Ostrava was very different, with only the dozen disembarking passengers making their way to the exit.

A minute later, he stepped out of the station and onto a small square where an ornate fountain was splashing a modest bit of water. Again, Felix was surprised by the lack of activity, and he continued, feeling somewhat exposed. The crowds of Vienna and Prague had always provided him with a sense of safety in numbers. If an SS patrol turned up from around the corner, he was quite certain they would ask him for his papers. Probably just because they were bored. It prompted him to pick up his pace, following the directions he had memorized before leaving.

Walking through the city center, he ran into slightly more people, but it still felt very quiet. He was also surprised by the lack of German troops. It was nothing like what he'd been used to in Prague, where the uniforms of the Wehrmacht and SS were a common sight, the soldiers vying for the attention of the local women. Ostrava was clearly not as interesting, although Felix was certain the German influence extended to this city as well. It had to, with the amount of coal dug up, fueling the industries of the Protectorate.

He continued, turning down a few more streets, taking himself farther from the city center. While he enjoyed the solitude, each step toward the safe house made him more anxious. Adela insisted the Communists were aware that he would be arriving, and they would be waiting for him. But given that this was an underground operation, Felix was well aware the situation could change at any minute. If something had happened, he had few alternatives, and no way of contacting Adela. It was a frightening thought, and he pushed it aside as he checked the street name at the next intersection. This was his street, and his throat went dry in anticipation. Almost at the end of the street he found number fifty.

The curtains were drawn, and it was eerily quiet. Felix listened for any sounds of people moving about inside, but he heard nothing but the chirping of birds in the trees. Felix took a deep breath, steadied himself, and knocked on the door. He leaned in, his ears straining to catch the expected footsteps on the other side.

The silence remained, and he shifted on his feet. He knocked again, this time more forcefully. His eyes went up and down the quiet street as he felt intently aware of his presence. He could almost feel the neighbors peering down from behind their drawn curtains.

Felix was about to give up when he thought he heard the faint sound of footsteps approaching on the other side of the door. His heart leaped, hope rising, and he momentarily forgot his concerns about the endeavor. A key turned and the door swung open, revealing a large man wearing shoddy clothes. His wrinkled face made him appear older than he probably was, and his fingernails were blackened with coal dust. He looked Felix up and down, then signaled him inside.

"You must be the Austrian from Prague." The man spoke gruffly, the Moravian-Silesian accent challenging for Felix to understand. He made out enough to nod and stepped inside. "Follow me." The man was already halfway up the narrow stairs, and Felix sensed his impatience. The stairs creaked loudly with every step, further underlining the silence in the rest of the house. An uneasy feeling crept into Felix's mind, but he ignored it as he reached the landing on the second floor. The big man was waiting for him and opened a door, making a sweeping motion. "In here."

Felix walked into the room, and the first thing he noticed was the lack of furniture. With just a dining table and four chairs, something felt off. He turned around, but the large man had disappeared. Confused, Felix took a step back into the hallway. That's when two men appeared out of nowhere. It took Felix a second to process what he was looking at as they moved closer. One of the men drew back his jacket, revealing a pistol strapped to his belt, and nodded at him.

"Why don't you step back into the room, and we can have a little chat."

If the sight of the pistol wasn't alarming enough, the man's crisp Berlin accent chilled his bones to the core.

SIXTY-TWO

Prague
8 June 1939

Karl rushed into the castle and bounded up the stairs, his feet barely touching the steps as he took them two at a time. His aide was waiting at the top, his face flushed.

"He just walked in, I didn't even know he was in town." The young man looked overwhelmed. "I told him he could wait in your office, and that you should be in momentarily. That's when I sent for you."

Karl listened without slowing down, his eyes focused on his office door. "How long has he been waiting?"

"About half an hour, sir."

"He'll be in a mood, then." Karl reached his closed office door. "You did offer him refreshments, right?"

"Of course. He refused everything but water. Said he didn't have that much time and preferred I made sure to get you in here as quickly as possible." The aide looked mortified. "Sorry about this, sir, there really wasn't any indication he'd be here today. I double-checked."

"It's fine." Karl reached for the door handle, his heart pounding in his chest. It was bad enough that he hadn't been aware of the visit, but it was even more unfortunate that he'd been on an errand when he arrived. "I'll handle it. Make sure you get some coffee in here now. Anything to improve his mood." He stepped inside, his young assistant hurrying off down the hallway.

"Sir! This is an unexpected, pleasant surprise." Karl found Reinhard Heydrich peering out the window. "I'm terribly sorry to keep you waiting. Did we miss any announcements of your visit, somehow?"

The Brigadeführer turned and shook his head. "Not at all. I decided to fly down this morning." He sounded surprisingly upbeat, and Karl relaxed a little. "I thought it was high time to check in with you, and some of the other agents working in Prague. The operation has expanded quite a bit since I was last here. I'd also like to address everybody in the office later. Can you arrange for them to assemble?"

"I'll have my secretary summon everyone. What time would you prefer?"

"Let's do two p.m. I'd like you to introduce me to your contacts in the Czech police. Perhaps we can do that right away?"

"Absolutely, sir."

At that point there was a cautious knock at the door, and Karl's aide walked in with a tray of coffee and sandwiches. He placed them on a table in the corner of the room and quickly left. Heydrich took one of the sandwiches and looked at Karl. "Let's take some for the road."

KARL FELT self-conscious as he sat in the back seat next to one of the most powerful men in the Reich. The last time he had shared a car with Heydrich was when he'd welcomed him and Himmler to Vienna, the morning after Austria had joined the Reich. That felt like a lifetime ago, but he was aware of the significance of his boss showing up unannounced and demanding his time.

"You've been in the Protectorate for seven months now, Vogt. It seems you're feeling quite at home. Things are running smoothly, and from what I can tell, a lot of what's happening here has your touch."

"That's perhaps a little too much credit, sir. I have some very capable people working alongside me. The team from Berlin has integrated into the administration rather well. We've recently been able to remove many of the former Czechoslovak government employees, replacing them with more of our own people."

"Yes. And the Czech police is proving to be more capable than we expected. How is that going?"

"Quite well." After the ambush at the warehouse, Karl had kept a close eye on his new allies. Leopold maintained he had known nothing about the ambush, and the truth had come out quite quickly, courtesy of Karl's colleagues at the Gestapo. When they started interrogating the men arrested at the warehouse, they quickly found none of the men were actual regional leaders of their districts. A low-level clerk at the police station with communist ties had tipped them off at the last minute. Instead of canceling the meeting, they overestimated their ability to strike a blow against the Nazi government. They hadn't expected the well-trained and armed SS troopers. "They're perfectly capable foot soldiers, and their intelligence network is valuable. These men are well integrated in the community."

"Good. I look forward to meeting them." Heydrich gazed out the window as they drove along the Vltava River. He looked deep in thought, then spoke again. "I think it's safe to say you've set up a well-functioning machine in Prague, with its influence spreading nicely into the rest of Bohemia."

"Thank you, sir, but the Czech resistance still bothers me. It continues to grow, and I'm looking into ways to combat it effectively."

Heydrich let out a soft, disapproving grunt, the first of his visit, putting Karl on alert. "Eradicating resistance networks is something many of your colleagues at the Sicherheitsdienst can work on."

"Don't get me wrong, sir, I enjoy the challenge. Just the other day, we discovered an illegal printing press. After scoping it out for a few days, we managed to arrest most of those responsible." In reality, Karl had little to do with the actual arrests, but he felt the need to give his boss a tangible result in his battle against the resistance.

"That's all well and good, Vogt, but that's not what I sent you to the Protectorate for."

"Sir?" Karl's cheeks flushed, the space in the back of the car suddenly feeling cramped.

Heydrich turned to him, his sharp eyes showing amusement. "Oh, I think you misunderstand what I'm trying to say. I'm not criticizing your work. In fact, I think you've done a great job, much as expected. But when you talk about hunting down resistance networks, it means you've probably overstayed your welcome here."

Karl wasn't sure how to respond. An uncomfortable silence descended onto the car, only interrupted by the steady humming of the engine. They were still a good ten minutes from the police station. "Are you pulling me from the Protectorate?" Speaking the words filled him with dread. The power he yielded as Heydrich's man on the ground was beyond anything he'd experienced before. He'd been given full control in building up his network prior to the invasion, allowing him to pick and choose those useful and—most importantly—loyal to him. Karl couldn't imagine leaving Prague would allow him to operate with the same autonomy.

"You make it sound like a bad thing." Heydrich's attention was drawn to the crowd on the square next to them, while they waited for a streetcar to start moving again. "You're welcome to stay in Prague and hunt resistance networks, if that's what you prefer." He paused, leaving the words hanging in the air. It was obvious he disapproved of this option. "But if you're really looking to move up the party ranks, and perhaps rise beyond being a field agent, you may want to consider my alternative proposal."

They started moving again, and while they passed the spires of the Church of Our Lady of the Snows, Karl sensed Heydrich's proposal was something special. "I like Prague, but I'm even more curious to hear what you have to offer."

"Karl." The significance of Heydrich addressing him by his first name wasn't lost on him. "You've been one of my most trusted agents since I sent you to Vienna. Everywhere you've gone, you exceeded expectations. It would be a tremendous waste to see your ascent up the chain grind to a halt in Prague. I understand, this is a great city, and I also know you've got a very good thing going here. I wouldn't be surprised if you'd found yourself a nice Czech girl to keep your bed warm at night." Heydrich smiled, but when Karl shook his head, he continued. "Then it shouldn't be too difficult a choice. We'll send someone to take over your duties. But I need you to work alongside me on what will be the biggest leap forward our country has ever seen."

A wave of excitement swept through Karl, and he sat up a little straighter. "What are you suggesting, sir?"

"Forget everything you've done so far." Heydrich's excitement was infectious: It was exhilarating to see his boss express himself without restraint. "That was just your preparation for what's to come. Join me on the plane back to Berlin tomorrow, and together we will draw up the plans to truly change the course of history. Together, we will secure the future of the Reich for centuries to come."

Reinhard Heydrich was not a man of hyperboles. For Karl's boss to be this passionate, the project had to be extraordinary. There could only be one response.

SIXTY-THREE

Pilsen, Protectorate of Bohemia and Moravia
12 June 1939

The air was thick with oil and diesel fumes, but it hardly bothered Adela as she walked across the factory floor, greeting the workers handling heavy machinery. She smiled at Emil, a fiftysomething-year-old engineer who'd been at the Skoda Works for over thirty years. He roamed the factory floor, inspecting the work of his more junior, less experienced colleagues. Adela was especially impressed with his patience; he was always willing to explain what needed to be done, or could be improved. She'd spent plenty of time with Emil since arriving at the factory two months ago, eager to learn the details of the products she distributed across Europe.

"Ms. Beran, always a pleasure to see you on the floor." He addressed her more formally than required, ignoring her pleas to tone it down. "Of all the people working in the offices, you're certainly down here the most."

"It's a good way to know what's happening in the factory, and I like to see how things are made. Besides, the men working down here often have interesting stories to share." Adela nodded to the rows of offices on the floor above them. "Everybody's only talking numbers up there. It's nice to be out here."

"That attitude is exactly why the men are happy to have you join them during their break." He winked at her. "Well, that, and the fact that you're probably the only attractive woman from upstairs showing an interest in their work."

"You flatter me, Emil." She looked to the end of the hall, where a large number of wooden crates were stacked five high in neat rows taking up much of the loading dock. "Is that the shipment for Munich?"

Emil shook his head. "I believe those are barrels that need to be moved to the other side of the factory." They walked to the crates and Emil inspected the labels. "These will be mounted on artillery guns."

"Right. Makes sense." Adela made a mental note to check on the destination of the final product later. "Everything going well otherwise? How's your wife?"

"All good, Ms. Beran. Our daughter is taking us on a surprise week away next month, and we're looking forward to it. Do you have any plans for the summer?"

Adela couldn't believe it was that time of the year already. It felt like yesterday when she arrived in Pilsen and started her job at the factory. She hadn't even considered a summer vacation, with everything going on. But Emil didn't have to know that, and she smiled, answering in an airy tone, "Nothing solid yet, but I may look to take a few days when the weather improves. I've yet to explore the surroundings of my new home."

"If you need anything, let me know. I've spent my entire life here."

"Will do. See you later, Emil."

Adela continued along the factory floor, then stepped outside into the comfortable June weather. The sky was clear, and the warmth of the sun invigorated her. She spent so much time inside the factory's halls that it was easy to forget how nice it was to be outside. Adela upped her pace and effortlessly navigated her way through the maze of roads between the buildings of the Skoda Works. She waved at the guard at the exit, who wished her a nice evening, and she ran to catch the streetcar heading into the city.

She was lucky to secure a window seat and looked outside as the industrial complex made way for homes and shops. It was a short ride into town, and Adela especially liked the part where it crossed the Radbuza River into the city center. Although Pilsen was much smaller than Prague, the clattering of the streetcar's wheels over the bridge, with water on both sides of the tram, reminded her of home.

It had been two months since she'd moved to Pilsen, and it still felt surreal at times. After her meeting with Václav, she hadn't gone into work. Instead, he'd accompanied her to her home instead. She'd quickly packed her essentials, and then Václav had driven her to Pilsen the very same day. She spent the first few nights in a safe house on the outskirts of the city, questioning whether she'd made the right decision, but she trusted Moravec's judgment. Václav had stayed in Pilsen with her, and he told her more about the operation he—and she, now—was a part of. It had been encouraging, for the men who founded the *Obrana Národa*—Defense of the Nation—resistance group all had ties to the Czechoslovak armed forces. It was no coincidence Moravec had connected her with them.

After three days, Václav announced he'd found her a new job at the Skoda Works factory. She didn't ask how, but she was certain the group had connections within the highest echelons of Czech society. She was hired to oversee shipments of the various goods produced across the Reich, her knowledge of languages again securing her a strategically placed job.

Although the factory produced a modest amount of civilian hardware, such as delivery carts and cars, it was soon evident to Adela that its main purpose was the production of weapons. It was clear why she had been placed here.

The tram stopped in the middle of the city and Adela disembarked. It was only a short walk to Republic Square, where many of the restaurants had placed outside tables on the cobblestones. On a beautiful late afternoon as today, they were packed, with many of the patrons enjoying their first beers of the day.

Adela enjoyed the scene but walked on, entering a small tavern just off the main square. While most of the patrons at the tables on the main square were affluent *Plzeňáci*, the crowd in this tavern was more working class. She felt very much at home here, scanning the faces until she found the person she was looking for at a small table near the wall.

The man looked up from his newspaper when she slid back a chair and sat. He made a show of checking his watch, then put the paper aside. "You're late. I thought you'd forgotten about our meeting."

"Oh, come on, Milan, it's only a few minutes. I discovered an interesting shipment on my way out." A waiter appeared and she ordered a beer. Noticing Milan's glass was almost empty, she ordered him one, too.

He sat up and grinned. "I like you, Adela. You don't take any crap. Tell me about this shipment." As Adela told him about the barrels and their intended use, he nodded, as if nothing of what she was saying was a surprise. "That all makes a lot of sense."

"How so?"

The waiter appeared with two large mugs of Pilsner Urquell, and Milan waited for him to leave before answering. "Our sources at the other factories across the country are reporting the same increase in weapons production." He took a sip of his beer. "Can you look into the records of your factory's production of tanks and related material?"

"I think so. It's not my department, but I can run it by some colleagues. They'll be happy to tell me." Adela took a sip as well, listening in on the conversations around them. The men were boisterous, clearly happy they had finished another day, and paid them no attention. "There's another thing I noticed at the factory. Lots more Germans coming in. In our office alone, we've had a host of new managers join, and it's rumored there will be many more arriving."

"Well, the Czech management is forced to work along with the new German directors, reporting directly to Hermann Göring in Berlin these days, so it was only a matter of time."

Adela held up her hand. "That reminds me. One of the senior engineers I spoke to just now said many of the weapons produced in the factory aren't being shipped to Germany. The Germans are keeping them in Moravia. That's odd, don't you think?"

"Hmm." Again, Milan didn't seem too surprised. "Adela, I have a message from Moravec. He wants you to go to Prague tomorrow."

"Really?" Adela felt a mix of excitement and anxiety at the thought of returning home for the first time in two months. "What for?"

"He needs you to meet with your German agent."

"Really?" Adela hadn't heard from Dieter for a long time, and she'd assumed Moravec had found a different way to communicate with him from London. "He's in Prague?"

"Yes. And he won't speak to anyone but you."

Dieter looked much the same, maybe a few more gray hairs, but otherwise healthy. Adela sat opposite him in the small cafe.

"It's good to see you. It's been a while. I'll admit I was surprised to hear you wanted to speak with me. Did you speak with Moravec?"

"I have, a while back, but it takes some planning to set up meetings with him. The last time we spoke was in the Netherlands. I thought it would be easier to travel to Prague and meet with you."

Adela couldn't contain her curiosity. "What happened to you? It's been three months since we last spoke. I thought you abandoned us."

"I apologize, but I thought I was compromised, so I needed to lie low for a while. I couldn't leave the country, and certainly couldn't travel to Czechoslovakia. I sent word to Moravec through his Dutch and Swiss channels."

Adela nodded, as if this information wasn't new to her. In reality, if Moravec received Dieter's message, he hadn't informed her. It didn't matter. He was here now, and he had something to share. "And you're confident you weren't followed?"

"As confident as one can be." When he saw Adela's response, he quickly held up his hands. "I was careful. I'm in Prague on official business. Nobody knows about our meeting, and I certainly wasn't followed here."

It was as good a guarantee as Adela was going to get. "What did you want to tell me that you couldn't tell the other people Moravec sent?" She held her breath in anticipation, hoping her trip from Pilsen hadn't been in vain.

"Before I share my information, I want to make something clear first—" he started, but Adela interrupted him.

"Dieter, you don't have to worry about money. You know we pay you handsomely for the information you provide." In her impatience to hear his news, she couldn't contain her annoyance, and she immediately regretted it. "I'm sorry. I mean we value your information."

The German looked a little hurt. "That's not what this is about. The money is of secondary importance to me. I don't want to see Europe collapsing into war again. It didn't end well last time."

Although Adela doubted Dieter didn't care about the money—it was clear from their previous interactions that he did—there was something in his voice that made her sit up. He'd never spoken about a European war with such finality before.

"What makes you think there will be a European war?" Her question was loaded with the hope that she had misunderstood him.

He slowly shook his head and looked away for a few agonizing seconds. When his gaze returned to Adela, he spoke the words she would never forget.

"Hitler has ordered the German High Command to make plans for the invasion of Poland."

Dieter spoke with such certainty that Adela had no doubt the statement was true. She also knew why he was so certain of a European war. If Hitler indeed moved for Poland, the great European powers that were happy to look away when he took Austria and Czechoslovakia would no longer be able to ignore him.

SIXTY-FOUR

Five kilometers from the Czech-Polish border
15 June 1939

The broom felt heavier than ever before, but Felix wouldn't allow himself a moment of rest. He continued sweeping the yard, which really was as clean as it would ever get. He'd been at the task for over two hours, but he didn't dare put the broom down. The guards in the watchtowers spaced at even intervals atop the looming walls were ever vigilant, and the slightest infraction could—and usually would—result in a severe beating, at the very least.

For Felix, life in the prison had become strangely familiar. It was spartan, and he was currently harried by the guards, but it was nowhere near as barbarous as Buchenwald. The food was as barely edible, but at night he was sheltered in a brick building, not the drafty, wooden structures that passed for barracks in Buchenwald.

He shook his head while he brushed more imaginary dirt around the yard. Despite the dwellings being somewhat better, his situation was as hopeless as it was in Buchenwald. After his arrest in the compromised safe house in Ostrava, he was taken to a large police station in the city. The Gestapo agents were remarkably gentle in their interrogation, especially considering they found his Austrian passport sewn into his jacket almost immediately. His case was quite clear, and after some perfunctory questioning they placed him in a large holding cell. He spent a week there, and when they came for him, Felix was certain he was on his way to one of the camps—perhaps even back to Buchenwald.

Instead, the truck took him an hour's drive from the city, finally arriving in the very yard he was sweeping now. The towering walls with evenly barred windows had left no doubt that he was in a prison. Processing had gone relatively quickly, although none of the guards seemed in the least bit of a hurry—something that hadn't changed in the nearly three months he'd been here. At first, Felix was convinced his stop at the prison was temporary. The authorities were likely collecting prisoners in the region before putting them on a train to one of the camps in Germany. But as the first weeks turned into a month with no sign of anything changing, he slowly started to accept that the tiny, cold cell he shared with two other prisoners might be his home for a longer time.

The guards showed little interest in the prisoners, leaving them in their cells for days on end. It beat being worked to death in the Buchenwald quarry, but the days also dragged on forever, and when Felix was offered the opportunity to join the cleaning crew after two months, he jumped at the chance. That's how he ended up spending most of his days roaming the prison grounds, pretending to clean.

It was also where he learned that the sentries in the towers were the only ones who cared about their jobs. During the afternoons spent sweeping the yard he'd seen multiple prisoner bodies dragged away after getting too close to the fence.

Felix made sure to stay well clear, but as he looked out, he saw the rolling hills that he'd seen from the train on his arrival three months ago. The Polish border was less than five kilometers away, yet it might as well be the other side of the world. His mind wandered to thoughts of escape, as it did every day. One look at the closest guard tower underlined the futility of such fantasies. Two guards had a clear view of the yard on one side, and the open fields on the outside. They were equipped with long-range rifles, and Felix had seen them practice on any wildlife that made the mistake of venturing too close to the prison. They hardly ever needed more than a single bullet.

While the thought of escaping came and went, it was impossible not to think of the women he'd left behind. He'd promised Adela and his mother he'd let them know when he arrived safely in Poland. At the time, he wasn't sure how he'd manage that, but he figured he'd find a way. Poland was a free country. But from his hopeless position behind bars there was no opportunity to send any mail. His mother would be sick with worry, for even in Buchenwald he was maintaining contact. Adela, he knew, would most likely blame herself. He held on to the hope that she had inquired with her contacts in the Ostrava resistance. At least she might know what had happened.

"All prisoners, back to your cells. Line up outside entrance one," a metallic, disembodied voice shouted from the loudspeakers, echoing between the yard's walls. "On the double!"

Felix was relieved at the command, and he made his way toward the door, along with some twenty other prisoners that were allowed to get some air. He joined the group waiting near the door and looked back to the hills of freedom. That's when he caught the eye of one of the guards on the other side of the fence, the young man's piercing gaze uncomfortably settled on Felix. The man moved along the fence and disappeared into the prison through one of the side doors.

A little shaken, Felix waited for the door leading into the prison to open. Two bulky guards appeared and counted the prisoners as they shuffled back into the prison. The guards appeared disinterested, a little bored even, crossing off prisoner numbers on their lists. When Felix passed and stated his number, the man looked up.

"You're wanted in interrogation one. Wait over there." He pointed at a corner next to the door. "I'll take you in just a minute."

Felix's mouth went dry. He hadn't been interrogated once since arriving in the prison, but he'd passed through the small hallway in the northeastern corner of the prison numerous times on cleaning duty. One of the rooms he'd been assigned to clean had been splattered with blood. It was on the floor and walls and even a bit was on the ceiling, which he'd only been able to reach by climbing on what appeared to be a torture table. His mind was racing: He'd done nothing to warrant a trip to that area of the prison. Was this a mistake? He didn't dare ask the guard, and he waited anxiously while the last prisoners passed by. The guards double-checked their lists, and when all was well, one escorted the other men back to their cells. The guard that had spoken to him earlier nodded at Felix.

"Are you going to give me trouble?" He waved at a set of handcuffs. "Or are you going to come along peacefully?"

Fifteen minutes later, Felix found himself in small, damp room. The single light bulb in the middle of the room gave off barely enough of a glow to illuminate the room.

The escorting guard hadn't given any indication as to why he was brought here, which had only increased Felix's anxiety. When the man left without another word, after simply pointing at the chair in the middle of the room, Felix's mind went into overdrive.

When the door opened again a few minutes later, Felix had come up with at least ten reasons why he found himself in the room. The light streaming in from the hallway concealed the face of the man entering, only providing an outline as he entered. Felix's eyes immediately went to the large bag he carried in his left hand, taking him back to the tortures in Buchenwald's Bunker, where Martin Sommer carried his doctor's bag with his vicious tools in much the same manner.

When he closed the door and turned to reveal his face, Felix gasped softly. The eyes were unmistakable. It was the guard who'd eyed him from behind the fence earlier. The man took a few steps toward Felix, who inched back in his chair.

"Don't worry. I'm not here to hurt you." His voice was softer than Felix had expected. "I just want to talk. Your name is Felix, isn't it?"

Felix eyed the man with suspicion. Any interrogator worth his salt would try to win his subject's trust. *Just talk?* Despite his misgivings, there was little sense in denying his identity in here. "I am."

"And you're originally from Vienna, aren't you?" The man crouched down, drawing his face level with Felix's, centimeters away, uncomfortably close. He could feel the man's breath on his face.

"Yes."

"Quite some way from home." The man rose, returning to his full height. He pulled up a chair from the wall and sat opposite Felix. "I'm from Salzburg. You can call me Olaf."

Felix looked at him in disbelief. If the casual mention of his first name was odd, nothing in the man's manner of speaking hinted at Salzburg origins. It must've shown, for the man smiled.

"I spent the past six years in Germany. My father was an early supporter of Hitler, and let's just say that opinion wasn't shared broadly in Austria back then. He considered it a good career move to apply for a job just across the border." Olaf chuckled. "Turns out, he was right."

Felix didn't know how to respond. He looked at the guard, who appeared deep in thought for a moment. They were about the same age, and apart from the uniform, there was little separating them in terms of appearance. Both athletically built, in different circumstances they might've faced each other on the football pitch. The guard snapped back to the present and looked at Felix with a knowing expression. He held up his hand, then reached into the large bag. Felix averted his eyes, expecting the worst.

An odd clacking Felix recognized but couldn't place sounded. "Here, have some of this."

Felix looked up and thought his eyes were deceiving him. Olaf held out a small bottle of beer. Felix blinked hard, but the man moved the bottle closer.

"Please, have a sip, share a drink with me." He looked around the room. "Nobody knows, and nobody will disturb us in here. Come on, two Austrians far from home."

Felix reluctantly took the bottle and held it, not daring to move it to his lips. The guard reached into his bag again, producing a second bottle. He uncapped it, then took a large swig.

"I promise it's fine." He nodded at Felix's beer again, and this time Felix took a small, careful sip. The sensation of the cold, bitter liquid stinging his throat was delightful, and Felix couldn't help but close his eyes in pleasure. His last beer had been in Prague, more than three months ago. He took another sip, fearing the guard would take it away, as part of a cruel joke. He didn't. Instead, the young man looked at him with interest.

"You've been in the prison for quite a while now, haven't you?" the guard said casually. "It must be difficult to see the border every day, knowing freedom is so close, yet so far."

"I don't allow myself any thoughts of freedom," Felix lied. "Not as long as this country and my own are occupied."

"That's fair." The answer sounded sincere. "I would feel the same way if I were in your shoes. To be honest, I'm not even that much of a supporter of the party myself. I didn't have much of a choice when we moved to Munich, though. I joined the Hitler Youth, and my father made sure my career path was set up beyond that."

"Is that how you ended up here?" Felix took another sip, the beer giving him the courage to speak more freely than he would normally feel in this situation.

"More or less. It's all part of my training to join the SS proper. I was sent here because I speak Czech. My mother is from Prague." He reached into the bag and handed Felix a large block of cheese. "Have this, it's pretty good."

That description didn't even come close to how Felix experienced it. He couldn't recall tasting anything this good, his sense of taste completely overwhelmed after a steady diet of prison food.

"You must be wondering why I had you brought here." The guard nodded at their surroundings. "To this room."

Felix's guard went up, but he answered neutrally, "It crossed my mind."

"That's fair." The guard smiled. "The thing is, when I saw you in the yard a few days ago, you reminded me of someone. Imagine my surprise when I found out you were Austrian." Emotion creeped into the guard's voice.

"Who's that?" Felix tilted his head.

"My best friend growing up in Salzburg." The guard shook his head and chuckled. "For a moment, I thought you might be him, under a new identity, somehow ending up in my prison. But when I looked into your file, I knew it couldn't be."

Felix took another bite of his cheese, unsure how to respond. "When was the last time you saw him?"

"About six years ago, when we moved to Munich." Sadness crossed the guard's face, and he evaded Felix's gaze as he focused his attention on the label of his bottle. "Ernst and I did everything together. Our friendship started in the school playground, and we experienced everything up to chasing girls in middle school. But in the last year living in Salzburg, things changed."

Felix took a sip of his beer, noticing with regret the bottle was almost empty. "What changes?"

"My father became openly hostile about our friendship. At one point, he made it clear Ernst was no longer welcome in our home. A few weeks later, he demanded I end the friendship."

"Ernst was Jewish."

Olaf nodded sadly. "As my father radicalized, Ernst became the enemy. It was something I couldn't accept. He was still the same person he'd always been. My best friend."

"You defied your father?"

"Not openly." Olaf's gaze hardened, and he clenched his jaw. "I continued to see Ernst, of course. We would still go fishing, hiking, and chase girls in the city. But it wasn't the same. I needed to look over my shoulder every time, and despite never admitting it to anyone, I was afraid of my father. Of what he'd do when he found out." He paused, taking a deep breath. "As it turned out, I was right to fear him."

Felix finished his beer and set the empty bottle on the table. It was a surreal situation, and he wasn't certain if his tired mind was conjuring up the situation. Would he wake up soon?

"One evening, I arrived home to find my parents waiting for me.

It was immediately clear something was wrong. My mother looked chastised, my father was fuming. He announced I had sullied the family's good name by consorting with Jews. His friends in the Austrian NSDAP were asking questions, and he blamed me for putting his prospects within the party in danger."

Felix made a quick calculation. "This must've been around the time the party was banned in Austria."

"Yes, but we wouldn't be around to witness that. My father announced we were leaving for Bavaria the very next day. I had destroyed his chances to rise up through the Austrian Nazi Party. The ironic part of it all is that our early move to Germany was essential to his quick rise in Hitler's party in Germany."

"You beat the Austrian Nazis fleeing the country a few months later."

"Exactly." Olaf was silent, his eyes glassy, as if he were somewhere else. Felix saw, for the first time, an actual person behind the façade of the Nazi uniform. In another life, they could've been friends. But what did the young Salzburger want from him?

"Did you have any contact with Ernst after you left?"

"A few letters back and forth, before they stopped abruptly." Olaf's mouth twisted. "I don't know if they were somehow intercepted, or if something happened to him." A shadow crossed the guard's face. "I'm ashamed of not trying harder to find out. Maybe he needed my help. Now, I pray he managed to find his way to safety somehow." Olaf then met Felix's eyes with a determined gaze, his expression hard. "I can't help my friend, but when I saw you in the yard, it was a sign. I can help you."

Felix's heart skipped a beat, his mouth turning dry. He hardly dared dream, but looking at Olaf's face, there was no hint of malice. Finally, he managed, "How?"

A FEW HOURS LATER, Felix and Olaf stood in the pitch black, with only the lights of the prison behind them in the distance visible.

"You run that way, Felix." He pointed up at the clear sky.

"That's Ursa Major." Felix looked up, easily identifying the Great Bear constellation. He nodded while Olaf continued. "Once you reach the trees, keep moving. The ground will rise, which means you're moving in the right direction. Whenever you can, look up and search for the star. If you keep moving at a steady pace, you should reach the top of the hills after about an hour or two. From there, you should see the lights of a small city. That will be Gołkowice, in Poland. Keep moving."

Felix nodded, then realized Olaf couldn't see his face in the darkness. "Got it." He still couldn't believe the guard would just let him go like that, the sight of Olaf strapping a pistol to his belt before leaving the camp worrying him. Was this all just an elaborate and sick ploy to amuse the guard?

"Go. You should make it there before sunrise. Good luck, Felix. I wish you well." Olaf gave him an encouraging pat on the shoulder.

Without another word, Felix moved in the direction of the star, praying Olaf's intentions were true. He half expected the sound of a gunshot behind him, but the night remained quiet, only the sound of his breathing remaining. It grew more ragged as he pushed his tired legs harder, willing himself toward Poland, toward freedom.

SIXTY-FIVE

Berlin
20 August 1939

The air was thick with tension, despite the three men taking up little space in the large conference room at the Sicherheitsdienst headquarters at number 8 Prinz-Albrecht-Straße. Karl listened while Heydrich and Heinrich Müller, the chief of operations for the Gestapo, discussed the logistics of their new plan.

"We'd just need to find enough men to make it plausible. It shouldn't be that hard," Müller said with confidence.

"Ten, fifteen? That should do it." Reinhard Heydrich looked pensive. "And where would we get them, without raising any suspicions?"

"How about the camps?" Karl cut in, and both men turned to him. Müller looked as if he'd forgotten Karl's presence at the table. "We could ask for volunteers."

Heydrich tilted his head, but it was Müller who responded first. "That's not a bad idea. But most of the prisoners would be hesitant to take an offer from the camp leadership. They'll be wary."

"What if we frame it so that it doesn't appear to come from the SS men in the camp? Perhaps have someone they don't know come in and offer a way out?" Karl could imagine it working, and he was pleased to see Heydrich was nodding along.

"A chance at freedom for joining the mission?" Heydrich said. "What do you think, Müller?"

"Might be too little, still." Müller appeared reluctant to go with Karl's proposal, and he found his irritation growing. "We could tell them they'll be pardoned after participating in the mission. That would really make it worth their while."

"I think most prisoners would jump at the chance of freedom, but you're more knowledgeable about the situation inside the camps," Heydrich said without conviction, and Karl suppressed a smile. The concentration camps were run by the SS, which was one of the few institutions his boss did not oversee, but was under the management of his direct superior, Heinrich Himmler. He was also the man they needed to convince of the value of the plan they were finalizing today. They had until tomorrow morning, and while plenty of ideas had been immediately rejected by Heydrich, Karl was certain they were onto something now.

It had been interesting to return to Berlin. He'd spent the first weeks familiarizing himself with the situation in Poland. Heydrich expected him to know everything from the strongest fortifications on the border to strategically positioned cities and towns located farther into the country. His boss didn't explicitly tell him why this information was vital, and he didn't need to. It was clear what they were preparing for, and it excited Karl. Heydrich hadn't exaggerated when he said his new task would change the course of history. If executed well, this project would see the Reich's borders expand eastward like never before. It would push German *Lebensraum*—living space—and its new borders all the way to the Joseph Stalin's Russia. Karl had expressed his concerns, but Heydrich had told him not to worry about it: They were working on it. It would all become clear soon.

"Shall we ask the Reichsführer's input on the matter? He has the final say about anything that happens in the camps." It was a smart way to pass the buck by Müller, who appeared hesitant to commit to the idea. Karl found it odd that the Gestapo chief took this position: Was there something more to it? He was pleased to see Heydrich shake his head.

"No, I want our plan to be complete when we present it to Himmler tomorrow. We'll present the recruitment of concentration camp prisoners as our solution to the Polish problem."

"We could recruit from the *Straffbarracken*, the disciplinary blocks. They have nothing to lose. They'll jump at any chance to escape their punishment," Karl said, seeing both men's eyes light up at the idea. "Perhaps recruit them from those awaiting death sentences. It won't change their fortune."

"Excellent idea, Vogt." Heydrich nodded, and now even Müller had to agree. His eyes shot daggers at Karl, who pretended not to notice.

"Right, with that sorted, let's move on to some more of the logistics." Heydrich sounded pleased and keen to continue. The plan was taking shape, and Karl was confident they would have something for Himmler in the next few hours.

THE NEXT MORNING, Karl entered the SS headquarters and made straight for the stairway. His stomach was in knots as he focused on keeping his balance, taking the steps one at a time. He'd hardly slept that night, his mind not giving him any respite from the plan he was about to present to Reichsführer Himmler. It reminded him of his final exams at the *Gymnasium*, just before he would join the Sicherheitsdienst. It had felt like the most important moment of life back then, for failing to demonstrate his secondary school education would mean the route into Reinhard Heydrich's organization would be blocked.

That all seemed so trivial now, as he reached the top floor of the building. What he was about to propose to Himmler would change the landscape of Europe forever. It dwarfed the annexations of Austria and Czechoslovakia, demoting them to trivial victories building up to this pivotal moment ahead. He took a deep breath and turned the corner into the hallway leading to Heinrich Himmler's office.

Karl had never been there before, but he wasn't surprised to find two SS troopers standing guard, demanding his credentials.

"It's fine, let him pass." The authoritative voice of Reinhard Heydrich behind him had the troopers jumping to attention before moving out of the way to allow Karl and his boss to pass.

"Are you ready?" Heydrich said in an uncharacteristically light tone as they moved toward a junior SS officer sitting behind a desk. The young man stood and saluted Heydrich, then quickly moved to the large double doors that Karl assumed led into Himmler's office.

"I'm feeling confident, sir," Karl said, as Himmler's secretary pushed down the door handles. It gave Heydrich just enough time to give Karl an encouraging nod, before they stepped in together.

Karl was surprised to see Müller was already there, chatting with Himmler. The chief of the Gestapo stood with his hands resting on the small of his back, the smile on his face widening as Karl and Heydrich entered. Although Heydrich's face remained impassive, Karl was certain his boss was fuming at his subordinate going into the meeting ahead of him.

"Reichsführer, *Guten Morgen*, it's good to see you." Heydrich, impressively, took control of the situation, steering Himmler's attention away from Müller. "I hope you haven't started without us." The jibe was delivered without the faintest trace of humor in his voice, and Karl could see Müller's mouth twitch faintly. *Good.* "I'm sure you remember Standartenführer Vogt."

"Karl, of course." Himmler extended his hand, and Karl shook it, awestruck to be addressed by his first name. "The last time we met was in Sudetenland, wasn't it?"

"Yes, sir." *He remembers?* "It's good to see you again, sir."

"Likewise." Himmler kept his eyes on Karl a moment longer, then turned and pointed at a table in the corner. "Shall we begin? I've gone through your preliminary plans, and I have some questions." He took the thin folder that Karl, Müller, and Heydrich had sent ahead the evening prior. It contained the outline of the plan, highlighting the most important actions and requirements. Karl tried to read Himmler as they sat, but the face of Hitler's second-in-command revealed nothing as he turned to the first page.

"Before we go into the details, I'd like to point out that I missed one crucial element in your briefing."

That wasn't the start Karl had hoped for, and he swallowed hard.

"What's that, sir?" Heydrich didn't waver, his voice as sharp and controlled as ever.

"The Einsatzgruppen. I'm not seeing them in your approach."

"They're not part of this first operation. They'll accompany the Wehrmacht as usual, once the command to move is given."

"I understand that, Reinhard." Himmler's tone was terse, the use of Heydrich's first name anything but familiar. "Are you saying you'll require none of the Einsatzgruppen's support for this operation?"

"That's correct, sir. The missions will be carried out at several spots across the border, coordinated by experienced SD agents, supported by SS troopers. I'd like to keep the circle as small as feasible. This gives us the best possible chance of success." His eyes went between the men at the table before continuing. "This operation requires stealth and discretion. With all due respect, the Einsatzgruppen are a very useful tool, but they are not the most covert element."

Himmler nodded, seemingly pleased with Heydrich's reasoning, and Karl let out a silent sigh of relief. "These concentration camp prisoners you need. I like the idea. It gives plausibility to our planned response. Have you thought about the Poles possibly finding out these men's real identities?"

"We'll make sure they are beyond recognition, sir. They are dispensable." The finality of Heydrich's statement required no further questions, and Himmler turned the page, moving on.

"How long would you need to prepare? The Führer will want to know."

That was encouraging, and Karl sat up as Heydrich answered.

"Until the end of the month. We have a short list of SD and SS personnel that will lead the operations. Considering their experience, I don't think we need more than a day, maybe two, for briefing and training them. Meanwhile, I was hoping you could grant us permission to send Müller's men to Dachau and Buchenwald to recruit the concentration camp prisoners required."

"Done. How many do you need?"

"Twenty would do, sir."

"Perfect." Himmler scanned the pages, pausing at times, making Karl anxious he'd have more questions. In the end, he looked up and said, "It seems the Gleiwitz tower is the most crucial target. The rest will draw much less attention, but will work to amplify what you're planning at Gleiwitz."

"Correct, sir. We'll use it to broadcast the message."

"I like it. I'm quite certain the Führer will consent to it but I will brief him this afternoon, and anticipate his approval shortly after." Himmler closed the file. "Have you picked the agent leading the Gleiwitz operation yet?"

Heydrich turned to Karl. "We have, sir."

SIXTY-SIX

Prague
23 August 1939

The riverfront was crowded. An eclectic mix of Praguers made the best of the warm, sunny day, seeking the cooler air along the Vltava River. Adela had secured a seat on a wooden bench underneath a small tree providing enough shade for her to observe those passing by. The castle towering above on the opposite bank reminded her of the time she roamed those halls, feeling a lifetime ago. The soldiers in their field-gray uniforms walked among the crowd, their youthful appearance masking the danger they represented.

Adela scanned the other faces in the crowd, and she was pleased to see the man she was meeting making his way toward her. Václav Morávek had become more than her highly placed contact in the resistance group that had moved her to the relative safety of Pilsen. Whenever she met him, she was struck by his charm and the ease with which he held himself. Adela wasn't surprised he'd gathered a loyal following across the country. His Obrana Národa group had contacts in all major cities, and their military backgrounds meant their leaders possessed an impressive sense of discipline. Unlike many of the smaller resistance groups that had popped up all across the country, they had managed to stay out of the Nazis' grasp. František Moravec's influence was clearly felt, even all the way from London.

"Miss Beran, a rather pleasant day." Václav sat next to her, his eyes on the river. "I trust your trip went without incident?"

"It's nice to be back in Prague."

"You've settled into your job at the Skoda Works well, I hear." Adela met with Milan every week, sometimes more often, and she was certain her reports were relayed to the leadership immediately after. Václav stood and signaled to the river. "Shall we take a short walk? I prefer to keep moving."

"Of course." Adela fell into step with the tall man, and they walked close to the riverbank, where slightly fewer people ventured. Most of the crowd gathered around the little stalls selling refreshments. "I noticed something interesting yesterday, just before I left for the weekend." Václav turned his face to her but didn't slow his pace, inviting her to continue. "There's been a significant increase in the production of weaponry these past months. At first, most remained in the country, but just this week, more was sent west."

"This isn't anything we weren't aware of. The factory's been shipping weapons to Germany since they took over." He sounded unimpressed, even a little disappointed.

"I think it might be linked to something bigger going on at the factory. Some of my colleagues were discussing changes in the top of the company. According to what they heard, the Czech leadership is being replaced by more Germans coming in."

Václav frowned. "I've heard of no such thing. From what I understand, the Germans are keen to maintain the factory is run by Czechs."

"They're not firing the directors. They're keeping them on, but taking away their responsibilities. They're puppets."

"Hmm." Václav looked thoughtful, and Adela wondered if he knew more than he was letting on. They walked for a few minutes, and Adela felt a pang of jealousy as she watched couples strolling along, holding hands, seemingly without a care in the world. Felix's face appeared in her mind, and a cold feeling grew in her stomach. There wasn't a day that went by without her thinking, and worrying, about him. She refused to believe he was dead, although with every passing day, worry gnawed more at her conviction. Still, she knew it was nearly impossible for him to contact her. The only address he had was of her apartment in Prague, and she hadn't gone back since she moved to Pilsen.

She was so caught up in her thoughts that she hadn't noticed Václav stopping a few meters back. He stood overlooking the river, and when she returned to him, his face was lined with concern.

"The truth is, Adela, what you're saying isn't that big a surprise for me. We've received similar reports from other locations in the country. Production is ramped up everywhere, whether it's at the coal mines or the factories. It was a matter of time before the same happened at the Skoda Works." He paused, then looked at her with a sad smile. "It's a big place, and there's probably been quite some changes without you noticing."

"I try to keep my eyes and ears open." Adela couldn't hide her annoyance at his suggestion that she was missing things, although she knew it was impossible for her to know everything that was happening within the enormous factory.

"I'm sorry, I didn't mean to offend you. You're a great asset, and your information is valuable. What you just told me confirms that we'll need to become more active in your region." Adela wondered what that meant, and it seemed Václav read her mind. "Do you have connections within the factory that might be able to, say, slow things down?"

"You mean sabotage production?"

"Yes, but not in an obvious way. We don't want to expose ourselves, nor do we want retributions against the workforce. Czech livelihoods depend on these jobs, even if their efforts strengthen the German army."

Adela considered his words. "I know a lot of the men working the factory floor. And plenty in the offices, of course. But I'm not sure any of them would be willing to sabotage production."

"What about you? Could you influence what happens once it leaves the factory floor?"

Adela returned to Pilsen two days later, walking into the factory at eight a.m. sharp. She entered her office and barely had a chance to sit down when her boss walked in. He had a big smile on his face, looking more than a little excited.

"Adela, did you have a good weekend?" He continued without waiting for her answer. "I have some great news. The leadership is rather impressed by your handling of the shipments across the Reich, and they've decided to promote you."

"Really?" Adela felt no excitement at the thought of leaving her post. After her talk with Václav, she spent most of the weekend considering her approach. She'd settled on further cultivating her relationships with her colleagues in the office and the factory floor. "What's the new job?"

He responded like he didn't hear her, almost beside himself with excitement. "Oh, and just so you know, I'm not talking about the local leadership. The leadership in Berlin noticed our productivity and efficiency, and they're sending someone down here to further expand operations."

Adela's heart sank even further. "What does that mean for me?"

He looked at her, his eyes and ears properly registering her for the first time. "Oh, you'll stay on here, don't worry. In fact, you've been assigned to work with the new export director."

"And he's from Berlin as well?"

"Not sure. But he is German, and rather well connected. This is a great opportunity, Adela."

"I'm sure." Adela had no energy to fake any excitement. "What will I be doing? And when do I start?"

"You'll be his personal assistant. And you're starting right now. He's settling into his office, and this would be a great time to introduce yourself, and see if you can help with anything." Her boss was beaming. "He's only just arrived in the city last night, so I'm sure he has plenty of questions. Congratulations, Adela!" With those words, he disappeared from her office, and Adela sat in stunned silence for a moment.

Deciding there was nothing to do but face her new, German, boss, she got up and headed in the direction of one of the corner offices where she saw a man moving about, rearranging furniture and unpacking a single box.

Adela reached the highly ranked German official's open door and knocked on the glass panel.

The man turned around, and the first thing she noticed was how attractive he was. Certainly a good ten to fifteen years older than her, he carried himself with unmistakable confidence, almost gliding across the room.

"If I'm not mistaken, you must be Miss Beran." His accent was unexpected. There was certainly the crispness of the German upper classes, but there was something else that sounded very familiar.

"I am Adela Beran, yes."

He moved closer to her, and as he extended his hand, she realized what the familiar tones in his accent were. Viennese. Like Felix. She shook his hand, surprised by his gentle touch, squeezing hers ever so lightly.

"Very pleased to meet you, Miss Beran. My name is Göring, Albert Göring." Adela's chest constricted at the casual mention of a name every person in Europe knew. She'd seen it in newspapers and newsreels for years, belonging to the brother who looked nothing like the handsome man in front of her. He flashed a self-assured smile. "I'm confident we're going to make a fine team."

SIXTY-SEVEN

Gdynia, Poland
26 August 1939

The harbor of Gdynia was much larger than Felix had expected. He'd found a table at one of the many seaside restaurants overlooking the Baltic Sea. The promenade lining the harbor was crowded: People were about for different purposes. The affluent walked while porters carried their large trunks; families on day trips bought ice cream at one of the many vendors, while youngsters ran around chasing each other. This all played out to the constant cawing of flocks of seagulls flying overhead, looking to pick up any scraps.

Felix closed his eyes and took a deep breath of the fresh, salty sea air.

"Don't you fall asleep on me!" The familiar voice of Mattias made him open his eyes. His friend placed a large glass of beer in front of him. "The service is atrocious here."

"Good thing you're not above getting our drinks yourself." Felix held out his glass, which Mattias promptly clinked while sitting down next to him.

Felix took a sip, enjoying the thick, foamy head touching his lips before the refreshing beer filtered through. He looked at Mattias and was grateful for meeting him on his journey through Poland. It was pure coincidence that they met on the train from Łódź to Warsaw, when Mattias overheard Felix struggling to explain to the ticket inspector where he was going. Mattias had intervened, translating and helping Felix out of a challenging situation. They had gotten to talking, and it turned out Mattias was in a situation very similar to Felix's. As a German Jew, he'd escaped to Poland two years earlier, and with rumors abounding about the German army assembling on the western Polish border, he was looking for a way to leave the country. He had been traveling to Warsaw to apply for a British visa at the embassy, just like Felix.

"How long until our ship departs? It's that one, right?" Mattias pointed at a medium-sized steamer docked in front of two much larger ocean liners.

"I think we still have an hour or two." Felix took another sip. "But we'll probably need to leave after this beer." He couldn't wait to board, and he was even more excited about the moment the ship would enter the calm waters of the Baltic Sea. The journey through Poland hadn't been without its challenges, and he checked his inside pocket for the ticket securing his passage to Denmark, and then on to England.

The queue at the British embassy in Warsaw hadn't been anywhere near what Felix was used to from Vienna. He was even more surprised when the kind woman manning the reception desk called their names within an hour of their arrival. The embassy employee that took their applications warned that it might take a few weeks before they heard back, and that the government was restricting the inflow of refugees. They should prepare for rejection. Nevertheless, she suggested it was a good idea to conduct an interview to decide their eligibility for a British visa, and add that to their application. Felix's journey genuinely appeared to shock her, and she marked something on his application, without explaining to him what it was.

Felix and Mattias spent a week in Warsaw, stopping at the

embassy to check on their visa applications every day. To their surprise and delight, they were informed after a week that their applications had been approved. The same woman that had submitted their applications took them into a room and let them know they received visas because they were considered refugees with exceptional skills deemed beneficial to the development of the British economy. When Felix asked what that meant, she told him they would need to come up with their skills on the way over. She'd handed them a list of potential trades that qualified, and she wished them well in their new lives in England.

The journey to Gdynia by train had filled Felix with hope, and when they disembarked, the pair journeyed straight to the harbor in search of passage to England. That's how they ended up waiting at the dock now, a week later.

They finished their drinks, and Mattias stood. "Let's get to the ship. Don't want to miss it!" Felix felt the same, and they made the walk down the quay, where a short queue of passengers had formed. They slowly made their way up the gangplank, and Felix held on to the handrailing as he watched the sea gently splash against the docks below.

Mattias went first, and he was quickly waved through by a sailor at the top of the gangplank. Felix handed the man his ticket and British visa and waited. The man took his time inspecting his documents, then tutted and looked up at Felix.

"Where's your passport?" The sailor spoke with the bored tone of someone asking a routine question, but it felt nothing like that to Felix. He was acutely aware of the stares of the people waiting behind him.

"My passport was taken from me on my journey here." He pointed at the British papers. "Those are the only papers I have, and I was told that would be sufficient to enter Britain."

"Hmm, I'm not so sure about that. You need a passport to travel." The man handed the papers and ticket back. "I'm afraid you can't sail with us today." His eyes went to the next person in line, dismissing Felix.

Felix felt like the gangplank under his feet disappeared, his hopes crashing into the water below. After everything he'd gone through, was he really falling at the final hurdle? Mattias' face a few meters away, on board the ship, mirrored his own, as despair filled Felix. He refused to move and addressed the sailor.

"I'm sorry, but the British embassy said they would accept me with these papers. Please let me board."

The man shook his head resolutely. "You can't come with us without a passport. It's the law."

Felix felt his despair turn into rage, but it was clear the sailor wouldn't budge, and starting an argument wouldn't change anything. It would only make the situation worse.

"Felix, I'll come with you, we'll get this sorted, and we'll take the next ship!" Mattias began walking toward him, but Felix shook his head.

"No! Get back, Mattias. You don't know when you might get another chance." He wouldn't let his friend miss out on this opportunity. "I'll sort this out somehow." Defeated, he turned around on the gangplank, a mass of faces looking up at him. He took a step down and struggled as people reluctantly moved so he could return to the docks. Felix kept his head down, avoiding the pitiful looks. He didn't look back.

He placed his feet on the dock and forced himself to look up, to send his friend off well. Mattias deserved as much; they had shared an important part of each other's journey, and Felix didn't begrudge him his place on the ship. Scanning the railing around the top of the gangplank, he didn't see Mattias. His eyes darted left and right, but his friend was nowhere to be found. Felix let out a deep sigh: Mattias must've decided he didn't want his own papers scrutinized again, and headed indoors. With a deep sense of loss, Felix slowly started walking away from the gangplank.

"Felix!" The wind carried the shout from atop the ship, making it sound as if Mattias stood only a few meters away. Felix turned around and saw his friend waving from the boarding area atop the ship. "Come back!" He was smiling and furiously waving his arms.

Moving as in a dream, Felix didn't allow himself the promise of hope yet, despite his friend's enthusiasm. The gangplank was nearly empty, as most passengers had boarded by now, and he ascended it with great strides. The same sailor stood waiting at the top, and Felix's heart skipped a beat. Next to him stood an older man and Mattias, looking confident, pointing at his friend.

"You say this young man has a ticket and valid papers for England as well?" It was only now that Felix noted the older man wore a maritime uniform similar to the one on the sailor inspecting tickets, but the markings on his shoulder straps made it obvious he was more senior.

"He doesn't have a passport." The younger sailor looked unsure, shifting his weight between his feet. "Just a ticket and a British visa."

The older man let out an exasperated sigh and signaled for Felix to hand him the papers. As the man thumbed through the documents, Felix held his breath. His heart pounded in his ears, and he anxiously studied the man. The senior sailor hummed and appeared to double-check something, then handed the papers back to Felix.

"These are all in order. Come on board, young man." He smiled at Felix, then shot the younger sailor an annoyed look. "Don't ever deny people with the correct papers boarding again. Do you have any idea what this young man has been through?"

Felix finally stepped on board, and inclined his head. "Thank you, sir. I can't thank you enough."

The man shook his head and nodded to Mattias. "Thank your friend. If it wasn't for his quick thinking, you'd still be down there."

THE TRIP to Denmark went without a hitch, and they transferred to their DFDS ferry bound for London four days later. Felix had been nervous about arriving in Denmark without a passport, but when he was about to disembark, the man who had allowed him to board in Poland was waiting at the exit. He wanted to make sure Felix would be allowed on board the DFDS ferry.

On the way to their next ship, Felix learned the man was the captain of the ship, and he knew plenty of the other captains sailing the Baltic Sea and North Sea regions. Felix couldn't believe his luck, and this time, there were no issues when boarding their vessel to England.

Mattias and Felix stood at the stern of the ship as it pulled out of the Esbjerg harbor early in the evening. The sun was still quite high up in the sky and cast a golden glow on the city and the calm waters below.

"It's really happening this time," Mattias said as he watched the ship's propellers send thick white waves from underneath them. "In a few days, we'll be in England. Can you believe it?"

"I wasn't so sure when I was on that dock in Gdynia. You really saved me, Mattias. I'll never forget it."

"Oh, don't worry. I won't let you forget." His friend laughed. "The first round in England is on you!"

"The first few will be on me." Felix smiled. Maybe he did have a future. He had a little bit of the money Adela had lent him left, after he'd successfully hidden it inside his shoes in the prison. He didn't know how expensive England would be, but he was certain the money wouldn't last very long. He would need to find a job, and he wondered how receptive the English people would be.

"When we get to England, what's the first thing you'll do?" Mattias asked, interrupting his thoughts, and Felix smiled.

"I need to post some letters."

"To your mother and the woman in Prague? What's her name again?"

Felix nodded. "Adela." Just mentioning her name made his heart race.

"That's right. You did the same in Warsaw, didn't you?"

"Yes, but this time, I'll have a return address." He'd written to his mother and Adela at every opportunity, but he never spent enough time in one place to receive any replies. That would be different in England, where he hoped to find lodging, or at least a post office where they could send letters. His heart swelled at the thought of hearing from them. "What about you? What are you looking forward to in England?"

"I haven't really thought about it much." Mattias shrugged. "I was so focused on getting there that I think I'll just see what happens when we do."

It was an enviable attitude, but it was exactly why Felix liked his new friend so much.

Esbjerg turned into a blip on the coast as the ship ventured farther into the North Sea. Soon, the men would need to step inside, for stormy weather was forecast, but for now they could enjoy the smell of the sea, the seagulls cawing overhead, and the chugging of the engine that powered their passage to freedom.

For the first time in a very long while, Felix was optimistic about the future. He would arrive in England with a friend, and together they would navigate life in their new country. As the European continent slowly disappeared from sight, he silently bid it farewell. Felix was certain he would return, but until it was safe enough to do so, England would be his new home.

SIXTY-EIGHT

Slawentzitz, Germany
31 August 1939

T he grandeur of the location masked the true purpose of the men in Schloss Slawentzitz. Hidden away in Upper Silesia, near the Polish border, the small palace was the perfect location to prepare for the most important mission of Karl's career.

He'd arrived four days ago and spent most of the time making sure the palace was ready to receive his guests. The SS troopers involved arrived two days ago, and they had spent their time going through the practical matters of the operation, as well as getting to know each other a little better in the evenings. Karl had enjoyed his time with the men, who came across as highly intelligent and capable, but who also possessed plenty of core social skills. It was clear why Himmler had volunteered them: These were no simple brutes. They were the elite of the SS, and Karl was confident they would execute his orders flawlessly.

It was early in the evening, and Karl descended the steps into the large basement of the castle. A guard stepped aside, and he entered a room where four men, dressed in Polish army uniforms, had their ankles and wrists strapped to metal chairs. They looked up fearfully when Karl inspected them. One of the men even spoke.

"What's happening? We were promised we would be free after we helped with your mission." His eyes shot to the small instrument table that was positioned a few meters away from them. A man wearing a doctor's coat stood alongside it, passively following the proceedings.

"And free you will be." Karl looked at the man with disdain. He had no time for common criminals, and he nodded at the man in the doctor's coat, who immediately sprang into action. Karl took a step back and watched as he picked up the first of four syringes and, without a word of warning, injected its contents into the arm of the first prisoner. The man yelped in pain, but his restraints were strapped so tightly that it didn't matter. The doctor set aside the empty syringe before moving to the next man.

In less than two minutes, they sat slumped in their chairs, unconscious and only held up by their restraints. Karl nodded appreciatively. "How long will they be out for?"

"At least twelve hours, sir."

"Perfect." He opened the door, where six SS troopers stood waiting. "Load them into the truck."

He bounded up the stairs, his pulse racing. He cared nothing for the fate of the prisoners below, for they would have died in Dachau's sooner rather than later anyway. The injections marked the start of the mission. Karl stepped out into a long hallway on the second floor and made his way to the first door to his right. He was pleased to see the six SS men poring over a map. Like Karl, they were already fully dressed in their Polish army uniforms. They looked up when he entered, snapping to attention.

"At ease. It's time." Karl moved to the table with the map. "Are you ready? The trucks are waiting."

"We're ready, sir," their leader, a man named Alfred Naujocks, said, while the others nodded. They looked calm, confident, and keen to get started. It filled Karl with confidence, and he nodded before turning toward the door.

"Let's make history."

―――

The two trucks stopped about a kilometer from the objective, killing their engines and lights as they parked on a dirt road in the forest. The SS soldiers silently disembarked and moved to the truck carrying the unconscious prisoners. They had little trouble as each hoisted a single, emaciated concentration camp prisoner over his shoulder. One of the men struggled somewhat with the fifth prisoner, whom they had picked up at the local police station: a German-Polish farmer the Gestapo had arrested the night prior. He would play an integral role in the operation.

The group made the short trek through the wooded area, and it soon opened up to a small building surrounded by a high fence. In the distance a large, wooden radio tower was visible. They had arrived.

Naujocks glanced at Karl, who nodded and moved to the main gate. He produced a key and, hands trembling from anticipation, placed it in the lock. It clicked, and a wave of relief washed over Karl as he pushed open the gate. The SS men entered silently, and Karl shut the gate behind them. Things now moved very quickly, as the troopers went into full operational mode. Karl hung back while the men dropped their prisoners by the side of the building.

They reached the front door of the transmitting building and Naujocks tried the handle. Locked. Karl quickly took another key and opened the door. The operation had been prepared well, and the men stormed into the building. A surprised shriek sounded seconds later, followed by a crunching sound. When Karl turned the corner of the narrow hallway, he found a man lying unconscious on the floor, his head bleeding. He stepped over the man and followed the SS men farther into the building.

They had studied the map of the building in detail, and they soon entered the transmission room. Surprised shouts, and the two men in the room were quickly overpowered. Their hands were bound, and they were removed from the room.

One of the SS men turned to the transmitting equipment, pressing several buttons. Naujocks and Karl looked on, while the other troopers returned.

"The radio experts are secured, sir. What do you want us to do with them?"

"Nothing. Leave them where they are. They're German citizens, and not to be hurt," Karl said, his eyes glued to the activities of his own radio operator. "Is it working?"

The man's hands moved furiously, turning the knobs and dials of the panel, but his face betrayed that something wasn't quite right. "I'm not seeing a signal. I've switched on everything that should have us transmitting." He sounded composed, but Karl didn't appreciate the doubt in his voice. Feeling the operation slip from his control, he turned to Naujocks.

"Let's prepare the situation outside. No matter what happens, we need to make sure that everything appears correct. This was a Polish attack on German territory."

"Understood. All of them, sir?"

"Yes. And make sure the farmer is positioned prominently in the doorway. He's one of the Polish sympathizers in the region. We need to make that very clear."

"We're on it." Naujocks disappeared with the other troopers, while Karl stayed in the control room. The SS radioman continued turning the dials, and Karl was starting to lose his patience when the man lifted a finger, handing a set of headphones to Karl.

"I think I've got it, sir." Karl placed the headphones on his ears and heard a soft buzzing sound, and he gave the trooper a questioning look. "You're hearing the static, sir." He pointed at a display with a needle that was moving left to right. "It'll change to whatever we're broadcasting."

Outside, the sound of gunshots rang in the quiet night air, and Karl nodded to the operator. "Do it. Send the message."

The SS man picked up the microphone, pushed the transmission button, then spoke in perfect Polish.

"This is Gliwice. We've taken over the broadcasting station. This is a Polish station now."

THE EAGLE'S SHADOW

Karl watched as the needle moved furiously, the words coming through his headphones a few seconds later. Gunshots sounded outside. He closed his eyes for a moment, savoring the success of the mission.

THEY LEFT the broadcasting station minutes later. Karl almost tripped over the body of the German farmer, who was placed in front of the door. His corpse was riddled with bullet holes. The bodies of concentration camp prisoners were strewn haphazardly along the perimeter fence. They were in a much worse state, their faces unrecognizable from gunshots at close range. Karl nodded his approval: There would be no way to identify these men.

Karl was last to leave the broadcasting site. He took one last look, noting with satisfaction the carnage on display. The front door swung lightly in the wind. The concentration camp prisoners looked every bit the Polish soldiers they were supposed to be. Inside, the frightened radio operators would soon tell the German police and Gestapo they were overpowered by Polish soldiers.

Satisfied, Karl left the main gate open before disappearing into the forest with Naujocks and his men.

THE SMALL PLANE was waiting for Karl at the nearby Gleiwitz-Trinneck airstrip and took off the moment he boarded. He arrived in Berlin a little after midnight, where a large Mercedes-Benz was waiting on the tarmac. It whisked him to the Reich Chancellery, where an aide was waiting outside, opening the door for him.

"Sir, welcome home. Please follow me. They're waiting for you." The young man sounded nervous and excited, and despite his exhaustion, Karl matched the man's quick pace through the building. At a set of high doors, the aide paused. "They're in here. Are you ready?"

Karl smiled, unfazed. "Of course."

The door swung open and Karl entered a spacious room with an oversized conference table as the main focal point. The corners of the rooms were furnished with comfortable chairs. The walls were lined with portraits of prominent Nazis, with the largest, a painting of the Führer in full military uniform, dominating the farthest wall.

"Vogt! You're here!" Reinhard Heydrich's voice thundered through the space, and his boss appeared from nowhere in the far corner. In reality, he had been hidden from view by the large armchair where he had been sitting. "Come here." Another man rose beside him, Heinrich Himmler.

Karl saluted them, and they casually returned the gesture. Himmler took his hand and shook it fiercely.

"Well done, Karl. Well done."

Heydrich slapped his shoulder, then looked serious. "The first reports from Gleiwitz are coming in. Our Gestapo agents took pictures before the police arrived. They're sending them over now, but from everything I'm hearing, the local police are reporting a Polish attack on the radio tower."

"How did the other operations fare?" It was Karl's first opportunity to hear of the other planned attacks across the border.

Himmler smiled. "To perfection. It's quite clear Poland carried out numerous attacks on the Reich's soil."

Karl felt elated. They had done it. His exhaustion almost overpowered him, but he was given no respite, as Himmler moved toward the door and gestured for him to follow.

"There's someone who wants a word, Karl."

The three men moved through the hallway, until they arrived at another large set of double doors. Himmler knocked, and a voice answered promptly. The Reichsführer opened the door and held it for Karl, urging him inside.

Karl thought his tired mind was deceiving him when he spotted the man rising behind the ornate desk at the far end of the room. His breath caught, his throat instantly dry, and his feet turned leaden. His heart was pounding in his chest as he watched the man move from his desk and toward him, dressed in the uniform Karl knew so well from the photos and newsreels. His brain struggled to comprehend what was happening. Until it did, and he clicked his heels, his right arm shooting into the air with newfound vigor.

"Heil Hitler!" he almost shouted, catching the faint sound of Heydrich and Himmler echoing the words behind him. They might as well have been in another room, for the aura of the man now less than a few meters away took every bit of his attention.

"Karl Vogt." The voice was so familiar, although they had never spoken before. "I wanted to thank you personally. Your efforts have not gone unnoticed, and you have truly outdone yourself this evening." The smile that appeared on the man's face was genuine, and Karl's heart swelled with pride. "We are on the brink of greatness, thanks to you. In a few hours, we will claim what is rightfully ours." He placed a hand on his shoulder, a surge of adrenaline shooting through Karl's body. Struggling to come up with something remarkable to say, in the end, he settled for the only thing that seemed appropriate.

"I live only to serve you." He bowed his head. "My Führer."

EPILOGUE

London, United Kingdom
1 September 1939

It was often said that England was a dreary, rainy place, but none of that was on display as Felix stepped outside. The sun was high in the clear blue sky, the warm summer air a welcome change from the stuffiness inside the post office. It could be pouring rain for all Felix cared, and it still wouldn't dampen his spirits. The envelope he held felt like mana from heaven, and he had to control himself not to immediately tear it open.

He crossed into the park across the street, careful to look right first before crossing. It still felt unnatural, and he'd suffered—and caused—a few scares when he crossed looking in the wrong direction first. This time, he made it across without incident, and he found a bench near a large pond filled with ducks.

Felix turned to the envelope, his mother's distinct handwriting clear from the moment the clerk handed it to him. He carefully opened it and took out the piece of paper with its neat handwriting. He started reading, purposefully slowing down to savor the words from Vienna. As he did, his eyes became misty, and he choked up as she described life back home. As always, Rebecca Wolff was keen to stress she was doing well, even if everything she described painted a very different picture. The most important thing, she wrote, was that Felix was alive and safe. She had indeed received all his previous letters, and she hoped he would receive hers this time. With love from Leopoldstadt, she signed off, again stressing she was doing well.

    Holding the letter in his hand, Felix observed the people in the park. A young couple walked their dog, while a mother with a pram fussed over her crying baby. A group of teenagers sat by the pond, sipping on drinks while a toddler approached the ducks with pieces of stale bread. Felix knew he should be grateful. He had escaped the Nazis, and his mother was alive, and surviving. He read the letter again. There was no indication she was being harassed by the Gestapo or SS. Perhaps they had given up on tracking him down? He stood, putting the letter in his pocket. He tried to convince himself that he should take his mother's words at face value. Maybe she really was doing alright. The positive thing was that she had friends nearby, who could help her.

    Felix left the park, and the more he considered his mother's letter, the more he was convinced this was simply how it had to be. He reflected on his journey to England, and he decided that his mother's decision to stay in Vienna was probably, in hindsight, the right one. He would write to her every week. In a surge of optimism, he wondered if there might be a way for her to visit in the future. If he secured a job, he might be able to secure a visa for her. He looked up at the sun and smiled, wondering what Mattias would say. Probably something along the lines of "Why not?"

    His first two weeks in London had been eventful. Mattias and he found cheap lodging in a home for refugees, which was both a blessing and a curse. Some of the men had been there for months, and they'd grown bitter about England after failing to secure jobs. Others were more encouraging, remaining in their cheap accommodations while they saved as much of their pay as possible before moving into their own places. Both groups provided advice, but Felix had been keen to listen to the latter group. He had sent out a number of applications and was awaiting a decision from yesterday's interview at a bank. The owner was Jewish, and he was keen to hire from among his own people. The only problem, for Felix, was that there were many young Jewish men vying for the role.

He returned to the refugee home and found Mattias in the shared living room. Mattias greeted him warmly, and he opened his mouth to ask the same question he always posed when Felix returned from the post office. Felix beat him to it by waving his mother's letter in front of him.

"Felix, that's fantastic!" Mattias' face lit up. "Who is it from?"

"My mother, and she says she's doing well." Felix sat down, forcing a smile. "I'm not sure I'd call it doing well, but she's keen to make sure I worry as little about her as possible. She always says it's not my job to worry about her, but the other way around."

"I'm not sure I agree with your mother, but it must be a relief to hear from her. To know she's alive and free enough to receive and write you letters!" Mattias looked thoughtful. "Anything special she mentioned?"

Felix shook his head. "I'm sure mail to Britain is censored, so she kept it pretty general."

"If your mother received your letter, there's a good chance Adela did, too."

"Yes." It had been the first thing he considered when he received the envelope at the post office. "I hope she's okay." He worried about Adela more than his mother, for he knew she would continue covertly opposing the Nazis. She had probably looked into ways to bring Greta and her family to safety. Felix couldn't help but smile. Adela would look after herself. *It would just be so good to know she's alive.*

"Patience, my friend." Mattias smiled sympathetically from across the table, reading his mind. "One of these days, her letter will arrive. How do you feel about heading out with me? I have some good news as well."

Felix looked up. "Did you get the job?"

"Yessir! I start in the jewelers next week. They were impressed with my eye for detail."

"Congratulations! I'm so happy for you!" Felix got up and clasped his friend's hand. "That certainly calls for a small celebration."

They departed, heading toward their favorite pub, just around the corner.

"Perhaps we should look into moving out of the shelter." Mattias was in especially good spirits. "It would be nice to have some privacy. Those miserable old bums are really getting on my nerves."

"You can probably afford it."

Mattias gave him an odd look. "I'm not moving alone, you're coming with me. You'll have a job before you know it, and then we'll be living really comfortably. Best start looking."

They turned the corner onto the street of the pub, where people had gathered around a newsstand.

"I wonder what's going on," Mattias said, and Felix shared his surprise. It was nearly five in the afternoon, an unusual time for a crowd at a newsstand. An uncomfortable, familiar feeling built in the back of Felix's mind as they squeezed through the group, making their way to the front. It was impossible to miss the headlines blaring from the special evening edition papers stacked in the front rows of the newsstand. Felix blinked hard, hoping this was a bad dream he was about to wake from. He felt physically sick as he picked up the *Evening Standard*.

Germans Invade and Bomb Poland. Britain Mobilises.

The words were printed without emotion, a dry stating of facts. For Felix, they turned his world upside down, the air squeezed from his lungs like a punch to the gut. He looked to Mattias, whose face had gone as pale as his own no doubt was.

All thoughts of celebration abandoned, they turned away from the newsstand.

Two days later, on 3 September, Great Britain declared war on Germany. For Felix, his latest escape from the Nazis had lasted a pitiful two weeks.

But this time, he wouldn't run away.

He would fight.

AUTHOR'S NOTE

Most of the initial ideas for my books originate from something I read. It might be while doing research, or it could be a random article popping up in my news feed. For *The Eagle's Shadow*, it was bit different.

Walking Vienna's streets for the better part of nine years, I was surrounded by Austria's history every day. The country's role in WWII is one that still drives fierce discussions, even today. Were they Hitler's first victim, or his most willing accomplice when 99 percent of the country ostensibly voted in favor of the unification with Nazi Germany?

It seemed logical to write a story with a connection to the city I consider my second home, and this first book in my Covert War Chronicles series is just that. And yes, if you've read my previous works, you'll have noticed that this is the first time I've put down the marker for a series from the first book onward. I've committed to Felix, Karl, and Adela, and I hope you feel the same way.

Few books covering World War II start as early as March 1938, and even fewer give an insight into the events that took place in Austria and Czechoslovakia. Centrally located in Europe, both countries served multiple purposes in Hitler's aggressive foreign policy that would escalate into the Second World War.

The annexation of Austria was Hitler's first test of the main European powers, Great Britain and France. When their response could best be described as indifferent, it emboldened the Führer to continue into the Sudetenland. With France and Great Britain deciding on a policy of appeasement to Hitler, instead of keeping their promises to Czechoslovakia, it was hardly a surprise when, a few months later, he invaded the rest of the country as well.

The territorial advances, along with the incredible production facilities of the Sudetenland now within the Reich's borders, meant Nazi Germany was supremely positioned to continue its expansion eastward, into Poland.

The proceedings in Austria and Czechoslovakia shaped the careers of a number of prominent Nazis. Reinhard Heydrich, Adolf Eichmann, Odilo Globočnik, and Walter Stahlecker would go on to play pivotal roles as the war progressed. While their interactions with Karl are fictional, I've spent considerable time researching these individuals to feel confident I've portrayed them in a realistic way. Most of the events depicted in the book actually happened, and I have used Karl as a vessel to show how these men were involved.

On the other side, I was delighted to find the memoirs of František Moravec at a secondhand bookstore in London. As I was transported back to the early 1930s through the stained, dark-yellow pages, I stumbled upon a treasure trove of firsthand knowledge, captured in the words of the head of the Czech military intelligence himself. Without this book, I wouldn't have been able to detail Adela's dealings with Dieter, the German spy.

Dieter is based on the legendary German double agent Paul Thümmel, known as Agent A-54. The clandestine meetings between Adela and him are based on real events, and he really did warn Czech intelligence about the impending invasions. For most of these meetings, A-54 met directly with Moravec or his operatives. Because little is known about Thümmel, I crafted Dieter in his image to give me more creative freedom, and to allow Adela to take on the role of his handler.

I'd like to extend a word of gratitude to Caroline Heller, whose excellent memoir *Reading Claudius* provided much of the inspiration for Adela's life. Her vivid descriptions of the streets, apartments, and coffeehouses of 1930s Prague had me walking through the city in my imagination.

Felix, Karl, and Adela are fictional. They've been created using multiple pieces of research, allowing me to craft narratives incorporating true events and historical figures. There were many men like Felix Wolff in Vienna, and the rest of Austria, suffering greatly after the Nazis took over.

Between the many German agents operating within the Sicherheitsdienst and those in other Nazi-affiliated organizations, it's easy to see Karl Vogt as one of them, albeit a very successful one.

And government employees like Adela Beran were essential to František Moravec's intelligence network, as well as the Czech resistance.

In this first book, you've witnessed their mostly ordinary lives turned upside down by the events leading up to World War II. Things are about to be turned up a notch as the war starts in earnest in the next book. I hope you'll join me for the continuation of their journey.

All my very best,
Michael

A NOTE TO THE READER

Dear Reader,

I want to thank you for picking up your copy of *The Eagle's Shadow* - readers mean everything to authors, and I appreciate you more than I can say.

    As an author I depend on you to leave an honest review on your favorite online bookstore. If you've got the time to do so, I would be very grateful.

    If you would like to reach out to me with questions or comments, please feel free to contact me via my website – michaelreit.com or reach out to me on Facebook – www.facebook.com/MichaelReitAuthor. I love hearing from readers, and look forward to hearing what you have to say about *The Eagle's Shadow*!

Warmly and with Gratitude,
Michael Reit

ABOUT THE AUTHOR

Michael Reit writes page-turning historical fiction. His books focus on lesser-known events and people in World War II Europe.
Michael and his family live in the Netherlands.

Connect with Michael via his website:
www.michaelreit.com

Or via Facebook:

facebook.com/MichaelReitAuthor

ALSO BY MICHAEL REIT

The Covert War Chronicles

1. The Eagle's Shadow

Beyond the Tracks Series

1. Beyond the Tracks
2. Tracks to Freedom
3. The Botanist's Tracks

Orphans of War Series

1. Orphans of War
2. They Bled Orange
3. Crossroads of Granite

Stand-alones

Warsaw Fury

Printed in Great Britain
by Amazon